Robert Smythe Hichens

Flames

A London Phantasy

Robert Smythe Hichens

Flames
A London Phantasy

ISBN/EAN: 9783743310735

Manufactured in Europe, USA, Canada, Australia, Japa

Cover: Foto ©ninafisch / pixelio.de

Manufactured and distributed by brebook publishing software
(www.brebook.com)

Robert Smythe Hichens

Flames

Flames

A London Phantasy

By

Robert Hichens

Author of

"The Green Carnation," "An Imaginative Man"
&c.

"And the souls mounting up to God
Went by her like thin flames"
DANTE GABRIEL ROSSETTI

London
William Heinemann
1899

First Impression, 1897
Second Impression, 1897
Third Impression, 1898

CONTENTS

BOOK I—VALENTINE

BOOK II—JULIAN

BOOK III—THE LADY OF THE FEATHERS

BOOK IV—DOCTOR LEVILLIER

BOOK V—FLAMES

BOOK I—VALENTINE

CHAPTER I

THE SAINT OF VICTORIA STREET

REFINEMENT had more power over the soul of Valentine Cresswell than religion. It governed him with a curious ease of supremacy, and held him back without effort from most of the young man's sins. Each age has its special sins. Each age passes them, like troops, in review, before it decides what regiment it will join. Valentine had never decided to join any regiment. The trumpets of vice rang in his ears in vain, mingled with the more classical music of his life as the retreat from the barracks of Seville mingled with the click of Carmen's castanets. But he heeded them not. If he listened to them sometimes, it was only to wonder at the harsh and blatant nature of their voices, only to pity the poor creatures who hastened to the prison, which youth thinks freedom and old age protection, at their shrieking summons. He preferred to be master of his soul, and had no desire to set it drilling at the command of painted women, or to drown it in wine, or to suffocate it in the smoke at which the voluptuary tries to warm his hands, mistaking it for fire. Intellectuality is to some men what religion is to many women, a trellis of roses that bars out the larger world. Valentine loved to watch the roses bud and bloom as he sat in his flower-walled cell, a deliberate and rejoicing prisoner. For a long time he loved to watch them. And he thought that it must always be so, for he was not greatly given to moods, and therefore scarcely appreciated the thrilling meaning of the word change, that is the keyword of so many a life cipher. He loved the pleasures of the intellect so much that he made the mistake of opposing them, as enemies, to the pleasures of the body. The reverse mistake is made by the generality of men ; and those who deem it wise to mingle the sharply contrasted

A

ingredients that form a good recipe for happiness are often dubbed incomprehensible, or worse. But there were moments at a period of Valentine's life when he felt discontented at his strange inability to long for sin; when he wondered, rather wearily, why he was rapt from the follies that other men enjoyed; why he could refuse, without effort, the things that they clamoured after year by year with an unceasing gluttony of appetite. The saint quarrelled mutely with his holiness of intellectuality, and argued, almost fiercely, with his cold and delicate purity.

"Why am I like some ivory statue?" he thought sometimes, "instead of like a human being, with drumming pulses, and dancing longings, and voices calling for ever in my ears, like voices of sirens, 'Come, come, rest in our arms, sleep on our bosoms, for we are they who have given joy to all men from the beginning of time. We are they who have drawn good men from their sad goodness, and they have blessed us. We are they who have been the allegory of the sage and the story of the world. In our soft arms the world has learned the glory of embracing. On our melodious hearts the hearts of men have learned the sweet religion of singing.' Why cannot I be as other men are, instead of the saint—the saint of Victoria Street that I am?"

For, absurdly enough, that was the name his world gave to Valentine. This is not an age of romance, and he did not dwell, like the saints of old centuries, in the clear solitudes of the great desert, but in what the advertisement writer calls a "commodious flat" in Victoria Street. No little jackals thronged about him in sinful circle by night. No school of picturesque disciples surrounded him by day. If he peeped above his blinds he could see the radiant procession of omnibuses on their halting way towards Westminster. The melodies of wandering organs sang in his ascetic ears, not once, nor twice, but many times a week. The milk-boy came, it must be presumed, to pay his visit in the morning; and the sparrows made the air alive, poising above the chimneys, instead of the wild eagles, whose home is near the sun. Valentine was a modern young man of twenty-four, dealt at the Army and Navy Stores, was extremely well off, and knew everybody. He belonged to the best clubs and went, occasionally, to the best parties. His tailor had a habitation in Sackville Street, and his gloves came from the Burlington Arcade. He often lunched at the Berkeley and frequently dined at Willis's. Also he had laughed at the antics of Arthur Roberts, and gazed through a pair of gold-mounted opera-glasses at Empire ballets and at the discreet juggleries of Paul Cinquevalli. The romance of cloistered saintliness was not his. If it had been he might never have rebelled. For how often it is romance which makes a home for religion in the heart of man, romance which feathers the nest of purity in which the hermit soul delights to dwell! Is it not that bizarre silence of the Algerian waste which leads many a Trappist to his fate, rather than the strange thought of God calling his soul to heavenly dreams and ecstatic renunciations? Is it not the wild poetry of the sleeping snows by night that gives to the St. Bernard monk his holiest meditations? When the organ murmurs, and he kneels in that remote chapel of the clouds to pray, is it not the religion of his wonderful earthly situation and prospect that speaks to him loudly, rather than the religion of the far-off Power whose hands he believes to hold the threads of his destinies? Even the tonsure is a psalm to some, and the robe and cowl a litany. The knotted cord is a mass and the sandal a prayer.

But Valentine had been a saint by temperament, it seemed, and would be a saint by temperament to the end. He had not been scourged to a prayerful attitude by sorrow or by pain. Tears had not made a sea to float him to repentance or to purity. Apparently he had been given what men call goodness, as others are given moustaches or a cheerful temper. When his contemporaries wondered at him, he often found himself wondering still more at them. Why did they love coarse sins? he thought. Why did they fling themselves down, like dogs, to roll in offal? He could not understand, and for a long time he did not wish to understand. But one night the wish came to him, and he expressed it to his bosom friend, Julian Addison.

CHAPTER II

A QUESTION OF EXCHANGE

MOST of us need an opposite to sit by the hearth with us sometimes, and to stir us to wonder or to war. Julian was Valentine's singularly complete and perfect opposite, in nature if not in deeds. But, after all, it is the thoughts that are of account rather than the acts, to a mind like Valentine's. He knew that Julian's nature was totally unlike his own, so singularly unlike that Julian struck just the right note to give the strength of a discord to the chord—that often seemed a common chord—of his own harmony. Long ago, for this reason, or for no special reason, he had grown to love Julian. Theirs was a fine, clean specimen of friendship. How fine, Valentine never rightly knew until this evening.

They were sitting together in Valentine's flat in that hour when he became serious and expansive. He had rather a habit of becoming serious towards midnight, especially if he was with only one person ; and no desire to please interfered with his natural play of mind and of feeling when he was with Julian. To affect any feeling with Julian would have seemed like being on conventional terms with an element, or endeavouring to deceive one's valet about one's personal habits. Long ago Julian and he had, in mind, taken up their residence together, fallen into the pleasant custom of breakfasting, lunching, and dining on all topics in common. Valentine knew of no barriers between them. And so, now, as they sat smoking, he expressed his mood without fear or hesitation.

The room in which they were was small. It was named the tent-room, being hung with dull green draperies, which hid the ceiling and fell loosely to the floor on every side. A heavy curtain shrouded the one door. On the hearth flickered a fire, before which lay Valentine's fox terrier, Rip. Julian was half lying down on a divan in an unbuttoned attitude. Valentine leaned forward in an arm-chair. They were smoking cigarettes.

" Julian," Valentine said, meditatively, " I sometimes wonder why you and I are such great friends."

" How abominable of you! To seek a reason for friendship is as

inhuman as to probe for the causes of love. Don't, for goodness'
sake, let your intellect triumph over your humanity, Valentine. Of
all modern vices, that seems to me the most loathsome. But you
could never fall into anything loathsome. You are sheeted against
that danger with plate armour."

" Nonsense ! "

" But you are. It sometimes seems to me that you and I are
like Elijah and Elisha, in a way. But I am covetous of your
mantle."

" Then you want me to be caught from you into heaven ? "

" No. I should like you to give me your mantle, your powers,
your nature, that is, and to stay here as well."

" And send the chariot of fire to the coach-house, and the horses
of fire to the nearest stables ? "   .

" Exactly ! "

" Well, but give me a reason for this rascally craving."

" A reason ! Oh, I hate my nature and I love yours. What a
curse it is to go through life eternally haunted by oneself ; worse
than being married to an ugly, boring wife."

" Now you are being morbid."

" Well, I'm telling you just how I feel."

" That is being morbid, according to some people who claim to
direct Society."

" The world's County Council, who would like to abolish all the
public bars."

" And force us to do our drinking in the privacy of our bed-
rooms."

" You would never do any drinking, Valentine. How could you
the saint of Victoria Street ? "

" I begin to hate that nickname."

And he frowned slowly. Tall, fair, curiously innocent looking,
his face was the face of a blonde ascetic. His blue eyes were certainly
not cold, but nobody could imagine that they would ever gleam with
passion or with desire as they looked upon sin. His mouth seemed
made for prayer, not for kisses ; and so women often longed to kiss
it. Over him, indeed, intellectuality hung like a light veil, setting
him apart from the uproar which the world raises while it breaks the
ten commandments. Julian, on the other hand, was brown, with
bright, eager eyes, and the expression of one who was above all
things intensely human. Valentine had ever been, and still remained,
to him a perpetual wonder, a sort of beautiful mystery. He actually
reverenced this youth who stood apart from all the muddy ways of
sin, too refined, as it seemed, rather than too religious, to be attracted
by any wile of the devil's, too completely artistic to feel any impulse
towards the subtle violence which lurks in all the vagaries of the

body. Valentine was to Julian a god, but in their mutual relations this fact never became apparent. On the contrary, Valentine was apt to look up to Julian with admiration, and the curious respect often felt by those who are good by temperament for those who are completely human. And Julian loved Valentine for looking up to him, finding in this absurd modesty of his friend a crowning beauty of character. He had never told Valentine the fact that Valentine kept him pure, held his bounding nature in leash, was the wall of fire that hedged him from sin, the armour that protected him against the assaults of self. He had never told Valentine this secret, which he cherished with the exceeding and watchful care men so often display in hiding that which does them credit. For who is not a pocket Byron nowadays? But to-night was fated by the Immortals to be a night of self-revelation. And Valentine led the way by taking a step that surprised Julian not a little. For, as Valentine frowned, he said:

" Yes, I begin to hate my nickname, and I begin to hate myself."

Julian could not help smiling at the absurdity of this bemoaning.

" What is it in yourself that you hate so much? " he asked, with a decided curiosity.

Valentine sat considering.

" Well," he replied at length, " I think it is my inhumanity, which robs me of many things. I don't desire the pleasures that most men desire, as you know. But lately I have often wished to desire them."

" Rather an elaborate state of mind."

"Yet a state easy to understand, surely. Julian, emotions pass me by. Why is that? Deep love, deep hate, despair, desire, won't stop to speak to me. Men tell me I am a marvel because I never do as they do. But I am not driven as they are evidently driven. The fact of the matter is that desire is not in me. My nature shrinks from sin; but it is not virtue that shrinks, it is rather reserve. I have no more temptation to be sensual, for instance, than I have to be vulgar."

" Hang it, Val, you don't want to have the temptation, do you? "

Valentine looked at Julian curiously.

" You have the temptation, Julian? " he said.

" You know I have—horribly."

" But you fight it and conquer it? "

" I fight it, and now I am beginning to conquer it, to get it under."

" Now? Since when? "

Julian replied by asking another question.

" Look here, how long have we known each other? "

"Let me see. I'm twenty-four, you twenty-three. Just five years."

"Ah! For just five years I've fought, Val, been able to fight."

"And before then?"

"I didn't fight, I revelled, in the enemy's camp."

"You have never told me this before. Did you suddenly get conversion, as Salvationists say?"

"Something like it. But my conversion had nothing to do with trumpets and tambourines."

"What then? This is interesting."

A certain confusion had come into Julian's expression, even a certain echoing awkwardness into his attitude. He looked away into the fire and lighted another cigarette before he answered. Then he said rather unevenly:

"I daresay you'll be surprised when I tell you. But I never meant to tell you at all."

"Don't, if you would rather not."

"Yes, I think I will. I must stop you from disliking yourself at any cost, dear old boy. Well, you converted me so far as I am converted; and that's not very far, I'm afraid."

"I?" said Valentine, with genuine surprise. "Why, I never tried to."

"Exactly. If you had, no doubt you'd have failed."

"But explain."

"I've never told you all you do for me, Val. You are my armour against all these damned things. When I'm with you, I hate the notion of being a sinner. I never hated it before I met you. In fact, I loved it. I wanted sin more than I wanted anything in heaven or earth. And then—just at the critical moment when I was passing from boyhood into manhood, I met you."

He stopped. His brown cheeks were glowing, and he avoided Valentine's gaze.

"Go on, Julian," Valentine said. "I want to hear this."

"All right, I'll finish now, but I don't know why I ever began. Perhaps you'll think me a fool, or a sentimentalist."

"Nonsense!"

"Well, I don't know how it is, but when I saw you I first understood that there is a good deal in what the parsons say, that sin is beastly in itself, don't you know, even apart from one's religious convictions, or the injury one may do to others. When I saw you, I understood that sin degrades oneself, Valentine. For you had never sinned as I had, and you were so different from me. You are the only sinless man I know, and you have made me know what beasts we men are. Why can't we be what we might be?"

Valentine did not reply. He seemed lost in thought, and Julian continued, throwing off his original shamefacedness:

" Ever since then you've kept me straight. If I feel inclined to
throw myself down in the gutter, one look at you makes me loathe
the notion. Preaching often drives one wrong out of sheer ' cussed-
ness,' I suppose. But you don't preach and don't care. You just
live beautifully, because you're made differently from all of us. So
you do for me what no preachers could ever do. There—now you
know."

He lay back, puffing violently at his cigarette.

" It is strange," Valentine said, seeing he had finished. " You
know, to live as I do is no effort to me, and so it is absurd to
praise me."

" I won't praise you, but it's outrageous of you to want to feel as
I and other men feel."

" Is it ? I don't think so. I think it is very natural. My life is
a dead calm, and a dead calm is monotonous."

" It's better than an everlasting storm."

" I wonder ! " Valentine said. " How curious that I should protect you. I am glad it is so. And yet, Julian, in spite of what you
say, I would give a great deal to change souls with you, if only for a
day or two. You will laugh at me, but I do long to feel a real,
keen temptation. Those agonising struggles of holy men that one
reads of, what can they be like ? I can hardly imagine. There
have been ascetics who have wept, and dashed themselves down on
the ground, and injured, wounded their bodies to distract their
thoughts from vice. To me they seem as madmen. You know the
story of the monk who rescued a great courtesan from her life of
shame. He placed her in a convent and went into the desert. But
her image haunted him, maddened him. He slunk back to the
convent, and found her dying in the arms of God. And he tried to
drag her away, that she might sin only once again with him, with
him, her saviour. But she died, giving herself to God, and he went
out cursing and blaspheming. This is only a dramatic fable to me.
And yet I suppose it is a possibility."

" Of course. Val, I could imagine myself doing as that monk did,
but for you. Only that I could never have been a monk at all."

" I am glad if I help you to any happiness, Julian. But—but—
oh ! to feel temptation ! "

" Oh, not to feel it ! By Jove, I long to have done with the
infernal thing that's always ready to bother me. Fighting it is no
fun, Val, I can tell you. If you would like to have my soul for a
day or two, I should love to have yours in exchange."

Valentine smoked in silence for two or three minutes. His pure,
pale, beautiful face was rather wistful as he gazed at the fire.

" Why can't these affairs be managed ? " he sighed out at length.
" Why can't we do just the one thing more ? We can kill a man's

body. We can kill a woman's purity. And yet here you and I sit, the closest friends, and neither of us can have the same experiences as the other, even for a moment. Why isn't it possible ? "

" Perhaps it is."

" Why ? How do you mean ? "

" Well, of course I'm rather a sceptic, and entirely an ignoramus. But I met a man the other day who would have laughed at us for doubting. He was an awfully strange fellow. His name is Marr. I met him at Lady Crichton's."

" Who is he ? "

" Haven't an idea. I never saw or heard of him before. We talked a good deal at dessert. He came over from the other side of the table to sit by me, and somehow, in five minutes, we'd got into spiritualism and all that sort of thing. He's evidently a believer in it, calls himself an occultist."

" But do you mean to tell me he said souls could be exchanged at will ? Come, Julian ! "

" I won't say that. But he set no limit at all to what can be done. He declares that if people seriously set themselves to develop the latent powers that lie hidden within them, they can do almost anything. Only they must be *en rapport*. Each must respond closely, definitely, to the other. Now, you and I are as much in sympathy with one another as any two men in London, I suppose."

" Surely ! "

" Then half the battle's won—according to Marr."

" You are joking."

" He wasn't. He would declare that, with time and perseverance, we could accomplish an exchange of souls."

Valentine laughed.

" Well, but how ? "

Julian laughed too.

" Oh, it seems absurd—but he'd tell us to sit together."

" Well, we are sitting together now."

" No ; at a table, I mean."

" Table turning ! " Valentine cried with a sort of contempt. " That is for children; and for all of us at Christmas, when we want to make fools of ourselves."

" Just what I am inclined to think. But Marr—and he's really a very smart, clever chap, Val—denies it. He swears it is possible for two people who sit together often to get up a marvellous sympathy, which lasts on even when they are no longer sitting. He says you can even see your companion's thoughts take form in the darkness before your eyes, and pass in procession like living things."

" He must be mad."

" Perhaps. I don't know. If he is, he can put his madness to you very lucidly, very ingeniously."

Valentine stroked the white back of Rip meditatively with his foot.

" You have never sat, have you ? " he asked.

" Never."

" Nor I. I have always thought it an idiotic and a very dull way of wasting one's time. Now, what on earth can a table have to do with one's soul ? "

" I don't know. What is one s soul ? "

" One's essence, I suppose ; the inner light that spreads its rays outward in actions, and that is extinguished, or expelled, at the hour of death."

" Expelled, I think."

" I think so too. That which is so full of strange power cannot surely die so soon. Even my soul, so frigid, so passionless, has, you say, held you back from sins like a leash of steel. And I did not even try to forge the steel. If we could exchange souls, would yours hold me back in the same way ? "

" No doubt."

" I wonder," Valentine said thoughtfully. After a moment he added, " Shall we make this absurd experiment of sitting, just for a phantasy ? "

" Why not ? It would be rather fun."

" It might be. We will just do it once to see whether you can get some of my feelings, and I some of yours."

" That's it. But you could never get mine. I know you too well, Val. You're my rock of defence. You've kept me straight because you're so straight yourself ; and, with that face, you'll never alter. If anything should happen, it will be that you'll drag me up to where you are. I shan't drag you down to my level, you old saint ! "

And he laid his hand affectionately on his friend's shoulder.

Valentine smiled.

" Your level is not low," he said.

" No, perhaps ; but, by Jove, it could be, though. If you hadn't been chucked into the world, I often think the devil must have had me altogether. You keep him off. How he must hate you, Val. Hulloh ! What's that ? "

" What ? "

" Who's that laughing outside ? Has Wade got a friend in to-night ? "

" Not that I know of. I didn't hear anything."

Valentine touched the electric bell, and his man appeared.

" Any one in with you to-night, Wade ? " he asked.

The man looked surprised.

" No, sir, certainly not, sir."

"Oh! Don't sit up; we may be late to-night. And we don't want anything more, except—yes, bring another couple of sodas."

" Yes, sir."

He brought them and vanished. A moment later they heard the front door of the flat close. The butler was married and slept out of the house. Valentine had no servant sleeping in the flat. He preferred to be alone at night.

CHAPTER III

EPISODE OF THE FIRST SITTING

"Now then," said Valentine, "let us be absurd and try this sitting. Shall we clear this little table?"

"Yes. It's just the right size. It might do for three people, but certainly not for more."

"There! Now then."

And, as the clock struck twelve, Valentine turned off the electric light, and they sat down with their hands upon the table. The room was only very dimly illuminated by the fire on the hearth, where Rip slept on, indifferent to their proceedings.

"I suppose nothing could go wrong," Julian said, after a moment of silence.

"Wrong!"

"Yes. I don't know exactly what Marr meant, but he said that if unsuitable people sit together any amount of harm can result from it."

"What sort of harm?"

"I don't know."

"H'm! I expect that is all nonsense, like the rest of his remarks. Anyhow, Julian, no two people could ever hit it off better than you and I do. Wait a second."

He jumped up and drew the curtain over the door. Wade had pulled it back when he came in.

"I must have that curtain altered," Valentine said. "It is so badly hung that whenever the door is opened, it falls half way back, and looks hideous. That is better."

He sat down again.

"We won't talk," he said.

"No. We'll give the—whatever it is, every chance."

They were silent.

Presently—it might have been a quarter of an hour later—Julian said suddenly:

"Do you feel anything?"

"'M—no," Valentine answered, rather doubtfully.

" Sure ? "

" I think so."

" You can't merely think you are sure, old chap."

" Well then—yes, I'll say I am sure."

" Right," rejoined Julian.

Again there was a silence, broken this time by Valentine.

" Why did you ask me ? " he said.

" Oh ! no special reason. I just wanted to know."

" Then you didn't ? "

" Didn't what ? "

" Feel anything ? "

" No, nothing particular."

" Well, what do you mean by that ? "

" What I say. I can't be sure it was anything."

" That's vague."

" So was my—I can't even call it exactly sensation. It was so very slight. In fact, I'm as good as sure I felt nothing at all. It was a mere fancy, nothing more."

And then again they were silent. The fire gradually died down until the room grew quite dark. Presently Valentine said :

" Hulloh ! here is Rip up against my foot. He is cold without the fire, poor little beggar."

" Shall we stop ? " asked Julian.

" Yes, I vote we do—for to-night."

Valentine struck a match, felt for the knob of the electric light and turned it on. Julian and he looked at each other, blinking.

" Think there's anything in it ? " asked Julian.

" I don't know," said Valentine. " I suppose not. Rip ! Rip ! He is cold. Did you ever see a dog shiver like that ? "

He picked the little creature up in his arms. It nestled against his shoulder with a deep sigh.

" Well, we have made a beginning," he said, turning to pour out a drink. " It is rather interesting."

Julian was lighting a cigarette.

" Yes, it is—very," he answered.

Valentine gave him a brandy and soda ; then, as if struck by a sudden thought, asked :

" You really didn't feel anything ? "

" No."

" Nor I. But then, Julian, why do we find it interesting ? "

Julian looked puzzled.

" Hang it ! I don't know," he answered, after an instant of reflection. " Why do we ? I wonder."

" That is what I am wondering."

He flicked the ash from his cigarette.

"But I don't come to any conclusion," he presently added meditatively. "We sit in the dark for an hour and a quarter, with our hands solemnly spread out upon a table; we don't talk; the table doesn't move; we hear no sound; we see nothing; we feel nothing that we have not felt before. And yet we find the function interesting. This problem of sensation is simply insoluble. I cannot work it out."

"It is awfully puzzling," said Julian. "I suppose our nerves must have been subtly excited because the thing was an absolute novelty."

"Possibly. But, if so, we are a couple of children, mere schoolboys."

"That's rather refreshing, however undignified. If we sit long enough, we may even recover our long-lost babyhood."

And so they laughed the matter easily away. Soon afterwards, however, Julian got up to go home to his chambers. Valentine went towards the door, intending to open it and to get his friend's coat. Suddenly he stopped:

"Strange!" he exclaimed.

"What's the row?"

"Look at the door, Julian."

"Well?"

"Don't you see?"

"What?"

"The curtain is half drawn back again."

Julian gave vent to a long, low whistle.

"So it is!"

"It always does that when the door is opened."

"And only then, of course?"

"Of course."

"But the door hasn't been opened."

"I know."

They regarded each other almost uneasily. Then Valentine added, with a short laugh:

"I can't have drawn it thoroughly over the door when Wade went away."

"I suppose not. Well, good-night, Val."

"Good night. Shall we sit again to-morrow?"

"Yes, I vote we do."

Valentine let his friend out. As he shut the front door, he said to himself:

"I am positive I did draw the curtain thoroughly."

He went back into the tent-room and glanced again at the curtain.

"Yes, I am positive."

After an instant of puzzled wonder, he seemed to put the matter deliberately from him.

" Come along, Rip," he said. " Why, you are cold and miserable to-night! Must I carry you, then ? "

He picked the dog up, turned out the light, and walked slowly into his bedroom.

CHAPTER IV

THE SECOND SITTING

ON the following night Valentine sat waiting for Julian's arrival in his drawing-room, which looked out upon Victoria Street, whereas the only window of the tent-room opened upon some waste ground where once a panorama of Jerusalem, or some notorious city, stood, and where building operations were now being generally carried on. Valentine very seldom used his drawing-room. Sometimes pretty women came to tea with him, and he did them honour there. Sometimes musicians came. Then there was always a silent group gathered round the Steinway grand piano. For Valentine was inordinately fond of music, and played so admirably that even professionals never hurled at him a jeering "amateur!" But when Valentine was alone, or when he expected one or two men to smoke, he invariably sat in the tent-room, where the long lounges and the shaded electric light were suggestive of desultory conversation, and seemed tacitly to forbid all things that savour of a hind-leg attitude. To-night, however, some whim, no doubt, had prompted him to forsake his usual haunt. Perhaps he had been seized with a dislike for complete silence, such as comes upon men in recurring hours of depression, when the mind is submerged by a thin tide of unreasoning melancholy, and sound of one kind or another is as ardently sought as at other times it is avoided. In this room Valentine could hear the vague traffic of the dim street outside, the dull tumult of an omnibus, the furtive, flashing clamour of a hansom, the cry of an occasional newsboy, explanatory of the crimes and tragedies of the passing hour. Or, perhaps, the eyes of Valentine were, for the moment, weary of the monotonous green walls of his sanctum, leaning tent-wise towards the peaked apex of the ceiling, and longed to rest on the many beautiful pictures that hung in one line around his drawing-room. It seemed so, for now, as he sat in a chair before the fire, holding Rip upon his knee, his blue eyes were fixed meditatively upon a picture called "The Merciful Knight," which faced him over the mantelpiece. This was the only picture containing a figure of the Christ which Valentine possessed. He had no holy children, no Madonnas. But he loved this Christ, this exquisitely imagined dead, drooping figure, which, roused into life by an act of noble renunciation, bent down and kissed the armed hero who had been great enough to forgive his enemy. He loved those weary, tender lips, those faded limbs, the sacred tenuity of the ascetic figure, the wonderful posture of benign familiarity that was more majestic than any reserve. Yes, Valentine loved this Christ, and Julian knew it well. Often, late at night, Julian had leaned back lazily listening while Valentine played, improvising in a light so dim as to be near to darkness. And Julian had noticed that the player's eyes perpetually sought this picture, and rested on it, while his soul, through the touch of the fingers, called to the soul of music that slept in the piano, stirred it from sleep, carried it through strange and flashing scenes, taught it to strive and to agonise, then hushed it again to sleep and peace. And as Julian looked from the picture to the player, who seemed drawing inspiration from it, he often mutely compared the imagined beauty of the soul of the Christ with the known beauty of the soul of his friend. And the two lovelinesses seemed to meet, and to mingle as easily as two streams one with the other. Yet the beauty of the Christ soul sprang from a strange parentage, was a sublime inheritance, had been tried in the fiercest fires of pity and of pain. The beauty of Valentine's soul seemed curiously innate, and mingled with a dazzling snow of almost inhuman purity. His was not a great soul that had striven successfully and must always strive. His was a soul that easily triumphed, that was almost coldly perfect without effort, that had surely never longed even for a moment to fall, had never desired and refused the shadowy pleasures of passion. The wonderful purity of his friend's face continually struck Julian anew. It suggested to him the ivory peak of an Alp, the luminous pallor of a pearl. What other young man in London looked like that? Valentine was indeed a unique figure in the modern London world. Had he strayed into it from the fragrant pages of a missal, or condescended to it from the beatific vistas of some far-off Paradise? Julian had often wondered, as he looked into the clear, calm eyes of the friend who had been for so long the vigilant, yet unconscious guardian of his soul.

To-night, as Valentine sat looking at the Christ, a curious wonder at himself came into his mind. He was musing on the confession of Julian, so long withheld, so shyly made at last. This confession caused him, for the first time, to look self-consciously upon himself, to stand away from his nature, as the artist stands away from the picture he is painting, and to examine it with a sideways head, with a peering, contracted gaze. This thing that protected a soul from sin—what was it like? What was it? He could not easily surmise. He had a clear vision of the Christ soul, of the exquisite

B

essence of a divine individuality that prompted life to spring out o
death for one perfect moment that it might miraculously reward :
great human act of humanity. Yes, that soul floated before hin
almost visibly. He could call it up before his mind as a man cai
call up the vision of a supremely beautiful rose he has admired
And there was a scent from the Christ soul as ineffably delicious a
the scent of the rose. But when Valentine tried to see his owi
soul, he could not see it. He could not comprehend how its aspec
affected others, even quite how it affected Julian. Only he coul
comprehend, as he looked at the Christ, its imperfection, and :
longing, not felt before, came to him to be better than he was
This new aspiration was given to him by Julian's confession. H
knew that well. He protected his friend now without effort
Could he not protect him more certainly with effort? Can a soul b
beautiful that never strives consciously after beauty? A child'
nature is beautiful in its innocence because it has never striven to b
innocent. But is not an innocent woman more wonderful, mor
beautiful than an innocent child? Valentine felt within him tha
night a distinct aspiration, and he vaguely connected it with th
drooping Christ, who touched with wan, rewarding lips the arden
face of the merciful knight. And he no longer had the desire t
know desire of sin. He no longer sought to understand the powei
of temptation or the joy of yielding to that power. A subtle changi
swept over him. Whether it was permanent, or only passing, h
could not tell.

A tingling cry from the electric bell in the passage told o:
Julian's arrival, and in a moment he entered. He looked gay
almost rowdy, and clapped Valentine on the shoulder rathei
boisterously.

"Why on earth are you in here?" he exclaimed. "Have you
been playing?"

"No."

"Are you in an exalted state of mind, that demands the besi
parlour for its environment?"

"Hardly."

"But why then have you let out the fire in the den and
enthroned yourself here?"

"A whim, Julian. I felt a strong inclination to sit in this room
to-night. It seems to me a less nervous room than the other, and I
want to be as cold-blooded as possible."

"Oh, I see! But, my dear fellow, what is there nervous about
the tent? Do you imagine ghosts lurking in the hangings, or
phantoms of dead Arabs clinging, like bats, round that rosette in
the roof? You got it up the Nile, didn't you?"

"Yes. Where have you been?"

" Dining out. And, oddly enough, I met Marr again, the man I told you about. It seems he is in universal request just now."

" On account of his mystery-mongering, I suppose."

" Probably."

" Did you tell him anything about our sitting ? "

" Only that we had sat, and that nothing had happened."

" What did he say ? "

" He said, ' Pooh, pooh ! these processes are, and always must be, gradual. Another time there may be some manifestation.' "

" Manifestation ! Did you ask him of what nature the manifestation was likely to be ? These people are so vague in the terms they employ."

" Yes. I asked him; but I couldn't get much out of him. I must tell you, Val, that he seemed curiously doubtful about my statement that nothing had happened. I can't think why. He said, ' Are you quite sure ?' "

" Of course you answered Yes ? "

" Of course."

Valentine looked at him for a moment, and then said :

" You didn't mention the—the curtain by any chance ? "

" No. You thought you had left it only partially drawn, didn't you ? "

Valentine made no reply. His face was rather grave. Julian did not repeat the question. He felt instinctively that Valentine did not wish to be obliged to answer it. Oddly enough, during the short silence which followed, he was conscious of a slight constraint such as he had certainly never felt with Valentine before. His gaiety seemed dropping from him in this quiet room to which he was so often a visitor. The rowdy expression faded out of his face, and he found himself glancing half furtively at his friend.

" Valentine," he presently said, " shall we really sit to-night ? "

" Yes, surely. You meant to when you came here, didn't you ? "

" I don't believe there is anything in it."

" We will find out. Remember that I want to get hold of your soul."

Julian laughed.

" If you ever do, it will prove an old man of the sea to you," he said.

" I will risk that," Valentine answered.

And then he added :

" But, come, don't let us waste time. I will go and send away Wade. Clear that little table by the piano."

Julian began removing the photographs and books which stood on it, while Valentine went out of the room and told his man to go.

As soon as they heard the front door close ı
down opposite to each other as on the previous ni

They kept silence, and sat for what seemed a v
last Julian said :

"Val ! "

"Well ? "

"Let us go back into the tent-room."

"Why ? "

"Nothing will ever happen here."

"Why should anything happen there ? "

"I don't know. Let us go. The fire is bu
here. We ought to have complete darkness."

"Very well, though I can't believe it will :
difference."

They got up and went into the tent-room, w
cheerless with its fireless grate.

"I know this will be better," Julian said. "T
table as last night."

Valentine carefully drew the green curtain q
and called Julian's attention to the fact that he I
they sat down again. Rip lay on the divan ir
rug over him, so that he might not disturb them
in search of warmth and of companionship.

The arrangements seemed careful and comp
absolutely isolated from the rest of the world. '
ness, and the silence might almost be felt. A
were safe from trickery, and, as Valentine re|
voix d'or, they were, therefore, probably also safe
had mysteriously called "manifestations."

Dead, numb silence. Their four hands,
loosely on the oval table. Rip slept unutteral
and body in his cosy rug. So—till the last glean
So—till another twenty minutes had passed. T
exchanged a word, had scarcely made the sl
Could a stranger have been suddenly introduced iı
and have remained listening attentively, he migh
deceived into the belief that, but for himself, it
both Valentine and Julian the silence seemed |
each gliding moment they could have declared t
more dense, more prominent, even more grot
There seemed to be a sort of pressure in it wl
more and more definitely. The sensation was int
Each gave himself to it, and each had a, perh
sciousness of yielding up something, something
escent, fluent. Valentine, more especially, felt as

away from himself, by this act of sitting, a vital liquid, and he thought with a mental smile :

" Am I letting my soul out of its cage, here and now ? "

" No doubt," his common sense replied, " no doubt this sensation is the merest fancy."

He played with it in the darkness, and had no feeling of weariness.

Nearly an hour had passed in this morose way, when, with, it seemed, appalling abruptness, Rip barked.

Although the bark was half stifled in rug, both Valentine and Julian started perceptibly.

" 'Sh ! " Valentine hissed to the little dog. " 'Sh ! Rip ! Quiet ! "

The response of Rip was, with a violent scramble, to disentangle himself from his covering, emerging from which he again barked with shrill and piercing vehemence, at the same time leaping to the floor. By the sound, which he could locate, Valentine felt certain that the dog had gone over to the door.

" What on earth is he barking at ? " Julian said in the darkness.

" I can't imagine. Hush, Rip ! S-sh ! "

" Val, turn on the light, quick ! You're nearest to it."

Valentine stretched out his hand hastily, and in a flash the room sprang into view. He was right. Rip was crouched—his front legs extended along the floor, his hind legs standing almost straight —close to the door, and facing it full. His head was down, and moving, darting this way and that, as if he were worrying the feet of some person who was trying to advance from the door into the centre of the room. All his teeth showed, and his yellow eyes were glaring fiercely.

Julian, who had thrown a hasty and searching glance round the room when the light was turned on, sprang forward and bent down to him.

" Rip ! Rip ! " he said. " Silly ! What's the matter ? Silly dog ! " and he began to stroke him.

Either this action of his, or something else not known by the young men, had an effect on the terrier, for he suddenly ceased barking, and began to snuffle eagerly, excitedly, at the bottom of the door.

" It's as if he were mad," said Julian, turning round. " Hulloh, Val ! What the devil's come to you ? "

For he found Valentine standing up by the table with an expression of deep astonishment on his face.

He pointed in silence to the door.

" By Jove ! that curtain again ! " said Julian, with an accent of amazement. " I'm damned ! "

The curtain was, in fact, drawn back from the door. Valentine

struck a match and put it to a candle.   Then he opened the door.
Rip immediately darted out of the room and pattered excitedly down
the passage, as if searching for something, his sharp nose investigating
the ground with a vehement attention.   The young men followed
him.   He ran to the front door, then back into Valentine's bedroom;
then, by turns, into the four other apartments—bedroom, drawing-
room, bath-room and kitchen, that formed the suite.   The doors of
the two latter were opened by Valentine.   Having completed this
useless progress, Rip once more resorted to the passage and the
front door, by which he paused, whimpering, in an uncertain, almost
a wistful attitude.

"Open it!" said Julian.

Valentine did so.

They looked out upon the broad and dreary stone steps, and
waited, listening.   There was no sound.   Rip still whimpered, rather
feebly.   His excitement was evidently dying away.   At last Valentine shut the door, and they went back again to the tent-room,
accompanied closely by the dog, who gradually regained his calmness,
and who presently jumped of his own accord into his basket, and,
after turning quickly round some half-dozen times, composed himself
once more to sleep.

"I wish, after all, we had stayed in the other room by the fire,"
Julian said.   "Give me some brandy."

Valentine poured some into a glass and Julian swallowed it at a
gulp.

"We mustn't have Rip in the room another time," he added.
"He spoilt the whole thing."

"What whole thing?" Valentine asked, sinking down in a chair.

"Well, the sitting.   Perhaps—perhaps one of Marr's mysterious
manifestations might have come off to-night."

Valentine did not reply at first.   When he did, he startled Julian
by saying:

"Perhaps one of them did come off."

"Did?"

"Yes."

"How?"

"What was Rip barking at?"

"There's no accounting for what dogs will do.   They often bark
at shadows."

"At shadows—yes, exactly.   But what cast a shadow to-night?"

Julian laughed with some apparent uneasiness.

"Perhaps a coming event," he exclaimed.

Valentine looked at him rather gravely.

"That is exactly what I felt," he said.

"Explain.   For I was only joking."

" I felt, perhaps it was only a fancy, that this second sitting of ours brought some event a stage nearer, a stage nearer on its journey."

" To what ? "

" I felt—to us."

" Fancy."

" Probably. You didn't feel it ? "

" I ? Oh, I scarcely know what I felt. I must say, though, that squatting in the dark, and saying nothing for such an age, and—and all the rest of it, doesn't exactly toughen one's nerves. That little demon of a Rip quite gave me the horrors when he started barking. What fools we are! I should think nothing of mounting a dangerous horse, or sailing a boat in rough weather, or risking my life as we all do half our time in one way or another. Yet a dog and a dark room give me the shudders. Funny, Val, isn't it ? "

Valentine answered, " If it is a dog and a dark room."

" What else can it possibly be ? " Julian said, with an accent of rather unreasonable annoyance.

" I don't know. But I did draw the curtain completely over the door to-night. Julian, I am getting interested in this. Perhaps—who knows ?—in the end I shall have your soul, you mine."

He laughed as he spoke, then added.

" No, no, I don't believe in such an exchange, and, Julian, I scarcely desire it. But let us go on. This gives a slight new excitement to life."

" Yes. But it is selfish of you to wish to keep your soul to yourself. I want it. Well, *au revoir*, Val, to-morrow night."

" *Au revoir.*"

After Julian had gone Valentine went back into the drawing room and stood for a long while before " The Merciful Knight." He had a strange fancy that the picture of the bending Christ protected the room from the intrusion of—what ?

He could not tell yet. Perhaps he could never tell.

CHAPTER V

THE THIRD SITTING

"Isn't it an extraordinary thing," Julian said, on the following evening, "that if you meet a man once in London you keep knocking up against him day after day? While, if——"

"You don't meet him, you don't."

"No. I mean that if you don't happen to be introduced to him, you probably never set eyes on him at all."

"I know. But whom have you met to-day?"

"Marr again."

"That's odd. He is beginning to haunt you."

"I met him at my club. He has just been elected a member."

"Did he make any more inquiries into our sittings?"

"Rather. He talked of nothing else. He's an extraordinary fellow, extraordinary."

"Why? What is he like?"

"In appearance? Oh, the sort of chap little pink women call Satanic; white complexion showing blue where he shaves, big dark eyes rather sunken, black hair, tall, very thin and quiet. Very well dressed. He is that uncanny kind of man who has a silent manner and a noisy expression. You know what I mean?"

"Yes, perfectly."

"I think he's very morbid. He never reads the evening papers."

"That proves it absolutely. Does he smoke?"

"Always. I found him in the smoking room. He showed the most persistent interest in our proceedings, Val. I couldn't get him to talk of anything else, so at last I told him exactly what had happened."

"Did you tell him that we began to sit last night in a different room?"

"Yes. That was curious. Directly I said it he began making minute inquiries as to what the room was like, how the furniture was placed, even what pictures hung on the walls."

"The pictures!"

"Yes. I described them."

"All of them?"

"No, one or two; that favourite of yours, 'The Merciful Knight,' the Turner, those girls of Solomon's with the man playing to them, and—yes, I think those were all."

" Oh ! "

" He said, ' You made a great mistake in changing your venue to that room, a great mistake.' Then I explained how we moved back to the tent-room in the middle of the sitting and all about Rip."

" Did he make any remark ? "

" One that struck me as very quaint, ' You are *en route.*' "

" Enigmatic again. He was playing the wizard."

" He spoke very gravely."

" Of course. Great gravity is part of the business."

" Afterwards he said, ' Turn that dog out next time.' "

" And that was all ? "

" I think so."

Valentine sat musing. Presently he said,

" I should rather like to meet this Marr."

" Oh, I don't think—I fancy——"

" Well ? "

" I'd as soon you didn't." .

" Why ?"

" I don't think you'd get on. You wouldn't like him."

" For what reason ? "

" I don't know. I've a notion he's something exceptional in the way of a blackguard. Perhaps I am wrong. I haven't an idea what sort of a reputation he has. But he is black, Valentine, not at all your colour. Oh ! and, by the way, he doesn't want to meet you."

" How charming of him ! "

" I had half suggested it, I don't know why, and he said, ' Thanks ! Thanks ! Chance will bring us together later on if we ought to meet.' And now I am glad he wasn't keen. Shall we begin ? Put Rip into your bedroom, as he advised. Besides, I can't stand his barking."

Valentine carried the little dog away. When he came back he shut the tent-room door and was about to draw the curtain over it. But Julian stopped him.

" No, don't," Julian said.

" Why not ? "

" I would rather you didn't. I hate that curtain. If I were you I would have it taken down altogether."

Valentine looked at him in surprise. He had uttered the words with an energy almost violent. But even as Valentine looked Julian switched off the electric light and the leaping darkness hid his face.

" Come now. Business ! Business ! " he cried.

And again they sat with their hands loosely on the table, not touching each other.

Valentine felt that Julian was being less frank with him than usual. Perhaps for this reason he was immediately conscious that they were not so much in sympathy as on the two former occasions of their sittings. Or there might have been some other reason which he could not identify. It is certain that he gradually became acutely aware of a stifling sense of constraint, which he believed to be greatly intensified by the surrounding darkness and silence. He wondered if Julian was conscious of it also, and at moments longed to ask. But something held him back, that curious something which we all feel at times like a strong hand laid upon us. He made up his mind that this discomfort of his soul, unreasonably considerable though it was, must be due solely to Julian's abrupt demeanour and obvious desire to check his curiosity about the drawing of the curtain. But, as the moments ran by, his sense of uneasiness assumed such fantastic proportions that he began to cast about for some more definite, more concrete, cause. At one instant he found it in the condition of his health. The day had been damp and dreary and he had suffered from neuralgia. Doubtless the pain had acted upon his nervous system, and was accountable for his present and perpetually increasing anxiety. A little later he was fain to dismiss this supposition as untenable. His sense of constraint was changing into a positive dread, and not at all of Julian, around whom he had believed that his thoughts were in flight. Something, he knew not at all what, interposed between him and Julian, and so definitely that Valentine felt as if he could have fixed the exact moment in which the interposition had taken place, as one can fix the exact moment in which a person enters a room where one is sitting. And the interposition was one of great horror, entirely malignant, Valentine believed.

He had an impulse to spring up from the table, to turn on the light, and to say, " Let us make an end of this jugglery!" Yet he sat still, wondering why he did so. A curiosity walked in his mind, pacing about till he could almost fancy he heard its footsteps. He sat, then, as one awaiting an arrival, that has been heralded in some way, by a telegram, a message, a carrier pigeon flown in at an open window. But the herald, too, was horrible. What then would follow it? What was coming? Valentine felt that he began to understand Marr's queer remark, " You are *en route.*" At the first sitting he had felt a very vague suggestion of immoderate possibilities, made possibilities by the apparently futile position assumed at a table by himself and Julian. To-night the vague seemed on march towards the definite. Fancy was surely moving towards fact.

With his eyes wide open Valentine gazed in the direction of Julian, sitting invisible opposite to him. He wondered how Julian was feeling, what he was thinking. And then he remembered that strange saying of Marr's that thoughts could take form, materialise. What would he give to witness that monstrous procession. of embodied brain actions trooping from the mind of his friend! He imagined them small, spare, phantom-like things, fringed with fire as weapon against the darkness, silent-footed as spirits, moving with a level impetus, as pale ghosts treading a sea, onward to the vast world of clashing minds, to which we carelessly cast out our thoughts as a man who shoots rubbish into a cart. The vagrant fancies danced along with attenuated steps and tiny, whimsical gestures of fairies, fluttering their flame-veined wings. The sad thoughts moved slowly with drooped heads and monotonous hands, and tears fell for ever about their feet. The thoughts that were evil—and Julian had acknowledged them many, though combated—were endowed with a strangely sinister gait, like the gait of those modern sinners who express, ignorantly, in their motions the hidden deeds their tongues decline to speak. The wayward thoughts had faces like women, who kiss and frown within the limits of an hour. On the cheeks of the libertine thoughts a rosy cloud of rouge shone softly, and their haggard eyes were brightened by a cunning pigment. And the noble thoughts, grand in gesture, god-like in bearing, did not pass them by, but spoke to them serene words, and sought to bring them out from their degradation. And there was no music in this imagined procession which Valentine longed to see. All was silent as, from the gulf of Julian's mind, the inhabitants stole furtively to do their mission. Yes, Valentine knew to-night that he should feel no wonder if thought took form, if a disembodied voice spoke, or a detached hand moved into ripples the air. Only he was irritated and alarmed by the abiding sense of some surrounding danger, which stayed with him, which he fought against in vain. His common sense had not deserted him. On the contrary, it was argumentative, cogent in explanation and in rebuke. It strove to sneer his distress down with stinging epithets, and shot arrows of laughter against his aimless fears. But the combat was nevertheless tamely unequal. Common sense was routed by this enigmatic enemy, and at length Valentine's spirits became so violently perturbed that he could keep silence no longer.

"Julian," he said, with a pressure of chained alarm in his voice, "Julian!"

"Yes," Julian replied, tensely.

"Anything wrong with you?"

"No, no. Or with you?"

"Nothing definite."

"What then?"

"I will confess to you that to-night I feel—I feel, well, horribly afraid."

" Of what ? "

" I have no idea. The feeling is totally unreasonable. That gives it an inexplicable horror."

" Ah ! then that is why you joined your left hand with my right five minutes ago. I wondered why you did it."

" I !   Joined hands ! "

" Yes."

" I haven't moved my hand."

" My dear Val !   How is it holding mine then ? "

" Don't be absurd, Julian ; my hand is not near yours. Both my hands are just where they were when we sat down, on my side of the table."

" Just where they were !   Your little finger has been tightly linked in mine for the last five minutes. You know that as well as I do."

" Nonsense ! "

" But it is linked now while I am speaking."

" I tell you it isn't."

" I'll soon let you know it, too. There ! Ah ! no wonder you have snatched it away. You forget that my muscles are like steel and that I can pinch as a gin pinches a rabbit's leg. I say, I didn't really hurt you, did I ? It was only a joke to stop your little game."

" I tell you," Valentine said, almost angrily, " your hand has never once touched mine, nor mine yours."

His accent of irritable sincerity appeared suddenly to carry conviction to the mind of Julian, for he sprang violently up from the table, and cried, in the darkness :

" Then who the devil's in the room with us ? "

Valentine also, convinced that Julian had not been joking, was appalled. He switched on the light, and saw Julian standing opposite to him, looking very white. They both threw a rapid glance upon the room, whose dull green draperies returned their inquiry with the complete indifference of artistic inanimation.

" Who the devil's got in here ? " Julian repeated, with the savage accent of extreme uneasiness.

" Nobody," Valentine replied. " You know the thing's impossible."

" Impossible or not, somebody has found means to get in."

Valentine shook his head.

" Then you were lying ? "

" Julian, what are you saying ? Don't go too far."

" Either you were, or else a man has been sitting at that table between us, and I have held his hand, the hand of some stranger. Ouf ! "

He shook his broad shoulders in an irrepressible shudder.

" I was not lying, Julian. I tell you so, and I mean it."

Valentine's eyes met Julian's, and Julian believed him.

" Put your hands on the table again," Julian said.

Valentine obeyed, and Julian laid his beside them, linking one of his little fingers tightly in one of Valentine's, and, at the same time, shutting his eyes. After a long pause he grew visibly whiter, and hastily unlinked his finger.

" No, damn it, Val, I hadn't hold of your hand. The hand I touched was much harder, and the finger was bigger, thicker. I say, this is ghastly."

Again he shook himself, and cast a searching glance upon the little room.

" Somebody has been in here with us, sitting between us in the dark," he repeated. " Good God, who is it ? "

Valentine looked doubtful, but uneasy too.

" Let us go through the rooms," he said.

They took a candle, and, as on the previous night, searched, but in vain. They found no trace of any alien presence in the flat. No book, no ornament, had been moved. No door stood open. There was no sound of any footsteps except their own. When they came to Valentine's bedroom, Rip leaped to greet them, and seemed in excellent spirits. He showed no excitement until he had followed them back into the tent-room. But, arrived there, he suddenly stood still, raised one white paw from the ground, and emitted a long and dreary howl. The young men stared at him, and then at each other.

" Rip knows somebody has been here," Julian said.

Valentine was much more uncomfortably impressed by the demeanour of the dog than by Julian's declaration and subsequent agitation. He had been inclined to attribute the whole affair to a trick of his friend's nerves. But the nervous system of a fox terrier was surely, under such circumstances as these, more truth-telling than that of a man.

" But the thing is absolutely impossible," he repeated, with some disturbance of manner.

" Is anything that we can't investigate straight away absolutely impossible ? "

Valentine did not reply directly.

" Here is a cigarette," he said. " Let us sit down, soothe our nerves, and talk things over calmly and openly. We have not been quite frank with each other about these sittings yet."

Julian accepted Valentine's offer with his usual readiness. The fire was relit with some difficulty. Rip was coaxed into silence.

Presently, as the smoke curled upward with its lazy demeanour, the horror that had hung like a thin vapour in the atmosphere seemed to be dissipated.

" Now I think we are ourselves again, and can be reasonable,"

Valentine began. "Don't let us be hysterical. Spiritualists always suffer from hysteria."

"The sceptics say, Val."

"And probably they are generally right. Now—yes, do drink some more of that brandy and soda. Now, Julian, do you still believe that a hand held yours just now?"

Julian answered quietly, showing no irritation at the question:

"I simply know it as surely as I know that I am sitting with you at this moment. And—look here, you may laugh at me as much as you like—although I supposed the hand to be yours, until you denied it, I had previously felt the most curious sensation."

"Of what?"

"Well, that something was coming, even had actually come, into the room."

Valentine answered nothing to this, so Julian went on.

"I thought it was a trick of the nerves, and determined to drive it away, and I succeeded. And then, just as I was internally laughing at myself, this hand, as if groping about in the dark, was first laid on mine, full on it, Val, and then slid off on to the table and linked its little finger tightly in mine. I, of course, supposed the hand was yours, and this finger was crooked round mine for fully five minutes, I should say. After you spoke, thinking that you were trying to deceive me for a joke, I caught the hand in mine, and pinched it with all my strength until it was forcibly dragged away."

"Strange," Valentine murmured.

"Deucedly strange! and, what's more, diabolically unpleasant."

"I wonder what that fellow, Marr, would say to this."

"Marr! By Jove, is this one of the manifestations which he spoke about so vaguely?"

"It seems like it."

"But describe your sensations. You say you felt horribly afraid. Why was that?"

"I can't tell. That, I think, made part of the horror. There was a sort of definite vagueness, if you can imagine such a seeming contradiction, in my state of mind. But the feeling is really indescribable. That it was more strange and more terrible than anything I have known is certain. I should like to ask Dr. Levillier about all this."

"Levillier—yes. But he would——"

"Be reasonable about it, as he is about everything. Dear, sensible, odd, saintly, emotional, strong-headed, soft-hearted little doctor. He is unique."

They talked on for some time, arriving at no conclusion, until, it seemed, they had talked the whole matter thoroughly out. Yet Valentine, who was curiously instinctive, had, all the time, a secret knowledge that Julian was keeping something from him, was not being perfectly frank. The conviction pained him. At last Julian got up to go. He stood putting on his overcoat.

" Good-night," he said.

" Good-night, Julian."

" Now—is this to be our last sitting ? "

Valentine hesitated.

" What do you wish ? " he asked, at length.

" What do you ? "

" Well, I—yes, I think I would rather it was the last."

Julian caught his hand impulsively.

" So would I. Good-night."

" Good-night."

Julian went out into the hall, got as far as the front door, opened it, then suddenly called out :

" Valentine ! "

" Yes."

" Come here for a moment."

Valentine went, and found him standing with his hand on the door, looking flushed and rather excited.

" There is one thing I haven't told you," he began.

" I knew that."

" I guessed you did. The most horrible sensation I have had. During our sitting to-night—don't be vexed—an extraordinary apprehension of—well, of you, came over me. There ! Now I have told you."

Valentine was greatly astonished.

" Of me ? " he said.

" Yes. There was a moment when the idea that I was alone with you made my blood run cold."

" Good heavens ! "

" Do you wish I hadn't told you ? "

" No, of course not. But it is so extraordinary, so unnatural."

" It is utterly gone now, thank God. I say, we have resolved that we won't sit again, haven't we ? "

" Yes ; and what you have just told me makes me hate the whole thing. The game seems a game no longer."

When the door had closed upon Julian, Valentine sat down and wrote a note.

He addressed it to

" DOCTOR HERMANN LEVILLIER,

Harley Street, W.,"

and laid it on his writing-table so that it might be posted early the next morning.

CHAPTER VI

A CONVERSATION AT THE CLUB

DOCTOR LEVILLIER was not a materialist, although he concerned himself much with the functions of the body, and with that strange spider's web of tingling threads which we call the nervous system The man who sweeps out the temple, who polishes the marble steps and dusts the painted windows, may yet find time to bend in prayer before the altars he helps to keep beautiful, may yet find a heart to wonder at the spirit which the temple holds as an envelope holds a letter. Reversing the process of mind which seems to lead so many medical students to atheism, Dr. Levillier had found that the more he understood the weaknesses, the nastinesses, the dreary failures the unimaginable impulses of the flesh, the more he grew to believe in the existence, within it, of the soul. One day a worn out dyspeptic, famous for his intellectual acquirements over two continents, sat with the little great doctor in his consulting-room. The author, with dry, white lips, had been recounting a series of sordid symptoms, and, as the recital grew, their sordidness seemed suddenly to strike him with a mighty disgust.

"Ah, doctor," he said. "And do you know there are people thousands of miles away from Harley Street who actually admire me, who are stirred and moved by what I write, who make a cult and a hero of me. They say I have soul, forsooth. But I am all body; you know that. You doctors know that it is only body that we put on paper, body that lifts us high, or drags us low. Why, my best romances come straight from my liver. My pathos springs from its condition of disorder, and my imaginative force is only due to an unnatural state of body which I can deliberately produce by drinking tea that has stood a long while and become full of tannin. When my prose glows with fiery beauty, the tea is getting well hold of my digestive organs, and by the time it has begun to prove its power by giving me a violent pain in the stomach, I have wrung from it a fine scene which will help to consolidate my fame. When a man wins the Victoria Cross, his healthy body has done the deed, unprompted by anything higher. Good air, or a muscular life, has strung his nerves strongly so that he can't, even if he would, appreciate danger. On the other hand, when a man shows funk, turns tail and bolts, and is dubbed a coward, it's his beastly body again. Some obscure physical misfortune is the cause of his disgrace, and if he'd only been to you he would have won the Cross too. Isn't it so? How you doctors must laugh at mystics, and at those who are ascetics, save for sake of their health. Why, I suppose even the saint owes his so-called goodness to some analysable proceeding that has gone on in his inside, and that you could diagnose. Eh?"

Dr. Levillier was writing a prescription in which bismuth was an item. He glanced up quietly.

"The more I know of the body, the more I think of, and believe in, the power of the soul," he said. "Have that made up. Take it three times a day, and come to me again in a fortnight. Good morning."

Indeed, this little man was writing prescriptions for the body and thinking prescriptions for the soul all day long. Within him there dwelt a double mind, the mind of a great doctor and the mind of a great priest, and these two minds linked hands and lived as friends. The one never strove against the other. There was never a moment of estrangement. And if there were frequent arguments and discussions between the two, they were the arguments and discussions that make friendship firmer, not enmity more bitter. And, as Dr. Levillier very well knew, it was often the mind of the priest within him that gave to him his healing power over the body. It was the mind of the priest that had won him testimonial clocks and silver salvers from grateful patients. Often as he sat with some dingy-faced complainant, listening to a recital of sickness, or uttering directions about avoidance of green meat, sauces, pastry and liquids, till the atmosphere seemed that of a hospital, a pastrycook's shop and a bar combined, he was silently examining the patient's soul, facing its probable vagaries, mapping out the tours it had taken, scheming for its welfare. And, perhaps, after the dietary was arranged and the prescription was written, he would say carelessly :

"Do you read much? What do you read? Ah! such and such books. Yes, very interesting. Do you know this book which has struck me greatly? No? Allow me to lend it to you. Good-bye."

And the patient departed, ignorant that he had received a pill for his soul from the priest as well as a pill for his body from the doctor.

In appearance Dr. Levillier was small, slight, and delicate looking. His complexion was clear and white. His eyes were blue. What hair he possessed was rather soft, fluffy, and reddish, with a dash of light brown in it. He wore neither beard nor moustache, was always very neatly and simply dressed, and was remarkable for his polished boots, said to be the most perfectly varnished in London. Although he must have been nearly fifty-five, he had never married, and some

C

people declared he had the intention of starting a new "order" of medical celibates, who would be father confessors as well as physicians, and who would pray for the souls of their patients after tending their bodily needs.

For some years Valentine had been very intimate with the doctor, whom he admired for his intellect and loved for his nature. So now he resolved to lay the case of the sittings with Julian before him, and hear his opinion of the matter. In all their conversations Valentine could not remember that they had ever discussed spiritualism or occultism. As a rule they talked about books, painting, or music, of which Dr. Levillier was a devoted lover. Valentine's note asked the doctor to dine with him that night at his club. The messenger brought back an acceptance.

They dined at a corner table, and the room was rather empty. A few men chatted desultorily of burlesques, horses, the legs of actresses, the chances of politics. The waiters moved quietly about with pathetic masks of satisfied servitude. Valentine and the doctor conversed earnestly.

At first they spoke of a new symphony composed by a daring young Frenchman, who had striven to reproduce vices in notes, and to summon up visions of things damnable by harmonic progressions which frequently defied the laws of harmony. Levillier gently condemned him for putting a great art to a small and degraded use.

"His very success makes me regret the waste of his time more deeply, Cresswell," he said. "He is a marvellous painter in sound. He has improved upon Berlioz, if it is improvement to cry sin with a clearer, more determinate voice. Think what a heaven that man could reproduce in music."

"Because he has reproduced a hell. But do you think that follows? Can the man who wallows with force and originality, soar with force and originality too?"

"I believe he could learn to. The main thing is to possess genius in any form, the genius to imagine, to construct, to present things that seize upon the minds of men. But to possess genius is only a beginning. We have to train it, to lead it, to coax it even, until it learns to be obedient."

"Genius and obedience. Don't the two terms quarrel?"

"They should not. Obedience is a very magnificent thing, Cresswell, just as to have to struggle, to be obliged to fight, is a very magnificent thing."

"Yes," Valentine answered thoughtfully. "I believe you are right. But, if you are right, I have missed a great deal."

"How do you deduce that?"

"In this way. I have never had to be obedient. I have never had to struggle."

"Surely the latter," the little doctor said, fixing his clear, kind eyes on Valentine's face. "I don't think in all my experience that I have ever met a man who lived a fine, pure life without fixing the bayonet and using the sword at moments. There must be an occasional *mêlée*."

"Indeed not; that is to say," Valentine rather hastily added, "as regards the pure life. For I cannot lay claim to anything fine. But I assure you that my life has been pure without a struggle."

"Without one? Think!"

"Without one. Perhaps that is what wearies me at moments, doctor, the completeness of my coldness. Perhaps it is this lack of necessity to struggle that has at last begun to render me dissatisfied."

"I thought you were free from that evil humour of dissatisfaction, that evil humour which crowds my consulting-rooms and wastes away the very tissues of the body."

"I have been, until quite lately. I have been neither pessimist nor optimist, just myself, and I believe happy."

"And what is this change, and what has it led to?"

"It was to tell you that I asked you here to-night."

They had finished dinner, and rose from the table. Passing through the hall of the club, they went into a huge, high room, papered with books. Valentine led the way to a secluded corner, and gave the doctor a cigar. When he had lit it and settled himself comfortably, his rather small feet, in their marvellously polished boots, lightly crossed, his head reposing serenely on the back of his chair, Valentine continued, answering his attentive silence.

"It has led to what I suppose you would call an absurdity. But first, the change itself. A sort of dissatisfaction has been creeping over me, perhaps for a long while, I being unconscious of it. At length I became conscious. I found that I was weary of being so free from the impulse to sin—to sin, I mean, in definite, active ways, as young men sin. It seemed to me that I was missing a great deal, missing the delight sin is said to give to natures, or at least missing the invigorating necessity you have just mentioned, the necessity to fight, to wage war against impulses."

"I understand."

"And one night I expressed this feeling to Julian."

"To Addison?" the doctor said, an expression of keen interest sliding into his face. "I should much like to know how he received it."

"He said, of course, that such a dissatisfaction was rather monstrous."

"Was that all?"

"No. He told me he considered temptation rather a curse than otherwise, and then he surprised me very much."

" He told you a secret ? "

" Why, yes."

" The secret of your great influence over his life ? "

" You knew of this secret then ? "

" He didn't tell it to me. Long ago I divined it. Addison is a very interesting fellow to a doctor, and the fact of his strong friendship with you has made him more interesting even than he would otherwise have been. His physique is tremendous. He has a quite unusual vitality, and stronger passions by far than most Englishmen. I confess that my knowledge of human nature led me to foresee a very troubled and too vehement future for him. My anticipation being utterly falsified led me naturally to look round for the reason of its falsification. I very soon found that reason in you."

" I had never suspected it."

" Your lack of suspicion was not the least reason of the influence you exercised."

" Possibly. He told me of the strength of his evil impulses, of how he hated their assaults, and of how being with me enabled him to conquer them. Apparently the contemplation of my unnatural nature is an armour to him."

" It is."

" Well, I continued to bewail my condition, which he envied, and it ended in our sitting down, in jest, to make an experiment, to try to exchange our souls."

" What means did you take ? "

And then Valentine told Dr. Levillier the exact circumstances of the three sittings, without embellishment, without omission of any kind. He listened with keen attention, and without attempting interruption or intruding comment. When Valentine had finished, he made no remark.

" What do you think of it, doctor ? "

" Of what part of it ? "

" Of any part. Do you attach any importance to it ? "

" I do, certainly."

" I thought you would laugh at the whole thing."

" Why should I ? Why should I laugh at any circumstances which strongly affect men whom I know ; or, indeed, any men ? "

" But then, tell me, do you believe in some strange, unseen agency ? Do you believe that Julian absolutely held the hand of some being dwelling in another sphere, some being attracted to us, or, say, enabled to come to us by such an action as our sitting at a table in the dark ? "

" No. I don't believe that."

" You attribute the whole thing to bodily causes ? "

" I am inclined to attribute it to the action and reaction of mind and body, undoubtedly. If you had sat in the light, for instance, I don't think Addison would have felt that hand. The hand is indeed the least of the circumstances you have related, in my opinion. The incidents of the dog and of the curtain are far more mysterious. You are positive the door was securely shut ? "

" Quite positive."

" Could you, after having drawn the curtain, have allowed your hand to slip slightly back, pulling the curtain with it ? "

" I don't think so. I feel sure not."

" You know we all constantly make involuntary motions, motions that our minds are quite unaware of."

" I do feel sure, nevertheless. And the dog ? What do you say to that ? "

" I don't know what to say. But dogs are extraordinarily sensitive. I do not think it beyond the bounds of possibility that the tumult of your nerves—for there was tumult; you confess it—communicated itself to him."

" And was the cause of his conduct ? "

" Yes. In the course of my career I have been consulted by a great many patients whose nervous systems have been disastrously upset by the practices you describe, by so-called spiritualism, table-turning, and so forth. One man I knew, trying to cultivate himself on to what he called 'a higher plane,' cultivated himself into a lunatic asylum, where he still remains."

" Then you consider spiritualism —— ? "

" I have too much respect for the soul, too much belief in its great destiny, Cresswell, to juggle with it, or to play tricks with it. When one meets a genius one does not want to have a game at puss-in-the-corner with him. One is rather anxious to hear him talk seriously and display his mind. When I come into contact with a soul, I don't want to try to detach it from the home in which a divine power has placed it for a time. I glory in many limitations against which it is the prevailing fashion to fight uselessly. The soul can do all its work where it is—in the body. The influence you exercise over your friend Addison convinces me of the existence of spirits, things which will eventually be freed from the body, more certainly than any amount of material manifestations, sights, sounds, apparent physical sensations. Why should we not be satisfied with remaining, for a time, as we are ? I consider that you and Addison were ill-advised in making this—no doubt absurd—experiment. Supposing it to be absurd, the *raison d'être* of the sittings is gone at once. Supposing it not to be absurd——"

" Yes. What then ? "

" Then the danger is great. Imagine yourself with Addison's

soul, or nature, him with yours. To what might not you be led? How do you know that your nature in him would exert any control over his nature in you?"

"Why should it not?"

"There comes in the power of the body, which is very great. I believe, as you know, absolutely in the existence of the soul, and in its immortal destiny; but that does not blind me to the extraordinary influence, the extraordinary kingship, which a mere body, a mere husk and shell, as some good people call it—I don't feel with them—can obtain not only over another body, but, strangely, over the soul which is in that body. Your influence over Addison has been, and is, immense. Do you imagine that it is simply your nature which governs him?"

"I suppose so."

"Your mere appearance may have an immense deal to do with the matter. You have the look, the expression, of one who has not sinned. It is partly that which keeps Addison from giving the reins to his impulses. I consider that if it were possible for your nature to change secretly, and for your face to remain unchanged, if you sinned perpetually and retained your exact appearance, and if Addison did not know you sinned, you could still be his guardian, while, really, yourself far worse in every way than he."

"But surely that fights against your theory that the existence of a soul is proved by such an influence as I possess over Addison?"

"Not at all. I said if it were possible for the body not to express the soul, if—but that's just the difficulty, it is not possible. The body manifests the soul. Supposing it were not so, the power of evil, the devil, if you choose to name it and imply a personal existence for it, might have hold of the world even more tightly than now. Just conceive, under such conditions, how you might lure Addison to destruction if you desired to do so. Looking at you and seeing the same face in which he has learned to see what he thinks entire goodness, he would be unable to believe that any action you could suggest and take part in could be evil. You could wreck his future with a perfect ease. But, as things are, did your nature change and become malignant, your face would change too, and you might quickly cease to exercise a strong influence over Addison. He might even, having now been unconsciously trained into a curious integrity, learn to hate and to despise you. You remember our conversation to-night about that symphony?"

"Yes."

"I said that the soul which could reproduce hell should be able to reproduce heaven."

"I know."

" Well, my boy—for you are a boy to me—the reverse of that might happen also."

" Perhaps. But I don't quite see."

" The application—to you ? "

" To me ? "

" Yes, to you, Cresswell. You have been given a strangely perfect nature. As you say, you seem to have nothing to do with the matter. You have even been inclined to rebel against your gift. But, take my advice. Cherish it. Don't play with it, as you have been playing. Remember, if you lose heaven, the space once filled by heaven will not be left empty."

" Ah ! now I see. You think that I——"

" Might swing from a great height to an equally great depth. That has been my experience, that the man who is once extreme is always extreme, but not always in the same way. The greatest libertines have made the greatest ascetics. But, within my own experience, I have known the reverse process to obtain. And you, if you changed, might carry Addison with you."

" But then, doctor, you do believe in these manifestations ? "

" Not necessarily. But I believe that the minds of men are often very carefully, very deftly poised, and that a little push can send them one way or the other. Have you ever balanced one billiard ball on the top of another ? "

" Yes."

" Then you know that a breath will upset it and send it rolling. Be careful. Your mind, your very nature, may be poised like that billiard ball. Addison's may be the same. Indeed, I feel sure Addison's is. That curious dread of you which overcame him at your last sitting is a sign of it. The whole thing is wrong, bad for body and for mind."

" Perhaps. Well, we have definitely agreed to give it up."

" That's well. Eleven o'clock ! I must be going. Are you doing anything to-morrow night ? "

" No."

" I have got a box for this new play at the Duke's Theatre. Will you come ? "

" With pleasure."

" I will ask Addison also."

They put on their overcoats, and walked a little way along Pall Mall before they parted. Near the Athenæum they passed a tall, thin man, who was coming in the opposite direction. He turned round as they went by, and stood directly regarding them till they were out of sight.

CHAPTER VII

THE REGENT STREET EPISODE

THE things we do apparently by chance often have a curious applicability to the things we have thought. John the Baptist was sent to prepare the way of the Lord. These thoughts are the John the Baptists of the mind, and prepare the way for facts that often startlingly illustrate them. It is as if our thoughts were gradually materialised by the action of the mind, as if, by the act of thinking, we projected them.

When Dr. Levillier got a box for the first night of the new play at the Duke's Theatre, and when he invited Valentine and Julian to make up his party, he had no idea what the subject of the piece was, no notion that it would have anything to do with the conversation which took place between him and Valentine at the Club. But the plot applied with almost amazing fidelity to much that he had said upon that occasion. The play was a modern allegory of the struggle between good and evil, which has been illustrated in so many different ways since the birth of the Faust legend. But the piece had a certain curious originality which sprang from the daring of the author. Instead of showing one result of the struggle, a good man drawn gradually down, or a bad man drawn gradually up, he set forth, with a great deal of detail, a great deal of vividness, a modern wobbler, a human pendulum, and simply noted down, as it were, his slow swinging backwards and forwards. His hero, an evil liver, a modern man of wrath in the first act, dominated by a particular vice, was drawn, by an outside personal influence, from the mire in which he was wallowing to purity, to real elevation. But his author, having led him up to the pinnacle, had no intention of leaving him there, blessed by the proclaimed admiration of the gods in the gallery. In the succeeding acts he introduced a second personal influence, exerted this time on the side of evil, and permitted it to act upon his central figure successfully. The man fell again into the mire, and was left there at the conclusion of the piece, but hugging a different sin, not the sin he had been embracing when the curtain rose upon the first act. This dramatic scheme took away the breath of the house for a moment, but only for a moment. Then the lungs once more did their accustomed duty, and enabled a large number of excited persons to hiss with a wonderful penetration. Their well-meant efforts did not have the effect of terrorising the author. On the contrary, he quickly responded to the hostile uproar, and, coming forward in a very neat Jaeger suit, a flannel shirt, and a pair of admirably fitting doeskin gloves, bowed with great gravity and perfect self-possession. The hisses thereupon suddenly faded into piercing entreaties for a speech, in which a gallery lady with a powerful soprano voice became notorious as the leader. But the Jaeger author was not to be prevailed upon. He waved the doeskin gloves in token of adieu, and retreated once more into the excited obscurity of the wings, where his manager was trembling like an aspen in the midst of a perspiring company. The lights were turned down. The orchestra burst into a tuneful jig, and the lingering audience at length began to disperse.

Dr. Levillier, Julian, and Valentine left their box in silence. It seemed that this odd play, which dared to be natural, had impressed them. They walked into the vestibule without a word, and, avoiding many voluble friends who were letting off the steam as they gathered their coats and hats from a weary lady in a white cap, they threaded their way through the crowd and emerged into the street. Just as they reached the portico, Julian suddenly started and laid his hand on Valentine's arm.

" What is it ? " asked Valentine, looking round.

" Ah ! you're just too late. He's gone ! "

" He—who ? "

" Marr."

" Oh," Valentine said, showing considerable interest, " I wish I had seen him. Where was he sitting ? "

" I haven't an idea. Didn't know he was in the theatre."

Dr. Levillier made an exception to his rule of being in bed by twelve o'clock that night, and accepted Valentine's invitation to sup in Victoria Street. He had always been greatly drawn to Valentine, attracted by the latter's exceptional clarity of character, and he was scarcely less interested in Julian. Nor did the considerable difference between his age and the ages of the two youths in any way interfere with their pleasant intercourse. For Levillier had a heart that was ageless. The corroding years did not act as an acid upon it. All his sympathies were as keen, all his power of enjoyment was as great, as when he had been a delightfully gay, and delightfully pleasant boy at school. Youth always loved him, and age always respected him. He possessed the great secret of a beautiful life. He was absolutely genuine, and he meant nothing but good to all with whom he was brought into contact

The three friends spoke but little as they went back to the flat, but when they had sat down to supper, and Dr. Levillier had expressed his complete satisfaction with the champagne that Valentine's butler had politely insinuated into his glass, the silence took to itself wings and lightly departed. They talked of the play, and it appeared that they were all impressed by it, but in slightly different ways, and for different reasons. Valentine, who was intensely, but sometimes almost coldly, artistic, appreciated it, he said, because it did not obviously endeavour to work out a problem or to teach a lesson. It simply, with a great deal of literary finish and dramatic force, stated a curiously human character, showed the nature of a man at work, and left him, after some scenes of his life, still at work upon his own salvation or destruction, not telling the audience what his end would be, scarcely even trying to imply his innate tendency one way or the other. This satisfied Valentine. This had made him feel as if he had seen a block cut out of life.

"I do not want to learn what becomes of that man," he said. "I have known him, good and bad. That is enough. That satisfies me more than the sight of a thousand bombastic heroes, a thousand equally bombastic villains. Life is neither ebony nor ivory. That man is something to my mind for ever, as Ibsen's ' Master Builder ' is something. I can never forget the one or the other."

"Your life is ivory, Val," Julian said.

He had liked the play because the violent struggle between good and evil woke up many responsive memories in his mind. The hero of the play had been shown feeling precisely as Julian had often felt. That was enough. He did not very much care for the brilliant artifice, which Valentine had remarked with so much pleasure. He did not specially note the peculiar effect of nature produced by the simplicity and thoughtful directness of the dialogue. He only knew that he had seen somebody whose nature was akin to his own, although placed in different, perhaps more dramatic, circumstances.

Dr. Levillier combined, to some appreciable extent, the differing joys of his two companions, and obtained another that was quite his own. He had seen two horses running in double harness that night, the body and mind of the hero, and had taken delight in observing, what had practically escaped the definite notice of his companions, the ingenuity and subtlety with which the author, without being obtrusive or insistent, had displayed their *liaison ;* the effect of each upon the other, their answering excursions and alarums, their attempts at separate *amours, amours* that always had an inevitable effect upon the one which the other had, for the moment, endeavoured to exclude from its life. The doctor in him and the priest in him had both enjoyed a glorious evening of bracing activity. As they discussed the piece, and each advanced his reason of pleasure, the doctor expanded into a sort of saintly geniality, which was peculiarly attractive even to sinners. And when supper was over, and they strolled into the drawing-room to smoke and to make music, he sank into a chair, stretched out his polished boots with a sigh, and said :

" And people say there is so little joy in life ! "

Julian laughed at the satisfied whimsicality of his exclamation and of the expression which shadowed it.

" Light up, Doctor," he cried. " You are a boon to this modern world. For you see all the sorrows of life, I suppose, and yet you always manage to convey the impression that the joys win the battle after all."

Valentine had gone over to the piano and was dreamily opening it. He did not seem to hear what they were saying. The doctor obeyed the injunction to light up. He was one of the hardest and most assiduous toilers in all London, and he appreciated a good cigar and a comfortable arm-chair more than some men could appreciate Paradise, or some women appreciate love.

" And I believe that joy will win the battle in the end," he said, with a puff that proved successful.

" Why ? "

" I see evidences of it, or think I do. The colour will fade out of bad acts, Addison, but the colour of a good act is eternal. A noble deed will never emulate a Sir Jeshua Reynolds—never. Play to us, Cresswell."

" Yes, but I wish you to talk. I want to improvise to-night. The murmur of your conversation will help me."

Julian sat down by the doctor. He, too, looked very happy. It was a pleasant hour. Sympathy was in that pretty room, complete human sympathy, and a sympathy that sprang from their vitality, avoiding the dusky dumbness of the phlegmatic. Valentine sat down at the piano and began to play gently. The smoke from the cigars curled away towards the watching pictures; the room was full of soft music.

" Yes, Addison," Dr. Levillier continued, in a low voice, " I am perpetually sitting with sorrow, communing with disease. That consulting room of mine is as a pool of Bethesda, only not all who come to it, alas ! can be healed. I sit day by day in my confessional—I like to call it that ; perhaps I was meant to be a priest—and I read the stories of the lives of men and of women, most of them necessarily, from the circumstances which bring them to me, sad. And yet I have a belief in joy and its triumph which nothing can ever shake, a belief in the final glory of good which nothing can ever conquer."

" That's fine, Doctor. But do you know why you have it ? "

" I daresay that question is difficult to answer. I often seek for my reasons, Cresswell, and I find many, though I can hardly say which is the best, or whether any quite explains the faith that is always in me. *A propos* of this evening, by-the-by, I long ago found one of my reasons in the theatre, the theatre which some really good men hate and condemn."

" What was that ? "

" Oh, a very simple one. I believe that men in the mass express eternal truths more readily, more certainly, than men as individuals. Put a lot of bad men, or—we won't call them bad, why should we ?—loose, careless, thoughtless men, together in the pit of a theatre. Many of them, perhaps, drink, and are rendered cruel by drink. Many of them care nothing for morality and have wounded, in the worst way, the souls of women. Many of them show incessant hardness in most of the relations of life. What, then, is it that makes all these individuals respond so directly, so certainly, to every touch of goodness, and gentleness, and unselfishness, and purity, and faith, that is put before them upon the stage ? I think it must be that eternal truth—the rocks of good that lie for ever beneath the wild seas of evil. Those men don't know themselves, don't know that it is all useless for them to try to hide the nobility which has been put into them, to thrust it down, and metaphorically to dance on it. They can't get rid of it, do what they will. I like to think of goodness as the shadow of evil through life, the shadow that, at death, or perhaps long after death, becomes the substance."

" You think we cannot kill the good that is in us ? "

" Not quite. But I think we can go near to killing it, so near that it will take longer to recover and to be itself again, longer far than the most relapsing typhoid patient."

" And have you other reasons for your belief ? "

" Perhaps. But some of them are difficult to define, and would carry no conviction to any one but myself. There is one in this very room with us."

Julian glanced up surprised.

" What is that, Doctor ? " he said.

" You ought to know better than I," Levillier answered.

He was looking at Valentine, who, apparently quite unconscious of their presence, was still playing rather softly. Julian followed his eyes.

The light in the room was dim, a carefully manufactured twilight. It is strange how many things, and how slight, stir, control, influence, in one direction or another, the emotions. Light and the absence of light can divert a heart as easily as the pressing of a button can give a warship to the sea. Twilight and music can

change a beast into a man, a man into an angel for the moment.
Long after that evening was dead, both Julian and Dr. Levillier
anxiously and, in their different ways, analytically, considered it.
They submitted it to a secret process of probing, such as many men
enforce upon what they imagine to be great causes in their lives.
That hour became an hour of wonder, an hour of amazement, viewed
in the illumination of subsequent events. They found in it a
curious climax of misunderstanding, a culmination of all deceptive
things.

And yet, in that hour they only watched a young man of London,
a modern intellectual youth, playing in a Victoria Street drawing-
room upon a Steinway grand piano.

They were sitting sideways to Valentine, and a little behind him.
Therefore he could not easily see them unless he slightly turned his
head. But they could observe him, and, obeying Dr. Levillier's mute
injunction, Julian now did so.

Valentine was gazing straight before him over the top of the piano,
and his eyes seemed to be fixed upon the dim figure of Christ in the
picture of "The Merciful Knight." Was he not playing to the
picture, playing to that figure in it? And did not his musical
imagination seek to reproduce in sound the vision of the life of that
mailed knight who never lived and died? The purity of his expression, always consummate, was to-night more peculiar, more unearthly,
than before in any place, at any moment. And, as mere line can
convey to the senses of man a conception of a great virtue or of a
great vice, the actual shape of his features, thus seen in profile, was
the embodiment of an exquisitely ascetic purity, as much an embodiment as is a drop of water pierced by a sunbeam. This struck both
Dr. Levillier and Julian, and the doctor was amazed anew at the
silent decree that the invisible shall be made visible in forms comprehensible to the commonest minds. Sin would surely flee from a
temple sculptured in such a shape as the body of Valentine, as a
vampire would flee from the bloodless courts of the heaven of the
Revelation. Lust cannot lie at ease on a crystal couch, or rest its
dark head upon a pillow of pale ivory. And the message of this
strange, unearthly youth now given in music, and to the air and the
dusk—for Valentine had lost knowledge of his friends—was crystal-
line too. In his improvisation he journeyed through many themes
of varying characters. He hymned the Knight's temptation no less
than his triumph. But purity was in the hymn even at the hour of
temptation, and sang like a bird in every scene of the life; a purity
classical, detached, so refined as to be almost physically cold.

" I understand you," Julian whispered to the little doctor. " Yes,
you are right. He is a great reason why what you think may be
true. And yet——" here Julian lowered his voice to a breath, lest

he might disturb the player. "He is not religious as—as—well, a
you are. Forgive the allusion——."

"Are the angels religious?" said Dr. Levillier. "Why should
you refrain, my dear boy? But you are right. There is a curious
unconsciousness about Cresswell—about Valentine—which seems to
exclude even definite religious belief as something in a way self
conscious, and so impossible to him. There is an extraordinary
strain of the child in Cresswell, such as I conceive to be in unearthly
beings, who have never had the power to sin. And the best behaved
sweetest child in the world might catch flies, or go to sleep during a
Litany or a sermon. This very absence of controversial or dogmatic
religion gives Valentine much of his power, seems positively to lift
him higher than religionists of any creed."

"You think—you think that perhaps it is something in him of
which he is unconscious which does so much for me?"

"Perhaps it is."

Valentine now glided into an accompaniment, and began to sing.
And the doctor and Julian ceased to talk. Valentine certainly did
not sing with such peculiar skill as he showed in playing, but he had
a charming voice which he used with great ease, and he never sang
a single note, or phrased a passage, without complete intelligence
and understanding of his composer. Only he lacked power. This
scarcely interfered with the pleasure he could give in a drawing-room,
and to-night both Levillier and Julian were rather in a mood for
supreme delicacy than for great passion. They listened with silent
pleasure for a time. Then Levillier said:

"Do you remark how wonderfully the timbre of Cresswell's voice
expresses the timbre of his mind? The parallel is exact."

Julian nodded.

"That is his soul written in sound," the doctor added.

It was at this point that Valentine ceased and got up from the
piano.

"I must smoke too," he said. "No, not a cigar, I'll have a
cigarette to-night."

"You are fond of that picture, Cresswell?" said Dr. Levillier as
Valentine sat down.

"'The Merciful Knight'? Yes, I love it. Have you told Julian
your opinion of our sittings, Doctor?"

"No. He didn't ask me for it."

"I should be glad to have it, all the same," Julian said.

"Well, my opinion is entirely adverse to your proceedings,"
Levillier said, with his usual frankness.

"You are, in fact, at the opposite pole from Marr," Julian
answered.

"Marr! Who is Marr? I never heard of him."

" Nor I, until the other evening," Julian said. " But now I see him every day. He was at the theatre to-night. I saw him as we came out."

" What is he, a spiritualist ? A professional ? "

" Oh dear, no ! He calls himself an occultist. He goes out in society a great deal, apparently. I met him at dinner first. Since then he has taken the keenest interest in my sittings with Valentine."

" Indeed ! You know him, Cresswell ? "

Valentine shook his head, and Julian laughed.

" The fun of it is that Marr doesn't wish to know Valentine," he said.

" Why ? " the doctor asked.

Julian told him the words Marr had used in reference to Valentine, and gave a fairly minute description of Marr's attitude towards their proceedings. Levillier listened with great attention.

" Then this man urges you to go on with your sittings ? " he said when Julian had finished.

" Scarcely that. But he certainly seems anxious that we should."

" You have both resolved to give them up, haven't you ? "

" Certainly, Doctor," Valentine replied.

" Does Marr know that ? " Levillier asked of Julian.

" No. I haven't seen him to speak to since our final sitting."

The little doctor sat in apparent meditation for two or three minutes. Then he remarked, with abruptness :

" Addison, will you think me an impertinent elderly person if I give you a piece of advice ? "

" You—Doctor ! Of course not. What is it ? "

" Well, you young fellows know me, know that I am not a mere sentimentalist or believer in every humbug that is the fashion of the moment. But one thing I do firmly believe, that certain people are born with a power to command, or direct others, which amounts to force. The world doesn't completely recognise this. The law doesn't recognise, perhaps ought not to recognise it. Some call it hypnotism. I call it suggestion."

He paused, as if he had finished.

" But your advice, Doctor ? " Julian said, wondering.

" Oh, h'm ! I don't mean to give it you after all."

" Why ? "

Dr. Levillier became enigmatic.

" Because I have just remembered that to warn is often to supply a cause of stumbling," he said.

Dr. Levillier and Julian drove together as far as the latter's chambers that evening, and, after bidding Julian good night, the doctor dismissed the cab and set out to walk to Harley Street. He

proceeded at a leisurely pace along Piccadilly, threading his way
abstractedly among the wandering wisps of painted humanity that
dye the London night with rouge. Occasionally a passing man in
evening dress would bid him good night, for he was universally
known in the town. But he did not reply. With his firm round
chin pressed down upon his fur coat, and his eyelids lowered, he
moved thoughtfully. The problem of the relations existing between
youth and life eternally fascinated him. He pondered over them
now. What a strange, complicated *liaison* it was, sometimes so
happy, sometimes so disastrous, always, to him, pathetic. Youth
sets up house with life as a lover sets up house with his mistress,
takes an attic near the stars, or builds a mansion that amazes the
street urchins. And they dwell together. And youth strives in
every way to know his mistress. He tests her, tries her, kisses and
cuffs her, gives her presents, weeps at her knees. And at first she
is magical, and a wonder, and a dream and eternity. And then,
perhaps, she is a faded creature, and terrible as a lost girl whom one
has known in innocence. She is grim and arid. She fills youth
with a great horror and with a great fear. He dare not kiss her
any more. And then, perhaps, at last he prays, "Deliver me from
this bondage!" And he thinks that he knows his mistress. But,
happy or sad, does he ever quite know her? Is she not always a
mystery, this life, a sphinx who jealously guards a great secret?

His evening with the two boys, for so the doctor called them in
his thoughts, had set him musing thus definitely. Was there not a
wonder and a secret in their dual life of friendship? For is not the
potent influence of one soul over another one of the marvels of time?
The doctor loved Valentine as a human saint loves another saint.
But he loved Julian as a saint loves a sinner. Not that he named
Julian sinner, but it was impossible to be with him, observantly,
sensitively, and not to feel the thrill of his warm, passionate humanity,
which cried aloud for governance, for protection. Julian could be
great, with the greatness only attained by purged humanity,
superior surely to the peaceful purity of angels. But he could be a
castaway, oh ! as much a castaway as the fainting shipwrecked man
whom the hoarse surf rolls to the sad island of a desert sea.

Without Valentine what might he not have been? And the
little doctor let his imagination run loose until his light eyes were
dim with absurd tears. He winked them away as he turned into
Regent Street. The hour was nearly two, and the great curved
thoroughfare was rather deserted. Those few persons who were
about had a curious aspect of wolves. Their eyes were watchful;
their gait denoted a ghastly readiness for pause, for colloquy. Poor
creatures ! What was their *liaison* with life? A thing like a cry
for help in the dark. The doctor longed to be a miracle-worker, to

lift up his hands, just there where he was by the New Gallery, and to say, "Be ye healed!" He had a true love for every human thing. And that love sometimes seared his heart, despite his fervent faith and hope.

But now, as he pursued his way, a physical sensation intruded itself upon his mind, and gradually excluded all his reflections. A sense of bodily uneasiness came upon him, of a curious irritation and contempt, mingled with fear. He at first ascribed it to the coffee he had imprudently drunk at Valentine's flat, and to the strength of the two cigars he had smoked, or to some ordinary, trifling cause of diet. But by the time he crossed Oxford Street, and was in the desert of Vere Street, he felt that there was a reason for his distress, outside of him.

" I am being followed," he said to himself. " I am being followed, and by some utterly abominable person."

He went by the Chapel and struck across to the right, not looking behind him, but analysing his feelings. Being strongly intuitive, he had no need to turn his head. He knew now for certain the cause of his uneasiness. Some dreadful human being was very near to him, full of hateful thoughts, sinister recollections, possibly evil intentions. Something, the very vibrations of the night air, it might be, carried, as a telegraph wire conveys a message, the soul aroma of this human being to the doctor. As he walked on, not hurrying, he mutely diagnosed the heart of this unseen being. It seemed full of deadly disease. Never had he suspected man or woman of such wickedness as he divined here ; never had he felt from any of his kind such a sick repulsion as from this unseen monster who was journeying steadily in his steps. Dr. Levillier was puzzled at the depth of the horror which beleaguered him. He remembered once driving a staid, well-behaved horse in a country lane. The animal ambled forward at a gentle pace, flicking its ears lazily to circumvent the flies, apparently at ease with its driver and with the world. But suddenly it raised its head, drew the air into its distended nostrils, stopped, quivered in every limb, and then, with a strange cry, bolted like a mad thing. Far away a travelling menagerie was encamping. It had scented the wild animals.

Dr. Levillier felt like that horse. A longing to bolt for his life came upon him. He had an impulse to cry out, to run forward, to escape out of the atmosphere created by this evil nature, this deadly life. He could have crept like a coward into the shadow of one of the areas of Henrietta Street, and sheltered there till the thing went past. And, just because he had this almost over-mastering desire to flee, he stood still, paused abruptly, and, without turning his head, listened. At a distance and, he judged, round the corner of the street, he heard the sound of a quickening footstep advancing in his direction. He waited, under the obligation of exerting all his powers of self-control; for his limbs trembled to movement, his heart beat to the march, and every separate vein, every separate hair of his body seemed crying out piercingly to begone. The footstep appproached. Dr. Levillier heard it turning the corner.

"Now," thought he, "this person will see me waiting here. Will he come on? Will he pass me? And, if he does, shall I be able to await, to endure the incident?"

And he listened, as a scout might listen in the night for sounds of the hidden enemy. Upon turning the corner, the footsteps advanced a pace or two, faltered, slackened, stopped. For an instant there was silence. The doctor knew that the man had been struck by his attentive figure, and was pausing to regard it, to consider it. What would be the result of the inspection? In a moment the doctor knew. The footsteps sounded again, this time in retreat.

On this the impulse of the doctor to flee changed, giving way to a strict desire and determination. He was resolved to interview this night wanderer, to see his face. A greedy anxiety for view, for question, of this person came upon him. He, too, wheeled round and followed hastily in pursuit. The man had already escaped from his sight into Vere Street, and the doctor broke into a soft run until he reached the corner, skirting which the man was immediately in his view, but at a considerable distance from him. As the doctor sprang upon the pavement the man turned round, and, evidently observing that he was pursued, quickened his steps impulsively. The doctor was now absolutely determined to address him, and began openly to run. And he was not far from coming up with the fellow when he suddenly whistled a passing hansom, bounded in, and thrust up the trapdoor in the roof. The direction given was sufficiently obvious, for the cabby glanced round at the doctor, lifted his whip, brought it down with a sweep over the horse's loins, and the cab disappeared down Oxford Street at a rocking gallop.

The doctor paused. He was breathing hard, and the perspiration stood upon his face. His disappointment was absurdly keen, and for an instant he had even some idea of hailing another cab, and of following in pursuit. But, upon reflection, he deemed it more reasonable to return upon his steps, and to seek his bed in Harley Street. This accordingly he did, wondering what had moved him so strangely, and wondering also, not a little, at the abrupt flight of the unknown person. In the brief and distant view of him, which was all that the doctor had obtained, he judged him to be tall, spare, and pale of countenance, with the figure of a gentleman. The aspect of his face had not been revealed before the shelter of the cab concealed him.

CHAPTER VIII

PAUSE

It chanced that for three or four days after the night of the theatre expedition Valentine and Julian did not meet. They were rarely apart for so long a period, and each was moved to wonder at this unwonted abstinence of their friendship. What was the cause of it? Each found it in a curious hesitation that enveloped him and impelled him to avoidance of the other. Valentine went about as usual. He looked in at White's, dined out, rode in the Park, visited two theatres, lived the habitual London life which contents so many and disgusts not a few. But he did not ask Julian to share any of these well-worn doings, and at first he did not acknowledge to himself why he did not do so. He sought, more definitely than ever before, to gain amusement from amusements, and this definite intention of course frustrated his purpose. His power of pleasure was, in fact, clogged by an abiding sense of dissatisfaction and depression. And it was really his eventual knowledge of this depression's cause that led him to bar Julian out from these few days of his life. All that he did bored him, and the more decidedly because he came to know that there was something which did not bore, which even excited him, something which he had resolved to give up. He was, in fact, strangely pursued by an unreasonable desire to fly in the face of Dr. Levillier's advice and of his own secondary antagonistic desire, and to sit again with Julian. Everything in which he sought to find distraction lacked savour. As he sat watching a ballet that glittered with electricity, and was one twinkle of coloured movement, he found himself longing for the silence, the gloom, the live expectation of the tent-room, night, and Julian. At White's the conversation of the men struck him as even more scrappy, more desultorily scandalous, than usual. His morning ride was an active *ennui*, an *ennui* revolving, like a horse in a circus, round and round the weariness of the Park.

Yet he had made up his mind quite fully that it would be better not to sit any more. It was not merely Dr. Levillier's urgency that had impressed him thus. A personal conviction had gradually forced itself upon him that if anything resulted from such apparently imbecile proceedings it would certainly not be of an agreeable nature. But, too, this very sense that a secret danger might be lurking against him and Julian, if only they would consent together to give it power by the united action of sitting, spurred him on to restless desire. It is not only the soldier who has a bizarre love of peril. Many of those who sit at home in apparent calmness of safety seek perils with a maniacal persistence, perils to the intricate scheme of bodily health, perils to the mind. More human mules than the men of the banner and the sword delight in journeying at the extreme edge of the precipice. And Valentine now had to the full this secret hankering after danger. As he knew it, he despised himself for it, for this attitude of the schoolboy in which he held himself. Until now he had believed that he was free from such a preposterous and morbid bondage, free on account of his constitutional indifference towards vice, his innate love of the brooding calms of refinement and of the upper snow-fields of the intellect. The discovery of his mistake irritated him, but the irritation could not conquer its cause, and each day the longing to sit once more grew upon him, until it became almost painful. It was this longing which occasioned Valentine's avoidance of Julian. He knew that if they were together he would yield to this foolish, witless temptation, and at any rate try to persuade Julian into an act which might be attended with misfortune, if not with disaster. And then Valentine's profound respect for Dr. Levillier, a respect which the doctor inspired without effort in every one who knew him, was a chain almost of steel to hold the young man back from gratification of his longing. Valentine never sought any one's advice except the little doctor's, and he had a strong feeling of the obligation laid upon him by such sought advice. To ask it and to reject it was a short course to insult.

He resolved to avoid Julian until this gripping desire was shaken from the shoulders of his mind.

Once or twice he tacitly wondered whether Julian was also the prey of this desire, but then he felt certain that his friend could not be so afflicted. Had he been, Julian would surely have found a swift occasion to call. But he did not call. His feet did not turn their accustomed way to Victoria Street. And it did not occur to Valentine that Julian might be immersed in the same sort of struggle as himself. He thought he knew Julian well enough to be sure that he would not have joined issue with such an enemy without instant consultation. A council of war would certainly have been convened.

So Valentine believed himself lonely in his feeling. One night he returned from the theatre and a succeeding supper-party at half-past twelve, let himself into the flat with a latchkey, threw off his coat and stood before the fire. His usually smooth, white forehead was puckered in a frown. He contemplated the inevitable hours of bed with dissatisfaction. When a man has allowed a vice to obtain dominion over him, there are moments when an enforced abstinence from it, even of only a few hours, seems intolerably irksome. So Valentine felt now. It seemed to him that he must sit again, that he could not go to bed, could not rest and sleep, until he gratified his desire. Yet what was he to do? He thought at first of starting out, late as the hour was, to Julian's rooms. But that would be ridiculous, more especially after their mutual resolution. Julian might refuse, would probably, in any event, wish to refuse the request which he came to make. Valentine strove sincerely to dismiss the desire from his mind, but his effort was entirely vain. Presently he went into his bedroom with the intention of forcing himself to go, as usual, to bed. He began to undress slowly, and had taken off his coat and waistcoat when he felt that he must resume them, that he must remain, unnecessarily, up. He allowed the mental prompting to govern him, and hardly had he once more fully attired himself when the electric bell in the passage rang twice. Valentine went to the door, opened it, and descended the flight of stone steps to the main door of the house, which was locked at night. Julian was standing outside on the pavement.

" You are still up then," he exclaimed. "That's good. May I come in ? "

" Yes, of course. Where have you been to-night ? "

They were going up, their footsteps echoing hoarsely in the dim light.

" Nowhere."

" Then what made you turn out so late ? "

" Oh," Julian said with an elaborate carelessness, " I don't know. I thought we were becoming strangers, I suppose. And suddenly I resolved to look you up."

" I see," Valentine said, wondering why Julian was lying.

By this time they were in the flat and had shut the door behind them.

" Why haven't you been near me ? " Julian said.

" Why haven't you been near me ? "

" Oh !—well—do you want to know really ? "

" Yes, if you have got a definite reason."

" To tell the truth, I have ; but it is such an absurd one."

Julian looked at Valentine and then added, with a decidedly forced laugh :

" You'll be awfully surprised when I tell you what it is, Val. I want to sit again."

" Now I know why I stopped undressing just now," said Valentine.

" I must have had a sense that you were coming. Were you thinking very hard of me to-night and of our sittings ? "

" Rather ! It is the oddest thing, but ever since we had that talk with the doctor and agreed to give the whole thing up, I've been perfectly miserable. I haven't enjoyed a single thing I've done since that night."

" Nor I," said Valentine.

" What ! you have been as bad ? And without having Marr continually at your elbow ! "

" Marr again ! "

" Again ! Yes, I should think so. That chap has taken a fancy to me, I suppose. Anyhow, directly I walk into the club, morning, noon, or night, up he comes. He must live there. And the first thing he says is, ' Have you gone on with your sittings ? You should, you should.' To-day he changed his formula and said, ' You must,' and when I was going away, he looked at me in a damned odd way and remarked in his low, toneless voice, ' You will.' I declare I almost think he must have a sort of influence over me, for I couldn't go to bed for the life of me, and here I am. By the way, Marr seems to have a sort of power of divination. Last night, when I happened to see him, he began talking about doctors, and, by Jove, didn't he abuse them ! He says they stand more in the way of the development of the spiritual forces in man than any other body of people. He denounced them all as low materialists, immersed in the tinkering of the flesh. ' What does the flesh matter ? ' he said. ' It is nothing. It is only an envelope. And the more tightly it is fastened together, the more it stifles the spirit. I would like to catch hold of some men's bodies and tear them in pieces to get at their souls.' Val, as he made that cheerful remark, he looked more like a homicidal maniac than anything I ever saw."

" I suppose you didn't stand up for the doctors ? "

" But I did—for our little man. D'you think I wasn't going to say a word for him ? "

" What, you mentioned his name to this chap ? "

" Certainly. Why not ? "

" I don't know," Valentine said, hesitatingly.

" What objection could there possibly be ? "

" None, of course—none. I simply had a quite unreasonable feeling that I wished you hadn't. That is all."

And then Valentine relapsed into silence, the silence some men keep when they are needlessly, uselessly irritated. The mention of Marr's name had affected him oddly. He now felt a perverse desire not to sit, not to comply with the rather impertinent prediction of this dark-featured prophet whom he had never seen. To carry out this prediction would seem like an obedience to a stranger, governing, unseen and at a distance. Why did this man concern himself in the affairs of those over whom he had no sovereignty, with whom he had no friendship?

"Julian," Valentine said at last, abruptly, "I wish you would promise me something."

"What is it?"

"To drop this fellow, Marr. He has nothing to do with us, and it is a decided impertinence, this curiosity he shows in our doings. Don't answer any more of his questions. Tell him to keep his advice to himself. And if you really believe he is obtaining an influence over you, avoid him."

"You talk as if you disliked him."

"I feel as if I hated him."

"A man you have never even seen?"

"Yes."

"Well, I don't take to him and I have seen him. . I will drop him as much as I can. I promise you that."

"Thank you, old boy."

Julian fidgeted about rather uneasily, touching the ornaments on the mantelpiece, opening and shutting his silver cigarette case with a click. It was obvious that he felt restless and dissatisfied. Then he said:

"Well, are we going to——?"

"Surely you don't mean to say that you came here to-night to persuade me into doing again what we both decided not to do any more?" asked Valentine.

"I came to try," Julian replied with decision.

He looked at Valentine and then added:

"And do you know I have been thinking, especially to-day, that you were of the same mind as I."

"How?"

"That you wanted to sit again as much as I did."

"But I don't know Marr," Valentine said, with unusual sarcasm.

Julian flushed red, like a man who has been stung.

"Perhaps he influences you through me though," he said with a laugh.

"What nonsense, Julian! If I thought he had anything to do with the matter, I would never sit again. But he can have nothing to do with it."

"Of course not. So will you sit? You want to give in. I know that."

"I do."

"I was sure of it."

"At the same time, remember the doctor's advice."

"Oh, doctors are always against that sort of thing."

" Julian, I have a strong feeling that, should we ever get any manifestation at all, it will be inimical, even deadly to one or both of us. Each time we have sat a sensation of distress has taken hold of me, and each time with greater force."

" Nerves ! "

" Well, then, the hand which you say you held was nerves ? "

" Perhaps. But that is just it. I must know or, at least, try to know. It is inevitable. We can't stop now, Val, whether we are standing on the threshold of good, or evil, or—nothing at all We have got to go on. Besides, you and I have not effected an exchange."

" Of souls ? No. Perhaps it is an imbecile proceeding to try."

" No matter."

" Or a dangerous proceeding."

" You are temporising, and the night is running away as hard as it can. Come now, will you do what I want—yes or no ? "

After a long hesitation, Valentine slowly answered :

" Yes."

And, absurdly as he said it, he felt like a man who tosses the dice for life or death.

CHAPTER IX

THE FOURTH SITTING

They turned the light off and sat down in silence. Then Julian said:
" Keep your hands well away from mine, Val."

" I will."

They had not been sitting for five minutes before Valentine felt that the atmosphere was becoming impregnated with a certain heaviness of mystery, with a certain steady and unyielding dreariness hanging round them like a cloud. They were once again confronted by a strange reality. Surely they were. Valentine felt it, silently knew it.

In this blackness he seemed at length to step forward and to stand upon the very threshold of an abyss, beyond which, in vague vapours, lay things unknown, creatures unsuspected hitherto. From this darkness anything might come to them, angel or devil, nymph or satyr. So, at least, he dreamed for a while, giving his imagination the rein. Then, in a revulsion of feeling, he jeered at his folly, mutely scolded his nerves for spurring him to such flagrant imbecilities.

"This is all nonsense," he told himself, "all fancy, all a world created, peopled, endowed with life by my desirous mind, which longs for a new sensation. I will not encourage this absurdity. I will be calm, cold, observant, discriminating. This is the same darkness in which every night I sleep, with no sense of being surrounded by forms which I cannot see, pressed upon by the denizens of some other sphere, not that in which I breathe and live."

He deliberately detached himself from his mood of keen expectation, and ardently resolved to anticipate nothing. And at this moment the table began to shift along the carpet, to twist under their hands, to rap, to tremble and to pulsate, as if breath had entered into it. Like some live animal it stirred beneath their pressing fingers.

"It is beginning," Julian whispered.

"Animal magnetism," Valentine murmured.

"Yes, of course," Julian replied. "Shall I ask——?"

"Hush!" Valentine interrupted.

Julian was silent.

For some time the table continued its stereotyped performances. Then it tremblingly ceased, and stood, mere dead furniture of everyday wood on which lay the four hands made deliberately limp. A long period of unpopulated silence ensued, and through that silence, very gradually, came again to Valentine a growing sense of anxiety. At first he fought against it as most men, perhaps out of self-respect, fight against the entrance of fear into their souls. Then he yielded to it, and let it crawl over him, as the sea crawls over flat sands. And the sea left no inch of sand uncovered. Every cranny of Valentine's soul was flooded. There was no part of it which did not shudder with apprehension. And outwards flowed this invisible, unmurmuring tide, devouring his body, till the sweat was upon his face and his strained hands and trembling fingers were cold like ice, and his knees fluttered as the knees of palsied age, and his teeth clicked, row against row, and his hairs stirred, and his head, under its thatch, tingled and burned and throbbed. Every faculty, too, seemed to stand straight up like a sentinel at its post, staring into dust clouds through which rode an approaching enemy. Eyes watched, ears listened, brain was hideously alert. The whole body kept itself tense, stiff, wary. For Valentine had a secret conviction at this moment that he was about to be attacked. By what? He was hardly master of himself enough to wonder. His thoughts no longer ran free. They crept like paralysed things about his mind, and that despite the unnatural vitality of his brain. It was as if he thought intensely, violently, and yet could not think at all, as a man terrified may stare with wide open eyes and yet perceive nothing, lacking for a moment the faculty of perceiving. So Valentine waited, like some blind man with glaring eyeballs. And then, passing into another stage of sensation, he found himself vehemently and rapidly discussing possibilities of terror, forming mental pictures of all the things, of all the powers that we cannot see. He embodied, materialised, the wind, the voice of the sea, the angry, hot scent of certain flowers, of the white lily, the tuberose, the hyacinth. He created figures for light, for darkness, for a wail, for a laugh, and set them in array all round him in the blackness. But none of these imagined figures could cause the horror which he felt. He drove away the whole pack of them with a silent cry, a motionless dismissing wave of his hands. But there might be other beings round us, condemned to eternal invisibility lest the sight of them should drive men mad. We cannot see them, he thought. As a rule we have no sensation of these gaunt neighbours, no suspicion of their approach, of their companionship. We do not hear their footsteps. We are utterly unconscious of them. Yet may there not be physical or mental paroxysms, during which we become conscious of them, during which we know, beyond all power of doubt, that they are near us, with us. And, in such paroxysms, is it not possible for them to break through the intangible and yet all-powerful barriers that divide them from us, and to touch us, caress us, attack us? Valentine believed that he was immersed in such a paroxysm, and that the barriers were in process of being broken down. He seemed actually to hear the faint cry of an approaching being, the dim uproar of its violent efforts to obtain its sinister will, and gain the power to make itself known to him by some ghastly and malignant deed. He was unutterably afraid.

"The hand again!" Julian suddenly cried. "Valentine, is it yours? Why don't you answer? I say, is it yours?"

"No," Valentine forced himself, with difficulty, to reply.

"For God's sake then—the light!"

Valentine felt for it, but his hand shook, and did not find the button.

"Make haste, Val. What are you doing? Ah!"

The room sprang into view, and Julian's eyes, with a furious, sick eagerness, sought his hands.

"Valentine," he exclaimed hoarsely, "I see nothing, but I've got hold of the hand still. I've got it tight. Put your hand here—that's it—under mine. Now d'you feel the thing?"

Julian's hand, contracted as if grasping another, was in the air, about an inch, or an inch and a half, above the surface of the table. Valentine obediently thrust his hand beneath it. He now shook his head.

"I feel nothing," he said. "There is nothing."

"Then am I mad?" said Julian. "I'm holding flesh and blood. I'll swear that. Yes, I can feel the fingers twitching, the muscles, the bones. I can even trace the veins. What does this mean?"

"I can't tell."

"You look very strange, Valentine. You are certain you see and feel nothing?"

"Nothing whatever," Valentine forced himself to answer calmly.

"We'll see this through," said Julian with a sort of angry determination. "I won't be frightened by a hand. We'll see it through. Out with the light."

Valentine turned it off. The action was purely mechanical. He had to perform it, whether he would or no.

"Don't speak," he whispered to Julian in the darkness. "Don't speak whatever happens till I ask you to speak."

"Why?"

"Don't; don't!"

"All right."

They sat still.

And now the horror that had possessed Valentine so utterly began to fade away, making its exit from his body and soul with infinitesimally small steps. At length it had quite gone, and its place was taken by a numb calm, level and still at first, then curiously definite, almost too definite to be calm at all. Gradually this calm withdrew into exhaustion, an exhaustion such as dwells incessantly with the anæmic, with those whose hearts beat feebly and whose vitality flickers low to fading. That was like a delicious arrival of death, of death delicate and serene, ivory white and pure, death desirable, grateful. Valentine indeed believed that he was dying, there in the darkness beside his friend, and, impersonally as it seemed, something of him, his brain perhaps, seemed to be floating high up, as a bird floats over the sea, and listening, and noting all that he did in this crisis. This attentive spirit heard a strange movement of his soul in its bodily prison, heard his soul stir, as if waking out of sleep, heard it shift, and rise up slowly, noted its pause of hesitation. Then, as the vitality of the body ebbed lower, there grew in the soul an excitement that aspired like a leaping flame. It was as if a madman, prisoned in his narrow cell in a vast asylum, secluded with his company of phantoms, heard the crackling of the fire that devoured his habitation, and was stirred into an ignorant and yet tumultuous passion. As the madman, with a childish, increasing uneasiness, awed by the sinuous approach of the unseen fire, might pace to and fro, round and round about his cell, so it seemed to this poised watching faculty of Valentine that his soul wandered in its confined cell of the body, at first with the cushioned softness of an animal, moving mechanically, driven by an endless and unmeaning restlessness, then with an increasing energy, a fervour, a crescendo of endeavour. What drove his soul? Surely it was struggling with an unseen power. And the steady diminuendo of his bodily forces continued, until he was a corpse in which a fury dwelt. That fury was the soul. He had a strange fancy that he, unlike all the rest of humanity, would die, yet still retain his spirit in its fleshly prison, and that the spirit screamed and fought to be free on its wayward pilgrimage to heaven or hell. All its brother and sister spirits that had fled, since the beginnings of time, from their bodies at the crisis of dissolution, had gone to punishment or to reward. His soul alone was to meet a different fate, was to be confined in a decaying body, to breath physical corruption and to be at home in a crumbling dwelling to which no light, no air could ever penetrate. And the soul, which knows instinctively its eternal *métier*, rebelled with a fantastic violence. And still, ever, the body died. The pulses ceased from beating. The warm blood was mixed with snow until it grew cold and gradually congealed in the veins. The little door of the heart swung slower and slower upon its hinges, more feebly—more feebly. And then there came a supreme moment. The soul of Valentine, with a frantic vehemence, beat down at last its prison door, and, even as his body died, escaped with a cry through the air.

* * * * *

" Valentine, did you hear that strange cry ? "

* * * * *

" Valentine, what was it ? I never heard any sound like that before, so thin and small, and yet so horribly clear and piercing; neither like the cry of a child nor of an animal, nor like the wail that could come from any instrument. Valentine, now I see a little flame come from where you are sitting. It's so tiny and faint. Don't you see it? It is floating towards me. Now it is passing me. It's beyond. It's going. There, it has vanished. Valentine! Valentine!"

PART II—JULIAN

CHAPTER I

THE TRANCE

GAINING no reply to his call, Julian grew alarmed. He sprang up from the table and turned on the electric light. Valentine was leaning back nervelessly in his chair. His face was quite pale and cold. His lips were slightly parted. His eyes were wide open, and stared before him without expression. His head hung far back over the edge of the chair. He looked exactly like a man who had just died, and died in a convulsion. For though the lips were parted, the teeth set tightly together grinned through them, and the hands were intensely contracted into fists. Julian seized Valentine in his arms, lifted the drooping body from the chair and laid it out at length on the divan. He put a pillow under the head, which fell on it grotesquely and lay sideways, still smiling horribly at nothing. Then he poured out a glass of brandy, and strove to force some of it between Valentine's teeth, dashed water in the glaring eyes, beat the air with a fan which he tore from the mantelpiece. All was in vain. There came no sign of returning life. Then Julian caught Valentine's hands in his and sought to unclench the rigid, cold fingers. He laid his hand on the heart of his friend. No pulsation beat beneath his anxious touch. Then a great horror overtook him. Suddenly he felt a conviction that Valentine had died beside him in the dark, had died sitting up in his chair by the table. The cry he had heard, so thin, so strange and piercing, the attenuated flame that he had seen, were the voice and the vision of the flying soul which he had loved, seeking its final freedom, *en route* to the distant spheres believers dream of and sceptics deny.

"Valentine! Valentine!" he cried again, with the desperate insistence of the hopeless. But the cold, staring creature upon the green divan did not reply. With a brusque and fearful movement Julian shut the eyelids. Would they ever open again? He knelt upon the floor, leaning passionately over his friend, or that which had been his friend. He bent his head down on the silent breast, listening. Surely if Valentine were alive he would show it by some sign, the least stir, breath, shiver, pulse. There was none. Julian might have been clasping stone or iron. If he could only know for certain whether Valentine were really dead. Yet he dared not leave him alone and go to seek aid. Suddenly a thought struck him. In the hall of the flat was a handle which, when turned in a certain direction, communicated with one of those wooden and glass hutches in which sleepy boy messengers harbour at night. Julian sprang to this handle, set the communicator in motion then ran back into the tent-room. His intention was to write a note to Dr. Levillier. The writing-table was so placed that, sitting at it, his back would be turned to that silent figure on the divan. A shiver ran over him at the bare thought of such a blind posture. No, he must face that terror, once so dear. He caught up a pen and a sheet of note-paper, and swerving round was about to write, holding the paper on his knee, when the electric bell rang. The boy had been very quick in his run from the hutch. Julian laid down the paper and went to let the boy in. His knees shook as he descended the dark echoing stairs and opened the door. There stood the messenger, a rosy faced urchin of about twelve, with rather sleepy brown eyes.

' "Come up," Julian said, and he hurried back to the flat, the little boy violently emulating his giant stride up the stairs and arriving flushed and panting at the door. Julian, who was entirely abstracted in his agitation, made for the tent-room without another word to the boy, seized pen and paper and began to write, urgently requesting Dr. Levillier to come at once to see Valentine. Abruptly a childish voice intruded itself upon him.

"Lor', sir," it said. "Is the gentleman ill?"

Julian glanced up and found that the little boy had innocently followed him into the tent-room, and was now standing near him, gazing with a round-eyed concern upon the stretched figure on the divan.

"Yes," Julian replied, "ill, very ill. I want you to go for a doctor."

The boy approached the divan, moved apparently by the impelling curiosity of tender years. Julian stopped writing and watched him. He leaned down and looked at the face, at the inertia of hands and limbs. As he raised himself up from a calm and close inspection he saw Julian staring at him. He shook his round bullet head, on which the thick hair grew in an unparted stubble.

"No, I don't think he's ill, sir," he remarked, with treble conviction.

" Then why does he lie like that ? "

" I expect it's because he's dead, sir," the child replied with grave serenity.

This unbiased testimony in favour of his fears came to Julian's mind like a storm.

" How do you know ? " he exclaimed, with a harsh voice.

" Lor', sir," the boy said, not without a certain pride, " I knows a corpse when I sees it. My father died come a fortnight ago. Seo that ? "

And he indicated, with stumpy finger, the black band upon his left arm.

" Well, father looked just like the gentleman."

Julian was petrified by this urchin's intimacy with death. It struck him as utterly vicious and terrible. A horror of the rosy-faced little creature, with good conduct medals gleaming on its breast, came over him.

" Hush ! " he said.

" All right, sir ; but you take my word for it ; the gentleman's dead."

Julian finished the note, thrust it into an envelope, and addressed it to the doctor.

" Run and get a cab and take that at once to Harley Street," he said.

The boy smiled.

" I like cab riding," he said.

" And," Julian caught his arm, " that gentleman is not dead. He's alive, I tell you, only in a faint, and alive."

The boy looked into Julian's face, with the pitying grin of superior knowledge of the world.

" Ah, sir, you didn't see father," he said.

Then he turned and bounded eagerly down the stairs, in a hurry for the cab ride.

Loneliness and desolation descended like a cloud over Julian when he had gone, for the frank belief of the boy, who cared nothing, struck like an arrow of truth to his heart, who cared everything. Was Valentine indeed dead ? He would not believe it, for such a belief would bring the world in ruins about his feet. Such a belief would people his soul with phantoms of despair and of wickedness. Could he not cry out against God with blasphemy, if God took his friend from him ? The tears rushed into his eyes, as he sat waiting there in the night. As before a drowning man, scenes of the last five years flashed before him, painted in vital colours ; scenes of his life with Valentine, then scenes of all that might have been had he never met Valentine, never known his strange mastering influence. Could that influence have been given only to be withdrawn ? Of all the

E

inexplicable things of life the most inexplicable are the abrupt intrusions and disappearances of those lovely manifestations which give healing to tired hearts, to the wounded soldiers of the campaign of the world. Why are they not permitted to stay? Bitterly Julian asked that question. Of all the men whom he knew only Valentine did anything for him. Must Valentine, of all men, be the one who might not stay with him? The rest he could spare. He could not spare Valentine. He could not. The impotence of his patience tortured him physically like a disease. He sprang up from his chair. He must do something at once to know the truth. What could he do? He had no knowledge of medicine. He could not tabulate physical indications, and he would not trust to his infernal instinct. For it was that which cried to him again and again " Valentine is dead." What—what could he do?

A thought darted into his mind. Dogs are miraculously instinctive. Rip might know what he did not certainly know, might divine the truth. He ran into Valentine's bedroom.

" Rip," he cried, " Rip ! "

The little dog sprang from its lonely sleep and accompanied Julian energetically to the tent-room. Observing Valentine's attitude, it sprang upon the couch beside him, licked his white face eagerly, then, gaining no response, showed hesitation, alarm. It began to investigate the body eagerly with its sharp nose, snuffing at head, shoulders, legs, feet. Still it seemed in doubt, and paused at length with one forefoot planted on Valentine's breast, the other raised in air.

"Even Rip is at fault," Julian said to himself. But as the words ran through his mind, the little dog grew suddenly calmer. It dropped the hesitating paw, again licked the face, then nestled quietly into the space between Valentine's left breast and arm, rested its chin on the latter, and, with blinking eyes, prepared evidently for repose. A wild hope came again to Julian.

" Valentine is not dead," he said to himself. " He is in some strange hypnotic trance. Presently he will recover from it. He will be well. Thank God ! Thank God ! I will watch ! "

And so he kept an attentive and hopeful vigil, his eyes always upon Valentine's face, his hand always touching Valentine's. Already life seemed blossoming anew with an inexplicable radiance. Valentine would speak once more, would come back from this underworld of the senses. And Julian's hand closed on his cold hand with a warm, impulsive strength, as if it might be possible to draw him back physically to consciousness and to speech. But there was no answer. And again Julian was assailed with doubts. Yet the dog slept on happily, a hostage to peace.

Julian never knew how long that vigil lasted. It might have been five minutes or a lifetime. The vehemence of his mental debate slew his power of observation of normal things. He forgot what he was waiting for. He forgot to expect Dr. Levillier. Two visions alternated in glaring contrast before the eyes of his brain—life with Valentine, and life without him. It is so we watch the trance, or death—we know not which—of those whom we love, with a greedy, beautiful selfishness. They are themselves only in relation to us. They live, they die, in that wonderful relation. To live is to be with us, to die—to go away from us. There are women who love so much that they angrily expostulate with the dying, as if, indeed, the dying deliberately elected to depart out of their arms. Do we not all feel at moments the " You could stay with me, if only you had the will !" that is the last bitter cry of despairing affection ? Julian, sitting there, while Valentine lay silent and the dog slept by his breast, saw ever and ever those two lives, flashing and fading like lamps across a dark sea, life with, life without—him. The immensity of the contrast, the millions of airy miles between those two life-worlds, appalled him, for it revealed to him what mighty issues of joy and grief hung upon the almost visionary thin thread of one little life. It is ghastly to be so idiotically dependent. Yet who, at some time, is not ? And those who are independent lose, by their power, their possible Paradise. But such a time of uncertainty as that which Julian must now endure is a great penalty to pay for even the greatest joy, when the joy is past. He had his trance of the mind. He was hypnotised by his ignorance whether Valentine were alive or dead. And so he sat motionless, making the tour of an eternity of suffering, of wonder, of doubt, and hope, and yet, through it all, in some strange, indefinite way, numb, phlegmatic, and actually stupid.

At last the bell rang. Dr. Levillier had arrived. He was struck at once by Julian's heaviness of manner.

" What is it ? What is the matter ? " he asked.

" I don't know. You tell me."

" He is fainting—unconscious ? "

" Unconscious, yes."

They were in the little hall now. Dr. Levillier narrowly scrutinised Julian. For a moment he thought Julian had been drinking, and he took him by the arm.

" No, it is fear," he murmured, releasing him, and walking into the tent-room.

Julian followed with a loud footstep, treading firmly. Each step said to Death, " You are not here. You are not here."

He stood at a little distance near the door, while Levillier approached Valentine and bent over him. Rip woke up and curled his top lip in a terrier smile of welcome. The doctor stroked his head, then lifted Valentine's hand and held the wrist. He dropped it, and threw a glance on Julian. There was a scream of interrogation in Julian's fixed eyes. Dr. Levillier avoided it by dropping his own and again turning his attention to the figure on the divan. He undid Valentine's shirt, bared the breast, and laid his hand on the heart, keeping it there for a long time.

"Fetch me a hand-glass," he said to Julian.

Mechanically, Julian went into the bedroom, and groped in the dark upon the dressing-table.

"Well, have you got it? Why don't you turn up the light?"

"I don't know," Julian answered, drily.

Dr. Levillier saw that anxiety was beginning to unnerve him. When the glass was found the doctor led Julian back to the tent-room and pushed him gently down in a chair.

"Keep quiet," he said. "And—keep hoping."

"There is—there is—hope?"

"Why not?"

Then the doctor held the little glass to Valentine's lips. The bright surface was not dimmed. No breath of life tarnished it to dulness. Again the doctor felt his heart, drew his eyelids apart, and carefully examined the eyes, then slowly turned round.

"Doctor—Doctor!" Julian whispered. "Why do you turn away? What are you going to do?"

Dr. Levillier made a gesture of finale, and knelt on the floor by Valentine. His head was bowed. His lips moved silently. Julian saw that he was praying, and sprang up fiercely. All the frost of his senses thawed in a moment. He seized Levillier by the shoulders.

"Don't pray!" he cried out, "don't pray. Curse! curse as I do! If he's dead you shall not pray. You shall not! You shall not!"

The little doctor drew him down to his knees.

"Julian, hush! My science tells me Valentine is dead."

Julian opened his white lips, but the doctor, with a motion, silenced him, and added, pointing to Rip, who still lay happily by his master's side:

"But that dog seems to tell me he is alive, that this is some strangely complete and perfect simulation of death, some unnatural sleep of the senses. Pray, pray with me that Valentine may wake."

And, kneeling by his friend, with bent head, Julian strove to pray. The answer to that double prayer pierced the two men. It was so instant, and so bizarre, fighting against probability, yet heralding light, and the end of that night's pale circumstances.

Rip, relapsing quickly from his perfunctory smile on the doctor, had again fallen asleep with an evident exceeding confidence and comfort, snoring his way into an apparent peace that passed all understanding. But scarcely had the doctor spoken, giving Julian hope, than the little dog suddenly opened its eyes, shifted round in its nest of arm and bosom, smelt furtively at Valentine's hand. Then it turned from the hand to the side of its master, investigated it with a supreme anxiety, pursued its search as far as the white, strict face and bared bosom. From the face it recoiled and, with a piercing howl, like the scream of a dog run over by a cart, it sprang away, darted to the farthest corner of the room, and huddled close against the wall in an agony of terror.

Julian turned cold. He believed implicitly that the trance at that very moment had deepened into death, and that the sleepless instinct of the dog had divined it partially while he slept, and now knew it and was afraid. And the same error of belief shook Dr. Levillier. A spasm crossed his thin, earnest face. No death had ever hurt him so sharply as this death hurt him. He saw Julian recoil in horror from the divan, and he could say nothing. For he, too, felt horror.

But in this moment of despair Valentine's hands slowly unclenched themselves, and the fingers were gradually extended as by a man stretching himself after a long sleep.

The doctor saw this, but believed himself the victim of a delusion, tricked by the excitement of his mind into foolish visions. And Julian had turned quite away, trembling. But now Valentine moved slightly, pressed his elbows on the cushions that supported him, and half sat up, still with closed eyes.

" Julian," Dr. Levillier said in a low, summoning voice, " Julian, do you see what I see ? Is he indeed alive ? Julian."

Then Julian, turning, saw with the doctor Valentine sit up erect, open his eyes, and gaze upon his two friends with a grave, staring scrutiny.

" Valentine, Valentine, how you frightened me ! How you terrified me !" Julian at last found a voice to exclaim. " Thank God, thank God ! you are alive. Oh, Valentine, you are alive, you are not dead."

Valentine's lips smiled slowly.

" Dead," he answered. " No, I am not dead."

And again he smiled quietly, as a man smiles at some secret thought which tickles him or whips the sense of humour in him till, like an obeying dog, it dances.

Dr. Levillier, having regained his feet, stood silently looking at Valentine, all his professional instinct wide awake to note this apparent resurrection from the dead.

" You here, Doctor !" said Valentine. " Why, what does this all mean ?"

" I want you to tell me that," Levillier said. " And you," he added, now turning towards Julian.

But Julian was too much excited to answer. His eyes were blazing with joy and with emotion. And Valentine seemed still to be informed with a curious, serpentine lassitude. The life seemed to be only very gently running again over his body, creeping from the centre, from the heart, to the extremities, gradually growing in the eyes, stronger and stronger, a dawn of life in a full-grown man. Dr. Levillier had never seen anything quite like it before. There was something violently unnatural about it, he thought, yet he could not say what. He could only stand by the broad couch, fascinated by the spectacle under his gaze. Once he had read a tale of the revivifying of a mummy in a museum. That might have been like this; or the raising of Lazarus. The streams of strength almost visibly trickled through Valentine's veins. And this new life was so vigorous, so alert. It was as if during his strange sleep Valentine had been carpentering his energies, polishing his powers, setting the temple of his soul in order, gaining almost a ruthlessness from rest. He stretched his limbs now as an athlete might stretch them to win the full consciousness of their muscular force. When the doctor took hold of his hand to feel his pulse the hand was hard and tense like iron, the fingers gripped for a moment like thin bands of steel, and the life in the blue eyes bounded, raced, swirled as water swirls in a mill stream. Indeed, Dr. Levillier felt as if there was too much life in them, as if the cup had been filled with wine until the wine ran over. He put his fingers on the pulse. It was strong and rapid and did not fluctuate, but beat steadily. He felt the heart. That, too, throbbed strongly. And while he made his examination Valentine smiled at him.

"I am all right, you see," Valentine said.

"All right," the doctor echoed, still possessed by the feeling that there lurked almost a danger in this apparently abounding health.

"What was it all?" Julian asked eagerly. "Was it a trance?"

"A trance?" Valentine said. "Yes, I suppose so."

He put his feet to the floor, stood up, and again stretched all his limbs. His eyes fell upon Rip, who was still in the corner, huddled up, his teeth showing, his eyes almost starting out of his head.

"Rip," he said, holding out his hand and slapping his knee, "come here! Come along! Rip! Rip! What's the matter with him?"

"He thought you were dead," said Julian. "Poor little chap. Rip, it's all right. Come!"

But the dog refused to be pacified, and still displayed every symptom of angry fear. At last Valentine, weary of calling the dog, went towards it and stooped to pick it up. At the downward movement of its master the dog shrank back, gathered itself together, then suddenly sprang forward with a harsh snarl and tried to fasten its teeth in his face. Valentine jumped back just in time.

"He must have gone mad," he exclaimed. "Julian, see what you can do with him."

Curiously enough, Rip welcomed Julian's advances with avidity, nestled into his arms, but when he walked towards Valentine, struggled to escape and trembled in every limb.

"How extraordinary!" Julian said. "Since your trance he seems to have taken a violent dislike to you. What can it mean?"

"Oh, nothing probably. He will get over it. Put him into the other room."

Julian did so, and returned.

Dr. Levillier was now sitting in an armchair. His light, kind eyes were fixed on Valentine with a scrutiny so intense as to render the expression of his usually gentle face almost stern. But Valentine appeared quite unconscious of his gaze and mainly attentive to all that Julian said and did. All this time the doctor had not said a word. Now he spoke.

"You spoke of a trance?" he said interrogatively.

Julian looked as guilty as a cribbing schoolboy discovered in his dingy act.

"Doctor, Val and I have to crawl to you for forgiveness," he said.

"To me—why?"

"We have disobeyed you."

"But I should never give you an order."

"Your advice is a command to those who know you, Doctor," said Valentine, with a sudden laugh.

"And what advice of mine have you put in the corner with its face to the wall?"

"We have been table-turning again."

"Ah!"

Dr. Levillier formed his lips into the shape assumed by one whistling.

"And this has been the result?"

"Yes," Julian cried. "Never, as long as I live, will I sit again. Val, if you go down on your knees to me——"

"I shall not do that," Valentine quietly interposed. "I have no desire to sit again now."

"You both seem set against such dangerous folly at last," said the doctor. "Give me your solemn promise to stick to what you have said."

And the two young men gave it, Julian with a strong gravity, Valentine with a light smile. Julian had by no means recovered his usual gaiety. The events of the night had seriously affected him.

He was excited and emotional, and now he grasped Valentine by the arm as he exclaimed :

"Valentine, tell me, what made you give that strange cry just before you went into your trance? Were you frightened, or did something—that hand—touch you? Or what was it?"

"A cry?"

"Yes."

"It was not I."

"Didn't you hear it?"

"No."

Julian turned to the doctor.

"It was an unearthly sound," he said. "Like nothing I have ever heard or imagined. And, Doctor, just afterwards I saw something, something that made me believe Valentine was really dead."

"What was it?"

Julian hesitated. Then he avoided directly replying to the question.

"Doctor," he said, "of course I needn't ask you if you have often been at death-beds?"

"I have. Very often," Levillier replied.

"I have never seen any one die," Julian continued, still with excitement. "But people have told me, people who have watched by the dying, that at the moment of death sometimes a tiny flame, a sort of shadow almost, comes from the lips of the corpse and evaporates into the air. And they say that flame is the soul going out of the body."

"I have never seen that," Levillier said. "And I have watched many deaths."

"I saw such a flame to-night," Julian said. "After I heard the cry, I distinctly saw a flame come from where Valentine was sitting, and float up and disappear in the darkness. And—and afterwards, when Valentine lay so still and cold, I grew to believe that flame was his soul, and that I had actually seen him die in the dark."

"Imagination," Valentine said, rather abruptly. "All imagination. Wasn't it, Doctor?"

"Probably," Levillier said. "Darkness certainly makes things visible that do not exist. I have patients who are perfectly sane, yet whom I forbid ever to be entirely in the dark. Remove all objects from their sight and they immediately see non-existent things."

"You think that flame came only from my inner consciousness?" Julian asked.

"I suspect so. Shut your eyes now."

Julian did so. Dr. Levillier bent over and pressed his two fore-fingers hard on Julian's eyes. After a moment,

" What do you see ? " he asked.

" Nothing," Julian replied.

" Wait a little longer. Now what do you see ? "

" Now I see a broad ring of yellow light edged with ragged purple."

" Exactly. You see flame colour."

He removed his fingers and Julian opened his eyes.

" Yes," he said. " But that cry. I most distinctly heard it."

" Imitate it."

" That would be impossible. It was too strange. Are the ears affected by darkness ? "

" The sense of hearing is intimately affected by suspense. If you do not listen attentively you may fail to hear a sound that is. If you listen too attentively you may succeed in hearing a sound that is not. Now, shut your eyes again."

Julian obeyed.

" I am going to clap my hands presently," said the doctor. " Tell me as soon as you have heard me do so."

" Yes."

Dr. Levillier made no movement for some time. Then he softly leant forward, extended his arms in the air, and made the motion of clapping his hands close to Julian's face. In reality he did not touch one hand with the other, yet Julian cried out :

" I heard you clap them then."

" I have not clapped them at all," Levillier said.

Julian expressed extreme surprise.

" You see how very easy it is for the senses to be deceived," the doctor added. " Once stir the nervous system into an acute state of anticipation, and it will conjure up for you a veritable panorama of sights, sounds, bodily sensations. But throw it into that state once too often and the panorama, instead of passing and disappearing, may remain fixed for a time, even for ever, before your eyes, your ears, your touch. And that means recurrent or permanent madness. Valentine, I desire you most especially to remember that."

He uttered the words weightily, with very definite intention. Valentine, who still seemed to be in an unusually lazy or careless mood, laughed easily.

" I will remember," he said.

He yawned.

" My trance has made me sleepy," he added.

The doctor got up.

" Yes, bed is the best place for you," he said.

" And for us all, I suppose," added Julian. " Though I feel as if I could never sleep again."

The doctor went out into the hall to get his coat, leaving the friends alone for a moment.

"I am still so excited," Julian went on. "Dear old fellow! How good it is to see you yourself again. I made up my mind that you were dead. This is like a resurrection. Oh, Val, if you had been dead really!"

"What would you have done?"

"Done! I don't know. Gone to the devil, probably."

"Do you know where to find him?"

"My dear boy, he is in every London street to begin with."

"In Victoria Street even! I was only laughing."

"But tell me, what did you feel?"

"Nothing. As if I slept."

"And you really heard, saw, nothing?"

"Nothing."

"And that hand?"

Valentine smiled again, and seemed to hesitate. But then he replied quietly:

"I told you I could not feel it."

"I did, until I heard that dreadful cry, and then it was suddenly drawn away from me."

Dr. Levillier appeared in the doorway with his overcoat on, but Julian did not notice him. Again his excitement was rising. He began to pace up and down the room.

"My God!" he said, vehemently, "what would Marr say to all this? What does it mean? What can it mean?"

"Don't let us bother too much about it."

"Excellent advice," said Levillier from the doorway.

Julian stood still.

"Doctor, I can understand your attitude," he said. "But what an amazing being you are, Val. You are as calm and collected as if you had sat and held converse with spirits all through your life. And yet something has governed you, has temporarily deprived you of life. For you were to all intents and purposes dead while you were in that trance."

"Death is simply nothing then, and nothingness does not excite or terrify one. I never felt better than I do at this moment."

"That's well," said Levillier cheerfully.

Julian regarded Valentine's pure, beautiful face with astonishment.

"And you never looked better."

"I shall sleep exquisitely to-night, or rather this morning," Valentine said.

As he spoke he drew away the heavy green curtain that hung across the window. A very pale shaft of light stole in, and lit up his white face.

It was the dawn, and, standing there, he looked like the spirit of the dawn, painted against the dying night in such pale colours, white, blue, and shadowy gold, a wonder of death and of life.

In the silence Dr. Levillier and Julian gazed at him, and he seemed a mystery to them both, a strange enigma of purity and of unearthliness.

" Good-bye, Cresswell," Levillier said at last.

" Good-bye, Doctor."

"Good-bye, Valentine."

Julian held out his hand to grasp his friend's, but Valentine began looping up the curtain and did not take it. In his gentlest voice he said to Julian :

" Good-bye, dear Julian, good-bye. The dawn is on our friendship, Julian."

" Yes, Valentine."

Valentine added, after a moment of apparent reflection :

"Take Rip away with you just for to-night. I don't want to be bitten in my sleep."

And when Julian went away, the little dog eagerly followed him, pressing close to his heels, so close that several times Julian could not avoid kicking him.

As soon as the flat door had closed on his two friends, Valentine walked down the passage to the drawing-room, which was shrouded in darkness. He entered it, without turning on the light, and closed the door behind him. He remained in the room for perhaps a quarter of an hour. At length the door opened again. He emerged out of the blackness. There was a calm smile on his face. Two of his fingers were stained with blood, and to one a fragment of painted canvas adhered.

When Valentine's manservant went into the room in the morning and drew up the blinds, he found, to his horror, the picture of "The Merciful Knight" lying upon the floor. The canvas hung from the gold frame in shreds, as if rats had been gnawing it.

CHAPTER II

THE PICCADILLY EPISODE

Dr. Levillier and Julian bade each other good-
step. The doctor hailed a hansom, but Julian ʃ
He wished to be alone, to feel the cold touch of tʰ
The dawn was indeed just breaking, ever so wearilʃ
came up with it over the housetops, and Victoria Stː
in the faint, dusky, grey light, which grew as slo·
sky as hope in a long-starved heart. Julian lived
he now walked forward slowly towards Grosvenor
deliberate detour for the sake of exercising his liɪ
to be out under the sky, glad to feel the breeze oɪ
be free from the horror of that little room in whicʰ
appalling a vigil. The dull lines of the houseſ
through the foggy perspective were gracious to h
welcomed the hard fibre of the pavement. They h
night almost to shudder at the softness of a thick
his senses began to come out of their bondage aɪ
normal sanity. Only now did Julian realise hc
bondage had been, a veritable slavery of the soul.
could surely only have been possible within thɪ
building. An artificial environment must be neɪ
artificial condition of feeling. For Julian now g
believe that Dr. Levillier was right, and that he haɪ
himself to become unnaturally affected and struɪ
believe this in the air and in the dawn. For ʜ
prison as he walked, and heard the dirty sparrowſ
as they sank to the brown puddles in the roadway,
soot that clung round the chimneys which they lov
  And yet he had been communing with death, haɪ
completely realised the fact and the meaning of
demon of the world it was, sly, bitter, chuckling
one thing, surely, that has perfect enjoyment of all
scheme of the earth. What a trick it had played
Valentine. What a trick! And as this idea stɪ

nself on the pavement by the chemist's shop that
underground railway station of Victoria. His eyes
of the boy-messengers, and he beheld through the
: heads. He crossed the road, and tapped on the
nan pulled it up.
a message, sir ? "
o speak to one of your boys, if the one I mean is
ne is."
to his little Hermes of the midnight, who was
uneasily sleeping, his chin nestling wearily among
his exemplary conduct had won for him. The
the child by the shoulder.
" he yelled. " Here's a gentleman wants to speak

his dreams with a jerk, and stared upon Julian
i eyes. Presently he began to realise matters.
r doctor, sir ? It ain't no manner of good," he
eginning to search for his cap, and to glow in the
ir cab ride.
nid. " I stopped to tell you that you were wrong.
quite well again."
I into his pocket and produced half a crown.
hing for your mistake," he said.
mnly and, as Julian walked on, called after him :
fault, sir, it was father's."
isire to shine as an intellectual authority on great
tion than to respect the departed. Julian could
t the child's evident discomfiture as he pursued his
venor Place. On one of the doorsteps of the big
respect like a sharp nail into the hearts of the poor
ed old woman was tumultuously squatting. Her
came, like a scarlet cloud, to the view from the
abond black bonnet, braided with rags, viciously
I there with the stray bugles which survived from
of comparative respectability. Her penetrating
at she was oblivious of the lounging approach of
ose blue and burly form was visible in the extreme
stopped to observe her reflectively. His eye, which
e, was pleased by the bedragglement of her attitude,
its bursting boot, which protruded from the ocean
I petticoats, by the wisps of coarse hair wandering
ive her brazen wrinkles. Poor soul ! she kept a
, even though she could perhaps only make a mark
ire should have been. Julian stared at her very
e did so, he started violently, for, across the human

background which her sleeping dissipation supplied, there seemed to float the vague shadow, suggestion, call it what you will, of a tongue of flame.

He walked hastily on, angrily blaming his nerves. As he passed the policeman he fancied he noticed that the man glanced at him with a certain flickering suspicion. Was horror legibly written in his face? He wondered uneasily, confessing to himself that, even in the dawn and the lap of Grosvenor Place, a horror had again seized him. What did this shadow which he had now twice seen portend? Surely his nerves were not permanently upset. He was at first heartily ashamed of himself. Near St. George's Hospital, gaunt and grey in the morning, he stopped again, bent his left arm forcibly, and with his right hand felt the hard lump of muscle that sprang up like a ball of iron under his coat sleeve. And as he felt it he cursed himself for the greatest of all fools. Thin, meagre little men of the town, tea-party men whose thoughts were ever on their ties and their moustaches, no doubt gave themselves up readily to disturbances of the nerves. But Julian had always prided himself on being an athlete, able to hold his own in the world by mere muscular force, if need be. He had found it possible to develop side by side brain and biceps, each to an adequate end. It had seemed grand to him to hold these scales of his being evenly, to balance them to a hair. Those scales hung badly now, lopsidedly. One was up in the clouds. He resolved that the other should correct it. After a cold bath and a sleep he would go round to Angelo's and have an hour's hard fencing. Cold water, the Englishman's panacea for every ill, cold steel, the pioneer's Minerva, would tonic this errant brain of his and drill it into its customary obedience. So he said to himself.

And yet as he walked there came to him a notion that this little shadow of a flame was still his companion, that this night just passed, this day just begun, were the birthnight and the birthday of this small, ghostlike thing which had come into being to bear him company, to haunt him. Yes, as he walked, followed always closely by Rip, and saw the tall iron gates of the Park, Apsley House, the long line of Piccadilly, all uncertain, gentle, reduced to a whimsical mildness of aspect in the half-light of the dawning, he again recalled the fact, which he had mentioned that night to Dr. Levillier, of people watching an invalid who had seen, at the precise moment of dissolution, the soul escaping furtively from its fleshly prison like a flame which was immediately lost in the air. Surely wandering souls, if, indeed, there were such things, might still retain this faint semblance of a shape, a form. And if so, they might perhaps occasionally conceive a fantastic attachment to a human being, and companion him silently as the dog companions his master. He might have such a companion, whose nature he could not comprehend, whose object in seeking him out he could not guess. Perhaps it felt affection towards him; perhaps, on the other hand, enmity. A lover, or a spy—it might be either. Or it might have no definite purpose, but simply drift near him in the air, as some human beings drift feebly along together through life, because they have long ago loved each other, or thought each other useful, or fancied, in some moment of madness, that God meant them for each other. It might be an aimless, dreary soul, unable to be gone from sheer dulness of purpose, a soul without temperament, without character.

As this thought crossed Julian's mind he happened to glance at the front of a shop on his left, and against the iron shutters the flame was dimly but distinctly outlined. He stopped at once to look at it, but even as he stopped it was gone. Then he sternly brought himself back from the vague regions of fancy, and was angry that he had permitted himself to wander in them like a child lost in a forest. He bent down and patted Rip, and sought to wrench his mind from its wayward course, and to thrust it forcibly into its accustomed groove of healthy sanity. Yet sanity seemed to become abruptly commonplace, a sort of whining crossing-sweeper, chattering untimely, meaningless phrases to him. To divert himself entirely he paused beside a peripatetic coffee-stall, presided over by a grey-faced, prematurely old youth, with sharp features and the glancing eyes of poverty-stricken avarice.

" Give me a cup of coffee," he said.

The youth clattered his wares in excited obedience.

While he was pouring out the steaming liquid, there drifted down to Julian through the grey weariness of the morning a painted girl of the streets, crowned with a large hat, on which a forest of feathers waved in the weak and chilly breeze. Julian glanced at her idly enough and she glanced back at him. Horror, he thought, looked from her eyes as if from a window. As she returned his gaze she hovered near him in the peculiar desultory way of such women, and Julian, glad of any distraction, offered her a cup of coffee. She drew nearer and accepted it.

" And a bun, my dear," she hinted to the sharp-featured youth.

" And a bun," echoed Julian, seeing his doubtful pause of hesitation.

The bun came into view from a hidden basket, and the meal began, Julian, Rip, and the lady of the feathers forming a companionable group upon the kerb. The lady's curious and almost thrilling expression, which had seemed to beacon from some height of her soul some exceptional and dreary deed, faded under the influence of the dough and currants. A smile overspread her thin features. She examined Julian with a gracious interest.

"It's easy to see you've been makin' a night of it, Bertie," she remarked casually at length, in the suffocated voice of one divided between desire of conversation and love of food.

"You think so ? " said Julian.

"Think so, dear, I'm sure so ! Ask me another as I *don't* know; do, darlin'."

Julian took another draught from the thick coffee-cup that held so amazingly little.

"And what about yourself ? " he said. "Why are you out here so early ? "

The lady of the feathers cast a suspicious glance upon him. Then the horror dawned again in her eyes.

"I'm afraid to go home," she said. "Yes, that's a fact."

"Afraid; why ? " Julian spoke abstractedly. In truth he merely talked to this floating wisp of humanity to distract his mind, and thought of her as a strange female David of the streets sent to make a cockney music in his ears that his soul might be rid of its evil spirit.

"Never you mind why," the lady answered.

She shivered suddenly, violently, as a dog just come out of water.

"Have another cup ? " Julian said.

"And a bun, dearie," the lady again rejoined. She shook her head till all the feathers danced.

"Never you mind why," she said, reverting again to his vagrant question. "There's some things as don't do to talk about."

"I'm sure I've no wish to pry into your private affairs," Julian rejoined carelessly.

But again he noticed the worn terror of her face. Surely that night she too had passed through some unwonted experience, which had written its sign manual amid the paint and powder of her shame.

The lady stared back at him. Beneath her tinted eyelids the fear seemed to grow like a weed. Tears followed, rolling over her cheeks and mingling with the coffee in her cup.

"Oh dear," she murmured lamentably. "Oh, dear, oh ! "

"What's the matter ? " said Julian.

But she only shook her head, with the peevish persistence of weak obstinacy, and continued vaguely to weep as one worn down by chill circumstance.

Julian turned his eyes from her to the coffee-stall, in which the sharp-featured youth now negligently leant, well satisfied with the custom he had secured. Behind the youth's head it seemed to Julian that the phantom flame hung trembling, as if blown by the light wind of the morning. He laid his hand on the lady's left arm and unconsciously closed his fingers firmly over the flesh, while, in a low voice, he said to her :

" Look there ! "

The lady of the feathers stopped crying abruptly, as if her tears were suddenly frozen at their source.

" Where dearie ? " she said jerkily. " Whatever do you mean ? "

" There, where the cups are hung up. Don't you see anything ? "

But the lady was looking at him, and she now dropped her cup with a crash to the pavement.

" There's a go," said the sharp-featured youth. " You're a nice one, you are ! "

Without regarding his protest, the lady violently wrenched her arm from Julian's grasp and recoiled from the stall.

" Le-go my arm," she babbled hysterically. " Le-go, I say. I can't stand any more, no I can't."

" I'm not going to hurt you," said Julian, astonished at her outburst.

But she only repeated vehemently :

" Let go, let me go ! "

Backing away, she trod the fallen coffee-cup to fragments on the pavement, and began to drift down Piccadilly, her face under the feathers set so completely round over her shoulder, in observation of Julian, that she seemed to be promenading backwards. And as she went she uttered deplorable wailing sounds, which gradually increased in volume. Apparently she considered that her life had been in imminent danger, and that she saved herself by shrieks ; for, still keeping her face towards the coffee-stall, she faded away in the morning, until only the faint noise of her retreat betokened her existence any longer.

The sharp-featured youth winked wearily at Julian from the midst of his grove of coffee-cups.

" Nice things, women, sir," he ejaculated. " Good ayngels the books calls 'em. Oh Gawd ! "

Julian paid him and walked away.

And as he went he found himself instinctively watching for the fleeting shadow of a flame, trying to perceive it against the grey face of a house, against the trunk of a tree, the dark green of a seat. But the light of the mounting morning grew ever stronger and the flame-shaped shadow did not reappear.

Julian reached his chambers, undressed abstractedly and went to bed. Before he fell asleep he looked at Rip reposing happily at the foot of the bed, and had a moment of shooting wonder that the little dog was so completely comfortable with him. That it had

F

flown at its master, who had always been kind to it, whom it had always seemed to love hitherto, puzzled Julian.

But then so many things had puzzled him within the last few days.

He stroked Rip with a meditative hand and lay down. Soon his mind began to wander in the maze whose clue is sleep. He was with Valentine, with Dr. Levillier, with the sharp-featured youth and the lady of the feathers. They sat round a table and it was dark; yet he could see. And the lady's feathers grew like the beanstalk of Jack the giant-killer towards heaven and the land of ogres. Then Julian climbed up and up till he reached the top of the ladder. And it seemed to him that the feather ladder ended in blue space and in air, and that far away he saw the outline of a golden bar. And on this bar two figures leaned. One seemed an angel, one a devil. Yet they had faces that were alike, and were beautiful. They faded.

Julian seemed vaguely to hear the sharp-featured youth say, Good ayngels! Oh Gawd!"

Was that the motto of his sleep?

CHAPTER III

A DRIVE IN THE RAIN

When Julian returned from Angelo's the next morning he found lying upon the breakfast table a note, and, after the custom of many people, before opening it he read the address on the envelope two or three times and considered who the writer might be. It struck him at once that the writing ought to be familiar to him and capable of instant identification. The name of his correspondent was literally on the tip of his mind. Yet he could not utter it. And so at last he broke the seal. Before reading the note he glanced at the signature : "Valentine."

Julian was surprised. He knew now why he had seemed to remember, yet had not actually remembered the handwriting. Regarding it again, he found it curiously changed from Valentine's usual hand, yet containing many points of resemblance. After a while he came to the conclusion that it was like a bad photograph of the original, imitating, closely enough, all the main points of the original, yet leaving out all the character, all the delicacy of it. For Valentine's handwriting had always seemed to Julian to express his nature. It was rather large and very clear, but delicate, the letters exquisitely formed, the lines perfectly even, neither depressed nor slanting upwards. This note was surely much more coarsely written than usual. And yet of course it was Valentine's writing. Julian wondered he had not known. He read the note at last :

"Dear Julian,

"I am coming over to see you this afternoon about five, and shall try and persuade Rip to restore me to his confidence. I hope you will be in. Are you tired after last night's experiences ? I never felt better.

"Ever yours,
"Valentine."

"And yet," Julian thought, "I should have guessed by your writing that you were in some unusual frame of mind, either tired, or—or——" he looked again, and closely, at the writing,—— "or in a temper less delightfully calm and seraphic than usual. Yet, it looks actually a bad-tempered hand. Valentine's!" Then he laughed, and tossed the note carelessly into the fire that was crackling upon the hearth. Rip lay by it, quietly sleeping.

Punctually at five o'clock Valentine appeared. Rip was still lying happily before the fire, but directly the dog caught sight of its master all the hair along the middle of its back bristled on end, and it showed every symptom of acute distress and fury. Julian was obliged to put it out of the room.

"What can have come over Rip, Valentine?" he said as he came back. "This sudden hatred of you is inexplicable."

"Absolutely," Valentine answered. "But it is sure to pass away. There was something uncanny about that trance of mine which frightened the little beggar."

"Perhaps. But the oddest thing is that while you were insensible Rip lay with his head upon your arm as contented as possible. It was only just as you began to show signs of life that he seemed to turn against you. I can't understand it."

"Nor I. Have you seen Marr to-day?"

"No. I haven't been to the Club. I am so glad you don't know him."

Valentine laughed. He was lying back in a big chair, smoking a cigarette. His face was unclouded and serene, and he had never looked more entirely healthy. Indeed, he appeared much more decisively robust than usual. Julian noticed this.

"Your trance seems positively to have done you good," he said.

"It certainly has not done me harm. My short death of the senses has rested me wonderfully. I wonder if I am what is called a medium."

"I shouldn't be surprised if you are," Julian said. "But I don't think I could be surprised at anything to-day. Indeed, I have found myself dwelling with childish pleasure upon the most preposterous ideas, hugging them to my soul, determining to believe in them."

"Such as—what?"

"Well, such as this."

And then Julian told Valentine of his curious notion that some wandering soul was beginning to companion him, and described how he had thought he saw it when he was gazing at the old woman in Grosvenor Place, and again when he was with the lady of the feathers.

"But," Valentine said, "you say you were staring very hard at the old woman?"

"Yes."

" That might account for the matter of the first appearance of the flame in daylight. If you look very steadily at some object, a kind of slight mirage will often intervene between you and it."

" Perhaps. But I have seen this shadow of a flame when I was not thinking of it or expecting it."

" When ? "

" Just now. As you came into the room I saw it float out at that door."

" You are sure ? "

" I believe so. Yes, I am."

" But why should this soul, if soul it be, haunt you ? "

" I can't tell. Perhaps, Val, you and I ought not to have played at spiritualism as we should play at a game. Perhaps ——"

Julian paused. He was looking anxious, even worried.

" Suppose we have not stopped in time," he said.

Valentine raised his eyebrows.

" I don't understand."

Julian was standing exactly opposite to him, leaning against the mantelpiece and looking down at him.

" We ought never to have sat again after our conversation with the doctor," Julian said. " I feel that to-day, so strongly. I feel that perhaps we have taken just the one step too far, the one step in the dark that may be fatal."

" Fatal ! My dear Julian, you are unstrung by the events of the night."

But the calm of Valentine's voice did not seem to sway Julian. He continued:

" Valentine, now that I am with you, I am attacked by a strange idea."

" What is it ? "

" That last night may have its consequences ; yes, even though we strive to forget it, and to forget our sittings. If it should be so ! If anything ——"

He was curiously upset, and did not seem able to-day to take the influence of Valentine's mood. Indeed, this new anxiety of his was only born in Valentine's presence, was communicated apparently by him.

" Everything one does has its following consequence," Julian said.

" It is the fashion to say so. I do not believe it. I believe, on the contrary, that we often do things with a special view to the doctrine of consequence, and that our intentions are frustrated by the falseness of the doctrine. Suppose I kiss a woman. I may do so with intention to make her love me, or, on the other hand, to make her hate me. The chances are that she does neither the one nor the other. She simply forgets all about such a trifle, and we go on shaking hands politely for the rest of our natural lives. Julian, the memories of most people are like winter days—very short."

"Perhaps. But there is some hidden thing in life whose memory is everlasting. All the philosophers say so, especially those who are inclined to deny the Deity. They put their faith in the chain of cause and effect. What we have done, you and I, Valentine, must have an effect of some sort.

"It will have a very bad effect upon you, I can see," said Valentine smiling, "unless you pull yourself together. Come, this is nonsense. We have sat once too often and the consequence followed, and is over : I went into a trance. I have fortunately come out of it, so the penalty, which you so firmly believe in, has been paid. The score is cleared, Julian."

"I suppose so."

"I have no doubt of it. Let us forget the whole matter, since to remember it seems likely to affect those devils that make the hell of the physical man—the nerves. Let us forget it. Where are you dining to-night ? "

"Nowhere in particular. I have not thought about it," Julian said, rather listlessly.

"Dine with me then."

"Yes, Valentine."

Julian hesitated, then added.

"But not in Victoria Street, if you don't mind."

"At the Savoy then, or shall we say the Berkeley ? "

"Very well, the Berkeley."

"At eight o'clock. Good-bye till then. I must ask you to give the shelter of your roof to Rip till he returns to a more reasonable frame of mind about me."

When Valentine had gone Julian put on his coat, and walked down to the club, ostensibly to look at the evening papers, really because he had a desire to see Marr. His intention, if he did meet the latter, was to question him closely as to the consequences which might follow upon a sitting or series of sittings, undertaken by two people for some reason unsuited to carry out such an enterprise together. That Marr would be in the club he felt no shadow of doubt. Apparently the club had for Marr all the attraction that induces the new member to haunt the smoking- and reading-rooms of his freshly acquired home during the first week or two of its possession. He was incessantly there, as Julian had had reason to know.

But to-day proved to be an exception. Julian explored the club from end to end without finding the object of his search. Finally he went to the hall porter.

" Is Mr. Marr in the club to-day ? "

" No, sir, he has not been in at all since yesterday afternoon."

" Oh, thanks."

Julian felt strongly, even absurdly, disappointed, and found himself wishing that he possessed Marr's private address. He would certainly have called upon him. However he had no idea where Marr lived, so there was nothing to be done. He went back to his rooms, dressed for dinner, and was at the Berkeley by five minutes past eight. The restaurant was very crowded that night, but Valentine had secured a table in the window, and was waiting when Julian arrived. The table next to theirs was the only one unoccupied in the room.

The two friends sat down and began to eat rather silently in the midst of the uproar of conversation round them. Valentine seemed quite unconscious of the many glances directed towards him. He never succeeded in passing unnoticed anywhere, and although he had never done anything remarkable, was one of the best known men in town merely by virtue of his unusual personality.

" There's the Victoria Street Saint," murmured a pretty girl to her companion. " What a fortune that man could make on the stage."

" Yes, or as a pianist," responded the man rather enviously. " His looks would crowd St. James's Hall even if he couldn't play a note. I never can understand how Cresswell manages to have such a complexion in London. He must take precious good care of himself."

" Saints generally do. You see we live for time, they for eternity. We only have to keep the wrinkles at bay for a few years, but they want to look nice on the Judgment Day."

She was a little actress, and at this point she laughed to indicate that she had said something smart. As her laugh was dutifully echoed by the man who was paying for the dinner she felt deliciously clever for the rest of the evening.

Presently Julian said,

" I went to the club this afternoon."

" Did you ?

" Yes. I wanted to have a talk with that fellow, Marr."

Valentine suddenly put down the glass of champagne which he was in the act of raising to his lips.

" But surely," he began, with some appearance of haste. Then he seemed to check himself, and finished calmly.

" You found him, I suppose ? "

" No."

" I thought he was perpetually there, apparently on the look-out for you."

" Yes, but to-day he hadn't been in at all. Perhaps he has gone out of town."

"Ah, probably."

At this moment two men entered the restaurant and strolled towards the table next to that at which Valentine and Julian sat. One of them knew Julian and nodded as he passed. He was just on the point of sitting down and unfolding his napkin when a sudden thought seemed to strike him, and he came over and said to Julian:

"You remember that dinner at Lady Crichton's where we met the other night?"

"Yes."

"Startling bit of news to-night, wasn't it? Damned sudden!"

Julian looked puzzled.

"What—is Lady Crichton ill then?"

"Lady Crichton! No. I meant about that poor fellow, Marr."

Julian swung round in his seat and regarded the man full in the face.

"Marr! Why, what is it? Has he had an accident?"

"Dead!" the other man said laconically, arranging the gardenia in his coat, and taking a comprehensive survey of the room.

"Dead!" Julian repeated, without expression. "Dead!"

"Yes. Well, bye-bye. Going on to the Empire?"

He turned to go, but Julian caught his arm.

"Wait a moment. When did he die?"

"Last night. In the dead of the night, or in the early morning."

"What of?"

"They don't know. There's going to be an inquest. The poor chap didn't die at home, but in a private hotel in the Euston Road, the 'European.' He's lying there now. Funny sort of chap, but not bad in his way. I expect——"

Here the man bent down and murmured something into Julian's ear.

"Well, see you again presently. 'In the midst of life,' eh?"

He lounged away and began applying his intellect to the dissection of a sardine.

Julian turned round in his chair and again faced Valentine. But he did not go on eating the cutlet in aspic that lay upon his plate. He sat looking at Valentine, and at last said:

"How horribly sudden!"

"Yes," Valentine answered sympathetically. "He must have had a weak heart."

"I daresay. I suppose so. Valentine, I can't realise it."

"It must be difficult. A man whom you saw so recently, and I suppose apparently quite well."

"Quite. Absolutely."

Julian sat silent again and allowed the waiter to take away his plate with the untouched cutlet.

"I didn't like the man," he began at last. "But still I'm sorry, damned sorry about this. I wanted to see him again. He was an awfully interesting fellow, Val, and, as I told you, might, I believe, in time have gained a sort of influence over me; not like yours, of course, but he certainly had a power, a strength about him, even a kind of fascination. He was not like other people Ah—" and he exclaimed impatiently—"I wish now you had met him."

"Why?"

"I scarcely know. But I should like you to have had the experience. And then you are so intuitive about people, you might have read him. I could not. And he was a fellow worth reading, that I'm certain of. No, I won't have any mutton. I seem to have lost my appetite over this."

Valentine calmly continued his dinner, while Julian talked on about Marr rather excitedly. When they were having coffee Valentine said:

"What shall we do to-night? It is only a quarter past nine. Shall we go anywhere?"

"Oh no, I think not—wait—yes, we will."

Julian drank his coffee off at a gulp, in a way that would have made him the despair of an epicure.

"Where shall we go then?"

Julian answered:

"To the Euston Road. To the 'European.'"

"The 'European!'"

"Yes, Valentine, I must see Marr once more, even dead. And I want you to see him. It was he who made the strangeness in our lives. But for him these curious events of the last days would not have happened. And isn't it peculiar that he must have died just about the time you were in your trance?"

"I do not see that. The two things were totally uncon-nected."

"Perhaps. I suppose so. But I must know how he died. I must see what he looks like dead. You will come with me?"

"If you wish it. But we may not be admitted."

"I will manage that somehow. Let us go."

Valentine got up. He showed neither definite reluctance nor excitement. They put on their coats in the vestibule and went out into the street. While they had been dining the weather, fine during the day, had changed, and rain was falling in sheets. They stood in the doorway while the hall porter called a cab. Piccadilly on such a night as this looked, perhaps, more decisively dreary than a rain-soaked country lane, or storm-driven sand-dunes by the sea. For wet humanity, with wispy hair and swishing petticoats, draggled with desire for shelter, is a piteous vision as it passes by.

Valentine and Julian regarded it, turning up their coat collars and instinctively thrusting their hands deep into their pockets. Two soldiers passed, pursued by a weary and tattered woman, at whom they laughingly jeered as they adjusted the cloaks over their broad shoulders. They were hurrying back to barracks and disregarded the woman's reiterated exclamation that she would go with them, having no home. A hansom went by with the glass down, a painted face staring through it upon the yellow mud that splashed round the horse's feet. Suddenly the horse slipped and came down. The glass splintered as the painted and now screaming face was dashed through it. A wet crowd of roughs and pavement vagabonds gathered and made hoarse remarks on the woman's dress as she was hauled out in her finery, bleeding and half fainting, her silk gown a prey to the mud, her half naked shoulders a hostage to the wind. Two men in opera hats walked towards their club, discussing a divorce case, and telling funny stories through the rain. A very small, pale, and filthy boy stood with bare feet upon the kerb-stone, and cried damp matches.

" How horrible London is to-night," Julian said as he and Valentine got into their cab.

" Yes. Why add to our necessary contemplation of its horrors ? Why go on this mad errand ? "

" I want you to see Marr," Julian replied, with a curious obstinacy. He pushed up the trap in the roof.

" Drive to the European Hotel in the Euston Road," he said to the cabman. " D'you know it ? "

" Yes, sir," the cabman said. He was smiling on his perch as he cracked his whip and drove towards the Circus.

The glass had been let down and the two friends beheld a continuously blurred prospect of London framed in racing raindrops and intersected by the wooden framework of the movable shutter. It was at the same time fantastic and tumultuous. The glare of light at the Circus shone over the everlasting procession of converging omnibuses, the everlasting mob of prostitutes and of respectable citizens waiting to mount into the vehicles whose paint proclaimed their destination. Active walkers darted dexterously to and fro over the cobblestones, occasionally turning sharply to swear at a driver whose cab had bespattered their black conventionality with clinging dirt. The drivers were impassively insulting, as became men placed for the moment in a high station of life. At the door of the Criterion Restaurant an enormously fat and white bookmaker in a curly hat and diamonds muttered remarks into the ear of an unshaven music-hall singer. A gigantic "chucker-out" observed them with the dull gaze of sullen habit, and a beggar boy whined to them in vain for alms, then fluttered on into obscurity. Fixed with corner stones upon the wet pavement of the "island" lay in an unwinking row the contents bill of the evening papers, proclaiming in gigantic black or red letters the facts of suicide, slander, divorce, murder, railway accidents, fires and war complications. Dreary men read them with dreary, unexcited eyes, then forked out half-pence to raucous youths whose arms were full of damp sheets of pink paper. A Guardsman kissed "Good-bye" to his trembling sweetheart as he chivalrously assisted her into a Marylebone 'bus, and two shop-girls, going home from work, nudged each other and giggled hysterically. Four fat Frenchmen stood in the porch of the Monico violently gesticulating and talking volubly at the tops of their voices. Two English undergraduates pushed past them with a look of contempt, and went speechlessly into the *café* beyond. A lady from Paris, all red velvet and white ostrich tips, smoothed her cheek with her kid glove meditatively, and glanced about in search of her fate of the dark and silent hours. And then—Valentine and Julian were in the comparative dimness of Shaftesbury Avenue—a huge red cross on a black background started out of the gloom above a play-house. Julian shuddered at it visibly.

"You are quite unstrung to-night, Julian," Valentine said. "Let us turn the cab round and go home."

"No, no, my dear fellow, I am all right. It is only that I see things to-night much more clearly than usual. I suppose it is owing to something physical that every side of London seems to have sprung into prominence. Of course I go about every day in Piccadilly, St. James's Street, everywhere; but it is as if my eyes had been always shut, and now they are open. I can see London to-night. And that cross looked so devilishly ironical up there, as if it were silently laughing at the tumult in the rain. Don't you feel London to-night, too, Valentine?"

"I always feel it."

"Tragically or comically?"

"I don't know that I could say truly either. Calmly or contemptuously would rather be the word."

"You are always a philosopher. I can't be a philosopher when I see those hordes of women standing hour after hour in the rain, and those boys searching among them. I should be one of those boys probably but for you."

"If you were, I doubt whether I should feel horrified."

"Not morally horrified, I dare say, but intellectually disgusted. Eh?"

"I am not sure whether I shall permit my intellect quite so much licence in the future as I have permitted it in the past," Valentine said thoughtfully.

His blue eyes were on Julian, but Julian was gazing out on Oxford Street, which they were crossing at that moment. Julian, who had apparently continued dwelling on the train of thoughts waked in him by the sight of the painted cross, ignored this remark and said:

" It is not my moral sense which shuddered just now, I believe, but my imagination. Sin is so full of prose, although many clever writers have represented it as splendidly decorated with poetry. Don't you think so, Val? And it is the prose of sin I realise so vividly just now."

" The wet flowers on the waiting hats, the cold raindrops on the painted faces, the damp boots trudging to find sin, the dark clouds pouring a benediction on it. I know what you mean. But the whole question is one of weather, I think. Vanity Fair on a hot, sweet summer night, with a huge golden moon over Westminster, soft airs and dry pavements would make you see this city in a different light. And which of the lights is the true one?"

" I daresay neither."

" Why not both? The smartest coat has a lining, you know. I daresay there are velvet sins as well as plush sins, and the man who can find the velvet is the lucky fellow. Sins feel like plush to me, however, and I dislike plush. So I am not the lucky fellow."

" No, Valentine, you are wrong. I'm pretty sure all virtue is velvet and all vice is plush. So you stick to velvet."

" I don't know. Ask the next pretty dressmaker you meet. Bloomsbury is a genteel *inferno* on a wet night."

They traversed it smoothly on asphalte ways. All the time Valentine was watching Julian with a fixed and narrow scrutiny, which Julian failed to notice. The rows of dull houses seemed endless, and endlessly alike.

" I am sure all of them are full of solicitors," said Valentine.

Presently in many fanlights they saw the mystic legend, " Apartments." Then there were buildings that had an aged air and sported broken windows. Occasionally, on a background of red glass lit by a gas jet from behind, sat the word " Hotel." A certain grimy degradation swam in the atmosphere of these streets. Their aspect was subtly different from the Bloomsbury thoroughfares, which look actively church-going, and are full of the shadows of an everlasting respectability which pays its water rates and sends occasional conscience money to the Chancellor of the Exchequer. People looked furtive, and went in and out of the houses furtively. They crawled rather than pranced, and their bodies bore themselves with a depression that seemed indiscreet. Occasional men with dripping umbrellas knocked at the doors under the red glass, and disappeared into narrow passages inhabited by small iron umbrella stands. Night brooded here like a dyspeptic raven with moulting tail feathers and ragged wings. But London is eloquent of surprises. The cab turned a corner, and instantly they were in a wide and rain-swept street, long and straight and lined with reserved houses, that shrank back from the publicity of the passing traffic at the end of narrow alleys protected by iron gates. Over many of these gates appeared lit arches of glass on which names were inscribed : "Albion Hotel," "Valetta Hotel," "Imperial Hotel," "Cosmopolitan Hotel"—great names for small houses. These houses had front doors with glass panels, and all the panels glowed dimly with gas.

The cab flashed by them, and Julian read the fleeting names, until his eyes were suddenly saluted with "European Hotel."

Violently the cabman drew up. The smoking horse was squeezed upon its haunches, and its feet slithered harshly along the stones. It tried to sit down, was hauled up by the reins, and stood trembling as the right wheel of the cab collided with the pavement edge, and the water in the gutter splashed up as if projected from a spray.

"Beg pardon, gents. I thought it was a bit further on," said the cabby, leering down cheerfully. "Nice night, sir, ain't it ?"

He shook the reluctant drops of moisture from his waterproof shrouded hat, and drove off.

Valentine opened the damp iron gate, and they walked up the paved alley to the door.

CHAPTER IV

THE EUSTON ROAD EPISODE

OPENING the door they found themselves in a squalid passage. A room on the left was fronted by a sort of counter, above which was a long window giving on to the passage, and as the shrill tinkle of a bell announced their entrance this window was pushed up, and the large red face and furtive observant eyes of a man stared upon them inquiringly.

"Do you require a room for the night?" he asked, in a husky voice, invaded by a strong French accent. "Because——"

"No," interrupted Julian.

The man nodded, and, strange to say, with apparent content.

"There is trouble in my house," he said. "I am unlucky; I come to England from my country to earn an honest living, and before two years, I have the police here last night."

"Yes," said Julian. "I know."

"What? You know it? Well, it is not my fault. The gentleman come last night with a lady, his wife, I suppose. How am I to know? He ask for a room. He look perfectly well. I give them the room. They go to bed. At four o'clock in the morning I hear a bell ring. I get up. I go on the landing to listen. I hear the bell again. I run to the chamber of the lady and gentleman. The lady is gone. The gentleman falls back on the bed as I come in and dies. Mon Dieu! It is——"

He suddenly paused in his excited narrative. Valentine had moved his position slightly and was now standing almost immediately under the gas lamp that lit the glass door.

"You—you are relation of him?" he said. "You come to see him?"

"I have come to see him certainly," said Valentine. "But I am no relation of his. This gentleman," and he pointed to Julian, "knew him well, and wished to look at him once more."

The landlord seemed puzzled. He glanced from Valentine to Julian, then back again to Valentine.

"But," he began once more addressing himself to the latter, "you are like—there is something; when the poor gentleman fell on the bed and died he had your eyes. Yes, yes, you are relation of him."

" No," Valentine said, " you are mistaken."

" I should think so," exclaimed Julian. " Poor Marr's face was as utterly different from yours, Valentine, as darkness is different from light."

"No, no, it is not the eyes of the gentleman," the landlord continued, leaning forward through his window, and still violently scrutinising Valentine, " it is not the eyes. But there is something —the voice, the manner—yes, I say there is something, I cannot tell."

"You are dreaming, my friend," Valentine calmly interposed. "Now, Julian, what do you want to do?"

Julian came forward and leant his arm on the counter.

"I am the poor gentleman's great friend," he said. "You must let me see him."

The landlord held up his fat hands with a large gesticulation of refusal.

"I cannot, sir. To-morrow they remove him. They sit on the poor gentleman——"

"I know, the inquest. All this is very hard upon you, an honest man trying to make an honest living."

Julian put some money into one of the agitated hands.

"My friend and I only wish to see him for a moment."

"Monsieur, I cannot. I——"

Julian insinuated another sovereign into his protesting fingers. They took it as an anemone takes a shrimp, and made a gesture of abdication.

"Well, if Monsieur is the friend of the poor gentleman, I have not the heart, I am tender-hearted, I am foolish——"

He disappeared muttering from the window, and in a moment appeared at a door on the left, disclosing himself now fully as a degraded, flaccid looking, frowsy ruffian, of a very low type, flashily dressed, and of a most unamiable expression. Taking a candlestick from a dirty marble-topped slab that projected from the passage wall, he struck a match, lit the candle, and preceded them up the narrow flight of stairs, his boots creaking loudly at every step. On the landing at the top a smart maidservant with a very pale face reconnoitred the party for a moment with furtive curiosity, then flitted away in the darkness to the upper regions of the house.

The landlord paused by a door numbered with a black number.

"He is in here," he whispered hoarsely. "To-morrow they sit on him. After that he go from me. Mon Dieu ! I am glad when he is gone. My custom he is spoilt. My house get a bad name, and like a dog they hang him. Mon Dieu ! "

He opened the door stealthily, forming " St ! " with his fat, coarse lips.

" I light the gas. It is all dark."

" No, no," Julian said, taking the candle from him, " I will do that. Go down."

He motioned him away, and entered the room, followed by Valentine, at whom the landlord again stared with a greedy consideration and curiosity, before turning to retreat softly down the narrow stairs.

They found themselves in a good-sized room, typically of London. It was full of the peculiar and unmistakable metropolitan smell, a stale odour of the streets that suggests smuts to the mind. Two windows, with a long dingy mirror set between them, looked out towards the Euston Road. Venetian blinds and thin white curtains looped with yellow ribbon, shrouded them. On a slab that stuck out under the mirror was placed a bundle of curling-pins tied with white tape, a small brush and comb, and a bottle of Cherry Blossom scent. Near the mirror stood a narrow sofa covered with red rep. Upon this lay a man's upturned top hat, in the corner of which reposed a pair of reindeer gloves. A walking stick with a gold top stood against the wall in a corner by the marble mantelpiece. In the middle of the room lay a small open portmanteau, disclosing a disorder of shirts, handkerchiefs and boots, a cheque-book, a bottle of brandy and some brushes. By the fireplace there was a vulgar looking armchair upholstered in red. The room was full of the faint sound of London voices and London traffic.

Julian went straight up to the gas chandelier and lit all three jets. His action was hurried and abrupt. Then he set the candle down beside the bundle of curling-pins, and turned sharply round to face the bed. The room was now a glare of light, and in this glare of light the broad bed with its white counterpane and sheets stood out harshly enough. The sheets were turned smoothly down under the blue chin of the dead man, who lay there upon his back, his face, with fast shut eyes dusky white, or rather grey, among the pillows. As Julian looked upon him he exclaimed :

" Good God, it isn't Marr ! Valentine, it isn't Marr ! "

" Not ? "

" No. And yet—wait a moment——"

Julian came nearer to the bed and bent right down over the corpse. Then he drew away and looked at Valentine, who was at the other side of the bed.

" Oh, Valentine, this is strange," he whispered, and drawing a chair to the bedside he sank down upon it. " This is strange.

What is it death does to a man ? Yes, this is Marr. I see now ; but so different, so altered. The whole expression; oh, it is almost incredible."

He stared again upon the face.

It was long in shape, thin and swarthy, very weary looking, the face of a man who had seen much, who had done very many, very various things. No face with shut eyes can look, perhaps, completely characteristic. Yet this face was full of a character that seemed curiously at war with the shape of the features and with the position of the closed eyes, which were very near together. Julian, in describing Marr to Valentine, had pronounced him Satanic, and this dead face was, in truth, somewhat Mephistophelean. An artist might well have painted it upon his canvas as a devil. But he must have reproduced merely the features and colouring, the blue, shaven cheeks, and hollow eye-sockets ; for the expression of his devil he would have been obliged to seek another model. Marr dead looked serene, kind, gentle, satisfied, like a man who has shaken himself free from a heavy burden, and who stretches himself to realise the sudden and wonderful ease for which he has longed, and who smiles, thinking " that ghastly thrall is over. I am a slave no longer. I am free." The dead face was wonderfully happy.

Julian seemed entirely fascinated by it. After his last smothered exclamation to Valentine, he sat, leaning one arm upon the head of the bed, gazing till he looked stern, as all utterly ardent observers look.

Valentine, too, was staring at the dead man.

There was a very long silence in the room. The rain leaped upon the tall windows on each side of the mirror and ran down them with an unceasing chilly vivacity. Lights from the street flickered through the blinds to join the glare of the gas. All the music of the town wandered round the house as a panther wanders round a bungalow by night. And the thin stream of people flowed by on the shining pavement beyond the iron railing of the narrow garden. They spoke, as they went, of all the minor things of life, details of home, details of petty sins, details of common loves and common hopes and fears, all stirring feebly under umbrellas. And close by these two friends, under three flaring gas jets, watched the unwinking dead man, whose face seemed full of relief. Presently Julian, without looking up, said :

" Death has utterly changed him. He is no longer the same man. Formerly he looked all evil, and now it's just as if his body were thanking God because it had got rid of a soul it had hated. Yes, it's just like that. Valentine, I feel as if Marr had been rescued."

As he said the last words Julian looked up across the barrier of the bed at his friend. His lips opened as if to speak, but he said

G

nothing. For he was under the spell of a wild hallucination. It seemed to him that there, under the hard glare of the gas lamps, the soul of Marr spoke, stared from the pure, proud face of Valentine. That was like a possession of his friend. It was horrible, as if a devil chose for a moment to lurk and to do evil in the sanctuary of a church, to blaspheme at the very altar. Valentine did not speak. He was looking down on the dead serenity of Marr, vindictively. A busy intellect flashed in his clear blue eyes, meditating vigorously upon the dead man's escape from bondage, following him craftily to the very door of his freedom, to seize him surely if it might be.

This is what Julian felt in his hallucination, that Valentine was pursuing Marr, uselessly, but with a deadly intention, a deadly hatred.

" Valentine ! " Julian cried at last.

Valentine looked up.

And in an instant the spell was removed. Julian saw his friend and protector rightly again, calm, pure, delicately reserved. The death chamber no longer contained a phantom. His eyes were no longer the purveyors of a terrible deception to his mind.

"Oh, Valentine, come here," Julian said.

Valentine came round by the end of the bed and stood beside him. Julian examined him narrowly.

"Never stand opposite to me again, Valentine."

"Opposite to you ! Why not ? "

"Nothing, nothing. Or—everything. What is the matter with this room, and me, and you ? And why is Marr so changed ? "

"How is he changed ? You know I have never seen his face before."

"You do not see it now. He has gone out of it. All that was Marr as I knew him has utterly gone. Death has driven it away and left something quite different. Let us go."

Julian got up. Valentine took up the candle from its place beside the curling-pins and lifted his hand to the gas chandelier. He had turned out one of the burners, and was just going to turn out the two others when Julian checked him.

"No, leave them. Let the landlord put them out. Leave him in the light."

They went out of the room, treading softly. A little way up the staircase that led from the landing to the upper parts of the house a light flickered down to them, and they perceived the pale face of the housemaid diligently regarding them. Julian beckoned to her.

"You showed the gentleman—the gentleman who is dead—to his room last night ? "

"Yes, sir. Oh, sir, I can't believe he's really gone so sudden like."

"Then you saw the lady with him ? "

" Yes, sir, of course. Oh——"

" Hush ! What was she like ? "

The housemaid's nose curled derisively.

" Oh, sir, quite the usual sort. Oh, a very common person. Not at all like the poor gentleman, sir."

" Young ? "

" Not to say old, sir. No, I couldn't bring that against her. She wore a hat, sir, and feathers—well, more than ever growed on one ostrich, I'll be bound."

" Feathers ! "

A vision of the lady of the feathers sprang up before Julian, wrapped in the wan light of the early dawn. He put several rapid questions to the housemaid. But she could only say again that Marr's companion had been a very common person, a very common sort of person indeed, and flashily dressed, not at all as she—the housemaid—would care to go out of a Sunday. Julian tipped her and left her amazed upon the dim landing. Then he and Valentine descended the stairs. The landlord was waiting in the passage in an attentive attitude against the wall. He seemed taken unawares by their appearance, but his eyes immediately sought Valentine's face, still apparently questioning it with avidity. Julian noticed this, and recollected that the man had insisted on a likeness existing between Marr and Valentine. Possibly that fact, although apparently unremembered, had remained lurking in his mind and was accountable for his own curious deception. Or could it be that there really was some vague, fleeting resemblance between the dead man and the living which the landlord saw continuously, he only at moments ? Looking again at Valentine he could not believe it. No, the landlord was deceived now, as he had been in the death chamber above stairs.

" May we come into your room for a moment ? " Julian asked the man. " I want to put to you a few questions."

" But certainly, sir, with pleasure."

He opened the side door and showed them into his sanctum beyond the glass window. It was a small, evil-looking room, crowded with fumes of stale tobacco. On the walls hung two or three French prints of more than doubtful decency. A table with a bottle and two or three glasses ranged on it occupied the middle of the floor. On a chair by the fire the *Gil Blas* was thrown in a crumpled attitude. One gas burner flared, unshaded by any glass globe. Julian sat down on the *Gil Blas*. Valentine refused the landlord's offer of a chair, and stood looking rather contemptuously at the inartistic improprieties of the prints.

" Did you let in the gentleman who came last night ? " asked Julian.

"But sir, of course. I am always here. I mind my house. I
see that only respect——"

"Exactly. I don't doubt that for a moment. What was the
lady like, the lady who accompanied him?"

"Oh, sir, very *chic*, very pretty."

"Didn't you hear her go out in the night?"

The landlord looked for a moment as if he were considering the
advisableness of a little bluster. He stared hard at Julian and
thought better of it.

"Not a sound, not a mouse. Till the bell rang I slept. Then
she is gone!"

"Would you recognise her again?"

"But no. I hardly look at her and I see so many."

"Yes, yes, no doubt. And the gentleman. When you went into
his room?"

"Ah. He was half sitting up. I come in. He just look at me.
He fall back. He is dead. He say nothing. Then I—I run."

"That's all I wanted to know," Julian said. "Valentine, shall we
go?"

"By all means."

The landlord seemed relieved at their decision, and eagerly let
them out into the pouring rain. When they were in the dismal
strip of garden Julian turned and looked up at the lit windows of
the bedroom on the first storey. Marr was lying there in the bright
illumination at ease, relieved of his soul. But, as Julian looked, the
two windows suddenly grew dark. Evidently the economical
landlord had hastened up, observed the waste of the material he had
to pay for, and abruptly stopped it. At the gate they called a cab.

"No, let us have the glass up," Julian said. "A drop of rain
more or less doesn't matter. And I want some air."

"So do I," said Valentine. "The atmosphere of that house was
abominable."

"Of course there can be no two opinions as to its character,"
Julian said.

"Of course not."

"What a dreary place to die in!"

"Yes. But does it matter where one dies? I think not. I
attach immense importance to where one lives."

"It seems horrible to come to an end in such a place, to have had
that wretched Frenchman as the only witness of one's death. Still,
I suppose it is only foolish sentiment. Valentine, did you notice
how happy Marr looked?"

"No."

"Didn't you? I thought you watched him almost as if you
wondered as I did."

"How could I?　I had never seen him before."

"It was curious the landlord seeing a likeness between you and him."

"Do you think so?　The man naturally supposed one of us might be a relation, as we came to see Marr.　I should not suppose there could be much resemblance."

"There is none.　It's impossible.　There can be none!"

They rattled on towards Piccadilly, back through the dismal thoroughfares, towards the asphalte ways of Bloomsbury.　Presently Julian said :

"I wish I had seen Marr die."

"But why, Julian?　Why this extraordinary interest in a man you knew so slightly and for so short a time?"

"It's because I can't get it out of my head that he had something to do with our sittings, more than we know."

"Impossible."

"I am almost certain the doctor thought so.　I must tell him about Marr's death.　Valentine, let us drive to Harley Street now."

Valentine did not reply at once, and Julian said :

"I will tell the cabman."

"Very well."

Julian gave the order.

"I wonder if he will be in," Julian said presently.　"What is the time?"

He took out his watch and held it up sideways until the light of a gas lamp flashed on it for a moment.

"Just eleven.　So late?　I am surprised."

"We were a good while at the 'European.'"

"Longer than I thought.　Probably the doctor will have come in, even if he has been out dining.　Ah, here we are!"

The cab drew up.　Julian got out and rang the bell in the rain.

"Is Doctor Levillier at home?"

"No, sir.　He is out dining.　But I expect him every moment. Will you come in and wait?" said the manservant, who knew Julian well.

"Thanks, I think I will.　I rather want to see him.　I will just ask Mr. Cresswell.　He's with me to-night."

Julian returned to the cab, in which Valentine was sitting.

"The doctor will probably be home in a few minutes.　Let us go in and wait for him."

"Yes, you go in."

"But surely——"

"No, Julian," Valentine said, and suddenly there came into his voice a weariness, "I am rather tired to-night.　I think I'll go home to bed."

"Oh," Julian said. He was obviously disappointed. He hesitated.

"Shall I come too, old chap? You're sure—you're certain that you are not feeling ill after last night?"

He leant with his foot on the step of the cab to look at Valentine more closely.

"No, I am all right. Only tired and sleepy, Julian. Well, will you come or stay?"

"I think I will stay. I want badly to have a talk with the doctor."

"All right. Good night."

"Good night!"

Valentine called his address to the cabman, and the man whipped up his horse. Just as the cab was turning round Valentine leaned out over the wooden door and cried to Julian who was just going into the house:

"Give my best regards to the doctor, Julian."

The cab disappeared, splashing through the puddles.

Julian stood still on the doorstep.

"Who said that, Lawler?" he asked.

The servant looked at him in surprise.

"Mr. Valentine, sir."

"Mr. Valentine?"

"Yes, sir."

"Of course, of course. But his voice, didn't it—didn't you notice——"

"It was Mr. Valentine's usual voice, sir," Lawler said, with increasing astonishment.

"I'm upset to-night," Julian muttered.

He went into the house and Lawler closed the street door.

CHAPTER V

THE HARLEY STREET EPISODE

JULIAN was a favourite in Harley Street, so Lawler did not hesitate to show him into the doctor's very private room, a room dedicated to ease, and to the cultivation of a busy man's hobbies. No patient ever told the sad secrets of his body here. Here were no medical books, no appliances for the writing of prescriptions, no hints of the profession of the owner. Several pots of growing roses gravely shadowed forth the doctor's fondness for flowers. A grand piano mutely spoke of his love for music. Many of the books which lay about were novels, one, soberly dressed in a vellum binding, being Ouida's " Dog of Flanders." All the photographs which studded the silent chamber with a reflection of life were photographs of children, except one. That was Valentine's. The hearth, on which a fire flashed, was wide and had two mighty occupants, Rupert and Mab, the doctor's mastiffs, who took their evening ease, pillowing their huge heads upon each other's heaving bodies. The ticking clock on the mantelpiece was an imitation of the Devil Clock of Master Zacharius. There were no newspapers in the room. That fact alone made it original. A large cage of sleeping canaries was covered with a cloth. The room was long and rather narrow, the only door being at one end. On the walls hung many pictures, some of them gifts from the artists. Some foils lay on an ottoman in a far corner. The doctor fenced admirably, and believed in the exercise as a tonic to the muscles and a splendid drill-sergeant to the eyes.

As Julian came into the room, which was lit only by wax candles, he could not help comparing it with the room he had just left in which the body of Marr lay. The atmosphere of a house is a strange thing, and almost as definite to the mind as is an appearance to the eye. A sensitive nature takes it in like a breath of fœtid or of fresh air. The atmosphere of the European Hotel had been sinister and dreary, as of a building consecrated to hidden deeds, and inhabited mainly by wandering sinners. This home of a great doctor was open-hearted and receptive, frank and refined. The sleeping dogs, heaving gently in fawn-coloured beatitude, set upon it the best hall-mark. It was a house—judging at least by this room—for happy rest. Yet it was the abode of incessant work, as the great world knew well. This sanctum alone was the shrine of lotos eating. The doctor sometimes laughingly boasted that he had never insulted it by even so much as writing a postcard within its four walls.

Julian stroked the dogs, who woke to wink upon him majestically, and sat down. Lawler quietly departed and he was left alone. When he first entered the house he had been disappointed at the departure of Valentine. Now he felt rather glad to have the doctor to himself for a quiet half-hour. A conversation of two people is, under certain circumstances, more complete than a conversation of three, however delightful the third may chance to be. Julian placed Valentine before all the rest of the world. Nevertheless, to-night he was glad that Valentine had gone home to bed. It seems some-times as if affection contributes to the making of a man self-con-scious. Julian had a vague notion that the presence of his greatest friend to-night might render him self-conscious. He scarcely knew why. Then he looked at the mastiffs, and wondered at the extra-ordinary difference between men and the companion animals whom they love and who love them. What man, however natural, however independent and serene, could emulate the majestic and deliberate *abandon* of a big dog courted and caressed by a blazing fire and a soft rug ? Man has not the dignity of soul to be so grandly natural. Yet his very pert self-consciousness, the fringed petticoats of affecta-tion which he wears, give him the kennel, the collar, the muzzle, the whip, weapons of power to bring the dog to subjection. And Julian, as he watched Rupert and Mab, wrapped in large lethargic dreams, found himself pitying them, as civilised man vaguely pities all other inhabitants of the round world. Poor old things ! Sombre agitations were not theirs. They had nothing to aim at or to fight against. No devils and angels played at football with their souls. Their *liaisons* were clear, uncomplicated by the violent mental drum-taps that set the passions marching so often at a quick step in the wrong direction. And Julian knelt down on the hearth-rug and laid his strong young hands on their broad heads. Slowly they opened their veiled eyes and blinked. One, Rupert, struck a strict tail feebly upon the carpet in token of acquiescence and gratified goodwill. Mab heaved herself over until she rested more completely upon her side, and allowed an enormous sigh to rumble through her monotonously. Julian enjoyed that sigh. It made him for the moment an optimist, as a happy child makes a dreary old man shivering on the edge of death an optimist. Dogs are blessed things. That was his thought. And just then the door at the end of the room opened quietly, and Dr. Levillier came in, with a cloak on and his crush hat in his hand.

"I am glad to see you, Addison," he said.

The dogs shook themselves up on to their legs and laid their heads against his knees.

"Lawler, please bring my gruel."

"Yes, sir!"

"Addison, will you have brandy or whisky?"

"Whisky, please, Doctor."

Lawler took his master's cloak and hat and the doctor came up to the fire.

"So Valentine has gone home to bed?" he said.

"Yes."

"He's all right, I hope?"

"Yes. Indeed, Doctor, I thought him looking more fit than usual to-day, more alive than I have often seen him."

"I noticed that last night, when he revived from his trance. It struck me very forcibly, very forcibly indeed. But you——" and the doctor's eyes were on Julian's face—"look older than your age to-night, my boy."

He sat down and lit a cigar. The mastiffs coiled themselves at his feet rapturously. They sighed, and he sighed too, quietly in satisfaction. He loved the one hour before midnight, the hour of perfect rest for him. Putting his feet on Rupert's back, he went on:

"Last night's events upset you seriously, I see, young and strong though you are. But the most muscular men are more often the prey of their nervous systems than most people are aware. Spend a few quiet days. Fence in the morning. Ride—out in the country, not in the Park. Get off your horse now and then, tie him up at a lych-gate and sit in a village church. Listen to the amateur organist practising 'Abide with me,' and the 'Old Hundredth,' on the Leiblich Gedacht and the Dulciana, with the bourdon on the pedals. There's nothing like that for making life seem a slow stepper instead of a racer. And take Valentine with you. I should like to sit with him in a church at twilight, when the rooks were going home, and the organ was droning. Ah, well, but I must not think of holidays."

"Doctor, I like your prescription. Yes, I am feeling a bit out of sorts to-night. Last night, you see—and then to-day."

"Surely, Addison, surely you haven't been sitting—but no, forgive me. I've got your promise. Well, what is it?"

Julian replied quickly:

"That man I told you about, Marr, is dead."

Doctor Levillier looked decidedly startled. Julian's frequent allusions to Marr and evident strange interest in the man, had impressed him as it had impressed Valentine. However, he only said:

"Heart disease?"

"I don't know. There is going to be an inquest."

"When did he die?"

"Last night, or rather at four in the morning; just as Valentine came out of his trance, it must have been. Don't you remember the clock striking?"

"Certainly I do. But why do you connect the two circumstances?"

"Doctor, how can you tell that I do?"

"By your expression, the tone of your voice."

"You are right. Somehow I can't help connecting them. I told Valentine so to-night. He has been with me to see Marr's body."

"You have just come from that death-bed, now?"

"Yes."

Julian sketched rapidly the events of the European Hotel, but he left to the last the immense impression made upon him by the expression of the dead man.

"He looked so happy, so good, that at first I could not recognise him," he said. "His face, dead, was the most absolutely direct contradiction possible of his face, alive. He was not the same man."

"The man was gone, you see, Addison."

"Yes. But then what was it which remained to work this change in the body?"

"Death gives a strange calm. The relaxing of sinews, the droop of limbs and features, the absolute absence of motion, of breathing, work up an impression."

"But there was something more here, more than peace. There was a—well, a strong happiness and a goodness. And Marr had always struck me as an atrociously bad lot. I think I told you."

The doctor sat musing. Lawler came in with the tray, on which was a small basin of gruel and soda water bottles, a decanter of whisky, and a tall tumbler. Julian mixed himself a drink, and the doctor, still meditatively, took the basin of gruel on to his knees. As he sipped it, he looked a strange, little, serious ascetic, sitting there in the light from the wax candles, his shining boots planted gently on the broad back of the slumbering mastiff, his light eyes fixed on the fire. He did not speak again until he was half-way through his gruel. Then he said:

"And you know absolutely nothing of Marr's past history?"

"No, nothing."

"I gather from all you have told me that it would be worthy of study. If I knew it I might understand the startling change from the aspect of evil to the aspect of good at death. I believe the man must have been far less evil than you thought him, for dead faces express something that was always latent, if not known, in the departed natures. Ignorantly you possibly attributed to Marr a nature far more horrible than he ever really possessed."

But Julian answered:

"I feel absolutely convinced that at the time I knew him he was one of the greatest rips, one of the most merciless men in London. I never felt about any man as I did about him! And he impressed others in the same way."

"I wish I had seen him," Dr. Levillier said.

An idea, suggested by Julian's last remark, suddenly struck him.

"He conveyed a strong impression of evil, you say?"

"Yes."

"How? In what way exactly?"

Julian hesitated.

"It's difficult to say," he answered. "Awfully difficult to put such a thing into words. He interested me. I felt that he had a great power of intellect, or of will, or something. But in every way he suggested a bad, a damnably bad character. A woman said to me once about him that it was like an emanation."

"Ah!"

The doctor finished his gruel and put down the basin on the table beside him.

"By the way, where did Marr live? Anywhere in my direction? Would he, for instance, go home from Piccadilly, or the theatres, by Regent Street?"

"I don't know at all where he lived."

"Have you ever seen him with animals, with dogs, for instance?"

"No."

"If he had been as evil as you suppose, any dog would have avoided him."

"Well, but dogs avoid perfection too."

"Hardly, Addison."

"But Rip and Valentine!"

The remark struck the doctor, that was obvious. He pushed his right foot slowly backwards and forwards on Rupert's back, rucking up the dog's loose skin in heavy folds.

"Yes," he said. "Rip is rather an inexplicable beggar. But do you mean to tell me he hasn't got over his horror of Valentine to-day?"

"This afternoon he was worse than ever. If Valentine had touched him I believe he would have gone half mad. I had to put him out of the room."

"H'm!"

"Isn't it unaccountable?"

"I must say that it is. Dogs are such faithful wretches. If

Rupert and Mab were to turn against me like that I believe it would strike at my heart more fiercely than the deed of any man could."

He bent down and ran his hand over Rupert's heaving back.

" The cheap satirist," he said, " is for ever comparing the fickleness of men with the faithfulness of animals, but I don't mean to do that. I have a great belief in some human natures, and there are many men whom I could, and would, implicitly trust."

" There is one, Doctor, whom we both know."

" Cresswell. Yes. I could trust him through thick and thin. And yet his own dog flies at him."

Dr. Levillier returned to that fact, as if it puzzled him so utterly that he could not dismiss it from his mind.

" There must be some curious, subtle reason for that," he said, " yet with all my intimate and affectionate knowledge of dogs I cannot divine it. Watch Rip carefully when he is not with Cresswell. Look after his health. Notice if he seems natural and happy. Does he eat as usual ? "

" Rather. He did to-day."

" And he seems content with you ? "

" Quite."

" Well, all I can say is that Rip doesn't seem to possess a dog nature. He is uncanny."

" Uncanny," Julian said, seizing on the word. " But everything has become uncanny within the last few days. Upon my word, when I look back into the past of, say, a fortnight ago, I ask myself whether I am a fool, or dreaming, or whether my health is going to the deuce. London seems different. I look on things strangely. I fancy, I imagine——"

He broke off. Then he said :

" By Jove, Doctor, if half the men I know at White's could see into my mind they would think me fitted for a lunatic asylum."

" It doesn't matter to you what half the men, or the whole of the men at White's think, so long as you keep a cool head and a good heart. But it is as you say. You and Valentine have run, as a train runs into the Black Country, into an unwholesome atmosphere. In a day or two probably your lungs, which have drawn it in, will expel it again."

He smiled rather whimsically. Then he said :

" You know, Addison, men talk of their strength, and are inclined to call women nervous creatures, but the nerves play tricks among male muscles. Yes, you want the foils, the bicycle, the droning organ, and the village church. I advise you to go out of town for a week. Forget Marr, a queer fish evidently, with possibly a power of mesmerism. And don't ask Valentine to go away with you."

The last remark surprised Julian.

" But why not ? " he asked.

" Merely because he is intimately connected with the events that have turned you out of your usual, your right course. I see that your mind is moving in a rather narrow circle, which contains, besides yourself, two people only, Marr and Cresswell."

"Darkness and light. Yes, it's true. How rotten of me," Julian exclaimed, like a schoolboy. " I'm like a squirrel in a cage, going round and round. That's just it. Valentine and Marr are in that cursed circle of our sittings, and so I insanely connect them with one another. I actually began to think to-night that Marr died, poor fellow, because—well——"

" Yes."

" Oh, it's too ridiculous, that his death had something to do with our last sitting. Supposing, as you say, he had a hypnotic power of any kind. Could—could its exercise cause injury to his health ? "

But the doctor ignored the question in his quiet, and yet very complete and self-possessed, manner.

" Marr and Cresswell never met," he said. " It is folly to connect them together. It is, as you said," and he laughed, " rotten of you. Go away to-morrow."

" I will, you autocratic doctor. What fee do I owe you ? "

" Your friendship, my boy."

Dr. Levillier sat lower in his chair and they smoked in silence, both of them revelling in the warm peace and the ease of this night hour. Since he had come into the Harley Street house Julian had been much happier. His perturbation had gradually evaporated until now scarcely a vestige of it remained. The little doctor's talk, above all the sight of his calm, thoughtful face and the aspect of his calm, satisfied room, gave the *coup de grâce* to the uneasiness of a spurious and ill-omened excitement. When the power of wide medical knowledge is joined to the power of goodness and of umbrageous intellectuality a doctor is, among all men, the man to lay the ghosts that human nature is perpetually at the pains to set walking in their shrouds to cause alarm. All Julian's ghosts were laid. He smoked on and grew to feel perfectly natural and comfortable. The dogs echoed and emphasised all the healing power of their small and elderly master. As they lay sleeping, a tangle of large limbs and supine strength, the fire shone over them till their fawn-coloured coats gleamed almost like satin touched with gold. The delightful sanctity of unmeasured confidence, unmeasured satisfaction, sang in their gentle and large-hearted snores, which rose and fell with the regularity of waves on the sea. Now and then one of them slowly stretched a leg or expanded the toes of a foot, as if intent on presenting a larger surface of sensation to the embrace of comfort and of affection. And they, so it seemed to Julian, kept the pleasant silence now come into existence between him and the doctor alive. That silence rested him immensely. In it the two cigars diminished steadily, steadily as the length of a man's life, but glowing to the very end. And the grey ashes dropped away of their own accord, and Julian's mind shed its grey ashes too and glowed serenely. The dogs expanded their warm bodies on the hearth, and his nature expanded in a vague, wide-stretching generosity of mute evening emotion.

" How comfortable this is, Doctor," he murmured at last.

" Yes. It's a good hour," the doctor replied, letting the words go slowly from his lips. " I wish I could give to all the poor creatures in this city just one good hour."

They smoked their cigars out.

" I ought to go," Julian said lazily.

" No. Have one more. I know it is dangerous to prolong a pleasure. It loses its savour. But I think, Addison, to-night you and I can get no harm from the experiment."

He handed Julian the cigar box.

" We won't stir up the dogs for another half-hour," he added, looking at their happiness with a shining satisfaction. " Here are the matches. Light up."

Julian obeyed, and they began the delightful era of the second cigar, and sank a little deeper down, surely, into serenity and peace. Occasional coals dropping into the fender with a hot tick, tick, chirruped a lullaby to the four happy companions. And the men learnt a fine silence from the fine silence of the dogs.

Half-way through the second cigar Rupert shifted under his master's patent leather boots and raised his huge head. His eyes blinked out of their sleep, then ceased to blink and became attentive. Then his ears, which had been lying down on each side of his head in the suavest attitude which such features of a dog can assume, lifted themselves up and pointed grimly forward as he listened to something. His flaccid legs contracted under him, and the muscles of his back quivered. Mab, less readily alert, quickly caught the infection of his attention, rolled over out of her sideways position and couched beside him. The movement of the dogs was not congenial to the doctor. Rupert's curious back, alert under his feet, communicated an immediate sense of disquiet to the very centre of his being. He said to Julian :

" The acuteness of animal senses has its drawbacks. These dogs must have heard some sound in the street that is entirely inaudible to us. Well, Rupert, what is it? Lie down again and go to sleep."

Stooping forward he put his hand on the dog's neck, and gave him a push, expecting him to yield readily, and tumble over on to the warm rug to sleep once more. But Rupert resisted his hand, and instead, got up, and stood at attention. Mab immediately followed his example.

" What are they after, Doctor ? " said Julian.

As he spoke a bell rang in the house.

" Nemesis for prolonging the pleasure," Levillier said. " A summons to a patient, no doubt."

As if in reply to the twitter of the bell, Rupert sprang forward and barked. He remained beside the door waiting, while Mab barked too, nearer the fire. The bell sounded again, and the footstep of Lawler, who always sat up as late as his master, was heard on the stairs from the servants' part of the house. It passed them on its errand to the front door, but during its passage the excitement of the two dogs rapidly increased. They began to bark furiously, and to bristle.

" I never saw them like this before," the doctor said, not without anxiety.

As he spoke Lawler opened the hall door. They heard the latch go and the faint voice of somebody in colloquy with him. For the dogs were now abruptly silent, but displayed the most curious savage intentness, showing their teeth, and standing each by the door as if sentinels on guard. The colloquy ceasing, steps again sounded in the hall, but more than Lawler's. Evidently the man was returning towards the room accompanied by somebody from the street. The doctor was keenly observing the mastiffs, and just as Lawler's hand struck upon the handle of the door to turn it, he suddenly called out sharply :

" Lawler, you are not to open the door ! "

And as he called the doctor ran forward between the two dogs and caught their collars in his two hands. They tugged and leaped to get away, but he held on. The surprised voice of the obedient Lawler was heard on the hither side of the door, saying :

" I beg your pardon, sir."

The doctor said hastily to Julian :

" These dogs will tear the person who has just come into the house to pieces if we don't take care. Catch on to Mab, Addison."

Julian obeyed, and the dog was like live iron with determination under his grasp.

" Some one is with you, Lawler," the doctor said. " Does he wish to see me ? "

" If you please, sir, it is Mr. Cresswell, Mr. Valentine come back for Mr. Addison."

Julian felt himself go suddenly pale.

CHAPTER VI

THE STRENGTH OF THE SPRING

RATHER reluctantly Julian acted on the advice of Dr. Levillier and went out of town for a week on the following day. He took his way to the sea, and tried to feel normal in a sailing boat with a gnarled and corrugated old salt for his only companion. But his success was only partial, for while his body gave itself to the whisper of the ungoverned breezes, while his hands held the ropes, and his eyes watched the subtle proceedings of the weather, and his ears listened to the serial stories of the waves, and to the conversational peregrinations of his Ancient Mariner about the China Seas in bygone days, his mind was still in London, still busily concerned itself with the very things that should now undergo a sea change and vanish in ozone. Recent events oppressed him, to the occasional undoing of the old salt, well accustomed to the seasick reverence of his despairing clients on board the *Star of the Sea.* When the mind of a man has once fallen into the habit of prancing in a circle like a circus horse, it is difficult to drive it back into the public streets, to make it trot serenely forward in its ordinary ways. And Julian had with him a ring-master in the person of the ignorant Rip. Whenever his eyes fell on Rip, curled uneasily in the bottom of the swinging boat, he went at a tangent back to Harley Street, and the strange finale of his evening with the doctor.

It had been a curious tableau divided by a door. Levillier and he stood on one side tugging mightily at the intent mastiffs, which strained at their collars, dropping beads of foam from their grinning jaws, savages, instead of calm companions. On the other side, in the hall, Lawler and Valentine paused in amazement and a colloquy shot to and fro through the wooden barrier. On hearing the name of Valentine mentioned by the butler the doctor had cast an instant glance of unbounded amazement upon Julian. And Julian had returned it, feeling in his heart the dawning of an inexplicable trouble.

"Is anything the matter?" Valentine's voice had asked.

" No," said the doctor in reply. " But please go into the dining-room. We will come to you there. And Lawler——"

" Yes, sir."

" When you have shown Mr. Cresswell to the dining-room be careful to shut the door, and to keep it shut till I come."

" Yes, sir."

The butler's well-trained voice had vibrated with surprise and Julian had found himself mechanically smiling as he noted this. Th n the footsteps of servant and visitor had retreated. Presently a door was heard to shut. Lawler returned, and was passing discreetly by, to wonder if his master had gone mad in his pantry, when the doctor again called to him.

" Go downstairs, Lawler, and in a moment I shall bring the dogs to you."

" Yes, sir."

The butler's voice was now almost shrill with scarcely governable astonishment, and his footstep seemed to tremble uneasily upon the stairs as he retired. Then the doctor went to a corner of the room and took down from a hook a whip with a heavy thong.

" I haven't had to use this since they were both puppies," he said, with a side-glance at the dogs. " Now, Addison, keep hold of Mab and go in front of me down the servants' stairs. If the dogs once get out of hand we shall have trouble in the house to-night."

The door was opened, and then a veritable affray began. The animals seemed half mad. They tore at their collars, and struggled furiously to break loose, snarling and even snapping, their great heads turned in the direction of the dining-room. The doctor, firmest as well as kindest of men, recognised necessity, and used the whip unsparingly, lashing the animals through the door to the servants' quarters, and down the stairs. It was a violent procession to the lower regions. Julian could not get it out of his head. Entangled among the leaping dogs on the narrow stairway, he had a sense of whirling in the eddies of a stream, driven from this side to the other. His arms were nearly pulled out of their sockets. The shriek of the lash curling over and around the dogs, the dim vision of the doctor's compressed lips and eyes full of unaccustomed fire, the damp foam on his hands as he rocked from one wall to the other, amid a dull music of growls and fierce, low barks, came back to him now as he trimmed the sails to catch the undecided winds, or felt the tiller leap under his hold. Each moment he had expected to be bitten, but somehow they all tumbled together unhurt into Lawler's pantry, where they found that factotum standing grim and wire-strung with anticipation. Beyond the pantry were the dogs' night quarters, and they were quickly driven into them and shut up. But

H

they still bounded and beat against the door, and presently began to howl a vain chorale.

"Lord, Lord, sir, what's come to them?" Lawler exclaimed.

His fat face had become as white as a sheet, and the doctor was scarcely less pale as he leaned against the dresser, whip in hand, drawing panting breaths.

"I can't tell. They will be all right in a minute."

He pulled himself up.

"Go to bed now if you like, Lawler," he said, rather abruptly "Come, Addison."

They regained the hall, and made their way to Valentine. He was sitting by the dining-table in a watchful attitude, and sprang hastily up as they came in.

"My dear Doctor," he said, "what a pandemonium! I nearly came to your assistance."

"It's very lucky you didn't, Cresswell," the doctor answered, almost grimly.

"Why?"

"Because if you had you might chance to be a dead man by this time."

Out on the sea, under the streaming clouds that fled before the wind, Julian recalled the strange terseness of that reply, and the perhaps stranger silence that followed it. For Valentine had made no comment, had asked for no explanation. He had simply dropped the subject, and the three men had remained together for a few minutes, constrained and ill at ease. Then the doctor had said:

"Let us go back now to my room."

Valentine and he assented, and got upon their feet to follow him, but when he opened the door there came up from the servants' quarters the half-strangled howling of the mastiffs. Involuntarily Dr. Levillier paused to listen, his hand behind his ear. Then he turned to the young men, and held out his right hand.

"Good-night," he said. "I must go down to them, or there will be a summons applied for against me in the morning by one of my neighbours."

And they had let themselves out while he retreated once more down the stairs.

The drive home had been a silent one. Only when Julian was bidding Valentine good-night had he found a tongue to say to his friend:

"The devil's in all this, Valentine."

And Valentine had merely nodded with a smile and driven off.

Now, in the sea solitude that was to be a medicine to his soul, Julian went round and round in his mental circus, treading ever the same sawdust under foot, hearing ever the same whip crack to send him forward. His isolation bent him upon himself, and the old salt's hoarse murmurings of the " Chiney" seas in no way drew him to a healthier outlook. Why Valentine returned for him that night he did not know. That might have been merely the prompting of a vagrant impulse. Julian cursed that impulse on account of the circumstances to which it directly led ; for there was a peculiar strain of enmity in them which had affected, and continued to affect him most disagreeably. To behold the instinctive hostility of another towards a person whom one loves is offensively grotesque to the observer, and at moments Julian hated the doctor's mastiffs, and even hated the unconscious Rip, who lay, in a certain shivering dis-comfort and apprehension, seeking sleep with the determination of sorrow. There are things, feelings and desires, which should surely be kicked out of men and dogs. Such a thing, beyond doubt, was a savage hatred of Valentine. What prompted it, and whence it came, were merely mysteries, which the dumbness of dogs must for ever sustain. But what specially plunged Julian into concern was the latent fear that Dr. Levillier might echo the repulsion of his dogs and come to look upon Valentine with different eyes. Julian's fine jealousy for his friend sharpened his faculties of observation and of deduction, and he had observed the little doctor's dry reception of Valentine after the struggle on the stairs ; and his eager dismissal of them both to the street door on the howling excuse that rose up from the basement. Such a mood might probably be transient, and only engendered by the fatigue of excitement, or even by the physical exhaustion attendant upon the preservation of Valentine from the rage of Rupert and Mab. Julian told himself that to dwell upon it, or to conceive of it as permanent, was neither sensible nor acute, considering his intimate knowledge of the doctor's nature, and of his firm friendship for Valentine. That he did continue most persistently to dwell upon it, and with a keen suspicion, must be due to the present desolation of his circumstances, and to the vain babble of the blue-coated Methuselah, whose intellect roamed incessantly through a marine past, peopled with love episodes of a somewhat Rabelaisian character.

At the end of five days Julian abruptly threw up the sponge and returned to London, abandoning the old salt to the tobacco-chewing, which was his only solace during the winter season, now fast drawing to a close. He went at once to see Valentine, who had a narrative to tell him concerning Marr.

"You have probably read all about Marr in the papers ? " he asked, when he met Julian.

The question came at once with his hand-grasp.

" No," Julian said. " I shunted the papers, tried to give myself up entirely to the sea, as the doctor advised. What has there been ? "

" Oh, a good deal   I may as well tell it to you, or no doubt Lady Crichton will.   People exaggerate so much."

" Why—what is there to exaggerate about ? "

"The inquest was held," Valentine answered.   " And every effort was made to find the woman who came with Marr to the hotel, and evaporated so mysteriously, but there was no one to identify her. The Frenchman had not noticed her features, and the housemaid, as you remember, was a fool, and could only say she was a common-looking person."

" Well," Julian said rather eagerly, " but what was the cause of death ? "

"That was entirely obscure.   The body seemed healthy—at least the various organs were sound.   There was no obvious reason for death, and the verdict was simply, ' Died from failure of the heart's action.'"

" Vague but comprehensive."

" Yes, I suppose we shall all die strictly from the same cause."

" And that is all ? "

" Not quite.   It appears that a description of the dead man got into the papers, and that he was identified by his wife, who read the account in some remote part of the country, took the train to town, and found that Marr was, as she suspected, the man whom she had married, from whom she had separated, and whose real name was Wilson, the Wilson of a notorious newspaper case.   Do you re- member it ? "

" What, an action against a husband for gross cruelty, for in- credible, unspeakable inhumanity—some time ago ? "

" Yes.   The wife got a judicial separation."

" And that is the history of Marr ? "

" That is, such of his history as is known," Valentine said in his calm voice.

While he had been speaking his blue eyes had always been fixed on Julian's face.   When Julian looked up they were withdrawn.

" I always had a feeling that Marr was secretly a wretch, a devil," Julian said now.   " It seems I was right.   What has become of the wife ? "

" I suppose she has gone back to her country home.   Probably she is happy.   Her first mate chastised her with whips.   To fulfil her destiny as a woman she ought now to seek another who is fond of scorpions."

" Women are strange," Julian said, voluptuously generalising after the manner of young men.

Valentine leaned forward as if the sentence stirred some depth in his mind, and roused him to a certain excitement.

" Julian," he exclaimed, " are you and I wasting our lives, do you think? Since you have been away I have thought again over our conversation before we had our first sitting. Do you remember it?"

" Yes, Valentine."

" You said then I had held you back from so much."

" Yes."

" And I have been asking myself whether I have not, perhaps, held you back, held myself back, from all that is worth having in life."

Julian looked troubled.

" From all that is not worth having, old boy," he said.

But he looked troubled. When Valentine spoke like this he felt as a man who stands at a garden gate and gazes out into the world, and is stirred with a thrill of anticipation and of desire to leap out from the green and shadowy close, where trees are and flowers, into the dust and heat where passion hides as in a nest, and unspoken things lie warm. Julian was vaguely afraid of himself. It is dangerous to lean on any one, however strong. Having met Valentine on the threshold of life, Julian had never learnt to walk alone. He trusted another instead of trusting himself. He had never forged his own sword. When Siegfried sang at his anvil he sang a song of all the greatness of life. Julian was notably strong as to his muscles. He had arms of iron and the blood raced in his veins, but he had never forged his sword. Mistrust of himself was as a phantom that walked with him unless Valentine drove it away.

" I thought you had got over that absurd feeling, Val," he said. " I thought you were content with your soul."

" I think I have ceased to be content," said Valentine. " Perhaps I have stolen a fragment of your nature, Julian, in those dark nights in the tent-room. Since you have been away I have wondered. An extraordinary sensation of bodily strength, of enormous vigour has come to me. And I want to test the sensation, to see if it is founded upon fact."

He was sitting in a low chair, and as he spoke he slowly stretched his limbs. It was as if all his body yawned, waking from sleep.

" But how?" Julian asked.

Already he looked rather interested than troubled. At Valentine's words he too became violently conscious of his own strength, and stirred by the wonder of youth dwelling in him.

" How? That is what I wish to find out by going into the world with different eyes. I have been living in the arts, Julian. But is that living at all?"

Julian got up and stood by the fire. Valentine excited him. He leaned one arm on the mantelpiece. His right hand kept closing and unclosing as he talked.

" Such a life is natural to you," he said, " And you have made me love it."

"I sometimes wonder," responded Valentine, "whether I have not trained my head to slay my heart. Men of intellect are often strangely inhuman. Besides, what you call my purity and my refinement are due perhaps to my cowardice. I am called the Saint of Victoria Street because I live in a sort of London cloister with you for my companion, and in the cloister I read or I give myself up to music, and I hang my walls with pictures, and I wonder at the sins of men, and I believe I am that deadly thing, a Pharisee."

"But you are perfectly tolerant."

"Am I? I often find myself sneering at the follies of others, at what I call their coarsenesses, their wallowing in the mire."

"It is wallowing."

"And which is most human, the man who drives in a carriage, or the man who walks sturdily along the road, and gets the mud on his boots, and lets the rain fall on him and the wind be his friend? I suspect it is a fine thing to be out unsheltered in a storm, Julian."

Julian's dark eyes were glowing. Valentine spoke with an unusual, almost with an electric warmth, and Julian was conscious of drawing very near to him to-night. Always in their friendship, hitherto, he had thought of Valentine as of one apart, walking at a distance from all men, even from him. And he had believed most honestly, that this very detachment had drawn him to Valentine more than to any other human being. But to-night he began suddenly to feel that to be actually side by side with his friend would be a very glorious thing. He could never hope to walk perpetually upon the vestal heights. If Valentine did really come down towards the valley, what then? Just at first the idea had shocked him. Now he began almost to wish that it might be so, to feel that he was shaking hands with Valentine more brotherly than ever before.

"Extremes are wrong, desolate, abominable, I begin to think," Valentine went on. "Angel and devil, both should be scourged—the one to be purged of excessive good, the other of excessive evil, and between them, midway, is man, natural man. Julian, you are natural man, and you are more right than I, who, it seems, have been educating you by presenting to you for contemplation my own disease."

"Well, but is natural man worth much? That is the question! I don't know."

"He fights, and drinks, and loves, and, oftener than the renowned philosopher thinks, he knows how to die. And then he lives thoroughly, and that is probably what we were sent into the world to do."

"Can't we live thoroughly without, say, the fighting and the drinking, Val?"

Valentine got up, too, as if excited, and stood by the fire by Julian's side.

"Battle calls forth heroism," he said, "which else would sleep."

"And drinking?"

"Leads to good fellowship."

This last remark was so preposterously unlike Valentine that Julian could not for a moment accept it as uttered seriously. His mood changed, and he burst out suddenly into a laugh.

"You have been taking me in all the time," he exclaimed, "and I actually was fool enough to think you serious."

"And to agree with what I was saying?"

Valentine still spoke quite gravely and earnestly, and Julian began to be puzzled.

"You know I can never help agreeing with you when you really mean anything," he began. "I have proved so often that you are always right in the end. So your real theory of life must be the true one, but your real theory, I know, is to reject what most people ruu after."

"No longer that, I fancy, Julian."

"But then, what has changed you?"

Valentine met his eyes calmly.

"I don't know," he said. "Do you?"

"I? How should I?"

"Perhaps this change has been growing within me for a long while. It is difficult to say, but to-night my nature culminates. I am at a point, Julian."

"Then you have climbed to it. Don't you want to stay there?"

"No mere man can face the weather on a mountain peak for ever, and life lies rather in the plains."

Valentine went over to the window and touched the blind. It shot up, leaving the naked window, through which the gas-lamps of Victoria Street stared in the night.

"I wish," he said, "that we, in England, had the flat roofs of the East."

He thrust up the glass, and the night air pushed in.

"Come here, Julian," he said.

Julian obeyed, wondering rather. Valentine leaned a little out on the sill and made Julian lean beside him. It was early in the night and the hum of London was yet loud, for the bees did not sleep but were still busy in their monstrous hive. There was already a gentleness of Spring among the discoloured houses. Spring will not be denied even among men who dwell in flats. The cabs hurried past, and pedestrians went by in twos and threes or solitary, soldiers walking vaguely seeking cheap pleasures, or more gaily with adoring maidens, tired business men journeying towards Victoria Station, a desolate shop-girl, in dreary virtue defiant of mankind, but still unblessed, the Noah's ark figure of a policeman, tramping emptily, standing wearily by turns, to keep public order. Lights starred here and there the long line of mansions opposite.

"I often look out here at night," Valentine said, "generally to wonder why people live as they do. When I see the soldiers going by, for instance, I have often marvelled that they could find any pleasure in the servants, so often ugly, who hang on their arms, and languish persistently at them under cheap hats and dyed feathers. And I gaze at the policeman on his beat and pity him for the dead routine in which he stalks, seldom varied by the sordid capture of a starving cracksman, or the triumphant seizure of an unmuzzled dog. The boys selling evening papers seem to me imps of desolation, screaming through life aimlessly for halfpence, and the cabmen creatures driving for ever to stations, yet never able to get into the wide world. And yet they are all living, Julian; that is the thing, all having their experiences, all in strong touch with humanity. The newspaper boy has got his flower girl to give him grimy kisses, and the cabman is proud of the shine on his harness, and the soldier glories in his military faculty of seduction, and in his quick capacity for getting drunk in the glittering gin-palace at the corner of the street, and the policeman hopes to take some one up, and to be praised by a magistrate, and in those houses opposite intrigues are going on, and jealousy is being born, and men and women are quarrelling over trifles and making it up again, and children—what matter if legitimate or illegitimate?—are cooing and crying, and boys are waking to the turmoil of manhood, and girls are dreaming of the things they dare not pretend to know. Why should I be like a bird hovering over it all? Why should not I—and you—be in it? If I can only cease to be as I have always been, I can recreate London for myself, and make it a live city, fearing neither its vices nor its tears. I have made you fear them, Julian. I have done you an injury. Let us be quiet, and feel the rustle of Spring over the gas-lamps, and hear the pulsing of the hearts around us."

He put his arm through Julian's as they leaned out on the sill of the window, and to Julian his arm was like a line of living fire, compelling that which touched it to a speechless fever of excitement. Was this man Valentine? Julian's pulses throbbed and hammered as he looked upon the street, and he seemed to see all the passers by with eyes from which scales had fallen. If to die should be nothing to the wise man, to live should be much. Underneath two drunken men passed, embracing each other by the shoulders. They sang in snatches and hiccoughed protestations of eternal friendship. Valentine watched their wavering course with no disgust. His blue eyes even seemed to praise them as they went.

"Those men are more human than I," he slowly said. "Why should I condemn them?"

And, as if under the influence of a spell, Julian found himself thinking of the wandering ruffians as fine fellows, full of warmth of heart and generous feeling. A boy and girl went by. Neither could have been more than sixteen years old. They paused by a lamp-post, and the girl openly kissed the boy. He sturdily endured the compliment, staring firmly at her pale cheeks and tired eyes. Then the girl walked away, and he stood alone till she was out of sight. Eventually he walked off slowly, singing a plantation song: "I want you, my honey, yes I do!" Valentine and Julian had watched and listened, and now Valentine, moving round on the window-ledge till he faced Julian, said:

"That is it, Julian, put in the straightforward music-hall way. People are happy because they want things, yes, they do. It is a philosophy of life. That boy has a life because he wants that girl, and she wants him. And you, Julian, you want a thousand things——"

"Not since I have known you," Julian said.

He felt curiously excited and troubled. His arm was still linked in Valentine's. Slowly he withdrew it. Valentine shut down the window and they came back to the fire.

"You know," Valentine said, "that it is possible for two influences to work one upon the other, and for each to convert the other. I begin to think that your nature has triumphed over mine."

"What?" Julian said, in frank amazement. The Philistines could not have been more astounded when Samson pulled down the pillars.

"I have taught you, as you say, to die to the ordinary man's life, Julian. But what if you have taught me to live to it?"

Julian did not answer for a moment. He was wondering whether Valentine could possibly be serious. But his face was serious, even eager. There was an unwonted stain of red on his smooth, usually pale cheeks. A certain wild boyishness had stolen over him, a reckless devil danced in his blue eyes. Julian caught the infection of his mood.

"And what's my lesson?" Julian said.

His voice sounded thick and harsh. There was a surge of blood through his brain and a prickly heat behind his eyeballs. Suddenly a notion took him that Valentine had never been so magnificent, as now, now when a new fierceness glittered in his expression, and a wild wave of humanity ran through him like a surging tide.

"What's my lesson, Valentine?"

"I will show you this Spring. But it is the lesson the Spring teaches, the lesson of fulfilling your nature, of waking from your slumbers, of finding the air, of giving yourself to the rifling fingers of the sun, of yielding all your scent to others, and of taking all their scent to you. That's the lesson of your strength, Julian, and of all the strength of the Spring. Lie out in the showers, and let the clouds cover you with shadows, and listen to the song of every bird, and—and—Ah!" he suddenly broke off in a burst of laughter, "I am rhapsodising. The Spring has got into my veins even among these chimney-pots of London. The spring is in me, and, who knows? your soul, Julian. For don't you feel wild blood in your veins, sometimes?"

"Yes, yes."

"And humming passions that come to you and lift you from your feet?"

"You know I do."

"But I never knew before that they might lift you towards heaven. That's the thing. I have thought that the exercise of the passions dragged a man down, but why should it be so? I have talked of men wallowing in the mire. I must find out whether I have been lying when I said that. Julian, this Spring you and I will see the world at any rate with open eyes. We will watch the budding and blossoming of the souls around us, the flowers in the garden of life. We will not be indifferent or afraid. I have been a coward in my ice prison of refinement. I keep a perpetual season of winter round me. I know it. I know it to-night."

Julian did not speak. He was carried away by this outburst, which gained so much, and so strange, force by its issue from the lips and from the heart of Valentine. But he was carried away as a weak swimmer by a resistless torrent, and instinctively he seemed to be aware of danger and to be stretching out his arms for some rock or tree branch to stay his present course. Perhaps Valentine noticed this, for his excitement suddenly faded, and his face resumed its usual expression of almost cold purity and refinement.

"I generally translate this sort of thing into music," he said.

At the last word Julian looked up instinctively to the wall on which the picture of "The Merciful Knight" usually hung. For Valentine's music was inseparably connected in his mind with that picture. His eyes fell on a gap.

"Val," he exclaimed, in astonishment, "what's become of—?"

"Oh, 'The Merciful Knight'? It has gone to be cleaned."

"Why? It was all right, surely?"

"No. I found it wanted cleaning badly and I am having it reframed. It will be away for some time."

"You must miss it."

"Yes, very much."

The words were spoken with cutting indifference.

CHAPTER VII.

JULIAN VISITS THE LADY OF THE FEATHERS

FROM that night, and almost imperceptibly, the relations existing between Valentine and Julian slightly changed. It seemed to Julian as if a door previously shut in his friend's soul opened and as if he entered into this hitherto secret chamber. He found there an apparent strange humanity which, as he grew accustomed to it, warmed him. The curious refined saintliness of Valentine, almost chilly in its elevation, thawed gently as the days went by, but so gently that Julian scarcely knew it, could scarcely define the difference which nevertheless led him to alter his conduct almost unconsciously. One great sameness, perhaps, gave him a sensation of safety and of continuity. Valentine's face still kept its almost unearthly expression of intellectuality and of purity. When Julian looked at him no passions flamed in his blue eyes, no lust ever crawled in the lines about his mouth. His smooth cheeks never flushed with beaconing desire, nor was his white forehead pencilled with the shadowy writing that is a pale warning to the libertine. And yet his speech about the Spring that night as they leaned out over Victoria Street had evidently not been a mere reckless rhapsody. It had held a meaning and was remembered. In Valentine there seemed to be flowering a number of faint-hued wants, such wants as had never flowered from his nature before. The fig-tree that had seemed so exquisitely barren began to put forth leaves, and, when the warm showers sang to it, it sang in tremulous reply.

And the Spring grew in London.

Never before had Julian been so conscious of the growth of the year as now. The Spring stirred inside him, as if he were indeed the Mother Earth. Tumults of nature shook him. With the bursting of the crocus, the pointing of its spear of gold to the sun, a life gathered itself together within him, a life that held, too, a golden shaft within its colour-stained cup. And the bland scent of the innumerable troops of hyacinths in Hyde Park was a language to him as he strolled in the sun towards the Row. Scents speak to the young of the future as they speak to the old of the past, to the one with an indefinite excitement, to the other with a vague regret. And especially when he was in the company of Valentine did Julian become intensely alive to the march of the earth towards summer, and feel that he was in step with it, dragooned by the same music. He began to learn, so he believed, what Valentine had called the lesson of his strength and of all the strength of the Spring. His wild blood leaped in his veins, and the world was walking with him to a large prospect, as yet fancifully tricked out in mists and crowned with clouds.

The Spring brought to Valentine an abounding health such as he had never known before, a physical glory which, without actually changing him, gave to him a certain novelty of aspect which Julian felt without actually seeing. One day, when they were out riding together in the Park, he said :

" How extraordinarily strong you look to-day, Val."

Valentine spurred his horse into a short gallop.

" I feel robust," he said. " I think it is my mind working on my body. I have attained to a more healthy outlook on things, to a saner conception of life. For years you have been learning from me, Julian. Now I think the positions are reversed. I am learning from you."

Julian pressed his knees against his horse's sides with an iron grip, feeling the spirited animal's spirited life between them. They were now on a level with the Serpentine and riding parallel to it. A few vigorous and determined bathers swam gaily in the pale warmth of the morning sun. Two boys raced along the grassy bank to dry themselves, whooping with exultation, and leaping as they ran. A man in a broad boat, ready to save life, exchanged loud jokes with the swimmers. On a seat two filthy loafers watched the scene with vacant eyes. They had slept in the Park all night, and their ragged clothes were drenched with dew.

" I could race with those boys," Valentine said. " But not so long ago I was like the men on the bench. I only cared to look on at the bathing of others. Now I could swim myself."

He sent his horse along at a tremendous pace for a moment, then drew him in, and turned towards Julian.

" We are learning the lesson of the Spring," he said.

As he spoke a light from some hidden place shot for an instant into his eyes and faded again. Julian laughed gaily. The ride spurred his spirits. He was conscious of the recklessness created in a man by exercise.

" I could believe that you were actually growing, Val," he said, " growing before my eyes. Only you're much too old."

" Yes, I am too old for that," Valentine said.

A sudden weariness ran in the words, a sudden sound of age,

"The truth is," he added, but with more life, "my nature is expanding inside my body, and you feel it and fancy you can see the envelope echo the words of the letter it holds. You are clever enough to be fanciful. Gently, Raindrop, gently!"

He quieted the mare as they turned into the road. Just as they were passing under the arch into the open space at Hyde Park corner a woman shot across in front of them. They nearly rode over her, and she uttered a little yell as she awkwardly gained the pavement. Her head was crowned with a perfect pyramid of ostrich feathers, and as she turned to bestow upon the riders the contemptuous glance of a cockney pedestrian, who demands possession of all London as a sacred right, Julian suddenly pulled up his horse.

"Hulloh!" he said to the woman.

"What is it?" asked Valentine, who was in front.

"Wait a second, Val. I want a word with this lady."

"Rather compromising," Valentine said laughing, as his eyes took in with a swift glance the woman's situation in the economy of the town.

The woman now slowly advanced to the railing, apparently flattered at being thus hailed from horseback. Her kinsmen doubtless always walked.

"Don't you remember me?" Julian said.

She was in fact the lady of the feathers, with whom he had foregathered at the coffee-stall in Piccadilly. The lady leaned her plush arms upon the rail and surveyed him with her tinted eyes.

"Can't say as I do, my dear," she remarked. "What name?"

"Never mind that. But tell me have you ever had a cup of coffee and a bun in Piccadilly early in the morning?"

The mention of the bun struck home to the lady, swept the quivering chords of her memory into a tune. She pushed her face nearer to Julian, and stared at him hard.

"So it is," she said. "So it is."

For a moment she seemed inclined to retreat. Then she stood her ground. Her nerves, perhaps, had grown stronger.

"I should like to know you," Julian said.

The lady was obviously gratified. She tossed her head and giggled.

"Where do you live?" Julian continued.

The lady dived into the back part of her skirt, and, after a long and passionate pursuit, ran a small purse to earth. Opening it with deliberation she extracted a good-sized card, and handed it up to Julian.

"There you are, dearie," she said.

On the card was printed "Cuckoo Bright, 400 Marylebone Road."

"I will come at five this afternoon and take you out to tea," said Julian.

" Right you are, Bertie," the lady cried, in a voice thrilling with pride and exultation.

Julian rode off, and she watched him go, preening herself against the rail, like some gaudy bird. She looked up at a policeman and laughed knowingly.

" Well, copper," she said, " How's that, eh ? "

The policeman was equal to the occasion.

" Not out," he answered, with a stiff and semi-official smile. " Move along."

And Cuckoo Bright moved, as one who walked on air.

Julian had joined Valentine, who had observed the colloquy from afar, controlling with some difficulty the impatience of his mare, excited by her gallop.

" You know that lady ? " he asked, still laughing, with perhaps a touch of contempt.

" Very platonically. We met at a coffee-stall in Piccadilly as I was going home after your trance. She was with me when I saw that strange flame."

" When you imagined you saw it."

" If you prefer it, Val. I am going to see her this afternoon."

" My dear fellow—why ? "

" I'll tell you," Julian answered gravely. " I believe she is the woman who went to the ' European ' with Marr, who must have been with Marr when he was taken ill, and who fled. I have a reason for thinking so."

" What is it ? "

" I'll tell you later, when I have talked to her."

" Surely you don't suspect the poor creature of foul play ? "

" Not I. It's sheer curiosity that takes me to her."

" Oh."

They rode on a step or two. Then Valentine said :

" Are you going to take her out ? She's—well she is a trifle un- mistakable, Julian."

" Yes, I know. You are right. She is not for afternoon wear, poor soul. What damned scoundrels men are."

Valentine did not join in the sentiment thus forcibly expressed.

Between four and five that afternoon Julian hailed a cab and drove to Marylebone Road. The houses in it seemed endless, and drearily alike, but at length the cab drew up at number 400, tall, gaunt and haggard like the rest. Julian rang the bell, and immedi- ately a shrill dog barked with a piping fury within the house. Then the door was opened by an old woman, whose arid face was cabalistic, and who looked as if she spent her existence in expecting a raid from the police.

" Is Miss Cuckoo Bright at home ? "

" Miss Bright! I'll see."

The old dame turned tail, and slithered, flat-footed, to a room opening from the dirty passage. She vanished and Julian heard two voices muttering. The old gentlewoman returned.

" This way, sir ! " she said, in a voice that perpetually struggled to get the whip hand of an obvious bronchitis.

A moment more and Julian stood in the acute presence of the lady of the feathers. At first he scarcely recognised her, for she had discarded her crown of glory, and now faced him in the strange frivolity of her hatless touzled hair. She stood by the square table, covered with a green cloth, that occupied the centre of the small room, which communicated by folding doors with an inner chamber. A pastile was burning drowsily in a corner, and the shrill dog piped seditiously from its station on a black horsehair-covered sofa, over which a wool-work rug was thrown in easy *abandon*. Julian extended his hand.

" How d'you do ? " he said.

" Pretty bobbish, my dear," was the reply, but the voice was much less pert than he remembered it, and, looking at his hostess, Julian perceived that she was considerably younger than he had imagined, and that she was actually, amazing luxury !—a little shy. She had a box of safety-matches in her hand, and she now struck one, and applied it to a gas-burner. The day was dark.

" Pleased to see you," she added, with an attempt at a hearty and untutored air. " Jessie, shut up ! "

Jessie, the dog, of the toy species, and arched into the shape of a note of interrogation, obeyed, lay down and trembled into sleep. The gas light revealed the details of the sordid room, a satin box of sweetmeats on the table, a penny bunch of sweet violets in a specimen glass, one or two yellow backed novels, and a few photographs ranged upon the imitation marble mantelpiece. There was one armchair, whose torn lining indecently revealed the interior stuffing and there were three other chairs with wooden backs. The lady of the feathers did not dwell in marble halls, unless, perhaps imaginatively.

" You've got cosy quarters," Julian said, amiably lying.

" Yes, they're not bad, but they do cost money. Sit down, won't you ? "

The lady shoved the one armchair forward, and, after a polite skirmish, Julian was forced to take it. He sat down, disguising from his companion his sudden knowledge that the springs were broken. She, on her part, laid hold of Jessie, dumped the little creature into her lap, and assumed an air of abrupt gentility, pursing her painted lips, and shooting sidelong glances of inquiry at the furniture. Julian could not at once explain his errand. He felt

that caution was imperative. Besides, the lady doubtless expected
to be entertained at Verrey's or possibly even at Charbonnel's.
But Julian had resolved to throw himself upon the lady's hospi-
tality.

"It's an awful day," he said.

The lady assented, adding that she had not been out.

"We are very cosy here," Julian continued, gazing at the small
fire that was sputtering in the grate.

The lady looked gratified. She felt that the meagre abode which
she must name home had received the hall mark of a "toff's"
approval.

"Now I am going to ask you something," Julian said. "Will
you let me have tea with you to-day, and—and—come out with me
some evening, to the Empire or somewhere, instead?"

The lady nodded her fringed head.

"Certainly, my dear," she responded. "Proud to give you tea
I'm sure."

Suddenly she bounced up, scattering Jessie over the floor. She
promenaded to the door, opened it and yelled:

"Mrs. Brigg! Mrs. Brigg!"

The expostulating feet of the old person ascended wearily from
the lower depths of the house.

"Lord! Lord! Whatever is it now?" she wheezed,

"Please bring up tea for me and this gentleman."

The lady assumed the voice of a sucking dove.

"Tea! Why, I thought you'd be out to——"

The lady shot into the passage and shut the door behind her.
After a moment she put her head in and said to Julian:

"I'll be back in a minute. She's in a rare tantrum. I must go
down and help her. Pardon!"

And she vanished like a flash.

Julian sat feeling rather guilty. To distract himself he got up
and looked at the photographs on the mantelpiece. Most of them
were of men, but there were two or three girls in tights, and there
was one of a stout and venerable woman, evidently respectable,
seated in an armchair, with staring bead-like eyes, but a sweet and
gentle mouth. Her hair was arranged in glossy bands. Her hands
held a large book, probably a Bible. Julian looked at her and
wondered a little how she chanced to be in this *galère*. Then he
started and almost exclaimed aloud. For there, at the end of the
mantelpiece, was a cabinet photograph of Marr. He was right then
in his suspicion. The lady of the feathers was also the lady of the
"European."

"Sorry to keep you waiting," said a voice behind him.

There was a clatter of crockery. His hostess entered bearing a tray, which held a teapot, cups, a large loaf of bread, and some butter, and a milk-jug and sugar-basin. She plumped it down on the table.

"Mrs. Brigg *wouldn't* make toast," she explained. "And I didn't like to keep you."

"Let's make some ourselves," said Julian, with a happy inspiration.

He felt that to perform a common and a cosy act must draw them together, and awaken in the lady's breast a happy and progressive confidence. She was evidently surprised at the suggestion.

"Well, I never!" she ejaculated. "You are a queer one. You are taking a rise out of me now!"

"Not at all. I like making toast. Give me a fork. I'll do it and you sit there and direct me."

She laughed and produced the fork from a mean cupboard which did duty as a sideboard.

"Here you are then. Cut it pretty thick. It ain't so high class, but it eats better. That's it. Sit on this stool, dear."

She kicked an ancient leather one to the hearth, and Julian, tucking his long-tailed frock coat under him, squatted down and thrust forward the bread to the bars of the grate. The lady opened the lid of the teapot and examined the brew with an anxious eye.

"It's drawin' beautiful," she declared. "Well, I'm d——" She caught herself up short. "Well, this is bally funny," she said "Turn it, dearie."

Julian obeyed, and they began to talk. For the ice was broken now, and the lady was quite at her ease, and simple and human in her hospitalities.

"This is better than the bun," Julian said.

"I believe you, dear. And yet that bun did me a deal of good that mornin'."

Her voice became suddenly reflective.

"A deal of good."

"Are you often out at such a time?"

"Not I. But that night I'd—well, I didn't feel like bein' indoors. There's things—well, there, it don't matter. That toast's done, dearie. Bring it here, and let me butter it."

Julian brought it, and cut another slice from the loaf. He toasted while the lady buttered, a fine division of labour which drew them close together. Jessie, meanwhile, attracted by these pleasant preparations, hovered about, wriggling in pathetic anxiety to share the good things of life.

"Anything wrong that night?" Julian said carelessly.

The lady buttered, like an angry machine.

"Oh no, dearie," she said. "Make haste, or the tea'll be as black as a coal. Jessie, you're a pig! I do spoil her."

I

Julian called the little dog to him. She came voraciously, her minute and rat-like body tense with greed.

"She's a pretty dog," he said.

"Yes," the lady rejoined proudly. "She's a show dog. She was give to me, and I wouldn't part with her for nuts, no nor for diamonds neither. Would I, Jessie? Ah, well, dogs stick to you when men don't."

She was trying to be arch, but her voice was really quivering to tears, and in that sentence rang all the tragedy of her poor life. Julian looked across at her as she sat by the tray, buttering now almost mechanically. She was naturally a pretty girl, but was growing rapidly haggard, and was badly made up, rouged in wrong places consumptively, powdered everywhere disastrously. Her eyes were pathetic, but above them the hair was dreadfully dyed, and frizzed into a desolate turmoil. She had a thin young figure and anxious hands. As he looked Julian felt a profound pity and a curious manly friendship for her. She had that saddest aspect of a human being about whom it doesn't matter. Only it matters about every living creature so much.

The lady caught his eye, and extended her lips in a forced smile.

"You never know your luck!" she cried. "So it don't do to be down on it. Come on, dearie. Now then for the tea."

She poured it out, and Julian drew up to the table. Already he felt oddly at home in this poor room, with this poor life, into which he longed to bring a little hope, a little safety. Jessie sprang to his knees, and thence, naughtily, to the table, snuffling towards the plate of toast. The lady drew it away and approached it to her nose by turns, playfully.

"She is a funny one," she said. "Is your tea right, dearie?"

"Perfect," said Julian. "Is my toast right?"

"Right as ninepence, and righter."

She munched.

"I like you," she said. "You're a gentleman."

She spoke naturally, without coquetry. It was a fine experience for her to be treated with that thing some women never know—respect. She warmed under it and glistened.

"We must be friends," Julian said.

"Pals. Yes. Have some more sugar?"

She jumped two lumps into his cup, and laughed quite gaily when the tea spouted over into the saucer. And they chatted on, and fed Jessie into joy and peace. Gradually Julian drew the conversation round to the photographs. The lady was expansive. She gave short histories of some of the men, summing them up with considerable shrewdness, kodaking their characters with both humour and sarcasm. Julian and she progressed along the mantelpiece together. Presently they arrived at the old lady with the Bible.

" And this ? " Julian said.

The lady's fund of spirits was suddenly exhausted.

" Oh, that," she said, and a sort of strange, suppressed blush struggled up under the rouge on her face. " Well, that's mother."

" I like her face."

" Yes. She thinks I'm dead."

The lady turned away abruptly.

" I'll just carry the tray down to Mrs. Brigg," she said, and she clattered out with it, and down the stairs.

Julian heard her loudly humming a music-hall song as she went, the Requiem of her dead life with the old woman who held the Bible on her knees. When she returned her mouth was hard and her eyes were shining ominously. Julian was still standing by the mantelpiece. As she came in he pointed to the photograph of Marr.

" And this ? " he asked. " Who's this ? "

The lady burst into a shrill laugh of mingled fear and cunning.

" That's the old gentleman ! "

" What do you mean ? "

" What I say, the old gentleman, Nick, the devil, if you like it."

" Now you are trying to take a rise out of me."

" Not I, dear," she said. " That's the devil sure enough."

Either the tea and toast had rendered her exuberant, or the thought of the old woman who believed her to be dead had driven her into recklessness. She continued :

" I'd been with him that night I met you, and I was frightened, I tell you. I'd been mad with fright."

" Why ? What had he done to you ? "

Julian strove to conceal his eager interest under a light assumption of carelessness.

" Done !—never mind. It don't do to talk about it."

She laid her thin hand on his arm, as if impelled to be confidential.

" Do you believe in people being struck ? " she said.

" Struck ! I don't understand."

" Struck," she repeated superstitiously. " Down, from up there ? "

Her eyes went up to the ceiling, like the child's when it thinks of heaven.

" Was he ? " Julian asked.

She nodded, pursing her red lips.

" That's what I think. It came so sudden. Just when I was going to scream somethin' seemed to come over him, like madness it was. He seemed listening. Then he says, ' Now—now ! '

And he seemed goin' right off. He stared at me and didn't seem to know me. Lord, I was blue with it, I tell you, dear! I was that frightened I just left him and bunked for it, and never said a word to anybody. I ran downstairs and got out of the house, and I daren't go home. So I just walked about till I met you."

She sighed.

"I did enjoy that coffee, I tell you straight, but when you began about seein' things, I couldn't stow it. My nerves was shook. So off I trotted again."

Julian put a question to her.

"Do you know what has become of him?"

"Not I. He'll never get in here again. Mrs. Brigg won't let him. She never could abide him."

She shook her shoulders in an irrepressible shudder.

"I wish he was dead," she said. "I never go out but what I'm afraid I shall meet him, or come back late but what I think I shall find him standin' against the street door. I wish he was dead."

"I knew him. He is dead."

She looked at him, at first questioning, then awe-stricken.

"Then he was struck? Lord!"

Her red mouth gaped.

"It was in the papers," Julian said. "At the European Hotel."

"That was the place. Lord! I never see the papers. Dead is he? I am glad."

Her relief was obvious yet almost shocking, and Julian could not question her good faith. She had certainly not known. He longed to find out more about her relations with Marr, and his treatment of her, but she shied away from the subject. Obviously she really loathed and detested the remembrance of him.

"But why do you keep his photograph?" Julian asked at last.

The lady seemed puzzled.

"I dunno," she said at last. "I don't seem as if I could burn it. But if he is gone—dead I mean—really——"

"He is."

"I know."

She sat thoughtfully. Then she said:

"He didn't look a fellow to die. It seems funny. No, he didn't look it."

And then she dropped the subject, and nothing would induce her to return to it. Presently they heard a church clock strike. It chimed seven. Julian was astonished to find that time had gone so quickly.

"I must be going," he said.

The lady looked at him with an odd, half-impudent, half-girlish and wistful scrutiny.

' I say," she began, and stopped.

"Yes?"

" I say—why ever did you come?"

The short question that expressed her wondering curiosity might well have driven any thoughtful man into tears. And Julian, young and careless as he often was, felt something of the terror and the pain enshrined in it. But he did not let her see this.

" I wanted to have a talk with you," he answered.

"A talk; you like a talk with me?"

" Yes, surely."

She still stared at him with pathetic eyes. He had stood up.

"Oh," she said. " Well, dearie, I'm glad."

Julian took up his hat.

" I'm going out, too," she said.

" Are you?"

" Yes."

She threw a sidelong glance at him, then added hardily, although her painted lips were suddenly quivering:

" I've got to go to work."

" I know," Julian said. " Well, I will wait till you are ready and drive you wherever you want to go."

" *Want* to go," she began, with a little shrill, hideous laugh. Then, pulling herself up, she added in a subdued voice:

"Thank you, dearie. I won't be long."

She opened the folding doors and passed into the inner room, accompanied by Jessie. Julian waited for her. He found himself listening to her movements in the other room, to the creak of wood, as she pulled out drawers, to the rustle of a dress lifted from a hook, the ripple of water poured from a jug into a basin. He heard the whole tragedy of preparation, as this girl armed herself for the piteous battle of the London streets. And then his ears caught the eager patter of Jessie to and fro, and a murmured expostulation from her mistress. Evidently the little dog had got hold of some article of attire and was worrying it. There was a hidden chase and a hidden capture. Jessie was scolded and kissed. Then the sitting-room slowly filled with the scent of cherry blossom. A tooth brush in action was distinctly audible. This tragedy had its comic relief, like almost all tragedies. Julian sighed and smiled, but his heart was heavy with the desolate and sordid wonder of life, as his mind heard—all over London—a thousand echoes of the bedchamber music of the lady of the feathers.

The folding doors opened wide and she appeared, freshly painted and powdered, crowned once again with the forest of ostrich tips, and holding the struggling Jessie in her arms.

"Jessie must go to basket," she said, and she dropped the dog into a tiny basket lined with red flannel, and held up a warning finger.

"Naughty—go bials!" she cried. "Go bials, Jessie."

"What's that?"

"Bials—by-bye. She don't like bein' left. Well, dearie, we've had a nice time."

Suddenly she put her hands on Julian's shoulders and kissed his mouth.

"I wish there was more like you," she whispered.

He kissed her too, and put his arms around her.

"If I give you something will you—will you stay at home to-night, just to-night with Jessie?" he said.

But she drew away and shook her head.

"I won't take it."

"Yes."

"I won't. No—we're pals, not—not the other thing. You're the only one I've got—of that kind. I won't spoil it—no I won't."

Her decision was almost angry. Julian did not persist.

"I'll come again," he said.

She looked at him wistfully.

"Ah—but you won't," she answered.

"I will."

He spoke with energy. She nodded.

"I'd like you to."

Then they went out into the evening and hailed a hansom.

"Put me down at the Piccadilly end of Regent Street," said the lady of the feathers.

CHAPTER VIII

THE LADY OF THE FEATHERS VISITS VALENTINE

JULIAN was curiously touched by his interview in the Marylebone Road, and he did not fail to recount it to Valentine, whose delicate imagination would, he felt certain, feel the pity and the pain of it.

But Valentine did not respond to his generous emotion.

"I thought she looked a very degraded young person," he said, distantly. "And not interesting. The woman who is falling is interesting. The woman who has reached the bottom, who has completely arrived at degradation, is dull enough."

"But she is not utterly degraded, Val. For I know that she can see and understand something of the horror of her own condition."

Valentine put his hand on Julian's shoulder.

"I know what you are thinking," he said.

"What?"

"That you would like to rescue this girl."

A dull blush ran over Julian's face.

"I don't know that I had got quite so far as that," he said. "Would it be absurd if I had?"

"I am not sure that it would not be wrong. Probably this girl lives the life she is best fitted for."

"You surely don't mean——"

"That some human beings are born merely to further the necessities of sin in the scheme of creation? I don't know that. Nature, in certain countries, demands and obtains pernicious and deadly snakes to live in her bosom. Man demands and obtains female snakes to live in his bosom. Are not such women literally created for this *métier*? How can one tell?"

"But if they are unhappy?"

"You think they would be happy in purity?"

"I believe she would."

Valentine smiled and shook his head.

"I expect her sorrows are not caused by the loss of her virtue but merely by her lack of the luxuries of life. These birds always want their nests to be made of golden twigs and lined with satin."

But Julian remained unconvinced.

" You don't know her," he said. " Why, Valentine, you have never known such a woman ! You !—The very notion is ridiculous."

" I have seen them in their garden of Eden, offering men the fruit of the tree of knowledge."

" You mean ? "

" At the ' Empire.' "

" Ah ! I have half promised to take her there one night."

" Shall I come with you, Julian ? "

Julian looked at him to see if he was in earnest as he made this unutterable proposition. Valentine's clear, cold, thoughtful blue eyes met his eager, glowing, brown ones with direct gravity.

" You mean it, Val ? "

" Certainly."

" You will be seen at the ' Empire ' with her ? "

" Well—would not you ? "

" But you are so different."

" Julian, you remember that night when we leaned out over London, when we saw what are called common people having common experiences ?   I said then that they at any rate were living."

" Yes."

" You and I will try to live with them."

" But Valentine—you——"

" Even I may learn to feel the strength of the Spring if I order my life rather differently in the future. We three, you, I, the girl, will go one night to the Garden of Eden, where the birds wear tights and sing comic songs in French, and the scent that comes from the flowers is patchouli, and silk rustles instead of the leaves of the trees. We will go there on boat-race night. Ah, the strength of the Spring ! On boat-race night it beats with hammering pulses among the groves of the Garden of Eden."

Julian was surprised at this outburst, which sounded oddly deliberate, and was apparently spoken without real impulse. He was surprised, but, on consideration, he came to the conclusion that Valentine, having silently debated the question of his own life, had resolved to make a definite effort to see if he could change the course of it. Julian felt that such an effort must be useless. He knew Valentine so intimately he thought, knew the very ground-work of his nature—that that nature was too strong to be carved into a different, and possibly grotesque, form.

" Are you an experimentalist, Val ? " he asked.

Valentine threw a rapid glance on him.

" I ? I don't understand. Why should I experiment upon you ? "

'No, not on me, but on yourself."

"Oh, I see what you mean. No, Julian, I prefer to let fate experiment upon me."

"At the 'Empire'?"

"If fate chooses."

"I think you ought to know Cuckoo——"

"Is that her name?"

"Yes, Cuckoo Bright, before our meditated expedition."

Valentine seemed struck by this idea.

"So that we may all be at our ease. A capital motion. Julian, sit down, write a note asking her to come to tea on Thursday in the flat. I will show her my pictures, and you shall talk to her of Huxley and of Herbert Spencer."

Julian regarded Valentine rather doubtfully.

"Are you malicious?" he said, with a hesitating note in his voice.

"Malicious—no!"

"You won't chaff her?"

"Chaff a lady who wears more feathers than ever 'growed on one ostrich,' and who was the *intime* of the mysterious Marr? Julian, Julian!"

Then seeing that Julian still looked rather uncomfortable, Valentine added, dropping his mock heroic manner:

"Don't be afraid. We will give the lady one good hour."

"Ah," Julian cried, struck by the expression; "that's what the doctor wished to give to every poor wretch in London."

"We won't ask the doctor to our tea," Valentine replied, with a sudden coldness.

The invitation was conveyed to the lady of the feathers, and in due course an answer was received, a mosaic of mis-spelling and obvious gratification.

"My dear," ran the missive, "I will com. I shall be pleased to see you agane, but I thorght I shoold not. Men say—oh yes, I shall com back—but not many does, and I thorght praps you was like all the rest. Your friend is very good to ask me, and I am,

"Yr loving,
"Cuckoo."

Valentine read the letter without comment, and ordered an elaborate tea. Julian read it, and wondered whether he was a fool because he felt touched by the mis-spelt words, as he had sometimes felt touched when he saw some very poor woman attired in her ridiculous "best" clothes.

The tea time had been fixed for five o'clock, and Julian intended of course to be in Victoria Street with Valentine to receive the expected guest, but Cuckoo Bright threw his polite plans out of gear, and Valentine was alone when, at half-past four, the electric bell rang, and, a moment later, Wade solemnly showed into the drawing room a striking vision, such as had never "burst into that silent sea" of artistic repose and refinement before.

The lady undoubtedly wore what seemed to be her one hat, and the effect of it, at all times remarkable, was amazingly heightened by its proximity to the quiet and beautiful surroundings of the room. As a rule it merely cried out. Now it seemed absolutely to yell bank-holiday vulgarity and impropriety at the silent pictures. But her gown decidedly exceeded it in uproar, being of the very loudest scarlet hue, with large black lozenges scattered liberally over it. From her rather narrow shoulders depended a black cape, whose silk foundation was suffocated with bugles. A shrill scent of cherry blossom ran with her like a crowd, and in her hand she carried an umbrella and a plush bag with a steel snap. Her face, in the midst of this whirlpool of finery, peeped out anxiously, covered as it was with a smear of paint and powder, and when she saw Valentine standing alone to receive her, her nervous eyes ranged uncomfortably about in obvious quest of an acquaintance and protector.

"I am sorry that Mr. Addison has not come yet," Valentine said, holding out his hand. "I expect him every minute. Won't you come and sit down?"

An ironical courtesy vibrated in his voice. The lady grew more obviously nervous. She looked at Valentine through the veil which was drawn tightly across her face. His appearance seemed to carry awe into her heart, for she stood staring and attempted no reply, allowing him to take her hand without either protest or response.

"Won't you sit down?" he repeated, smiling at her with humorous contemplation of her awkward distress.

The lady abruptly sat down on a sofa.

"Allow me to put a cushion at your back," Valentine said. And he passed behind her to do so. But she quickly shifted round, almost as if in fear, and faced him as he stood with his hand on the back of the sofa.

"No," she said in a hurry, "I don't know as I want one, thanks."

She half got up.

"Have I come right?" she asked uneasily. "Is this the house?"

"Certainly. It's so good of you to come."

The words did not seem to carry any comfort to the lady. She passed the tip of her tongue along her painted lips and looked towards the door.

" Pray don't be alarmed," Valentine said, sitting down on a chair immediately opposite to her.

" I ain't. But—but you're not the friend, are you ? "

" I am, and the *ami des femmes*, too, I assure you. Be calm." .

He bent forward, looking closely into her face. . The lady leaned quickly back and uttered a little gasp.

" What is the matter ? Valentine asked.

"Nothin', nothin'," the lady answered, returning his glance as if fascinated into something that approached horror. " When's he comin' ? When's he comin' ? "

" Directly. But I trust you will not regret spending a few minutes alone in my company. What can I do to make you happy ? "

" I'm all right, thank you," she said, almost roughly. " Don't bother about me."

" Who could help bothering about a pretty woman ? " Valentine answered suavely, and approaching his chair a little more closely to her. " Do you know that my friend, Addison, can talk of nobody but you ? "

" Oh ! "

" Nobody. He raves about you."

" You're laughing," the lady said, still uncomfortably.

" Not at all. I never laugh."

As he made this last remark, Valentine slowly frowned. The effect of this change of expression upon the lady was most extraordinary. She leaned far back upon the sofa as if in retreat from the face that stared upon her, mechanically thrusting out her hands in a faltering gesture of self-defence. Then planting her feet on the ground, and using them as a lever, she succeeded in moving the sofa backwards upon its castors, which ran easily over the thick carpet. Valentine, on his part, did not stir, but, with immovable face, regarded her apparent terror as a man regards some spectacle neither new nor strange to him, silently awaiting its eventual closing tableau. What this would have been cannot be known, for at this moment the bell rang and the butler was heard moving in the hall. The frown faded from Valentine's face, and the lady sprang up from the sofa with a violent, almost a passionate, eagerness. Julian entered hastily.

" Why was you late ? " Cuckoo Bright cried out, hastening up to him, and speaking almost angrily. " Why was you late ? I didn't think—I didn't—oh ! "

Her voice sounded like the voice of one on the verge of tears. Julian looked astonished.

" I am very sorry," he began. " But I didn't know you would be here so soon."

He glanced from the lady to Valentine inquiringly, as much as to say:

"How have you been getting on?"

Valentine's expression was gay and re-assuring.

"I have been entertaining your friend, Julian," he said. "But she has been almost inconsolable in your absence. She was standing up because I was just about to show her the pictures. But now you are here we will have tea first instead. Ah, here is tea. Miss Bright, do come and sit by the fire, and put your feet on this stool. We will wait upon you."

Since the entrance of Julian, his manner had entirely changed. All the irony, all the mock politeness had died out of it. He was now a kind and delicately courteous host, desirous of putting his guests upon good terms and gilding the passing hour with a definite happiness. Cuckoo Bright seemed struck completely dumb by the transformation. She took the chair he indicated, mechanically put her feet up on the stool he pushed forward, and, with a rather trembling hand, accepted a cup of tea.

"Do you take sugar?" Valentine said, bending over her with the sugar basin.

"No, no," she said.

"Oh, but I thought you loved sweet things," Julian interposed. "Surely——"

"I won't have none to-day," she ejaculated, adding with an endeavour after gentility, "thank you all the same," to Valentine.

He offered her some delicious cakes, but she was apparently petrified by the grandeur of her surroundings, or by some hidden sensation of shyness or of shame, and was refusing to eat anything when Julian came to the rescue.

"Oh, but you must," he said. "Have some of these sugar biscuits."

She took some from him, and began to sip and munch steadily but still in silence. Julian began to fear that the festival must be a dire failure, for her obvious and extreme constraint affected him, and he was also seized with an absurd sense of shyness in the presence of Valentine, and, instead of talking, found himself immersed in a boyish anxiety as to Valentine's attitude of mind towards the girl. He looked at Cuckoo in the firelight, as she mutely ate and drank, and was all at once profoundly conscious of the dreary vulgarity of her appearance, against which even her original prettiness and her present youth fought in vain. Her hat cast a monstrous shadow upon the wall, a shadow so distorted and appalling that Julian almost grew red as he observed it, and felt that Valentine was probably observing it also. He wished poor Cuckoo had left the crying scarlet gown at home and those black lozenges, which were suited to the pavement of the hall of a financier. Everything she had on expressed a mind such as Valentine must become acquainted with in amazement, and have intercourse with in sorrow. The pathetic side of this preposterous feathered and bugled degradation he would fail to see. Julian felt painfully certain of this. All the details of the woman would offend him who was so alive to the value of fine details in life. He must surely be wondering with all his soul how Julian could ever have contemplated continuing the intercourse with Cuckoo which had been begun for a definite purpose already accomplished. Yet Julian's feeling of friendship towards this rouged scarecrow with the pathetic eyes and the anxious hands did not diminish as he blushed for her, but rather increased, fed, it seemed, by the discordant trifles in which her soul moved as in a maze. He was so much in the thrall of thought that he had become quite unconscious of the awkwardness of the brooding silence when he heard Valentine's voice say :

" Are you fond of art, Miss Bright ? "

The question sounded as if addressed to some society woman at home in Melbury Road. Addressed to Cuckoo it was entirely absurd, and Julian glanced at Valentine to deprecate the gay sarcasm which he suspected. But Valentine's face disarmed him. It was so gravely and serenely polite.

" Eh ? " said Cuckoo.

" Are you fond of art, or do you prefer literature ? "

" I don't know," she said nervously.

" Or perhaps music ? "

" I like singin'," she said. " And the organs."

" Do sing us something, Val," Julian said, to create a diversion. But Valentine shook his head.

" Not to-day. I have got a cold in my throat."

" Well then play something."

But Valentine did not seem to hear the last request. He had turned again to Cuckoo, who visibly shied away from him, and clattered the teacup and saucer, which she held like one alarmed.

" Music is a great art," he said persuasively. " And appeals essentially to one's emotions. I am certain now that you are emotional."

" I don't know, I'm sure," she said, with an effort at self-confidence.

" You feel strongly, whether it be love or hate."

This last remark seemed to reach her, even to stir her to something more definite than mere *mauvaise honte*. She glanced quickly from Julian to Valentine.

" Love and hate," she responded. " Yes, that's it, I could feel them both. You're right there, my d——, I mean yes."

And again she looked from one young man to the other. She had put up her veil, which was stretched in a bunched-up mass across her powdered forehead, and Julian had an odd fancy that in the firelight he saw upon her haggard young face the rapid and fleeting expression of the two violently opposed emotions of which she spoke. Her face, turned upon him, seemed to shine with a queer, almost with a ludicrous, vehemence of yearning which might mean passion. This flashed into the sudden frown of a young harridan as her eyes travelled on to Valentine. But the frown died quickly, and she looked downcast, and sat biting her thin lips, and crumbling a biscuit into the tiny blue and white china plate upon her knee.

"And do you give way to your impulses?" Valentine continued, still very gravely.

"What?"

"Do you express what you feel?"

A flash of childish cunning crept into her eyes and mouth, giving her the aspect of a *gamin*.

"No, I ain't such a fool," she answered. "Men don't like to be told the truth. Do they now?"

The question went to Julian.

"Why not?" he asked.

"Oh, they like to be fooled. If you don't fool them, they fool you."

"A sufficiently clear statement of the relations of the sexes through all time," said Valentine. "Have you ever studied Schopenhauer?"

"Ah, now you're kiddin' me!" was her not inappropriate answer.

She was getting a little more at her ease, but she still stole frequent furtive glances at Valentine from time to time, and moved with an uncomfortable jerk if he bent forward to her, or seemed about to come near to her. He seemed now really interested in her personality, and Julian began to wonder if its very vulgarity came to him with a charm of novelty.

"Kidding?" Valentine said interrogatively.

"Gettin' at me! Pullin' my leg! Oh, I know you!" cried Cuckoo. "I'm up to all them games. You don't get a rise out of me."

"The lady speaks in parables," Valentine murmured to Julian. "I assure you," he added aloud, "I am speaking quite seriously."

"Oh, seriously be hanged!" said Cuckoo recklessly. "You're a regular funny feller. Oh yes. Only don't you try to be funny with me, because I'm up to all that."

She seemed suddenly bent on turning the tables on one whom she apparently regarded as her adversary. Some people, when they do make an effort of will, are always carried forward by the unwonted exertion into an almost libertine excess. Miss Bright's timidity was now developing into violent impudence. She tossed her head till the gigantic shadow of the sarcophagus that crowned it aspired upon the wall almost to the ceiling. She stuck her feet out upon the stool aggressively, and her arms instinctively sought the akimbo position that is the physical expression of mental hardihood, in vulgar natures.

" Go along ! " she said.

Valentine pretended to take her at her word. He got up.

" Where shall I go ?   I am your slave ! "

She laughed shrilly.

" Go to blazes if you like."

Valentine crossed to the door, and, before Julian had time to speak, opened it and quietly vanished. Julian and Cuckoo were left staring at one another. The latter's impudence had suddenly evaporated. Her face was working as if she were astonished and afraid.

" What's he after ?   What's he after, I say ? " she ejaculated. " Go and see."

But Julian shook his head.

" It's all right. He has only done it for a joke. He will be back directly."

" Yes, but—but——"

She seemed really frightened. Julian supposed she realised her rudeness vaguely, and imagined she had made an abominable *faux pas.* Acting on this supposition he said reassuringly :

" He didn't mind your chaff. He knew you were only joking."

" Lord, it isn't that," she rejoined with trembling lips. " But what's he goin' to do ? "

" Do ? "

" Yes. Go and see. Hark ! "

She held up her hand and leaned forward in a strained attitude of attention. But there was no sound in the flat. Then she turned again to Julian and said :

" And he's your friend. Well, I never ! "

The words were spoken with an extraordinary conviction of astonishment that roused Julian to keen attention.

" Why, what do you mean ? " he asked.

" He's a wicked fellow," she said with a snatch of the breath. " A real downright wicked fellow, like Marr. That's what he is."

Julian was amazed.

" You don't know what are you saying," he answered.

But she stuck to her guns with the animation of hysteria.

" Don't I though ?   Don't I ?   A girl that lives like me has to know, I tell you. Where should I be if I didn't ?   Tell me that then. Why, there's men in the streets I wouldn't speak to, not for twenty pounds, I wouldn't. And he's one of them. Why didn't you come? Why ever did you let me be on my own with him? He's a devil."

"Nonsense," Julian said brusquely.

She laid her hand on his, and hers was trembling.

"Well, then, why's he gone off all sudden like that?"

"Only for a joke. Wait, I'll fetch him back."

Cuckoo Bright looked frankly terrified at the idea.

"No," she cried; "don't. I'm goin'. I'm off. Help me on with my cloak, dearie. I'm off."

Julian saw that it was useless to argue with her. He put the cloak round her shoulders. As he did so he was standing behind her, with his face to the fireplace. The leaping flames sprang from the coals in the grate and their light was reflected on the wall near the door, but only of course to a certain height. Julian's eyes were attracted to these leaping flames on the wall and he saw one suddenly detach itself from the shadows of its brethren, take definite shape and life, develop while he looked from shadow into substance, float up on the background of the wall higher and higher, reach the ceiling and melt away. As it faded the drawing-room door opened and Valentine re-appeared.

Miss Bright started violently, and caught at her cloak with both hands. Valentine came forward slowly.

"You are not going already, surely," he said.

"I must, I must," she ejaculated, already in movement towards the hall.

"But I have just been to get you a box of sugar plums."

He held a satin box in his hand and began to open it. But she hurried on with a nod.

"Good-bye. Sorry, but I can't stop."

She was in the hall and out of the flat in the twinkling of an eye, followed by Julian. Valentine remained in the drawing-room.

"Lord, I am glad to be out of it," said the lady when she had gained the street and stood panting on the pavement.

Julian hailed a hansom and put her into it. She gazed at him as if she was almost afraid to part from him.

"You'll—you'll come and see me again?" she said, wistfully.

"Yes, I'll come," he answered.

"For God's sake, don't bring him, dearie," she said, with an upward lift of her feathered head towards the block of mansions.

Then she drove off into the darkness.

CHAPTER IX

THE LADY OF THE FEATHERS WASHES HER FACE

IT was at this point in his career that Julian, just for a time, began keenly to observe Valentine and to wonder if there were hidden depths in his friend which he had never sounded. The cause of the dawning of this consideration lay in Cuckoo's strange assertion and fear of Valentine, primarily, but there were other reasons prompting him to an unusual attitude of attention, although he might not at first have been able to name them. He could not believe that there was any change in Valentine, but he fancied that there might be some side of Valentine's nature which he did not fully understand, which others vaguely felt and wrongly interpreted. For it was the instinctive creatures in whom Valentine's presence now seemed to awake distrust, and surely an instinct may be too violent, or move in a wrong direction, and yet be inspired by some subtlety in the character that awakens it and prompts it and drives it forward. Julian thought that he found a reason for Cuckoo's aversion in Valentine's lofty refinement, which would naturally jar upon her nature of the streets. For her pathos, her better impulses, which had touched him, and led him to sympathy with her, were perhaps only stars in a mind that must be a dust-heap of horrible memories and coarse thoughts. To protect Valentine from even the most diminutive shadow of suspicion, Julian was ready silently to insist that Cuckoo was radically bad, although he really knew that she was rather a weak sacrifice than an eager sinner.

Her declaration that Valentine was evil carried complete conviction of its sincerity. Indeed, her obvious fear of him proved this. And this fear of a woman reminded Julian of the fear exhibited towards Valentine by Rip, a terror which still continued, to such an extent indeed, that the little dog was now never permitted to be in the presence of its master.

" You are rather an awe-inspiring person, Valentine," Julian said one day.

Valentine looked surprised.

" I never knew it," he answered. " Who is afraid of me ? "

K

"Oh, I don't know—well, Rip, for one, and—and that girl, Cuckoo, for another."

"Why is she afraid?"

"I can't imagine."

"I could soon put her at her ease, and I will do so."

He went over to the mantelpiece and took up an envelope that was lying there. From it he drew a slip of coloured paper.

"This will be the talisman," he said. "Have you forgotten that Saturday is boat-race day?"

"What, you have really got a box for the 'Empire'?"

"Yes, and I mean to invite Miss Bright."

Julian exclaimed with his usual frankness.

"Why the devil do you think of asking her?"

"Because I am certain she will be amusing company on such an occasion."

"That's your real reason?"

"Yes. She will come, of course."

Julian looked rather doubtful.

"I don't know," he said. "She may."

"She must, Julian. Here is a note I have written to her. Do give it to her yourself. I can't be thought a bogey. She must come and learn that I am harmless."

As he said this Valentine's fingers unconsciously twisted the note they held so strongly that it was torn to shreds.

"Why, you have torn it up," Julian said, in surprise.

"Oh yes."

Valentine paused, then added,

"You had better ask her by word of mouth. Persuade her to come."

"I will try."

The lady of the feathers did indeed require a good deal of persuasion. When first Julian made the proposition her face shone with gratification, for he gave the invitation without mentioning Valentine's name. But then the clouds came down. The lady remembered him suddenly, and said:

"Are we two going alone, dearie?"

"Well—it's a big box, you see. We should be lost in it."

"Oh."

She waited for further explanation, an obvious anxiety in her eyes.

"My friend, Cresswell, is coming with us. It's his box."

The gratification died away from the painted face. Cuckoo shook her head and pursed her lips in obvious and absurd disapprobation.

"Then I don't think I'll go. No; I won't."

And, upon this, Julian had to launch forth over a sea of expostulation and protest. Cuckoo possessed all the obstinacy of an ignorant and battered nature, taught, by many a well-founded distrust, to rely upon its own feebleness rather than upon the probably brutal strength of others. She was difficult to move, although she had no arguments with which to defend her assumption of the mule's attitude. At last Julian grew almost angry in defence of Valentine.

"Half the women in London would be proud to go with him," he said hotly.

"Not if they knew as much about men as I do," she answered.

"But you know nothing whatever about him. That's just the point."

"Ah, but I feel a lot," she said, with an expressive twist of her thin, rather pretty face. "He's bad, rank bad. That's what he is."

Julian was suddenly seized with a desire to probe this outrageous instinct to its source, believing, like many people, that the stream of instinct must flow from some hidden spring of reason.

"Now look here," he said, more quietly. "I want you to try to tell me what it is in him that you dislike so much."

"It's everything, dearie."

"No, but that's absurd. For instance it can't be his looks."

"It is."

"Why he's wonderfully handsome."

"I don't care. I hate his face; yes I do."

Julian impatiently pitied her, as one pities a blind man who knocks up against one in the street. But he thought it best to abandon Valentine's appearance to its unhappy fate of her dislike, and sailed away on another tack.

"My friend likes you," he said, as he thought, craftily.

Cuckoo tossed her head without reply.

"He said he would rather go with you on Saturday than with any one in London."

This last remark seemed to produce a considerable effect upon the girl.

"Did he though?" she asked, one finger going up to her under-lip, reflectively. "Really, truly?"

"Really, truly."

"What should he want with me? He's—he's not one of the usual sort."

"Valentine usual! I should think not."

"And he wants me to go?"

Certainly she was impressed and flattered.

"Yes, very much."

Julian found himself again wondering, with Cuckoo, mightily at Valentine's vagary of desire. She touched his hand with her long, thin fingers.

" You'll stay with me all the time? "

" Why, of course."

" You won't leave me? Not alone with him, I mean."

" No, don't be so absurd."

A new hesitation sprang into her face.

" But what am I to go in? " she said. " He—he don't like my red."

So her awe and dislike prompted her to a desire of pleasing Valentine after all, and had led her shrewdly to read his verdict on her poorly smart gown. Julian, pleased at his apparent victory now ventured on a careful process of education, on the insertion of the thin edge of the wedge, as he mutely named it.

" Cuckoo," he said, " let me give you a present, a dress. Now,' as she began to shake her tangled head, " don't be silly. I have never given you anything, and if we are to be pals you mustn't be so proud. Can you get a dress made in three days, a black dress? "

" Yes," she said. " But black! I shall look a dowdy."

" No."

" Oh, but I shall," she murmured, dismally. " Colours suits me best. You see I'm thin now, not as I was when I—well, before I started. Ah, I looked different then, I did. I don't want to be a scarecrow and make you ashamed of me."

Julian longed to tell her that it was the rouge, the feathers, the scarlet skirt, the effusive bugles, that made a scarecrow of her. But he had a rough diplomacy that taught him to refrain. He stuck to his point, however. .

" I shall give you a black dress and hat——"

" Oh, my hat's all right now," she interposed. " Them feathers is beautiful."

" Splendid, but I'll give you a hat to match the dress, and a feather boa, and black suede gloves."

" But, dearie, I shall be a trottin' funeral, that I shall," she expostulated, divided between excitement and perplexity.

" No, you'll look splendid. And Cuckoo——"

He hesitated, aware that he was treading on the divine quicksand of woman's prejudices.

" Cuckoo, I want you to make a little experiment for my sake."

" Whatever is it, dearie? "

" Just on that one night take—take all that off."

With an almost timid gesture, and growing boyishly red, he indicated the art decoration, pink and pale, that adorned her face.

Poor Cuckoo looked completely flabbergasted.

" What! " she said uncertainly. " Don't you like me with it? "

" No."

"Well, but, I don't know."

Such an experiment evidently struck her as portentous, earth-shaking. She stared into the dingy glass that stood over the mantel-piece in Marylebone Road.

"I shall look a hag," she muttered with conviction. "I shall."

"You never had it, before you started."

Her eyes grew round.

"Ah, that was jolly different though," she said.

"Try it," he urged. "Go and try it now, then come and show me."

"I don't like to."

The idea reduced her almost to shyness. But she got up falter-ingly, and moved towards the bedroom. When she was by the fold-ing door she said :

"I say."

"Well ?"

"I say, you won't laugh at me ?"

"Of course not."

"You won't—honour ?"

"Honour ! "

She disappeared. And there was the sound of many waters. Julian listened to it, repeating under his breath that word of many meanings, that panorama word, honour. Among thieves, among prostitutes, among murderers, rebels, the lost, the damned of this world, still does it not sing, like a bird that is too hopeful of some great and beautiful end ever to be quite silent ?

Julian waited, while Cuckoo washed away her sin of paint and powder, at first nervously, then with a certain zest that was almost violent, that splashed the water on floor and walls, and sent the shivering Jessie beneath the bed for shelter. Cuckoo scrubbed and scrubbed then applied a towel, until her skin protested in patches. Finally, and with a disturbed heart, she approached the sitting-room. Her voice came in to Julian while she remained hidden :

"I say——"

"Yes."

"I know you will laugh."

"Honour, Cuckoo, honour."

"Oh, all right."

And she came in to him, hanging her head down, rather like a child among strangers, ashamed, poor thing, of looking respectable. Julian was astonished at the change the water had wrought. Cuckoo looked another woman, or rather girl, oddly young, thin, and haggard certainly, and the reverse of dashing, but pretty, even fascinating in her shyness. As he looked at her and saw the real red of nature run over her cheeks in waves of faint rose colour, Julian understood fully all that the girl gives up when she gives up herself, and the wish—smiled at by Valentine—came to him again, the wish to reclaim her.

" Ah ! " he said. " Now you are yourself."

He took her hand, and drew her in front of the mirror, but she refused to lift up her eyes and look at her reflection.

" I'm a scarecrow," she murmured, twisting the front of her gown in her fingers. Her lips began to twitch ominously. Julian felt uncomfortable. He thought she was going to cry.

" You are prettier than ever," he said. " Look ! "

" No, no. It's all gone—all gone."

" What ? "

" My looks, dearie. I could do without the paint once. I can't now."

Suddenly she turned to him with a sort of vulgar passion, that suspicion of the hard young harridan, typical of the pavement, which he had observed in her before.

" I should like to get the whole lot of men in here," she said, " and –and chew them up."

She showed her teeth almost like an animal. Then the relapse, characteristic of the hysterical condition in which she was, came.

" Never you treat me like the rest," she said, bursting into sobs. " Never you try anythin' on. If you do I'll kill myself."

This outburst showed to Julian that she was capable of a curious depth of real sentiment that gave to her a glimpse of purity and the divinity of restraint. He tried to soothe her and quickly succeeded. When she had recovered they went out together to see about the making of the new black dress, and before they parted he had persuaded Cuckoo to face the " Empire " multitude on the fateful evening without her panoply of paint and powder. She pleaded hard for a touch of black on the eyes, a line of red on the lips. But he was inexorable. When he had gained his point he comforted her anxiety with chocolates, a feat more easy than the soothing of her with reasoning could have been.

When he told Valentine of the success of his embassy, Valentine simply said :

" I am glad."

Julian did not mention the episode of the washing, the preparation of the black gown, or the promise wrung from the lady of the feathers. The result springing from these three events was to come as a surprise to Valentine on boat-race night.

CHAPTER X

THE DANCE OF THE HOURS

EVEN so huge a city as London, full of so many varying personalities and clashing interests, assumes upon certain days of the year a particular and characteristic aspect, arising from a community of curiosity, of excitement, or of delight felt by its inhabitants. Such days are Derby day and boat-race day. On the latter more especially London is leavened by a huge mob of juveniles from the universities and their female admirers from the country, who cast a sort of pleasant spell over the frigid indifference of town-bred dullards, and wake even the most vacuous of the Piccadilly loungers into a certain vivacity and boyishness. The cabmen blossom cheerily in dark and light blue favours. The butcher boys are partisans. Every *gamin* in the gutter is all for one boat or for the other, and dances excitedly to know the result. London, in fact, loses several wrinkles on boat-race day, and smiles itself into a very pleasant appearance of briskness and of youth. As a rule, Julian went to see the race and to lunch with his friends at Putney or elsewhere, without either abnormal experience of excitement or any unusual vivacity. He was naturally full of life, and had hot blood in his veins, loved a spectacle and especially a struggle of youth against youth. But no boat-race day had ever stirred him as this one did—found him so attentive to outside influence, so receptive of common things. For Julian had recently been half conscious that he was progressing, and with increasing rapidity, though he knew not in what exact direction. Simply he had the feeling of motion, of journeying, and it seemed to him that he had been standing comparatively still for years. And this boat-race day came to him like a flashing milestone upon the road of life. He felt as if it held in its hours a climax of episodes or of emotions, as if upon it either his body or his mind must prepare to undergo some large experience, to meet the searching eyes of a face new and unfamiliar.

Possibly the reason of his own excitement lay in the excitement of another, in the curious preparations, which he had oddly shared, for the transformation of the unmistakable into the vague. For the transformation of Cuckoo Bright had been preparing apace, and Julian was looking forward like a schoolboy to the effect which her novel respectability of appearance would have upon Valentine. The rouge box lay lonely and untouched in a drawer. Even the powder-puff suffered an unaccustomed neglect. The black gown had been tried on and taught to fit the thin young figure, and a hat—with only one feather—kept company with the discarded sarcophagus which had given to Cuckoo her original nickname. And Cuckoo herself was almost as excited as Francine when she received her muff. She had not seen Valentine since the day of the tea-party, yet her attitude of mind had undergone a change towards him, bent to it probably by her vanity. Ever since Julian had given her the invitation to the Empire she had displayed a furtive desire to meet him again, was perpetually talking of him and asking questions about him. Nevertheless her fear of him had not died away. Even now she sometimes exclaimed against him almost with vehemence, and made Julian renew his promise not to leave her during the evening. But Julian could see that she longed, as well as dreaded, to meet him again. After all, had he not picked her out from all the girlhood of London as one to whom he wished to do honour ? Had he been the Minotaur such a fact must have made her look upon him with desirous interest.

When the great day arrived poor Cuckoo had to struggle with a keen and a sore temptation. She longed to deck herself out in her usual borrowed plumage, to take the habitual brilliant complexion out of the accustomed drawer, to crown her frizzed head with feathers, and to look noisily dashing—her only idea of elegance and grace. Never before had she so desired to create an impression. Yet she had given Julian her most solemn promise, and she intended to keep it. As she slowly attired herself, however, she wondered very much why he was so set upon denuding her of her accustomed magnificence. Her mind was entirely unable to grasp his conception of beauty and of attractiveness. She thought all men preferred the peony to the violet. To-night it was very certain that she would be no peony, scarcely even a violet. Her new gown had been expensive, but it was terribly simple, and the skirt hung beautifully, but was surely most direfully sombre. Nevertheless, it rustled with a hand-some sound, a melody of wealth, when she had put it on and promenaded about her dingy bedroom, with Jessie at her heels, pretending to worry it playfully. The black bodice had some trimming. But it was all black. Cuckoo wished it had been scarlet, or, at the least, orange, something to catch the eye and hold it. When she was fully attired, and was staring into her glass, between two boldly flaring gas jets, she nearly resolved to break her promise to Julian. She even went so far as to paint her lips and eyes, and was charmed with the effect against the black. But then, with a sudden fury, she sponged her pale face clean, threw the new feather boa round her throat, and, without daring to glance again at her funereal image, turned out the gas, and went into the sitting-room. As usual, her last act was to ensconce the pensive Jessie in the flannel-lined basket, and to give her a kiss. To-night, as she did so, she let a tear fall on the little dog's head. She scarcely knew why she cried. Perhaps the quiet gown, the lack of paint and powder, the prospect of kind and even respectful treatment from at least Julian, if not from Valentine, gave to her heart a vision of some existence in which Piccadilly Circus had no part.

Jessie shivered as she felt the tear, and licked the face of her mistress eagerly. Then Cuckoo rustled forth, avoiding Mrs. Brigg, who might be heard laboriously ascending the kitchen stairs to view her in her gala attire. In the twinkling of an eye she was out in the street, and Mrs. Brigg returned, swearing gustily, to the lower regions.

Cuckoo was to join the young men in their box, of which she had received the number. She took a cab to the Empire, and was there in excellent time. As she paid the man, she saw several women going noisily in, dressed in bright colours and gigantic hats. She looked at them, and felt terribly mean and poor, and it was with no trace of her usual airy impudence that she asked her way of the towering attendant in uniform who stood at the bottom of the carpeted staircase.

Julian and Valentine were already there. They turned round as she came in, and stood up to receive her. Julian took her hand, but Valentine hesitated for a moment. Then he said:

" Is it—can it be really Miss Bright ?"

" Sure enough it is," Cuckoo answered, with an effort after liveliness.

But her eyes were fixed on his. She had seen a curious expression of mingled annoyance and contempt flit across his face as she came in. Why, why had she allowed Julian to over-persuade her ? She was looking horrible, a scarecrow, a ghost of a woman. She was certain of it. For a moment she felt almost angry with Julian for placing her in such a bitter position. But he was glowing with a consciousness of successful diplomacy, and was delighted with her neat black aspect, and with her smart, though small, hat. He was indeed surprised to find how really pretty she still was when she allowed her true face to be seen, and was only wishing that she had made a little less of her hair, which was more vigorously arranged even than usual. He glanced to see Valentine's surprise.

" You are so altered," the latter continued. " I scarcely recognised you."

Cuckoo's lips tightened.

"Altered or not, it's me, though," she said.

Valentine did not reply to this. He only made her come to the front of the box, and placed a chair for her. She sat down feeling like a dog just whipped. The young men were on each side of her, and the band played an overture. Cuckoo peered out over the bar of the box, shifting ever so little away from the side on which Valentine sat. In his presence all her original and extreme discomfort returned, with an added enmity caused by her secret certainty that he thought her looking her worst. She peered from the box and strove to interest herself in the huge crowd that thronged the house and in her own dignified and elevated position in it. For Valentine had taken one of the big boxes next the stage on the first tier, and Cuckoo had never been in such a situation before. She could survey the endless rows of heads in the stalls with a completeness of bird's-eye observation never previously attained. What multitudes there were. Endless ranks of men, all staring in the same direction, all smoking, all with handkerchiefs peeping out of their cuffs, and goldrings on their little fingers. Some of them looked half asleep, others, who had evidently been dining, threw themselves back in their stalls roaring with laughter, and leaning to tell each other stories that must surely have teemed with wit. Most of them were young. But here and there an elderly and lined figure-head appeared among them, a figure-head that had faced many sorts of weather in many shifting days and nights, and that must soon face eternity—instead of time. Yet at the gates of death it still sipped its brandy and soda, smiled over a French song with tired lips, and sat forward with a pale gleam dawning in its eyes to reconnoitre the charms of a *ballet*. And if it looked aside at youth and was pierced by the sword of tragedy, yet it was too well bred or too conventional to let even one of the world around witness the wound. There is much secret bravery in social life. But these elderly figure-heads were fewer than usual to-night. Youth seemed to have usurped the playing-grounds of pleasure, to have driven old age away into the shadows. With flag flying, with trumpet and drum, it gaily held the field. The lady of the feathers, Valentine, and Julian leaned out from their box as from the car of a balloon and saw below them a world of youth, hand in hand with the world of pleasure the gods offer to youth as wine. It was yet early in the evening, and the hours were only tripping along, as women trip in the pictures of Albert Moore. They had not begun to dance, although the band was playing a laughing measure from an opera of Auber that foams with frivolity. Men kept dropping in, cigar in mouth, walking to their seats with that air of well-washed and stiff composure peculiar to British youth grim with self-consciousness, but affecting the devil-may-care with a certain measure of success. Some of them escorted ladies, but by far the greater number were in couples, or in parties of three or four. The rose of health, or, in many cases, of repletion, sat enthroned upon their cheeks; on the upper lips of many the moustaches were budding delicately. These were just getting up on the box and gripping the reins for the great coach drive. Little wonder if the veins in the eager hands stood out. Little wonder if they flourished the whip with an unnecessary vehemence. But for them, too, so far the hours were only tripping, a slow and a dainty measure, a formal minuet. And they were but watching. Only later would they rise up and join the great dance of the hours, large, complicated, alluring, through whose measures the feet of eventual saints have trod, whose music rings in the ears of many who, long after, try to pray and to forget. Some who were with women made conversation jocosely, putting on travesties of military airs, and a knowingness of expression that might have put the wisdom of the Sphinx to shame. Nor did they hesitate to appear amorous in the public eye. On the contrary, their attitudes of attention were purposely assumed silently to utter volumes. They lay, to all intents and purposes, at the feet of their houris, as Samson lay shorn at the feet of Delilah. In loud, young voices they told the secrets of their hearts, until even the clash of the music could scarcely keep them hidden. And Delilah, who had shorn the locks of so many Samsons, and who had heard so many secrets, gave ear with a clever affectation of interested surprise that deceived these gay deceivers and set them high on the peaks of their own estimation. Two or three family parties, one obviously French, seemed out of place, indecently domestic, in the midst of such a throng, in which matrimony was a Cinderella before the ball, cuffed in curl-papers rather than kissed in crystal slippers. They sat rather silent. One consisted of a father, a mother, and two daughters, the latter in large flowered hats. The father smoked. The mother looked furtive in a bonnet, and the two daughters, with wide open eyes, examined the flirtations around them as a child examines a butterfly caught in a net. One of them blushed. But she did not turn away her eyes. Nor were her girlish ears inactive. Family life seemed suddenly to become dull to her. She wondered whether it were life at all. And the father still smoked domestically. He knew it all. That was the difference. And perhaps it was his knowledge that made him serenely content with domesticity and the three women who belonged to him. Two boys, who had come up from a public school for the race, and had forgotten to go back, sat at the end of a row in glistening white collars and neat ties, almost angrily observant of all that was going on around them. For them the dance of the hours was already begun. and already become a can-can. They watched it with an eager interest and excitement, and the calm self-possession with which some of the men near them made jokes to magnificently dressed women with diamond earrings, struck them dumb with admiration. Yet, later on, they too were fated to join in the dance, when the stars affected to sleep on the clouds and the moon lay wearily inattentive to the pilgrims of the night, like an invalid in a blue boudoir. On the thick carpet by the wall attendants stood loaded with programmes. One of them, very trim and respectable, in a white cap, was named Clara and offered a drink by an impudent Oxonian. She giggled with all the vanity of sixteen, happily forgetful of her husband and of the seven children who called her mother. Yet the dance of the hours was a venerable saraband to her, and she often wished she was in bed as she stood listening to the familiar music. In the enclosure set apart for the orchestra the massed musicians earned their living violently in the midst of the gaily dressed idlers, who heard them with indifference, and saw them as wound-up marionettes. The drummer hammered on his blatant instrument with all the crude skill of his tribe, producing occasional terrific noises with darting fists, while his face remained as immovable as that of a Punchinello. A flautist piped romantically an Arcadian measure while his prominent eyes stared about over the chattering audience as if in search of some one. Suddenly he gave a "couac." He had seen his sweetheart in the distance with a youth from Christ Church. The conductor turned on the estrade in the centre of the orchestra and scowled at him, and he hastened to become Arcadian once again, gazing at his flute as if the devil had entered into it. In a doorway shrouded with heavy curtains two acting managers talked warily, their hands in retreat behind their coat-tails. They surveyed the house and mentally calculated the amount of money in it, raising their eyes to the more distant promenade, at the back of which large hats covered with flowers and feathers moved steadily to and fro. One of them curled his lips and murmured the word "Chant." Then they both laughed and strolled out to the bar. More men passed in. Many could not get seats, and these stood, smoking and exchanging remarks in the broad space between the stalls and the wall. Some of them leaned nonchalantly against it and criticised the appearance of the seated audience, or nodded to acquaintances. Others gathered round the bar, and a few looked at the drop-curtain as if they thought their ascetic glances would cause it to roll up and disappear. The overture at length ended. The stage was disclosed, and a man came forward with a smirk, and a wriggle of gigantic feet, to sing a song.

But Cuckoo Bright, Valentine, and Julian, from their balloon car, still surveyed the world. Cuckoo had heard the man before. She was no stranger to the upper regions of the Empire, but the fascination of knowing herself watched and commented on from the stalls was a new experience and she wished to make the most of it. Forgetting that she was not painted and powdered, she stretched herself into view and believed she was creating a sensation. So absorbed was she in the grand effort of being seen that when Valentine drew his chair a little closer to her she did not notice it. One of her hands lay on her lap, the other being on the ledge of the box supporting her chin. She returned eagerly the glances of the stalls. The hand that was in her lap felt another hand close on it. Instinctively Cuckoo turned towards Julian ready to smile. But Julian was gazing absorbed at the crowd, and half abstractedly listening to the song of the man in the huge, distorted boots. It was Valentine who held her hand. She tried to draw it away. He merely tightened his grip on it and continued sitting in silence, not even looking towards her. And as he held her hand a sense of helplessness came over Cuckoo. Even through his kid glove she could feel the burning heat of his palm, of the fingers that clutched hers with the strength of an athlete. She gazed towards him through the new black veil that was drawn over her face, and it seemed even to her limited intelligence that the man who was so brutally holding her against her will could not be the man at whom she was now looking. For Valentine, whose profile was set towards her, was pale, calm, almost languid in appearance. His blue eyes were glancing quietly over the multitude, with an air of indifferent observation. His lips were slightly parted in a sort of dawning smile, and his whole attitude was that of a man lazily at ease and taking his pleasure in a desultory mood. Yet the hand on Cuckoo's knees was vicious in its grasp. This startling and silent contradiction threw her into a complete panic, but she did not dare to say anything in protest. She sat silently trembling and drawing her lips together in growing perturbation, till Julian happened to turn towards them. Then Valentine's fingers relaxed their grasp quietly, and slipped away. At the same time he moved with an air of energy, and broke into gay conversation. His languor vanished. His blue eyes sparkled. Julian was astonished at his intense vivacity. He laughed, made jokes, became absolutely boyish.

" Why, Val, how gay you are ! " Julian said.

" Every one is gay to-night."

He was interrupted by a roar of laughter. The man in the boots was becoming immoderately whimsical. His feet seemed to have escaped from control, and to be prancing in Paradise while he looked on in Purgatory.

" Every one is gay."

As Valentine repeated the words, and the huge theatre laughed like one enormous person, Julian felt again the strange thrill of over-

mastering excitement that had shaken him on the night when he and
Valentine had leaned out of the Victoria Street window. The
strength of the Spring and of his long tended and repressed young
instincts stirred within him mightily. Scales fell from his eyes.
From the car of the balloon he gazed down, and it seemed to him
that they—Valentine, Cuckoo, and himself—were drifting over a
new country, of which all the inhabitants were young, gay, careless,
rightly irresponsible. The rows of open-mouthed, laughing faces
called to him to join in their mirth, more, to join in their lives, and
in the lives of the pirouetting hours. He moved in his chair, as if
he were impelled to get up and leave his seat. And as he moved a
voice whispered in his ear :

" Let us eat and drink for to-morrow we die."

Was it Valentine's voice? He turned round hastily, curiously
perturbed.

" Val, was that you? Did you speak to me ? "

" No."

Julian looked at Cuckoo. Her cheeks were flushed, and her eyes
shone with dancing excitement.

" Did you, Cuckoo ? "

" Not I, dearie. I say, ain't he funny to-night ? "

Then the voice must have spoken in his own brain. He listened
for it and fancied he could hear it again and again, driving him on
like a phantom fate. But the voice was in timbre like the voice of
Valentine, and he felt as if Valentine spoke with a strange insistence
and reiteration. His heart, his whole being, made answer to the
whisper.

" To-morrow we die. It is true. Ah, then, let us—let us eat and
let us drink."

The man in the boots wriggled furiously into the wings, and the
curtain rose on the ballet. Wenzel had ascended to the conductor's
platform amid loud applause. The first weary melodies of " Faust "
streamed plaintively from the orchestra, and a gravity came over the
rows of faces in the stalls. Julian's face, too, was grave, but his
excitement and his sense of his own power of youth grew as he
looked on. The old Faust appeared, heavy with the years and with
the trouble of useless thought, and Julian felt that he could sneer at
him for his venerable age. As he watched the philosopher's grandi-
loquent pantomime of gesture, like a mist there floated over him the
keen imagination of the hell of regret in which the old age, that
never used to the full its irrevocable youth, must move, and a
passion of desire to use his own youth rushed over him, as fire
rushes over a dry prairie. Even a sudden anger against Valentine
came to him, against Valentine for the protection he had given
through so many years. For had he not been protecting Julian

against joy, and does not the capacity for joy pass away with a tragic swiftness? As Faust was transformed into a youth, and the ballet danced in the market-place, Julian turned to Valentine and said :

" We will live to-night."

Valentine laughed.

" You look excited."

" I feel excited? Don't you? "

Valentine answered :

" I may presently. We mustn't stay in here all the evening."

There was a knock at the door of the box. An attendant appeared to ask their orders. Valentine spoke some words to him, and in a few minutes he brought three long drinks to the box. Julian drank his mechanically. His eyes were always on the ballet. The betrayal of poor Margaret had now been accomplished and the soldiers were returning from the wars. Beyond the wall of the garden the tramp of their feet was heard, a vision of the tops of their passing weapons was seen. The orchestra played the fragment of a march. Cuckoo sipped her brandy and soda, and gazed sometimes at the stage indifferently, often at the audience eagerly, and then at Julian. When her eyes were on Julian's face a light came into them that made her expression young, and even pure. A simplicity hovered about her lips, and a queer dawning of something that was almost refinement spoke in her attitude. But if she chanced to meet the eyes of Valentine her face was full of fear.

And now the last great scene of the pageant approached, and the two schoolboys leant forward in their stalls in a passion of greedy excitement. Julian happened to see them, and instead of smiling at their frankly lustful attitudes, with the superiority of the drilled man over the child, he was conscious of an eager sympathy with their vigour of enjoyment and of desire. His nature retrograded and became a schoolboy's nature, with the whole garden of life flowering before its feet. Suddenly there came to him the need of touching something human. He stole his arm closely round Cuckoo's waist. She glanced at him surprised. But his eyes were turned away to the stage. Valentine pushed his chair a little backwards. He was watching them, and when he saw the movement of Julian's arm, he laughed to himself. The classical Sabbath sprang into view, and it seemed to be just then that the feet of the hours first began to move in the opening-steps of their great dance of that night. Was it the magnificent Cleopatra that gave them the signal? Or did Venus herself whisper in their ears that the time for their *fête* was come at length, that the paid vagaries of the stage demanded companionship, and that the audience too must move in great processions, whirl in demon circles, rise up in heart to the clash of

cymbals, bow down before the goddesses of the night, the women
who give to modern men the modern heaven that they desire in
our days. The stage was a waving sea of scarlet, through which one
white woman floated, like a sin with pale cheeks in the midst of the
rubicund virtues. She was, perhaps, not beautiful, but she was
provocative and alluring, and her whiteness made her as voluptuous
as innocence is when it moves through the habitations of the wicked.
Julian watched her come to Faust and win him from the scarlet
dancers and from the arms of Cleopatra, and the strange rejuvena-
tion of this philosopher who had been old, and known decaying
faculties, and the flight of the heart from the warm closes of the
summer to the white and iron winter plains, filled him with sympathy.
It must be easy to use your youth after you have known the enforced
reserve of age. For age is a bitter lesson. The dance grew more
wild and rattling. The *frou-frou* of the swinging scarlet skirts filled
the great house with sound as the glitter of spangles filled it with a
shimmering light. Faust was surrounded by fluttering women
moving in complicated evolutions with a trained air of reckless
devilry. And Julian gave himself to the illusion created by the
skill of Katti Lanner, ignoring entirely the real care of the dancers,
and choosing to consider them as merely driven by wild impulse,
vagrant desires of furious motion, and the dashing gaiety of keen
sensual sensation. They danced to fire a real Faust, and he was
Faust for the moment. His arm closed more firmly round the waist
of Cuckoo, and he could feel the throbbing of her heart against the
palm of his hand. He did not look at her, and so he did not see the
dawning anxiety with which she was beginning furtively to regard
him. Entirely engrossed with the stage spectacle, the movement of his
arm had been entirely mechanical, prompted by the hardening
pressure of excitement in his mind. If he had actually crushed
Cuckoo and hurt her he would have been unconscious that he was
doing it.

And Valentine all this time leaned back in his chair, that stood
in the shadow of the box, and looked at the enlaced figures before
him with an unvarying smile.

Contrast and surprise are the essence of the successful " spectacle."
Just as the scarlet dervish whirl was at its height the character of
the music changed, slackened, softened, died from the angrily sensuous
into an ethereal delicacy. The stage filled with clouds that faded in
golden light, and a huge and glittering stairway rose towards the
painted sky. On either side of it hung in the blue ether guardian
angels with outstretched wings, and between their attentive ranks
stood the radiant figure of the purified Margaret, at whose white feet
the red crowd of women, even the majestic Cleopatra and pale
voluptuous Venus, sank abashed. Harps sounded frostily. suggesting

that crystal heaven of St. John, in which the beauties we know in nature are ousted by unbreathing jewels, the lifeless pearl and chrysolite. The air filled with thin and wintry light, that deepened, and began to glow, through lemon to amber and to rose. The angels swam in it, and then the huge stairway leading up to heaven shone with the violence of a gigantic star. Faust fell in repentance before the girl he had ruined and failed to ruin, the girl who bent as if to bless him upon this fiery ascent to heaven. And Julian, absorbed, devoured the wide and glowing scene with his eyes, which were attracted especially by the living flames that were half veiled and half revealed beneath the feet of Margaret. The music of the orchestra rippled faintly, and then it seemed to Julian that, as if in answer, there rippled up from the golden stairs and from the hidden company of flames, that faint, thin riband of shadowy fire which had already so strangely been with him in the dawn and in the dusk. It came from beneath the pausing feet of the girl who blessed Faust, and trembled upwards slowly above her glittering hair. Julian felt a burning sensation at his heart, as if the tiny fire found its way there. He turned round sharply, withdrawing his arm from Cuckoo's waist with an abruptness that startled her.

"Valentine!" he exclaimed, in a whisper, "There; now you see it."

Valentine leaned to him.

"See what?"

"The flame. It's no fancy. It's no chimera. Look, it is mounting up behind Margaret. Watch it, Valentine, and tell me what it is."

"I see nothing."

Julian stared into his eyes, as if to make certain that he really spoke the truth. Then Valentine asked of Cuckoo:

"Miss Bright, can you see this flame of which Julian speaks?"

Cuckoo answered, with the roughness that always came to her in the company of alarm:

"Not I. There ain't nothing, no more than there was that day when I had the coffee."

She added to Julian, reproachfully:

"You've been drinkin'. Now, dearie, you have."

Suddenly his two companions became intolerable to Julian. He thought them stupid, boorish, dense, devoid of the senses of common humanity, not to see what he saw, not to feel as he felt—that this vague flame had a meaning and a message not yet interpreted, perhaps not even remotely divined. With an angry exclamation he sprang to his feet, turning once more to the stage. And as the curtain fell, he distinctly saw the flame glowing, like a long and curiously shaped star above the head of Margaret.

L

And this man and woman would not see it! A sudden enmity to them both came to him in that moment. He abruptly opened the door of the box, and went out without another word to either of them. Cuckoo's voice, shrilly calling to him to stop, did not affect his resolution and desire to escape from them if only for a moment.

Out in the corridor at the back of the dress circle people were beginning to circulate, relieved from the tension of examining the ballet. Julian was instantly swallowed up in a noisy crowd, hot, flushed, loud-voiced, bright-eyed. Masses of excited young men lounged to and fro, smoking cigarettes, and making fervent remarks upon the gaily-dressed women, who glided among them observantly. From the adjoining bar rose the music of popping corks and flowing liquids. The barmaids were besieged. Clouds of smoke hung in the air, and the heat was terrific. Julian felt it clinging to him as if with human arms as he slowly walked over the thick carpet, glancing about him. Humanity touched him on every side. At one moment an elderly woman, with yellow hair and a fat lined face, enveloped him in her skirts of scarlet and black striped silk. The black chiffon that swept about her neck and heaving shoulders fluttered against his face. Her high-heeled boots trod on his. He seemed one with her. Then she had vanished, and instantly he was in the arms of a huge racing man, who wore gigantic pink pearls in his shirt front, and bellowed the latest slang to a thin and dissipated companion. It seemed to Julian that he was kicked like a football from one life to another, and that from each life he drew away something as he bounded from it, the fragment of a thought, the thrill of a desire, the indrawn breath of a hope. Like a machine that winds in threads of various coloured silks, he wound in threads from the various coloured hearts about him—red, white, coarse and fine. And, half-unconsciously, was he not weaving them into a fabric? Never before had he understood the meaning of a crowd, that strange congregation of passions and of fates which speaks in movements and is melodious in attitudes, which quarrels in all its parts, silently, yet is swayed through and through by large impulses, and has an intellect far more keen and assertively critical than the intellect of any one person in it. And now, when Julian began to feel the meaning of this surging mob of men and women, the hours danced, and he and all the crowd danced with them. And the music that accompanied and directed the feet through the figures of that night's quadrille was the music of words and of laughter, of hissing enticements and of whispered replies. Irresistible was the performance of the hours and of the crowd that lived in them. Julian knew it when the dance began, marvelled at it for a little when the dance was ended. There was contagion in the air, furtive, but strong as the contagion of cholera—the contagion of human creatures gathered together in the night. Only the youth who dwells—like Will-o'-the-Mill—for ever by the lonely stream in the lonely mountain valley escapes it entirely. Aged saints look backward on their lives, and remember at least one night when it seized them in its embrace; and even the purest woman, through its spell, has caught sight of the vision behind the veil of our civilisation, and although she has shrunk from it, has had a moment of wonder and of interest, never quite effaced from her memory.

On every side the Oxford and Cambridge boys laughed and shouted, pushed and elbowed. They had begun to cast off restraint, and the god that is rowdy on a rowdy throne compelled them to their annual obeisance at his feet. Some of them moved along singing, and interrupting their song with shouts. Friends, when they met in the crowd, yelled shrill recognitions at each other, and nicknames sang in the air like noisy birds. Rows of men linked arms and, striding forward, compelled the throng to yield them difficult passage, swinging this way and that to make their progress more comprehensive. The attendants, standing by the wall like giants, calmly smiled on the growing uproar, into which they darted now and then with a sudden frenzy of dutiful agility, to eject some rude wit who had transgressed their code of propriety. The very spirit of lusty youth was in this crowd of hot, careless, blatant, roving youths, mad to find themselves away from the cool and grey Oxford towers, and from the vacant banks of the Cam, in passionate Leicester Square, fired by the scarlet ballet, and the thunder of the orchestra, and the sight of smart women. Sudden emancipation is the most flaming torch to human passions that exists in the world. It flared through all that mob, urging it to conflagration, to the flames that burst up in hearts that are fresh and ardent, and that so curiously confuse joy with wickedness.

Flames! flames! The word ran in Julian's mind, and in his breast flames surely burned that night, for, when he suddenly ran against Valentine and Cuckoo in the throng, he caught Valentine by the arm, and said:

" Val, you were right just now. There was no flame, there could have been no flame where Margaret stood. She was too pure. What can fire have to do with snow? Cuckoo, I was a fool. Catch hold of my arm."

He pulled her arm roughly through his, never noticing how pale the girl's face was, how horror-stricken were her eyes. He wanted to bathe himself, and her, and Valentine, in this crowd that influenced him and that he helped to influence. He felt as the diver feels, who, when he plunges, has a sacred passion for the depths. There are people who have an ardour for going down comparable to the ardour felt by those who mount. To-night such an ardour took hold of Julian.

Valentine fell in with it, seeing the humour of his friend, and Cuckoo, prisoned between the two men, did not attempt to resist them. As they moved on Valentine said, in a voice he made loud that it might be heard :

"Now you feel the strength of the Spring, Julian. Is it not better than all my teachings of ascetism ? "

" Yes, by —— it is."

And as he made that answer, Julian, for the first time, forgot to look up to Valentine, and felt a splendid equality with him, the equality that men of the same age and temper feel when they are bent on the same pursuit. How can one of two Bacchanals stoop in adoration of the other, when both are bounding in the procession of Silenus ? Valentine fell from his pedestal and became a comrade instead of a god. He was no longer the chaperon of the dancing hours but their partner. And a new fire shone in his blue eyes, an unaccustomed red ran over his cheeks, as he heard Julian's answer to his question. From that moment he ceased to play what, it seemed, had been but a part, the empty ivory *rôle* of saint. For Julian was no longer conscious or observant of him, no longer able to wonder at his abrupt transformation. In a flash he cast off his habitual restraint, and passed from the reserve of thought to the rowdyism of act.

He chattered unceasingly, dressing his English in all the slang embroidery of the day. He laughed and chaffed, exchanged repartees with the flowing multitude through which they passed, stopped to speak to the flaunting women and loaded them with extravagant compliments, elbowed loungers out of his way, and made the most personal remarks on those around him. Two men went by, and one of them exclaimed, with a surprised glance at Valentine:

" I'm damned ! Why, there goes the Saint of Victoria Street."

" Saint ! " said the other, " I should think devil the more appropriate name. That chap looks up to anything."

" Ah well, when a saint turns sinner——" answered the first speaker with a laugh.

Valentine heard the words, and burst into a roar of laughter. He drew Cuckoo to the left and Julian followed. They passed under an archway into the bar, which was crowded with men, drinking and talking at the tops of their voices. Valentine called for drinks in a voice so loud and authoritative that the barmaid hurried to serve him, deserting other customers, who protested vainly. He forced Cuckoo to drink, and Julian needed no urging. Clinking glasses noisily with them he gave as a toast :

" To the dance of the hours ! "

These words, uttered with almost strident force, attracted attention even amid the violent hubbub that was raging, and several young men pressed round Valentine as he stood with his back against the counter of the bar. They raised their glasses, too, half in ridicule, and shouting in chorus :
" To the dance of the hours ! " drained them to this toast, which they could not comprehend. Valentine dashed his glass down. It broke and was trodden under foot. The barmaid protested. He threw her a sovereign. The young men gathered round, broke theirs in imitation, and Julian, snatching Cuckoo's from her, flung it away. As he did so, Valentine thrust another, filled with champagne, into her hand, and again cried out the toast.
" What the deuce does he mean by it ? " one youth called out. " The dance of the hours ; what's that ? "
" The dance of the hours ! The dance of the hours ! " echoed other voices, and glasses were drained wildly. There was something exciting in the mere sound of the words that seemed to set brains jigging, and feet moving, and the world spinning and bowing. For if Time itself danced what could the most Puritan human being do but dance with it ? Seeing the crowd round Valentine, men who were drinking at the other end of the bar joined it, and the toast passed quickly from mouth to mouth. Uttered by every variety of voice, with every variety of accent, it filled the stifling atmosphere, and tickled many an empty brain, like the catch-word political that can set a nation behind one astute wire-puller. Boys yelled it, men murmured it, and an elderly woman in a plush gown and yellow feathers screamed it out in a piercing soprano that would have put many a trumpet blast to shame. Glasses were emptied and filled again in its honour. Yet nobody knew what it meant, and apparently nobody cared, except the Oxford boy, who had already expressed his desire to be better informed on the subject. He had gradually edged his way through the throng until he was close to Valentine, at whom he gazed with a sort of tipsy reverence.
" I say, you chap," he cried. " What are we drinking to—eh ? What the devil's the dance of the hours ? "
Valentine brought his glass down on the counter.
" What is it ? " he exclaimed. " Why, the greatest dance in the world, the dance that youth sends out the invitations for, and women live for, and old men die with longing for. We set the hours dancing in the night, we—all who are gay and careless, who love life in the greatest way, and who laugh at death, and who aren't afraid of the devil. The devil's only a bogey to frighten old women and children. What do the hours care for him ? Not a snap. It's only cowards who fear him. Brave men do what they will, and when the hours dance they dance with them, and drink with them all the

night through. Who says there'll be another morning? I don't believe it. Curse the sunshine. Give me the night and the dancing hours!"

The youth gave a yell, which was echoed by some of his rowdy companions, and by the two little schoolboys who had joined the throng in a frenzy of childish excitement, which they thought manly.

"The dancing hours! The dancing hours!" they cried, and one who was with a girl, suddenly caught her round the waist and broke into wild steps. Others joined in. The confusion became tremendous. Glasses were knocked over. Whiskies and sodas were poured out in libations upon the carpet. The protests of the barmaids were unheeded or unheard. Julian whirled Cuckoo into the throng, and Valentine, snapping his long white fingers like castanets, stamped his feet as if to the measure of a wild music. Against the wall some loungers looked on in contemptuous amusement, but by far the greater number of men present were young and eager for any absurdity, and not a few were half tipsy. These ardently welcomed anything in the nature of a row, and the romp became general and noisy. Men danced awkwardly with one another, roaring the latest music-hall tunes at the pitch of their voices. The women screamed with laughter, or giggled piercingly as they were banged and trodden on in the tumult. The noise penetrating to the promenade, drew the attention of the audience, many of whom hurried to see what was going on, and the block round the archways quickly became impenetrable. One or two of the gigantic chuckers-out forced their way into the throng and seized the dancers nearest to them, but they were entirely unable to stay the ridiculous impulse which impelled this mob of young human beings to capering and yelling. Indeed they merely increased the scuffle, which rapidly developed towards a free fight. Hats were knocked off, dresses were torn. The women got frightened and began to scream. The men swore, and some lost their tempers and struck out right and left. Valentine watched the scene with laughing eyes as if he enjoyed it. Especially he watched Julian, who, with scarlet face and sparkling eyes, still forced Cuckoo round and round in the midst of the tumult. Cuckoo was white, and seemed to be half fainting. Her head rested helplessly against Julian's shoulder, and her eyes stared at him as if fascinated. Her dress was torn, and her black veil hung all awry. If she danced with the hours it was without joy or desire.

But suddenly police appeared. The dancers, abruptly realising that a joke was dying in a disaster, ceased to prance. Some violently assumed airs of indifference and of alarming respectability. Many sinuously wound their way out to the promenade. A few, who had completely lost their heads, hustled the police, and were promptly taken into custody. Julian would have been among these had it not been for the intervention of Valentine, who caught him by the shoulder, and drew him and Cuckoo away.

" No, you mustn't end to-night in a cell," he said in Julian's ear. " The dancing hours want you still. Julian, you are only beginning your real life to-night."

Julian, like a man in an excited dream, followed Valentine to the bottom of the broad stairs, on, through the blooming masses of flowers, to the entrance. Two or three cabs were waiting. Valentine put Cuckoo into one. She had not spoken a word, and was trembling as if with fear.

" Get in, Julian."

Julian obeyed, and Valentine, standing on the pavement, leaned forward and whispered to him :

" Take her home, Julian."

Suddenly Julian shouted Cuckoo's address to the cabman hoarsely. The cab drove away.

Valentine walked slowly towards Piccadilly Circus, whistling softly, " I want you, my honey, yes, I do."

BOOK III—THE LADY OF THE FEATHERS

CHAPTER I

THE LADY OF THE FEATHERS WEEPS

THE thin afternoon light of an indefinite spring day shone over the Marylebone Road. A heavy warmth was in the air, and the weather was peculiarly windless, but the sun only shone fitfully, and the street looked sulky. The faces of the passers-by were hot and weary. Women trailed along under the weight of their parcels, and men returned from work grimmer than usual, and wondering almost with a fretfulness of passion why they were born predestined to toil. The cabmen about Baker Street Station dozed with nodding heads upon their perches, and the omnibus conductors forgot to chaff, and collected their tolls with a mechanical deliberation. At the crossings the policemen, helpless in their uniforms of the winter, became dictatorial more readily than on cooler days. Some sorts of weather incline every one to temper or to depression. The day after the boat-race lay under a malign spell. It seemed to feel all the weariness of reaction, and to fold all men and women in the embrace of its lassitude and heavy hopelessness.

At number 400, Jessie whined pitifully in her basket, and her arched back quivered perpetually as her minute body expanded and contracted in the effort of breathing. Her beady eyes were open and fixed furtively upon her mistress, as if in inquiry or alarm, and her whole soul was whirling in a turmoil set in motion by the first slap she had ever received in gravity at the hands of Cuckoo. Jessie's inner nature was stung by that slap. It knocked her world over like a doll hit by a child. Her universe lay prone upon its back.

And Cuckoo's? She was sitting in the one armchair with her thin hands folded in her lap. She wore the black dress given to her by Julian, but she did not look prepared to go out, for her hair was standing up over her head in violent disorder, her cheeks were haggard and unwashed, and her boots—still muddy from the previous night's promenading—stood in a corner near the grate in the first position, as if directed by a dancing mistress. Cuckoo was neither reading nor working. She was simply staring straight before her, without definite expression. Her face indeed wore a quite singularly blank look and her mouth was slightly open. Her feet, stuck out before her, rested on the edge of the fender, shoeless, and both her general appearance and attitude betokened a complete absence of self-consciousness, and that lack of expectation of any immediate event which is often dubbed stupidity. The lady of the feathers sitting in the horsehair-covered chair in the cheap sitting-room with the folding doors, looked indeed stupid, pale, and heavy. Fatigue lay in the shadows of her eyes, but something more than ordinary fatigue hovered round her parted lips and spoke in her posture. A dull weariness, in which the mind took part with the body, held her in numbing captivity. She had only broken through it in some hours to repulse the anxious effort of Jessie to scramble into the nest of her lap. That slap given, she had again relapsed without a struggle into this waking sleep.

The sun came out with a sudden violence, and an organ began to play a frisky tune in the street. Jessie whined and whimpered, formed her mouth into the shape of an O and, throwing up her head, emitted a vague and smothered howl. Below stairs, Mrs. Brigg, who was afflicted with a complaint that prompted her to perpetual anxious movement, laboured about the kitchen doing nothing in particular among her pots and pans. The occasional clatter of them mingled with the sound of the organ, and with the suffocated note of Jessie, in a depressing symphony. The sun went in again, and some dust, stirred into motion by a passing omnibus, floated in through the half-open window and settled in a light film upon the photograph of Marr. Presently the organ moved away, and faded gradually in pert tunes down the street. Jessie's nervous system, no longer played upon, ceased to spend its pain in sound, and a London silence fell round the little room. Then, at length, Cuckoo shifted in her chair, stretched her hands in her lap, and sat up slowly. The inward expression had not faded from her eyes yet, for, leaning forward, she still stared blankly before her, looking, as it seemed, straight at Marr's photograph. Gradually she woke to a consciousness of what she was looking at, and putting up one hand she took the photograph from its place, laid it in her lap, and, bending down, gazed at it long and earnestly. Then she shook her head as if puzzled.

"I don't know," she murmured, "I don't know."

Encouraged by the sound of her mistress's voice, Jessie stepped from her basket and gingerly approached, snuffling round Cuckoo's feet, and wriggling her body in token of anxious humility. Cuckoo picked her up and stroked her mechanically, but still with her eyes on the photograph. Two tears swam in them. She dashed the photograph down. It lay on the carpet, and was still there when a knock at the door was succeeded by the entrance of Julian.

He too looked pale and rather weary, but excited.

" Cuckoo," he said.

She sat still in the chair looking at him.

" Well ? " she said, and closed her lips tightly.

He came a step or two forward into the little room, and put his hat and stick down on the table.

" You expected me to come, didn't you ? "

" I don't know as I did."

Her eyes were on Jessie now, and she stroked the little dog's back steadily up and down, alternately smoothing and ruffling its short coat. Julian came over and stood by the mantelpiece.

" I told you I should come."

" Did you ? "

" Don't you remember ? "

She shifted round in the chair till he could only see her shoulder, and the side of her head and neck, on which the loose hair was tumbling in ugly confusion. Sitting thus she threw back at him the sentence :

" I don't want to remember nothing. I don't want to remember."

Julian stood hesitating. He glanced at Cuckoo's hair and at the back of her thin hand moving to and fro above the little contented dog.

" Why not ? " he said.

At first she made no answer to this question, and seemed as if she had not heard it, but presently it appeared that her silence had been caused by the effect of consideration, for at length she said, still retaining her aloof attitude :

" I don't want to remember, because it's like a beastly dream, and when I remember I know it ain't a dream."

Julian said nothing, and suddenly Cuckoo turned round to him, and took her hand from Jessie's back.

" I say. You were mad last night. Now, weren't you ? "

The words came from her almost pleadingly, and her eyes rested on Julian's insistently, as if demanding an affirmative.

" He'd made you mad," she continued.

" He," said Julian ; " who ? "

" Your friend."

"Valentine ! He had nothing to do with it."

"It was all his doing."

Her voice grew shrill with feeling.

"He's a devil," she said. " I hate him. I hate him worse than I hate that copper west side of Regent Street. And I hate you too, yes I do, to-day."

The tears gathered in her eyes and began to fall, tears of rage and shame and regret, tears of one who had lost a great possession. Julian looked embarrassed and pained, almost guilty too. He put out his hand and tried to take Cuckoo's. But she drew hers away and went on crying. She spoke again with vehemence.

"I told you what I wanted you to be, yes, I did," she exclaimed. Yes, I told you. You said you only come here to talk to me."

"It was true."

"No it wasn't. You're just like all the others. And I did so want to have a pal. I've never had one."

With the words the sense of her desolation seemed to strike her with stunning force. She leaned her head against the back of the chair, and cried bitterly, catching at the horsehair with violent hands, as if she longed to hurt something, to revenge her loss even upon an object without power of feeling. Julian sprang up and went over to the window. He looked out on to the road and watched the people moving by in the fitful sunshine beyond the dirty railings. That day, he, too, was in a tumult. He felt like a monk who had suddenly thrown off his habit, broken his vows and come forth into the world. The cell and the cloister were left behind, were things to be forgotten, with the grating of the confessional and the dim routine of service and of asceticism. He had been borne on by the wave of a brilliant, a violent hour, away from them. Let the angelus bell ring ; he no longer heard it. Let the drone of prayers and praises rise in a monotonous music by day and by night; he no longer had the will to heed them. For there was another music in his ears. Soon it would be in his heart. Imagine a Trappist suddenly transported from the desert of his long silence to a gay *plage* on which a brass band was playing. Julian was that Trappist in mind. And though he knew Cuckoo was sobbing at his back, and though his heart held a sense of pity for her trouble, yet he heard her grief with a strange cruelty, at which he wondered, without being able to soften it. That afternoon it seemed to him useless for anybody to cry. No grief was quite worth tears. The violence of life was present with him, gave him light and blinded him at the same time. He found delight in the thought of violence, because it held action in its grasp. Even cruelty was worth something. Was he cruel to Cuckoo ?

He turned from the window and looked at her, with the observa-

tion of a nature not generally his own. He noted the desolation of
her hair, and he noted, too, that she wore the gown he had given
to her. Would she have put it on if she had hated him as she said
she did ? Somehow it scarcely seemed to suit her to-day. It looked
draggled, and as if it had been up all night, he thought. The black
back of it heaved as Cuckoo sobbed, like a little black wave. Was the
eternal movement of the sea caused by some horrible, inward grief
which, though secret, must come thus to the eye of God and of the
world ? Julian found himself wondering in an unreasonable abstraction as he contemplated the crying girl. Then suddenly his mind
swerved to more normal paths ; he was seized by the natural feeling
of a man who has made a woman weep, and had the impulse to
comfort.

"Don't cry, Cuckoo," he said, coming over to her and sitting on
the edge of her chair. "You must not. Let us say I was mad last
night. Perhaps I was. Men are often mad surely. To-day I'm
sane, and I want you to forgive me."

He put his arm round her shoulder. She glanced up at him.
Then, with the odd penetration that so often gilds female ignorance
till it dazzles and distracts, she said quickly :

"You don't mean what you say ; you don't really care."

Julian was taken aback by her sharpness, and by the self-revelation
that immediately stabbed him.

"You mustn't say that," he began. But she stopped him on the
instant.

"You don't care ; you think it's nothing. So it ought to be to
me, I know."

That had perhaps actually been his thought, the thought of a
mind unimaginative to-day, because deadened by the excitement of
action. But if it was his thought he hastened to deny it.

"You know I don't think of you in that way," he said.

"You will now. You do."

That was the scourge that had lashed her all through this weary
day of miserable reaction, that now stung her to a passion that was
like the passion of purity. As she made this statement there was a
question in her eyes, but it was a question of despair, that scarcely
even asked for the negative which Julian hastened to give. He was
both perplexed and troubled by the unexpected violence of her
emotion, and blamed himself as the cause. But though he blamed
himself, his regret for what was irrevocable had none of the poignancy
of Cuckoo's. For a long time he had gloried in living in a cloister
with Valentine. Now he had left the cloister, he did not look back
to it with the curious pathos which so often gathers like moss upon
even a dull and vacant past. He did not, for the moment, look back
at all. Action had lifted scales from his eyes, had stirred the youth

in him, had stung him as if with bright fire, and given him, at a breath, a thousand thoughts, visions, curiosities. A sense of power came to him. He did not ask whether the power made for evil or for good. Simply he was inclined to glory in it, as a man glories in his recovered strength when he wakes from a long sleep following fatigue. Cuckoo, with feeble hands, seemed tugging to hold back this power, with feeble voice seemed crying against it as a deadly thing. And Julian, though he strove to console her, scarcely sympathised with her fully. He could not, if he would, be quite unhappy to-day. Only in Cuckoo's grief he began to read a curious legend. In her tears there was a passion, in her anger a vehemence that could only spring from the depths of a nature. Julian began to suspect that through all her sins and degradations this girl, his lady of the feathers, had managed to keep shut one door though all the others had been ruthlessly opened. And beyond this door was surely that holy of holies, an unspoiled woman's heart? From what other dwelling could rush forth such a passion for a man's respect, such a fury to be rightly and chivalrously considered. As he half vaguely realised something of the true position of Cuckoo and of himself, Julian felt stirred by the wonder of life, in which such strange blossoms flower out of the very dust. He looked at Cuckoo with new eyes. She looked back at him with the old ones of a girl who loves.

As he looked she stopped crying. Perhaps the sudden understanding in his gaze thrilled her. He put out his hand to touch hers, and again repeated his negative, but this time with greater conviction.

"I do not think of you in that way. I never shall," he said.

Her face was still full of doubt and thin with anxiety. She was not reassured, that seemed apparent; for in her ignorance she had a strange knowledge of life, and especially a strange intuition which guided her instincts as to the instinctive proceedings of men.

"They always do," she murmured. "Why should you be different?"

"All men aren't alike," he said, pretending to laugh at her.

"Yes, in some things though," she contradicted. "They all think dirt of you for doing what they want."

Seeing how unsatisfied she was, and how restlessly her anxiety paced up and down, Julian resolved on more plain speaking.

"Look here, Cuckoo," he said, and his voice had never sounded more boyish, "last night I was drunk. Last night I woke up, and I'd been asleep for years."

"Eh?" she interrupted, looking puzzled, but he went on:

"I was emancipated, and I was mad. Mind, I didn't mean to do you any wrong, but if you have thought of me in a different way,

I'm sorry. Tell me what you want me to be to you, and in future I'll be it."

Hope and eagerness sprang up in her eyes then.

" I say," she began.

" Yes."

" You promise."

" I promise."

The dull blood rose in her tired face.

" I want just a—just a friend," she said, as if almost ashamed.

Julian smiled.

" Not a lover," he said, with a fleeting air of gallantry. She shrank visibly from the word, and hurriedly went on :

" Not I. I've had too much of love." The last word was spoken with a violence of contempt. " I want a man as likes me, just really likes me, as he might another man. See ? "

" And you'll not love him ? "

His eyes searched hers with a gaiety of inquiry that was almost laughter. Cuckoo looked away.

" I'll not love him either," she said steadily. " I'll just like him too."

Seeing her earnestness and obvious emotion, Julian dropped his gently quizzing manner, and became earnest, too, in his degree.

" Then it's a bargain," he said. " You and I are to like each other thoroughly, never anything more, never anything less. Like two men, eh ? "

She began at last to look relieved and happier.

" Yes, like that," she said. " Ain't it—ain't it truer than the other thing ? There's something beastly about love, that's what I always think."

And she spoke with the sincerest conviction. When Julian left her that day, he shook hands with her by the door ; she stood after he had done it as if still half expectant.

" There's a man's good-bye to a man," he said. " Better sort of thing than a man's good-bye to a woman, isn't it ? "

" Rather ! " she said hastily, and moved back into the sitting-room. She stepped on something, and bent down to pick it up. It was Marr's photograph.

" What's that ? " Julian asked.

" Nothing," she said, concealing it. She had a foolish fancy that even the photograph of the creature she had feared and hated might spoil that good-bye of theirs. Yet even as it was, when Julian had gone she still seemed unsatisfied.

She was a woman after all, and woman is most feminine in her farewells.

CHAPTER II

VALENTINE SINGS

WHEN Valentine heard of the scene in Marylebone Road he smiled.

"How extraordinary women are," he said. "A man might give his life to them, I suppose, yet never understand them."

"It would be rather jolly—making that gift, I mean," said Julian.

"You think so? Since last night."

"I want to talk to you about that. Valentine, d'you blame me?"

"Not a bit."

"Only wonder at me?"

"I don't even say that."

"No, but of course you must wonder at me."

Julian spoke almost wistfully, and as if he wanted Valentine to sweep away the suggestion. Last night they had been comrades. To-day, in the light and in the calm of afternoon, Valentine seemed much more remote, and Julian felt for the first time a sense of degradation. He was uneasily conscious that he might have fallen in Valentine's esteem. But Valentine reassured him.

"I don't wonder at you either, Julian, I simply envy you, and metaphorically sit at your feet."

"That's absurd."

"Not quite; and I may not always be sitting there, for I believe I have really got a little bit of your soul. Last night I seemed to feel it stirring within me, and I liked its personality."

"You did seem different last night," Julian said, looking at Valentine with a keen interest. "Can it be possible that those sittings of ours have really had any effect?"

"On me they have, not on you. You haven't caught my coldness, but I have gained something of your warmth. Doesn't that perhaps show that mine was, after all, the wrong nature?"

"I don't know," Julian said doubtfully, "you look the same."

"Do I? Exactly?"

Valentine spoke with a sort of whimsical defiance, as if almost daring Julian to answer, yes. And Julian, too, seemed suddenly doubtful whether he had stated what was the fact. He looked closely at Valentine.

"Do you think your face has changed? Do you mean to say that?" he asked.

"I only fancied there might be a little more humanity in it, that was all."

"Once or twice I have thought I noticed something," Julian said, still doubtfully, "but I believe it's imagination. It doesn't stay."

"When it does, I suppose I shall be able thoroughly to appreciate all your temptations. Don't you begin to think now it's good to have them?"

"I don't know," Julian said. But he was conscious that there had come a change in his attitude of mind towards temptation. Some men glory in resisting temptation, others in yielding to it. Hitherto Julian had not been able to range himself in either of those two opposed camps. He had merely hated his faculty for being tempted. Did he entirely hate it now? He could not say so to himself, whatever he might say to others, but something kept him from making confession of the truth to Valentine. So he professed ignorance of his own exact state of feeling; really, had he analysed his reticence, it sprang from a fine desire to give forth no breath that might tarnish the clear mirror of Valentine's nature. He would not admit a change that might make his friend again fall into the absurd dissatisfaction which he had combated on the night of their first sitting in the tent-room. While they talked the afternoon had fallen into a creeping twilight. In the twilight the front-door bell rang.

"Some late visitor entreating entrance at my chamber door," Valentine said, quoting Poe. "It must be the doctor."

Julian reddened suddenly.

"I hope not," he said.

"What?" Valentine cried. "You don't want our little doctor?"

"Somehow not—to-day."

The door opened and Dr. Levillier entered. Valentine greeted him warmly. They had not met since the night of the affray with the mastiffs. In Julian's manner there was a touch of awkwardness as he shook hands with the doctor. Levillier did not seem to notice it. He looked very tired and rather depressed.

"Cresswell," he said, "I have come to you for a tonic."

"Doctor coming to patient!"

"Doctors take medicine oftener than you may suppose. I'm in

bad spirits to-day. I've been trying to cure too many people lately
It's hard work."

" It must be. Sit down and forget. Imagine the world beautifully incurable and your occupation consequently gone."

The doctor sat down, saying :

" My imagination stops short at that feat."

He kept silence for a moment, then he said :

" You know what I want."

" No," Valentine answered. " But I'll do anything. You know
that."

" I want your music."

Valentine suddenly became unresponsive. He didn't speak at
first, and both Julian and the doctor glanced at him in some
surprise.

" Oh, you want me to be David to your Saul," he said at length.

" Yes."

" Do, Val," said Julian. " I should like it too."

Valentine, who was sitting near the doctor, looked down thoughtfully on the carpet.

" I'm not in the mood to-day," he said slowly.

" You are always in the mood enough to cheer and rest me,'
Levillier said.

He had driven all the way from Harley Street for his medicine,
and it was obvious that he meant to have it. But Valentine still
hesitated, and a certain slight confusion became noticeable in his
manner. Moving the toe of his right boot to and fro, following the
pattern of the carpet, he glanced sideways at the doctor, and an odd
smile curved his lips.

" Doctor," he said, " d'you believe that talents can die in us while
we ourselves live ? "

" That's a strange question."

" It's waiting an answer."

" Well, my answer is : No, not wholly, unless through the approach
of old age, or the development of madness."

" I'm neither old nor mad."

Levillier and Julian both looked at Valentine with some amazement.

" Are you talking about yourself ? " the doctor asked.

" Certainly."

" Why ? What talent is dead in you ? "

" My talent for music. Do you know that for the last few days
I've been able neither to sing nor play ? "

" Val, you're joking," exclaimed Julian.

" I am certainly not," he answered, and quite gravely. " I am
simply stating a fact."

Dr. Levillier seemed unable to appreciate that he was speaking seriously.

"I have come all this way to hear you sing," he said. "I have never asked you in vain yet."

"Is it my fault if you ask me in vain now?"

Valentine looked him in the face, and spoke with a complete sincerity. The doctor returned the glance, as he sometimes returned the glance of a patient, very directly, with a clear and simple gravity. Having done this he felt completely puzzled.

"The talent for music has died in you?" he asked.

"Entirely. I can do nothing with my piano. I have even locked it."

As he spoke he went over to it and pulled at the lid to show them that he was speaking the truth.

"Where's the key?" asked the doctor.

"Here," said Valentine, producing it from his pocket.

"Give it to me," said the doctor.

Valentine did so, and the doctor quietly opened the piano, drew up the music-stool, and signed to Valentine to sit down.

"If you mean what you say the explanation must simply be that you are suffering from some form of hysteria," he said, rather authoritatively. "Now sing me something. No, I won't let you off."

Valentine, sitting on the stool, extended his hands and laid the tips of his long fingers upon the keys, but without sounding them.

"You insist on my trying to sing?" he asked.

"I do."

"I warn you, Doctor, you will be sorry if I do. My voice is quite out of order."

"No matter."

"Go on, Val," cried Julian, from his arm-chair. "Anybody would think you were a young lady."

Valentine bent his head, with a quick gesture of abnegation.

"As you will," he said.

He struck his hand down upon the keys as he spoke. That was the strangest prelude ever heard. In their different ways Dr. Levillier and Julian were both intensely fond of music, both quickly stirred by it when it was good music, not merely classical, but extravagant, violent, and in any way interesting. Each of them had heard Valentine play, not once only, but a hundred times. They knew not simply his large *répertoire* of pieces and songs through and through, but also the peculiar and characteristic progressions of his improvisations, the ornaments he most delighted in, the wildness of his melancholy, the phantasy of his gaieties: and they knew every tone of his voice, which expressed with an exquisite realism the temperament of his soul. But now, as Valentine's hands powerfully struck the keys, they both started and exchanged an involuntary glance of keen surprise. The first few bars gave the lie to Valentine's assertion that he could no longer play. A cataract of notes streamed from beneath his fingers, and of notes so curiously combined, or following each other in such a fantastic array, that they seemed arranged in the musical pattern by an intelligence of the strangest order. It is often easy for a cultivated ear to detect whether a given composition has sprung from the brain of a Frenchman, a German, a Hungarian, a Russian. The wildness of Bohemia, too, may be identified, or the vague sorrow of that northern melody which seems an echo of voices heard amid the fiords, or in pale valleys near the farthest Cape of Europe. And then there is that large and lofty music of the stars and the spheres, of the mightiest passions and of the deepest imaginings, that is of no definite country, but seems to be of its own power and beauty, and not of the brain and heart of any one man. It exists for eternity, and its creator can only wonder and worship before it, far from conceit as God was when He said, "Let there be light." Such music, too, is recognised on the instant by the men who have loved and studied the secrets of the most divine of the arts, for profound genius can utter itself as easily in five notes as in fifty. But the prelude now played by Valentine was neither the great music that is of all time and of all countries, nor the music that is of any one country. It was not even distinctively northern or southern in character, impregnated with the mystery of the tuneless, wonderful East, or with the peculiar homeliness that stirs western hearts. Both the doctor and Julian felt, as they listened, that it was music without an earthly home, without location, devoid of that sense of relation to humanity which links the greatness of the arts to the smallness of those who follow them. Eccentric the music was, but the eccentricity of it seemed almost inhuman, so unmannerly as to be beyond the range of the most uncouth man, in advance of the invention of any mind however coarse and criminal. That was the atmosphere of this prelude, excessive, unutterable, crude, sombre vulgarity of a detached and remote kind. As Levillier listened to it amazed, he found that he did not instinctively connect the vulgarity with any human traits, or translate the notes into acts within his experience. He was simply conscious of being brought to the verge of some sphere in which the sordidness attained by our race would be sneered at as delicacy, in which our lowest grovellings of the pigsty would be as lofty flights through the skies. And the hideous eccentricity of the music, its wanton desolation, deepened until both Levillier and Julian were pale under its spell, shrank from its ardent, its merciless and lambent sarcasm against all things refined or beautiful. The prelude was as fire and sword, as plague and famine, as plunder and war, as all instruments that lay waste and that wound, a destroying angel before whose breath the first-born withered and the very sun shrivelled into a heap of grey ashes.

As Dr. Levillier leaned forward, moved by an irresistible impulse, and stretched out his hand to enforce silence from this blare of deplorable melody, Valentine looked up at him, into his eyes, and began to sing. The doctor's movement was arrested, his hand dropped to his side, he remained tense, frigid, his eyes fastened on Valentine's like a man mesmerised. At first he knew that he was wondering whether his brain was playing him a trick, whether his sense of hearing had, by some means, become impaired, so that he heard a voice not dimly, as is the case with the partially deaf, but wrongly, as may be the case with the mad, or with those who have suffered under a blow or through an injury to the brain. For this voice was not Valentine's at all, but the voice of a stranger, powerful, harsh, and malignant. It rang through the room noisily. A thick hoarseness dressed it as in disease, and at moments broke it and crushed it down. Then it would emerge as in a sigh or wail, pushing its way up with all the mechanical power of the voice of a wild animal, and mounting to a desperate climax, sinister and alarming. So unlike ordinary singing was the performance of this voice that, after the first paralysis of surprise and disgust had passed away from the doctor and Julian, they both felt the immediate necessity of putting a period to this deadly song, to which no words gave the faintest touch of humanity. They knew that it must attract and rivet the attention of others in the mansions, even possibly of passers-by in the street. The doctor withdrew his gaze from Valentine's at length and turned hastily to Julian, whom he found regarding him with a glance almost of horror.

" Stop him," Julian murmured.

" You ! " answered Levillier.

And then each knew that the other was in some nervous crisis that rendered action almost an impossibility. And while they thus hesitated there came a loud, repeated, and unsteady knock at the door. Julian opened it. Valentine's man was standing outside, pale and anxious.

" Good God, sir," he ejaculated. " What is it ? What on earth is the matter ? "

The man's exclamation broke through Julian's frost of inaction. He whispered to Wade :

" It's all right," pushed him out and shut the door. Then he went straight up to the piano, seized Valentine's hands and dragged them from the key-board.

The silence was like a sweet blow.

"I said my voice was out of order," Valentine said, simply and with a smile.

"You did not say you had another voice, the voice of—of a devil," Julian said, almost falteringly, for he was still shaken by his distress of the senses, into a mental condition that was almost anger.

Dr. Levillier said nothing. More sensitive to musical sounds than Julian, he dared not speak, lest he should say something that might stand like a fixed gulf to separate him eternally from Valentine. He knew the future that stretches out like a spear beyond one word. So he sat quietly with his eyes on the ground. His lips were set firmly together. Valentine turned to observe him.

"Doctor, you're not angry?" he asked.

The doctor made no reply.

"You know I warned you," Valentine went on. "You brought this thing on yourself."

"Yes," said Levillier.

But Julian interposed.

"No, Valentine," he exclaimed. "For of course it is all a trick of yours. You didn't want to sing. We made you. This is your revenge, eh? I didn't know you had it in you to be so—so beastly and cantankerous."

Valentine shook his head.

"It's no trick. It's simply as I said. My talent for music is dead. You have been listening to the voice of its corpse."

Dr. Levillier looked up at length.

"You really mean that?" he said, and there was an awakening within him of his normal ready interest in all things.

"I mean it absolutely."

"That is the only event in which I can forgive the torture you have been inflicting upon me."

"That is the true event."

"But it's not possible," Julian said. "It's not conceivable. Surely, Doctor, you would not say——"

The doctor interrupted him.

"I cannot believe that Cresswell would deliberately commit an outrage upon me," he said. "And it would be an outrage to sing like that to a tired man. Weeks of work would not fatigue me as I am fatigued by Cresswell's music."

Julian was silent and looked uneasy. Valentine repeated again:

"I couldn't help it. I am sorry."

Dr. Levillier ignored the remark. His professional interest was beginning to be aroused. For the first time he felt convinced that some very peculiar and bizarre change was dawning over the youth he knew so well. He wanted to watch it grow or fade, to analyse it, to study it, to be aware of its exact nature. But he did not want to put either Valentine or Julian upon the alert. So he spoke lightly as he said :

" But I shall soon get the better of my fatigue, even without the usual medicine. Cresswell, take my advice, give your music a rest. Lock your piano again for a while. It will be better."

Valentine shut down the lid on the instant, and turned the little key in the lock.

" Adieu to my companion of many lonely hours ! " he said with a half whimsical pensiveness. Then, as if in joke, he held out his hand with the key in it, to the doctor.

" Will you take charge of this hostage ? " he asked.

" Yes," the doctor replied.

Quite gravely he took the key and put it into his pocket.

And so it was that silence fell round the Saint of Victoria Street.

CHAPTER III

THE FLIGHT OF THE BATS

JULIAN had resolved to keep his compact with the lady of the feathers. He had learned partially to understand the curious and beautiful attitude which her mind had assumed towards him, polluted as it must be by the terror and working out of her fate, by many dreary actions and by many vile imaginings. But although he held to his promise he did not, after that night of crisis, resume his former career of asceticism tempered by winds of temptation which could never blow his casement open. There are men who can vary the fine monotony of virtue by an occasional deliberate error, and who return from such an excursion into dangerous by-paths drilled and comforted, as it appears, for further journeying along the main road of their respectability. But Julian was not such a man. He resembled rather the morphia victim, or the inebriate, who must at all hazards abstain from any indulgence, even the smallest, in drug or draught, lest the demon who has such charm for him clasp him in imperturbable arms, and refuse with the steadfastness of a once tricked Venus ever to let him go again.

Valentine's empire of five years was broken in one night.

At first Julian was scarcely conscious that his descent was not momentary, but rather tending to the permanent. Certainly, at the first, he was inclined to have the schoolboy outlook upon it, and the schoolboy outlook is as a glance through the wrong end of a telescope, dwindling giant sins to the stature of pigmies, and pigmy sins to mere points of darkness which equal nothingness. But, strangely enough, it was his interview with the weeping Cuckoo, that Magdalen of the streets, which drove the schoolboy to limbo, and set virtue and vice for the moment rightly on the throne and in the gutter. Despite his comparatively dull mood and tendency to a calm of self-satisfaction in the Marylebone Road, Julian could not be wholly unmoved by the passion of Cuckoo's regret, nor entirely unaware that it was a passion in which he must have some share, whether now or at some more distant time, when the thrall of recently moved senses was weakened, and the numbness really born of excitement melted in the quiet expansion of a manly and a reasonable calm. His understanding of her passion, none too definite at first, gave him a moment's wonder, both at her and at himself. It seemed strange that the shattered influence of Valentine should be of less account to him who had known and loved it than to her who had never known it. It seemed stranger still that the streets—those wolves which tear one by one the rags of good from human nature, till it stands naked and tearless beneath the lamps, which are the eyes of the wolves—stranger that those streets should have left to one of their children a veil so bridal and so beautiful as that which hung round Cuckoo when she wept. Julian was almost driven to believe that sin and purity can dwell together in one woman, yet never have intercourse. Yet he knew that to be impossible. The fact remained that the tarnished Cuckoo, in the first moments of regret, was more conscious of his sin for him than he was conscious of it for himself; that she led him, with her dingy hands, to such repentance as he experienced, and that she, too, guarded him against repetition of the sin, so far as she was concerned. Julian considered these circumstances; and there was a time when they were not without effect upon him, and when, with the assistance of a word from Valentine, they might have worked upon him an easy salvation. But Valentine did not speak that word. His peculiar purity had saved Julian in the past by its mere existence. Its presence was enough. That *satis* was dead now. Julian did not ask why. Nor did he find himself troubled by its decease. There is nothing like action for making man unobservant. Julian was no longer a ship in dock, nor even a ship riding at anchor. The anchor was up, the sails were set, the water ran back from the vessel's prow.

Cuckoo was not conscious of this. Sometimes she was subtle by intuition; often she was not subtle at all. When she understood Julian's nature for the moment it was because his nature was, for the moment, in close relation to hers. Her fate was affected by it, or its passages of arms clashed near her heart. Then intuition, woman's guardian, had eyes and ears, saw and heard with a distinctness that was nearly brilliant. But when Julian's nature wandered, and the wanderings did not bring it where hers was dwelling, her observation slept soundly enough. So she was not conscious at first of Julian's gentle progress in a new direction. Whether Valentine was conscious of it did not immediately appear, for Julian said nothing. For five years he had not had a secret from Valentine. Now he had to have one. He ranked Valentine with Dr. Levillier as too good to be told of the evil thing. When he had had temptations and resisted them he had told Valentine of them frankly. Now he had temptations and was beginning not to resist them, he kept silence about them. This silence lasted for a little while, and then Valentine swept it away, involuntarily it seemed, and by means of action, not of words.

One day Julian met a man at his club, a lively, devil-may-care soldier of fortune in the world. The man came to where he was sitting and said:

"So, Addison, your god has fallen from his pedestal. He's only a Dagon, after all."

Julian looked at him ignorantly.

"What god?" he asked.

"Your saint has tumbled from his perch. I never believed in him."

He was of the species that never believes in anything except vice and the *Sporting Times.*

Julian rejoined:

"I don't understand you."

"Cresswell," said the man.

Julian began to wonder what was coming, and silently got ready for the defence, as he always did instinctively when Valentine was the subject of attack.

"What have you got to say about Cresswell?" he asked curtly.

"My dear chap, now don't you get your frills out. Nothing that I should mind being said about me, I assure you. Only Cresswell will soon lose his nickname if he goes on as he's going now."

"I'm in the dark."

"That's what he likes being, if what they say is true. Quite a night bird I'm told."

"You'd better be more explicit."

But the man glanced at Julian's face and seemed to think better of it. He moved off muttering:

"Damned rot, minding a little chaff. And when we're all in the same boat too."

Julian sat pondering over his veiled remarks. They surprised him, but at first he was inclined to consider them as meaningless and unfounded as so much of the gossip of the clubs. Men like Valentine must always be a target for the arrows of the cynical. Julian had heard his sanctity laughed at in billiard rooms and in bars many times, and had simply felt an easy contempt for the laughers, who could not understand that any nature could be finer than their own. But to-day his own faint change of life—as yet in its gentle beginnings—led him presently to wonder, literally for the first time, whether there was a side of Valentine's life that was not merely a side of feeling, but of action, and that he knew nothing of. If it were so, Julian felt an inward conviction that the very nearest weeks of the past had seen its birth. He remembered once more Valentine's idle remark about his weariness of goodness, and wondered whether —in violation of his nature, in violent revolt against his own nobility—

he was living at last that commonplace, theatrical puppet-play of the world, a double life.

Valentine a night bird! What did that mean?

And then Julian thought of the great wheeling army of the bats, whose evolutions every night of creation witnesses. In the day they do not sleep, but they are hidden. Their wings are folded so closely as to be invisible. Nobody could tell that they ever flew through shadowy places, seeking that which never satiates, although it may transform, the appetite. Nobody could tell how the twilight affects them when it comes, how, in their obscurity, they have to keep a guard lest the involuntary fluttering of a half-spread pinion betray them. And then when the twilight, the blessed one of the twin twilights, one in course towards day, one in course towards night, has deepened and has died, they can dare to be themselves, to spread their short wings, and to flutter on their vagrant and mono-tonous courses. It is a great though secret army, the army of the bats. It scours through cities. No weather will keep it quite restful in camp. No darkness will blind it into immobility. The main-spring of sin beats in it as drums beat in a Soudanese fantasia, as blood beats in a heart. The air of night is black with the movement of the bats. They fly so thickly round some lives that those lives can never see the sky, never catch a glimpse of the stars, never hear the wings of the angels, but always and ever the wings of the bats. Nor can such lives hear the whisper of Nature and of the sirens who walk purely with Nature. The murmur of the bats drowns all other sounds, and makes a hoarse and monotonous music. And the eyes of the bats are hungry, and the breath of the bats is poisonous, and the flight of the bats is a charade of the tragedy of the flight of the devils in hell.

How could Valentine be one of the bats? It seemed to Julian that if Valentine tried to join them they would fall upon him, as certain birds will fall upon one who is not of their tribe, and kill him. And yet?

Yet Julian began to know that he had been aware of a change in Valentine. He had believed it to be momentary. Perhaps it was not momentary. Perhaps Valentine was concealing his new mode of life from some strange idea of chivalry towards Julian. As Julian pondered he grew excited. He began to long to tell Valentine now what he had not liked to tell him before. Suddenly he got up and hastened out of the club. He drove to Victoria Street. But Valentine was not at home.

" I suppose Mr. Cresswell goes out every night, Wade?" he asked the man, after a moment of hesitation.

Wade looked very much astonished at such a question coming from Julian.

" Yes, sir. At least most nights," Wade answered.

" I see," Julian said.

He stood a minute longer. Then . he turned away, after an abrupt :

" Say I called; will you ? "

Wade looked after him as he went down the stairs, with the raised eyebrows of the confidential butler.

That night was warm and gentle, with a full moon riding in clear heavens. The season was growing towards its full height, and the streets were thronged with carriages till a late hour. There is one long pavement that is generally trodden by many feet at every time of the year, and in almost every hour of the wheeling twenty-four. It is the pavement on which the legend of London's disgrace is written in bold characters of defiance. Men from distant lands, having made the pilgrimage to our Mecca, the queen, by right of magnitude at least, of the world's cities, stare aghast upon the legend, almost as Belshazzar stared upon the writing on the wall. Colonists seeking for the first time the comfortable embrace of that mother country which has been the fable of their childhood and the dream of their laborious years of maturity, gaze with withering hearts at this cancer in her bosom. Pure women turn their eyes from it. Children seek it that they may learn in one sharp moment the knowledge of good and evil. The music of the feet on that pavement has called women to despair and men to destruction; has sung in the ears of innocence till they grew deaf to virtue, and murmured round the heart of love till it became the heart of lust. And that pavement is the camping-ground of the army of the bats. On wet nights they flit drearily through the rain. In winter they glide like shadows among the revealing snows. But in the time of flowers and of soft airs, when the moon at the full swims calmly above the towers of Westminster, and the Thames rests rocked in a silver dream among the ebony wharves and barges, the flight of the bats is gay and their number is legion. And their circle is joined by many who are but recruits, or as camp-followers, treading in the track of those whose names are on the roll-call.

The lady of the feathers rarely failed to join the evening flight of the bats. Her acquaintance with Julian, even her curious passion for his respect and distant treatment, had not won her to different evenings, or to a new mode of life. But her feeling for Julian led her to ignore now the fact of this fate of hers. She chose to set him aside from it, to keep him for a friend, as an innocent peasant girl might keep some recluse wandering after peace into her solitude. Julian was to be the one man who looked on her with quiet, habitual eyes, who touched her with calm, gentle hand, who spoke to her with the voice of friendship, demanding nothing, and thought of her with a feeling that was neither greed nor contempt. And that one fatal night in which Cuckoo's private and secluded heart was so bitterly wounded she put out of her recollection with a strength of determination soldier-like and almost fierce. It lay in the past, but she did not treat the past as a woman treats a drawer full of old, used things, opening it in quiet moments and turning over its contents with a lingering and a loving hand. She shut it, locked it almost angrily, and never, never looked into it. Julian was to be her friend of leisure, never associated in any way with her tragic hours. All other men were the same, stamped with a similar hall-mark. He only was unstamped and was beautiful.

On this evening of summer Cuckoo, as usual, joined the flight of the bats, with a tired wing. The heat tried her. Her cheeks were white as ivory under their cloud of rouge. Her mouth was more plaintive even than usual, and her heart felt dull and heavy. As she got out of the omnibus at the Circus one of her ankles turned, and she gave an awkward jump that set all the feathers on her hat in commotion, and made the newspaper boys laugh at her scornfully. They knew her by sight and joked her every evening when she arrived. At first—that was a long while ago—she had resented their remarks, still more their shrewd unboyish questions, and had answered them with angry bitterness. But—well, that was a long while ago. Now she simply recovered her footing, paused a moment on the kerb-stone to arrange her dress, and then drifted away into the crowd slowly, without even glancing at her nightly critics, who were aware of a new bow on her gown, recognised, with imperturbable *sang-froid*, the change in a trimming, or the alteration of a waist-belt.

Slowly she walked along. Piccadilly bats fly slowly. The moon went up. She had not met her fate. In the throng she saw Valentine pass. He looked at her with a smile. She turned her eyes hastily away. She had met him on several evenings of late, but had never told Julian so, for she began to understand now his reverence for Valentine and a new-born, lady-like instinct taught her not to hurt that reverence. Valentine disappeared. He had not tried to speak with her. Once, on encountering her, he had paused, but Cuckoo glided behind two large Frenchwomen and escaped with the adroitness of a snake in grass. Apparently he recognised her movement as one of retreat, and was resolved to leave her alone, for he had never followed her since that day, although he always lifted his hat when he saw her. The crowd grew thicker. It was very heterogeneous, but Cuckoo did not thread it with the attention of a psychologist, or examine it with the pains of a philosopher of the dark hours. She stared listlessly at the faces of the men, and, if they stared back at her, smiled mechanically with a thin and stereotyped coquetry, moving on vacantly the while in a sort of dream, such as a tired journalist may fall into as he drives his pen over the paper, leaving a train of familiar words and phrases behind it. There are many dreamers like Cuckoo on the thin riband of that pavement, moving in a maze created by everlasting custom, beneath their flowers, half-senseless to life, and yet alive to the least human notice, behind the stretched barriers of their veils. She walked from the Circus to Hyde Park Corner and back again, then turned, with an ever-growing lassitude, to repeat the desolate experience. By this time the playhouses had vomited their patrons into the night, and locomotion was becoming more difficult. Sometimes there was a block, and Cuckoo found herself "hung up" as she called it, squashed in a mass of people, all intent on some scheme of their own, and resentful of the enforced interruption to their movement. Then, by some unknown and mysterious means, the human knot was untied, and all the atoms murmured on again through the ocean of the town. And still Cuckoo was alone, and still the mechanical smile came and went upon her lips, and her feet seemed to grow heavier and heavier, till they were as cannon balls to be lifted and dragged by her protesting muscles. And still her senses seem to become more and more drugged by the familiarity of it all, the familiarity of smile, of tired limbs, of incessant slow motion, of staring faces and watchful eyes; the familiarity of the cabs rolling home towards Knightsbridge and farther Kensington, with a dull, harsh noise; the familiarity of personal, intense loneliness and longing for quiet, the familiarity of the knowledge that quiet could only be earned by failure, and that failure meant lack of food, debt, and deeper degradation.

At last, perhaps it was owing to the unusual heat of the night, Cuckoo became so over-fatigued that she was scarcely conscious what she was doing. Her smile was utterly devoid of meaning, and, had she been suddenly asked, she could not have told whether she was at the Regent Street end of Piccadilly, at Hyde Park Corner, or midway between the two. Once more there was a block. The people were pressed, or surged of their own will, together, and Cuckoo found herself leaning against some stranger. This sudden support gave to her an equally sudden knowledge of the extent to which she was fatigued, and when the block ceased and the stranger —unconscious that he was being used as a species of pillow—moved away, Cuckoo almost fell to the ground. Stretching out her hands to save herself she caught hold of a man's arm, and as she did so her eyes moved to his face. It was Julian, and, before her grasp had time to fix all his attention on her, Cuckoo saw why he was in Piccadilly. In an instant all her lassitude was gone, all the fatigue, so passionless and complete, vanished. An extraordinary warmth, that of fire, not of summer, swept into her heart. She stood still, and trembled as if from the accession of the abrupt strength that flows from an energy purely nervous.

"Hulloh, Cuckoo!" Julian said.

She nodded at him. He looked down at her not quite knowing what to say, for he knew, by this time, that she objected to any hint from him on the subject of her proceedings of the night. That was ignored between them, and when they met the situation was that of a lodger in the Marylebone Road holding friendly intercourse with a dweller in Mayfair, nothing more and nothing less.

"Taking a stroll?" Julian said at last. "Isn't it a lovely night?"

"Yes. I say, I'm tired," she answered.

"Shall I take you somewhere?" he asked.

"Yes, do," she said.

They moved towards the Circus.

"Where shall we go?" Julian said. "Have you any pet place?"

"I don't know—oh, the Monico," she replied.

The restaurant was right in front of them. They dodged across to the island, thence to the opposite pavement, and passed in silently. The outer hall was thronged with people. So was the long inner room, and for a moment they stood in the doorway looking for a table. At length Julian caught sight of an empty one far down under the clock at the end. They made their way to it and sat down.

"What will you have?" Julian asked Cuckoo.

She considered, sinking back on the plush settee.

"A glass of stout, I think, and——"

"And a bun," he interposed, smiling in recollection of their first interview.

But Cuckoo did not smile or seem to recognise the allusion.

"Please I'll have a sandwich," she said.

Julian ordered it, the stout, a cup of coffee and a liqueur brandy for himself. While the waiter was getting the things he noticed Cuckoo's extreme and active gravity, a gravity which seemed oddly to give her quite a formidable appearance under her feathers. Despite the obvious weariness written on her face, there was somehow a look of energy about her, the aspect of a person full of intention and purpose.

"Why, Cuckoo," he said, "you look like a young judge about to deliver a sentence on somebody."

And indeed that was just how her expression and pose behind the marble-topped table affected him. Just then the waiter brought the stout and the other things. Cuckoo removed her cheap kid gloves, took the tumbler in her thin fingers and sipped at it. After a sip or two she put the glass down, and said to Julian:

" I say."

" Well ? "

" What are you about to-night ? "

The question came from her painted lips very sternly. It seemed addressed by one who had a right to condemn and who was going to exercise that right. Julian was astonished by her tone, and had an instant's inclination to resent it. But then he thought that there was nothing in the words themselves, and that the odd manner probably sprang simply from fatigue or some other womanish, undivined cause. So he answered :

" Just taking a stroll. It's so fine," and began to drink his coffee.

But Cuckoo quickly showed that her manner meant all that it had seemed to say.

" That ain't it," she said, with emphatic excitement, though she spoke in a low voice, because of the people all round them. " You know it ain't."

Julian was just lighting a cigarette. The match was flaming in his hand. He let it go out as he looked at her.

" What do you mean ? " he asked. " What's the matter ? "

" What are you doin' ? " she retorted. " That's what I want to know. Not as I need to ask though," she added, bitterly.

Julian was distinctly taken aback by the emotion in her manner, and the passion that she tried to keep quiet in her voice. He flushed rather red, a boyish trick which he could never quite get over.

" I don't know what you're talking about," he said, lighting another match, and this time making it do its office on his cigarette.

Cuckoo tossed her head in a way that was not wholly free from vulgarity, but that was certainly wholly unconscious and expressive of real feeling.

" Oh yes, you do," she rejoined. Then after a moment's silence she added, with bitter emphasis, and a movement of her hand in the direction of the door :

" You out in that crowd, and doing the same as all of them ! "

As she said the words tears started under her blackened eyelashes. If Julian had been taken aback before she spoke the last sentence, he was ten times more astonished now. The whole situation struck him as unexampled, and, but for something so passionate in the girl's manner that it over-rode the natural feeling of the moment, his sense of humour must have moved him to a smile. It was strange indeed to sit at midnight under the electric moons of the Monico, and to be passionately condemned for dissipation by a girl with a painted face, dyed hair and that terribly unmistakable imprint of the streets. But Julian could not smile. Something in Cuckoo's demeanour, something so vehement and so unconscious as to be not far from dignity, impressed him and took him well beyond the gates of laughter.

"Why—but you were out in the crowd too," he said.

"I!" she said sharply, and with a touch of scathing contempt for herself, yet impatient, too, of any introduction of her entity into the discussion, "of course I've got to be there. What's that to do with it?"

"Really, Cuckoo," Julian began, but she interrupted him.

"I ain't you," she said.

"No, of course, but——"

"I'm different. It's nothing to me where I go of a night, or what I do. But you ain't got to be there. You needn't go, need you?"

"Nobody need," he said. "But——"

"Then what d'you do it for?" she reiterated, still in the same tone of one sitting on high in condemnation, and moved by her own utterance to an increasing excitement. This time she paused for a reply, and set her rouged lips together with the obvious intention of not speaking until Julian had plainly put forward his defence. Strange to say, her manner had impressed him with a ridiculous feeling that defence of some kind was actually necessary. It was a case of one denizen of the dock putting on the black cap to sentence another. Julian glanced at Cuckoo before he made any reply to her last question. If he had had any intention of not answering it at all, of calmly disposing, in a word or two, of her right to interrogate him on his proceedings, her fixed and passionate eyes killed it instantly. He moved his coffee-cup round uneasily in the saucer.

"Men do many things they needn't do, as well as women," he began. "I must have my amusements. Why not?"

At the word amusements she drew in her breath with a little hiss of contempt. Julian flushed again.

"You're the last person," he began, and then caught himself up short. It must be confessed that she was very aggravating, and that the position she took up was wholly untenable. Having checked himself, he said more calmly:

"What's the good of talking about it? I live as other men do, naturally."

"Are you a beast too, then?" she asked.

She still kept her voice low, and the sentence came with all the more effect on this account.

"I don't see that," Julian exclaimed, evidently stung. "Women are always ready to say that about men."

Cuckoo broke into a laugh. She picked up her glass, and drank all that was in it. Putting it down empty she laughed again, with her eyes on Julian. That sound of mirth chilled him utterly.

N

" Why d'you laugh ? " he said.

" I don't know—thinkin' that you're to be like all the rest, I suppose," she answered. " Like all them brutes out there, and him too."

" Him," said Julian. " Whom are you speaking of ? "

She had not meant to say those last words, and tried to get out of an answer by asking for something more to drink.

" Chartreuse," she said, with the oddest imaginable accent.

Julian ordered it hastily, and then immediately repeated his question.

" Never mind," Cuckoo replied. " It don't matter."

But he was not to be denied.

" D'you mean Valentine ? " he asked.

She nodded her head slowly. Although Julian had half suspected that Valentine might be there this confirmation of his suspicion gave him a decided shock.

" Oh, he was just walking home from some party," he exclaimed.

" P'raps."

" I'm certain of it."

" He don't matter," she said, with a hard accent.

She drank the Chartreuse very slowly, and seemed to be reflecting, and a change came over her face. It softened as much as a painted face can soften under dyed hair.

" Dearie," she said, " it makes me sick to see you like the rest."

" I never pretended to be anything different."

" But you was different," she asserted. " I know you was different."

How could she have divined the change in Julian that one night of the Empire had wrought ?

" I say," she went on, and her voice was trembling with eagerness, " you've got to tell me somethin'."

" Well ? "

" That night I—I—it wasn't me made you different, was it ? "

And as she spoke Julian knew that it was she. Perhaps a fleeting expression in his face—telling naked truth as expressions may, though words belie them—made her understand, for her cheeks turned grey beneath the paint on them.

" I wish I'd killed myself long ago," she said, in a whisper.

" Hush ! " he exclaimed, cursing his tell-tale features. " I'm not different ; and if I was you could have nothing to do with it."

She said no more, but he saw by her brooding expression that she clung to her intuition, and knew what he denied.

The hands of the clock fixed on the wall above their heads pointed to the half-hour after midnight. The pale and weary waiters were racing to and fro clearing the tables, dodging this way and that with trays, stealing along with arms full of long-stemmed, thick tumblers, eager for rest. The electric moons gave a sudden portentous wink.

"Time!" a voice cried.

People began to get up and move out, exchanging loud good-nights. The long room slowly assumed an aspect of desertion and greedy desolation.

"We must go," Julian said.

Cuckoo woke out of that reverie, which seemed so chilly, so terrible even. She glanced at Julian, and her eyes were again full of tears. He was standing, and he bent down to her with his two hands resting upon the marble of the table. He bent down and then suddenly stooped lower, lower, almost glaring into her eyes. She went back in her seat a little, half-frightened.

"What's it?" she murmured.

But Julian only remained fixedly looking into her eyes. In the pool of the tears of them he saw too tiny shadowy flames, flickering, as he thought, but quite clear, distinct, unmistakable. And there came a thick beating in his side. His heart beat hard. Each time he had seen the vision of the flame he had been instantly impressed with a sense of strange mystery, as if at the vision of some holy thing, a flame upon a prayer-blessed altar, a flame ascending from a tear-washed sacrifice. And now he saw this thing that he fancied holy burning behind the tears in Cuckoo's eyes!

Cuckoo got up.

"Come on," she said abruptly.

Julian followed her out of the *café*.

The dream of the moon was with them as they came to the entrance, clear as a quiet soul, directly above them in a clear sky. Julian looked up at it, but Cuckoo looked, with eyes that were almost sullen, at the night panorama of the Circus. They waited a moment on the step. Julian was lighting a cigar, and many other voluble men, most of them French or Italian, were doing likewise. Having lighted it, and given a strong puff or two, Julian said to Cuckoo:

"Shall I drive you home?"

"I ain't going home yet," she replied doggedly. "Are you?"

He hesitated.

"Are you, or aren't you?" she reiterated.

While she spoke, in her voice that was often a little hoarse, a young voice with a thread in it, he realised that somehow she—painted sinner as she was—had managed to make him ashamed of himself. Or was it that an awe had come to his soul with that strange flame? In any case his mood had risen from the old night mood of a young man to something higher, something that could not be satisfied in the sordid way of the world.

"I think I shall go home," he said.

"Right," she answered, and for the first time there was an accent of pleasure in her voice.

"But I'll walk a little way with you first," he added.

Together they crossed the Circus and mingled with the humming mob at the corner of Regent Street. They pushed their way toward Piccadilly with difficulty, for numbers of people at this hour do not attempt to walk, but stand stock still, despite the cry of the policeman, staring at the passers-by, or talking and laughing with the women who throng the pavement. Having elbowed their way along as far as the St. James's restaurant, they began to move with a little more ease, and could have talked as they went, but apparently neither of them felt conversational. Julian was comparing the vision of the moon with the vision of the street, a comparison no doubt often made even by young men in London on still nights of summer, suggestive to most people, perhaps, of much the same thoughts—yet a comparison to thrill, as all the wild and eternal contrasts of life thrill. And Julian was thinking, too, rather sombrely of himself. Cuckoo walked on beside him, looking straight before her. Quite unconsciously, with the unconsciousness of a mechanical toy, expressive at the turning of a key in its interior, she had assumed her thin, invariable, professional smile. It came to her face in a flash when the pavement of Piccadilly came to her feet. She did not know it was there.

The moon looked down on it, yet, if Julian had been able to see, perhaps the little flame still flickered in those eyes which had been full of tears. But a little beyond St. James's Hall their silent progress was arrested, for they both saw Valentine pass them swiftly in the crowd. He saw them, too, but did not attempt to speak to them. With a smile at Julian he walked on. Julian gazed after him, then turned to Cuckoo.

"And you saw him here to-night before I met you?" he asked.

"Yes."

"How long ago?"

"Two hours, I daresay."

After that Julian ceased to think of the vision of the moon. But presently he noticed that Cuckoo was walking more slowly.

"You're tired?" he said.

She nodded.

"Have you been out all the evening?"

She nodded again.

"Take a cab and go home. I'll pay the man."

"No, I can't go yet."

"Why not?"

"I can't." She repeated, and a mulish look of obstinacy came into her face.

Julian guessed the miserable reason.

" Let me——" he began, and in a moment his hand would have been in his pocket. She stopped him.

" I told you as I never would, not from you," she said. " And I wouldn't all the more since—since that night."

Then, after an instant, she added :

" But you'd better leave me to myself now."

And then Julian realised that his presence and company were ruining her chance. That thought turned him sick and dull.

" I can't," he began, almost desperately.

She gave with her hand a little twitch at his.

" I say," she whispered, and she spoke to him as if to Jessie in the tiny flannel-lined basket, " Go bials ! will you ? "

" But you ? " he said, and there was something that was half a sob in his voice.

" I can't. But you—go bials."

And then, to please her, he held up his hand and hailed a hansom. Getting in he gave the direction of his rooms, loud enough for her to hear. She stood at the edge of the pavement and nodded at him as she heard it.

Then she turned away, and Julian saw the feathers in her big hat waving, as she joined once more the flight of the bats.

CHAPTER IV

THE FLAME IN A WOMAN'S EYES

" THAT girl loves you," Valentine had said, when Julian told him of Cuckoo's strange fragmentary sermon in the Monico, and of its effect upon himself.

Valentine spoke without any emotion or sympathy, and the absence of feeling from his voice seemed almost to bring a certain slight vexation into his manner. The love of Cuckoo, perhaps naturally, was to his fine nature a thing of no account, or even of ill account. At least his look and manner faintly said so to Julian.

"But if she loves me," Julian said, and a certain wonder came into his heart at the thought, "surely she wouldn't behave to me as she does, turning me from a lover into a friend, and keeping me almost angrily in the latter relation."

"Perhaps not," Valentine said languidly.

No doubt he understood what Julian did not entirely understand, the subtleties of such a nature as Cuckoo's, a nature hammered out thin by cruel circumstance, drilled till it found the unspeakable ordinary and the loathsome inevitable, worn as a stone by dropping water till the water, ceasing to fall, must have left a loneliness of surprise. Julian did not fully realise that Cuckoo's life might well lead her to display real affection, if she possessed it, by ways the reverse of those naturally sought and gloried in by pure and protected women. To give is the act natural to the love of such women. It is at least their impulse, although restrained within strict limits, perhaps, by exigencies of conscience or of religion. But to give is the impulse, giving being the unusual act, the strange new act in them. Cuckoo's profession being an ordered routine of giving, how could she show her love better than by withholding? To be to Julian as she was to all men could prove nothing, either to him or to herself. To be to him as she was not to any other man whom she knew must mean something, argue something. So, at least, dimly and without mental self-consciousness, her mind reasoned rather instinctively, for the lady of the feathers was above all things instinctive. Instead of logic, ethics, morals, the equipment of sage, philosopher, good women, she had instinct only. Instinct told her the secret meaning of reticence in her relations with Julian. When she said good-bye to him, the hand-shake that passed between them had become something more to her than a kiss. She kissed so many whom she hated, so many who were dolls of vice to her, who were walking sins, incarnate lust shadows, scarcely men. To be to Julian what another woman might have been would be to seem to make him as all those dolls of horrible London. So Cuckoo set him apart by her relations towards him, as she had previously set him apart in her heart. She pushed the chair of her beloved from the hearth where the dolls sat night after night warming their expressive hands at the cheap and ever-burning fire. She pushed it out into a circle of cold that was the only sacred thing she could supply. The world and her situation in it had bereft her of the power of even proving the simplicity of love by simplicity of natural action. She had to find a new way to show an old worship. She found it in refusal where others find it in assent.

But, after all, she was a woman, and perhaps she wished Julian to be an anchorite. That was what Valentine meant when, after Julian's account of Cuckoo's anger on finding him in Piccadilly, he simply said:

"That girl loves you."

The sentence stirred Julian to a surprise warmer than seemed reasonable, for he had really known that Cuckoo had some feeling for him. But he had always at the back of his mind the idea common to so many, that such a girl as Cuckoo could not be capable of the real love, the love ascetic, not the love Bacchanalian. Love among the roses is easy, but not many can welcome love among the nettles, and whenever Julian, despite his knowledge of the thorny paths along which Cuckoo walked habitually, along which all her poor sisterhood walk incessantly, had not entirely disabused himself of the fallacy that a life such as hers was, in some vague, undefined and indefinable way, a life of pleasure. Even when we know a thing to be we often cannot feel it to be. Knowledge in the mind does not inevitably bring to the birth sensation in the heart, or even the mental apprehension, half reasonable and half emotional, on the base and foundation of which it is comparatively easy to ground acts that indicate an understanding.

From Valentine's remark Julian understood him to mean that Cuckoo's anger was entirely caused by jealousy, not at all by a fine desire of protecting some one stronger than herself from that which she knew so well through her own original weakness. Yet that was what Julian had been led to believe, not by any hint of Cuckoo's, but by something within himself.

"I don't see why she should love me," he said presently.

" You're well off, Julian," Valentine rejoined.

Almost for the first time in his life Julian felt angry with Valentine.

" You don't know her at all," he said, hotly.

" I know her class."

Julian looked at him, and his anger died, as his mind sailed off on a new tack.

" Her class! Then you must have been studying it lately, Val. Not long ago you could not have studied it. Your nature would not have let you."

" That is true enough."

" Were you studying it when we met you the other night? "

" Yes."

" With what result? " Julian asked with eager curiosity.

" That I understand something I never understood before—the charm of sin."

Julian was greatly surprised at this deliverance of his friend, who uttered it in his coldly pure voice, looking serenely high-minded and even loftily intellectual.

" You find the charm of sin in Piccadilly? "

" I begin to find it everywhere, in every place in which human beings gather together."

" You no longer feel yourself aloof from the average man, then? "

Valentine pressed his right hand slowly upon Julian's shoulder.

" No longer," he answered quietly. " Julian, you and I are emerging together from the hermitage in which we have dwelt retired for so long. I always thought you would emerge some day. I never thought I should. But so it is. Don't think that I am standing still while you are travelling. It is not so."

The strength of his hand's grip upon Julian's shoulder seemed to indicate a violence of feeling which the tones of his voice did not imply. Julian listened, and then said, in a hesitating, irresolute manner:

" Yes, I see, Val; but I say, where are we travelling? or, at least, where shall we travel if we don't pull up, if we keep on? That's the thing, I suppose."

As he spoke he did not tell himself that it was nothing less than the disconnected and ungrammatical remarks of the lady of the feathers which prompted this consideration, this prophetic movement of his mind. Yet so it was. And when Valentine replied he, the saint, was fighting against her, the sinner, and surely in the cause of evil. For he said lightly:

" After all, do human souls travel? I often think they are like eyes looking at a whirling zoetrope. It is the zoetrope that travels,"

" You think souls don't go up or down ? "

" I think that none of us know really much about souls, and that, after all, it is best not to bother ourselves too much about them."

" Marr thought a great deal about them. I used to fancy that, as some maniacs have been known to murder people in order to tear out their hearts, he could have murdered them to tear out their souls."

Valentine took his hand from Julian's shoulder.

" Marr is dead and forgotten," he said almost sternly.

" I can't quite forget him, Val, and I still feel as if he had had some influence over both of us. We have changed since those days of the sittings, since that night of your trance and his death."

Julian was looking at Valentine in a puzzled way while he spoke. Valentine met his eyes calmly.

" If I have changed," he said slowly, " it cannot be in essentials. Look at me. Is my face altered ? Is my expression different ? "

" No, Valentine."

Julian said the words with a sort of return to confidence and to greater happiness. To look into the face of his friend set all his doubts at rest. No man with eyes like that could ever fall into any- thing which was really and radically evil. Valentine perhaps was playing with life as a boy plays with a dog, making life jump up at him, dance round him, just to see the strength and grace of the creature, its possibilities of quick motion, its powers of varied move- ment. Where could be the harm of that ? And what Valentine could do safely he began to think he might do safely too. He gave expression to his thought with his usual frankness.

" You mean you are beginning to play with life ? " he said.

" That is it exactly. I am putting life through its paces. After all, no man is worth his salt if he shuts himself up from that which is placed in the world for him to see, to know, and perhaps—but only after he has seen and known it—to reject. To do that is like living in the midst of a number of people who may be either very agreeable or the reverse, and declining ever to be introduced to them on the ground that they must all be horrible and certain to do one an infinity of harm."

" Yes, yes, I see. Then you think that Cuckoo is jealous of me ? That that was all she meant ? "

Julian again returned to the old question. Valentine replied :

" I feel sure of it. Women are always governed by their hearts. So much so that my last sentence is a truism, scarcely worthy the saying. Besides, my dear Julian, what would it matter if she were not ? What could the attitude of such a woman on any subject under the sun matter to you ? "

The words were not spoken without intentional sarcasm. They stung Julian a little, but did not lead him, from any sense of false shame, to a feeble concealment of his real feeling.

"It does seem absurd, I dare say," he said. "But she's—well, she's not an ordinary woman, Val."

"Let us hope not."

"No, you don't understand. There's something strong about her. What she says might really matter, I think, to a cleverer man than I. She knows men, and then, Valentine, there's something else."

He stopped. There was a queer look of mystery in his face.

"Something else! What is it? What can there be?"

"I saw the flame as if it was burning in her eyes."

Valentine made an abrupt movement. It might have been caused by surprise, annoyance, anger, or simply by the desire to fidget which overcomes every one, not paralysed, at some time or another. His action knocked over a chair, and he stooped to pick it up and set it in its place before he spoke. Then he said:

"The flame, you say! What on earth is your theory about this extraordinary flame? You seem to attach a strange importance to it. Yet it can only be the fire of a fancy, a jet from the imagination. Tell me, have you any theory about it, honestly, and, if so, what is it?"

Julian was rather taken aback by this very sledge hammer invitation. Hitherto the flame, and his thought of it, had seemed to have the pale vagueness and the mystery of a dream. When the flame appeared, it is true, he was oppressed by a sense of awe; but the awe was indefinite, blurred, resisting analysis, and quite inexplicable to another.

"I did not say I had any theory about it," he answered.

"But then, why do you consider it at all? And why seem to think that its supposed presence in the eyes of a woman makes that woman in any way different from others?"

"But I did not say I thought so," Julian said, rather hastily. "How you jump to conclusions to-day!"

"You implied it, and you meant it. Now, didn't you?"

"Perhaps I may have."

"This is all too much for me," Valentine said, showing now a very unusual irritation. He even began to pace up and down the room with a slow, soft footstep, monotonous and mechanical in its regularity. As he was walking he went on:

"I do really think, Julian, that it is a mistake to allow any fancy to get upon your nerves. You know what the doctor thought about this flame."

"Yes,"

" And you know what I think."

" Do I ? "

" Yes, that it is a mere chimera. But my opinion on such a subject has no particular value. The doctor is different. He is a great specialist. The nerves have been his constant study for years. If this vision continues to haunt you, you really ought to put yourself definitely into his hands."

" Perhaps I will," said Julian.

He spoke rather seriously and meditatively Valentine, possibly because he was in the sort of peculiarly irritable frame of mind that will sometimes cause a man to dislike having his tendered advice taken, seemed additionally vexed by this reply, or at any rate struck by it. He paused in his walk, and seemed for an instant as if he were going to say something sharply sarcastic. Then suddenly he laughed.

"After all," he exclaimed, in a calmer voice, "we are taking an absurdity mighty seriously."

But Julian would not agree to this view of the matter.

" I don't know that we are," he said.

" You don't know ! "

" That it is an absurdity. No, Valentine, I don't, I can't think that it is. I saw it in Cuckoo's eyes only once, and that was—just——"

" Tell me just when you saw it."

The words came from Valentine's lips with a pressure, a hurry almost of anxiety. He seemed curiously eager about the history of this chimera. But Julian, eager too, and engrossed in thoughts that moved as yet in a maze full of vapours and of mists, did not find time to notice it.

"I noticed it just after, or when, she was begging me to go home."

" Like a good boy," Valentine hastily interposed. " Because her jealousy prompted her to hate the thought of your having any pleasure in which she did not share. Oh, you noticed the flame then. Did it, too, tell you to go home ? "

He spoke rather harshly and flippantly, and apparently put the question without desire of an answer, and rather with the intention of ridicule than for any other reason. But Julian took it seriously and replied to it.

"Somehow I felt as if, perhaps, it did wish to speak some message to me, and that the message came, or might come, through her."

He spoke slowly, for indeed it was this action of words that was beginning to make clear to himself his own impression, so vague and so unpresentable before. As he thus traced it out, like a man following the blurred letters of an old inscription with the point of his stick, and gradually coming at their meaning, his excitement grew. He said, speaking with a rising emphasis of conviction: ·

"I'm not a mere fool. There is—there is something in all this; I feel it; I cannot be simply imagining. There is something. But I'm like a man in the dark. I can't see what it is; I can't tell. But you, Valentine, you, with your nature, so much better than I am, with so much deeper an insight, how is it you don't see this flame? Unless——" And here Julian struck his hand violently on the table. "Unless it comes, as it seemed to come that night in the darkness, from you. If it's part of yourself—but then"—and his manner clouded again—"how can that be?"

"How indeed?" said Valentine, who had been watching him all through this outburst with a scrutiny that seemed almost uneasy, so narrow and so determined was it.

"Julian, listen to me; you trust me, don't you, and think my opinion worth something?"

"Worth everything."

"Well, I believe you're getting into an unnatural—if you weren't a man I should say a hysterical habit of mind. If you can't throw it off by yourself, I must help you to do so."

"Perhaps you're right. But how will you help me?"

Valentine seemed to think and consider for a moment. Then he exclaimed:

"I'll tell you. By making you join with me in putting this life, this old life—new enough to both of us—through its paces. Why should each of us do it alone? We are friends. We can trust one another. You know me through and through. You know the— chilliness I'll call it—of my nature, my natural bookishness, my bias towards contemning people too readily, and avoiding what all men ought to know. And I know you. Without you I believe I should never go any distance. Without me you might go too far. Together we will strike the happy medium. For us life shall go through lla his paces, but he shall never lame us with a kick, like a vicious horse, or give us a furtive bite when we're not looking. Men carry such bites and kicks, the wounds from them, to their graves. We'll be more careful. But we'll see the great play in all—all its acts. And, when we've seen it, we'll be as we were, only we'll be no longer blind. And we'll never forget our grand power of rejecting and refusing."

"Ah!" said Julian. "Perhaps I haven't that power."

"But I have."

"Yes, you have."

"And I'll share my power with you. We are friends and comrades. We ought to share everything."

"Yes," exclaimed Julian, carried away. "Yes, by Jove, yes!"

" And as to this flame——"

" Ah ! "

" We'll soon know if it's a vision or a reality. But it's a vision. You saw it in a woman's eyes."

" I'll swear I did."

" Then that proves it's a fraud. The flame in a woman's eyes never burnt true yet, never, Julian, since the days of Delilah."

CHAPTER V

JULIAN FEARS THE FLAME

ALTHOUGH Cuckoo knew well that Julian carried out his intention of going home after he left her in Piccadilly, the fact of his being there, of his making one of that crowd, that slowly moving crowd, troubled her. Valentine and Julian had argued the question of her real feeling about the matter. Cuckoo did not argue it. She never deliberately thought to herself, "I feel this or that. Why do I feel it?" She knew as much about astronomy as introspection, and that was simply nothing at all. Instead of diving into the depths of her mind and laboriously tracing every labelled and tabulated subtlety to its source, she sat in the squalid Marylebone Road sitting-room, with the folding doors open into the bedroom to temper the heat of summer with draughts from the frigid zone of the back area, and babbled her sensations to Jessie, who wriggled in response to every passing shadow that stole across the heart of her mistress.

Jessie had learned much about Julian in these latter days. Into her pricked and pointed ear, leaf shaped and the hue of india-rubber, had been whispered a strange tale of the dawning of love in a battered heart, of the blossoming of respect in a warped mind. She had heard of the meeting in Piccadilly, of the meal at the Monico of the farewell on the kerbstone. And she alone knew—or ought to have known—the mingling of intense jealousy and of a grander feeling that burnt in Cuckoo's breast whenever she thought of Julian's life, the greater part of it that lay beyond her knowledge, her sight or keeping.

For the lady of the feathers, in most things a strange mixture, had never driven two more contrasted passions in double harness than those which she drove around the circle of which Julian was the core, the centre. One was a passion of jealousy, the other a curious passion of protection. Each backed up the other, urged it to its work. It would have been a hard task indeed to tell at first which was the greater of the two. Cuckoo neither knew nor cared. She did not even differentiate the two passions or say to herself that there were two. That was not her way. She felt quickly and strongly, and she acted on her feelings with the peculiar and almost wild promptitude that such a life as hers seems to breed in woman's nature. It is the French lady of the feathers who scatters vitriol in the streets of Paris, the Italian or Spanish lady of the feathers who snatches the dagger from her hair to stab an enemy. The wind of Cuckoo's feelings blew her about like a dancing mote, and the feelings awakened by Julian were the strongest her nature was capable of.

Only Jessie knew that at present, unless indeed Valentine had divined it, as seemed possible from his words to Julian.

And these twin passions were fed full by the peculiar circum- stances of Cuckoo's relation to Julian, and by the depth of her knowledge concerning a certain side of life.

She went home that night of their meeting very late, and in the weariness of the morning succeeding it, and of many following mornings, she began to brood over the change in Julian that she had intuitively divined. Her street woman's instinct could not be at fault with a boy. For Julian was little more than a boy. She knew that when she first met him, when they made toast together on the foggy afternoon that she could never forget, Julian was unshadowed by the darkness that envelops the steps of so much human nature. Lively, bright, full of youth, strength, energy as he was, Cuckoo knew that then he had been free from the bondage of sense which demands and obtains the sacrifice of so many lives like hers. And she knew that now he was not free from that bondage, and that she, by an irony of fate, had, with her own hands, fastened the first fetter upon him.

Valentine had plotted that.

Cuckoo's belief said so ; but surely her curious instinct against Valentine must have tricked her here !

It was this knowledge of her unwilling action against Julian's peace that first woke in her the strong protective feeling towards him, a feeling almost akin to the maternal instinct. It was her strange love for him that prompted the fiery antagonism against his relations with others that could only be called jealousy. And though one of her passions was noble, the other pitiable, they could but work together for the same end, aim at a similar salvation.

Yet how could any salvation for a man come out of that dreary house in the Marylebone Road, from that piteous rouged agent of the devil ?

Cuckoo never stopped to ask such a question as that. She was a girl, and she began to understand love. She had no time to stop. And each passing day soon began to give fresh vitality to the vision of Julian's need.

Between him and her there had sprung up on the ruins of one

night's folly a tower of comradeship. Its foundations were not of sand. Even Cuckoo, despite her ceaseless jealousy, felt that. But after all, she had only come into his life as a desolate waif drifts into a settled community. She was neither of his class, his understanding, or his education. She was in the gutter; in the gutter to an extent that no man, as women feel at present, can ever be. And though through her inspiration he had not to come into the gutter to find her and to be with her, yet she sometimes writhed with the thought that he was so far above her. Nevertheless, her position never once tempted her, in the struggle that the future quickly brought with it, to shrink from effort, to fail in fight, to despair in endeavour for him.

There are flames that burn the dross from humanity and reveal the gold. There are flames in the eyes and in the hearts of women.

   *   *   *   *   *

Julian's visits to Cuckoo were irregular but fairly frequent. He always came in the afternoon, an hour or two before the psychological moment of her start out for the evening's duty. Sometimes he would take her out to tea at a small Italian restaurant near Baker Street Station. More often they would make tea together in the little sitting-room, with the ecstatic assistance of Jessie. And Rip, Valentine's dog, generally made one of the party. He and Jessie got on excellently together, and devoutly shared the scraps that fell from the Marylebone Road table. The first time that Julian brought Rip to number 400 Cuckoo fell in love with him.

"Why, you never said you had a dog," she exclaimed.

"Rip's not mine," Julian answered.

"Isn't he? Whose is he?"

"Valentine's."

"Then why d'you have him with you?" asked Cuckoo, suddenly and rather roughly pushing away Rip, who was swirling in her lap like a whirlpool.

"Oh, he's taken a stupid dislike to Valentine," Julian answered thoughtlessly. "He won't stay with him."

In a moment Cuckoo had caught the little dog back.

"That's funny," she said.

"Yes, isn't it?" said Julian.

Then, seeing her thoughtful gaze, and the odd way in which she suddenly caressed the dog, he was angry with himself for having told her anything about the matter.

"Rip's a little fool," he said. "Perhaps Jessie will take a dislike to you some day, Cuckoo.

"Not she, never!" said Cuckoo, with conviction. And, after that, she could never spoil Rip enough.

These visits and teas ought to have been pleasant functions, bright oases in the desert of Cuckoo's life, but a cloud fell over them at the beginning and deepened as the days went by. For Cuckoo, with her sharpness of the *gamin* and her quick instinct of the London streets, was perpetually watching for and noting the signs in Julian's face, manner, or language, that fed those two passions of jealousy and of protection within her. And, at first, she allowed Julian to see what she was doing.

One day, as they sat at the table in the middle of the room, Julian said to her :

" I say, Cuckoo, why d'you look at me like that ? "

" Like what ? "

" Why d'you stare at me ? Anything wrong ? "

" I wasn't staring at you," she asserted. " The sun gets in my eyes if I look the other way."

" I'll draw the blind down," he said.

He got up from the table and shut the afternoon sun out. The tea-tray, the photographs, the little dogs, they two, were plunged in a greenish twilight manufactured by the sun with the assistance of the Venetian blind.

" There," Julian said, sitting down again, " now we shall all look ghostly."

" But if I do take a fancy to look at you, why shouldn't I then ? " Cuckoo asked.

" I don't mind," he laughed. " But you didn't seem pleased with me, I thought."

" Rot ! "

" Oh ! you were pleased then ? "

" I don't say as I was, or wasn't."

" You're rather like the Sphinx."

" What's that ? "

" Enigmatic."

She didn't understand, and looked rather cross.

" I told you I wasn't looking at you," she exclaimed pettishly.

" Then you told a lie," Julian said, with supreme gravity. "Think of that, Cuckoo."

" And what would you ever tell me but lies if I was to ask you things ? " she rejoined quickly.

Julian began to see that there was something lurking in the background behind her show of temper. He wondered what on earth it was.

" Why should I tell you lies ? " he said.

"Oh ! to kid me. Men like that. You're just like the rest, I suppose."

" I suppose so."

She seemed vexed at his assent, and went on :

" Now aren't you, though ? "

" I say, yes."

" Well, you usen't to be," she exclaimed, with actual bitterness o‍ accent and of look. "That's just why I was lookin' at you—for] was lookin'—makin' out the difference."

" I'm just the same as I was," Julian said, and he spoke witl quite sincere conviction.

" No, you ain't."

Having uttered this very direct contradiction, Cuckoo proceedec with great energy :

" You've been lettin' him do it. I know you have."

Julian was completely puzzled.

" What do you mean ? " he asked, with a real desire fo‍ information.

" You know well enough. He's leadin' you wrong."

Julian reddened, with a sudden understanding. Her words touched him in his sorest place. In the first place, no man likes to think he has been doing a thing because he has been led by some one else. In the second, Julian had grown ardently to dislike Cuckoo's unreasoning antipathy to Valentine. Originally, and for some time, he had believed that she would get over it. Finding later that there was no chance of that, he had once told her that he could not hear Valentine abused. Since that day she had been careful not to mention his name. But now her bitterness against him peeped out once more, and seemed even to have been gathering force during the interval.

" Cuckoo, you're talking great nonsense," he said, forcing himself to speak quietly.

But she was in one of her most mulish moods, and was not to be turned from the subject or silenced.

" No, I ain't," she said. " Where was you last week ? You didn't come in once."

" I was in Paris."

Cuckoo's brow clouded still more. Her knowledge of Paris was not intimate, and, indeed, was confined to stories dropped from the lips of men who had been there for short periods, and for purposes the reverse of geographical or artistic. Julian's mention of the French capital drove a sword into her.

" With him ? " she exclaimed.

" Yes, with Valentine."

" Oh, what did you do there ? "

She spoke with angry insistence, and Julian could not help thinking of Valentine's remark, " That girl loves you." It seemed indeed that Cuckoo must have some deep and wholly personal reason prompting her to this strange demonstration of vexation.

" I can't tell you everything," Julian answered.

" Oh, you can't kid me over that. I know well enough what
men go to Paris for ! " she rejoined, with almost hysterical bitterness.

Julian was silent. It was curious, but this girl stirred his conscience from its sleep, as once Valentine alone could stir it. But by
how different a method ! The stillness and calm of one who was
sinless were replaced by the vehemence and the passion of one who
was steeped in sin. And yet the two opposites had, to some extent,
the same effect. Julian did not yet realise this thoroughly, and did
not analyse it at all. Had any one hinted to him that the waning
influence of Valentine for good could ever be balanced by the waxing
influence of the lady of the feathers, he would have laughed at the
crazy notion. And in the first place he would have denied that
Valentine's spell upon him had changed in nature ; for Valentine
was still as a god to him. And Cuckoo could never be a goddess,
either to him or to any one else. But, though he would scarcely
acknowledge it even to himself, he did not care for Cuckoo to know
fully the changing way of his life. Perhaps it was the curiously
strong line she had from the first taken with regard to his actions
that made him careful with her. Perhaps it was the incident of the
vision of the flame—but no; remembrance of that had been well-
nigh lulled to sleep by the lullabies of Valentine, by his disregard of
it, his certainty that it was an hallucination, a mirage. Whatever
the cause might be, Julian felt somewhat like a naughty boy in the
angry presence of Cuckoo. As he looked at her the greenish twilight
painted a chill and menacing gleam in her eyes, and made her twisting lips venomous and acrid to his glance. Her rouge vanished in
the twilight, or seemed only as a dull, darkish cloud upon her thin
and worn cheeks. She sat at the table almost like a scarecrow,
giving the tables of some strange law to a trembling and an unwilling
votary.

" I know ! " she reiterated.

Julian said nothing. He did not choose to deny what was in fact
the truth, that his stay in Paris had not been free from fault, and
yet he did not feel inclined to do what most men in his situation
must by all means have done, challenge Cuckoo's right to sit in
judgment, or even for a moment to criticise any action of his. There
was something about her, a frankness, perhaps, which made it.
impossible to put her out of court by any allusion to her own life.
And, indeed, that must have been cowardice and an impossibility.
Besides, she put herself and her own deeds calmly away as unworthy
and impossible of discussion, as things sunk down beneath the wave
of notice or comment, remote from criticism or condemnation, because
the life of their hopelessness had been so long and sunless

Cuckoo, with her eyes on Julian, was silent too now. She understood that what her suspicion had affirmed, without actually knowing, was true, and her stormy heart was swept by a whirlwind of jealousy, and of womanish pity for the man she was jealous of. In that moment she felt a sickness of life more sharp than she had ever felt before, and a dull longing to be a different woman, a woman of Julian's class, and clever, that she might be able to do something to keep him from sinking to the level of the men she hated.

How could she, in her nakedness of permanent degradation, give a helping hand to anybody? That was a clear rendering of the vague thought, vague as this twilight in which they sat, that ran through her mind. Suddenly she turned to the tray and poured herself out a cup of tea. The tea had been standing while they talked, and was black and strong. She drank it eagerly, and a wave of nervous energy rushed over her, surging up to her brain like light and electricity. It gave to her a sort of reckless valour to say just the thing she felt. She turned towards Julian with a manner that was half shrew, half wild-cat — street girls cannot always compass the impressive, though they may feel the great eternities nestling round their hearts—and cried out:

"I just hate you!"

All her jealousy rang in that cry, smothering the whisper of the maternal passion that went ever with it. Julian could no longer doubt the truth of Valentine's words.

"Cuckoo, don't be silly," he said hastily, and awkwardly enough.

"Silly!" she burst out. "What do I care for that? I ain't silly either, and I ain't blind like you are. I can see where you're goin'."

"I shall go away from here," Julian said, trying to laugh, "if you talk in this ridiculous way."

She sprang up and ran passionately in front of the door, as if she thought he was really going to escape.

"No, you don't," she said, and her accent seemed to draw near to that of Whitechapel as her voice rose higher. "Not till I've said what I mean."

"Hush, Cuckoo! We shall have Mrs. Brigg up thinking I'm murdering you."

"Let her come! And you are, that's what you are, murderin' me and worse, seein' you go where you're goin'. He's takin' you. It's all him. Yes, it is! He'll make you as he is."

"Cuckoo, I won't have it."

Julian spoke sternly and got up. The little dogs, alarmed by the tumult, had begun to whine uneasily, and at his movement Jessie barked in a thin voice. Julian went to Cuckoo, took her wrists in his two hands and drew her away from the door; but she tore herself from his grasp with fury, for the touch of his hands gave a clearer vision to her jealousy of his secret deeds, and made her understand better the depth of her present feeling.

"You shall have it," she cried. "You shall. I know men. I know what you'll be. I know what women'll make of you."

"A man makes himself," Julian interrupted.

"Rot! That's all you know about it. I've seen them begin so nice and go right down, like a stone in a well. And they never come up again. Not they. No more'll you. D'you hear that?"

"I shall hear you better if you speak lower."

Cuckoo suddenly changed from a sort of frenzy to a violent calm.

"You're different already," she said. "Can't I see it?"

As if to emphasise her remark she approached her face quite close to his in the twilight. While they had been arguing a cloud had passed over the sun and dimness increased in the little room. Both of them were still standing up, and now Cuckoo peered into Julian's eyes with almost hungry scrutiny. Her lips were still trembling with excitement and her mouth was contorted into a sideways grin, expressive of contemptuous knowledge of the descent of Julian's nature. She was a mere mask of passion, no doubt a ridiculous object enough, touzled, dishevelled, and shaken with temper, as she leaned forward to get a better view of him. And Julian was both vexed and disgusted by her outbreak, and sick of a scene which, like all men, he ardently hated and would have given much to avoid. He faced her coldly, endeavouring to calm her by banishing every trace of excitement from his expression.

And then, in the twilight of the dingy room and in the twilight of her eyes, he saw the flame once more. A thin glint of sunshine found its way in from the street, and threw a shadow near them. Cuckoo's eyes emitted a greenish ray like a cat's, and in this ray the flame swam and flickered, cold and pale, and, Julian fancied, menacing.

Perhaps, because he was already irritated and slightly strung up by Cuckoo's attack, he felt a sudden anger against the flame, almost as he might have felt a rage against a person. As he stared upon it, he could almost believe that it, too, had eyes, scrutinising, upbraiding, condemning him, and that in the thin riband and shade of its fire there dwelt a heart to hate him for the dear sin to which, at last, he began to give himself. For the moment Cuckoo and the flame were as one, and for the moment he feared and hated them both.

Abruptly he held up his hand to stop the further words that were fluttering on her thin and painted lips.

"Hush!" he said, in a little hiss of protest against sound.

For again, fighting with the anger, there was awe in his heart.

There was something unusual in his expression which held her silent, a furtive horror and expectation which she did not understand. And while she waited, Julian turned suddenly, and left the room and the house.

CHAPTER VI

THE LADY OF THE FEATHERS LEARNS WISDOM

JULIAN did not come again to the house in the Marylebone Road for at least a fortnight, and during that time the lady of the feathers was left alone with her life and with her sad thoughts. The summer days went heavily by, and the sultry summer nights. No rain fell, and London was veiled in dust. The pavements were so hot that they burned the feet that trod them. Sometimes they seemed to burn Cuckoo's very soul, and to sear her heart as she stood upon them for hours in the night, while the crowds of Piccadilly flitted by like shadows in an evil dream. She stared mechanically at the faces of those passing as she strolled with a lagging footstep along the line of houses. She turned to meet the eyes of the pale-faced loungers in the lighted entrance of the St. James's Restaurant "Jimmy's" as she called it. But her mind was preoccupied. A problem had fastened upon it with the tenacity of some vampire or strange clinging creature of the night. Cuckoo was wrestling with an angel, or was it a devil? And often, when she stopped on the pavement and exchanged a word or two with some casual stranger, she scarcely knew what she said, or to what kind of man she was speaking. She was possessed by one thought, the thought of Julian and of his danger. Valentine, in her thoughts, was strangely a pale shadow, incredibly evil, incredibly persistent, luring Julian downwards, beckoning him with the thin hand of a saint to depths unpierced by the gaze of even the most sinful. And that hand of the saint was only part of the appalling deception of his beautiful and tragically lying body, a crystal temple in which a demon dwelt secretly, peering from its concealment through the shadowy blue windows, in which Julian saw truth and honour, but in which Cuckoo read things to terrify and to dismay.

For she was not wholly unaware of the mystery of Valentine, of the sharp contrast between his appearance and the vision of his nature as it came to her. She understood that there was something in the fine beauty of his face and figure to account for Julian's blindness and refusal to be warned against him. Cuckoo's intuition, the intuition of an unlearned and instinctive creature trained by the hardest circumstances to rely on what she called her wits, laid the crystal temple in ruins, and drove the demon from its lurking place naked and shrieking into the open. But, after all, was not she rather deceived than Julian? Julian, from the first moment of meeting Valentine, looked upon him as saint. Cuckoo, from the first moment of meeting, looked upon him as devil. Each put him aside from the general run of humanity, the one in a heaven of the imagination, the other in a hell. Neither would allow him to be midway between the two, containing possibilities of both ; ordinary, natural man. Julian angrily scouted the notion of Valentine's being like other men. Cuckoo felt instinctively that he was not. And so they glorified and cursed him.

Cuckoo had at first cursed him plainly in the market-place, and upon the house-top. But that was before she had learnt wisdom. Slowly she learnt it on these hot days and nights, when the London dust filtered over the paint upon her cheeks and lips, clung round the shadows in the hollows beneath her eyes, and slept in the artificial primrose of her elaborate cloud of hair. Slowly she learnt it in many vague and struggling mental arguments, arguments in which logic was a dwarf and passion a giant, in which instinct strangled reason, and love wandered as a shame-faced fairy with tear-dimmed eyes.

Julian's prolonged absence and silence first taught the lady of the feathers the slow necessity of wisdom, otherwise, perhaps, her vehement ignorance could never have absorbed the precious thing. Women of her training and vile experience, nerve-ridden and clothed in hysteria as in a garment, often think to gain what they want by the mere shrillness of outcry, the mere grabbing of ostentatious, eager hands and frenzy of body. Their lives lead them through a wonder of knowledge and of danger to the demeanour of babyhood, and they cry for every rattle, much more for every moon. So Cuckoo had thrown her feelings down before Julian. She had dashed her hatred of Valentine in his face ; she had cried her fears of his downfall to that which she consorted with eternally and loathed—when she had still the energy to loathe it, which was not always—in his ears with the ardent shrillness of a boatswain's whistle. She had in fact done all that her instinct prompted her to do, and the result was the exit of Julian from her life. This set her, always in her sharp and yet childish way, sometimes oddly clear-sighted, often muddled and distressed, to turn upon instinct with a contempt not known before, to discard it with the fury still of a child. And instinct thus forsaken by an essentially instinctive creature opened the gates of distress and of confusion.

By day Cuckoo sat in her stuffy little parlour brooding wearily.

She waited in day after day, always hoping that Julian would return, full of resolutions, prompted by fear, to be gentle, even lively, to him when he did come, full of excited intention which could not be fulfilled ; for he did not come. And by night, while she tramped the streets, still Cuckoo's anxious mind revolved the question of her behaviour in the future. For she would not, passionately would not, allow herself to contemplate the possibility that Julian's anger against her would keep him for ever beyond reach either of her fury or of her tenderness. She insisted on contemplating his ultimate reappearance, and her wits were at work to devise means to win him from Valentine's influence without stirring his horror at any thought of disloyalty to his friend. Cuckoo in fact wanted to be subtle, intended to be subtle, and sought intensely the right way of subtlety. She sought it as she walked, as she hovered at street corners in the night, while the hours ran by, sometimes till the streets were nearly deserted, sometimes even till the dawn sang in the sky to the wail of the hungry woman beneath it. She sought it even in the company of those strangers who stepped for a night into her life as into a public room, and stepped from it on the morrow with a careless and everlasting adieu, half-drowned in the chink of money.

And sometimes she thought with a sick dreariness that she would never find it, and sometimes courage failed her, and despite her passionate resolution she did for a moment say to herself, " If he should never come again." There were moments, too, when every other feeling was drowned by sheer jealousy of Julian, when the tiger cat woke in this street girl who had always had to fight, when her thin frame shivered with the shaking violence of the soul it held. Then she clenched her hands, and longed to plant her nails in the faces of those other women, divined though never seen, those Frenchwomen who had sung him, like sirens, to Paris, away from the sea of her greedy love. Her similes were commonplace. In her heart she called such sirens hussies. Had she met them the battle of words would have been strong and singularly unclean. That she herself was a hussy to other men, not to Julian, did not trouble her. She did not realise it. Human nature has always one blind eye even when the other does not squint. This passion of jealousy circling round an absent man seized her at the strangest, the most inopportune, moments. Sometimes it came upon her in the street, and the meditation of it was so vital and complete that Cuckoo could not go on walking, lest she should, by movement, miss the keenest edge of the agony. Then she would stop wherever she was, lean against the down-drawn shutter of a shop, c. the corner of a public house, among the gaping loungers, let her powdered chin drop upon her breast, and sink into a fit of desperate detective duty, during which she followed Julian like a shadow through imagined

wanderings, and watched him committing all those imagined actions
that could cause her to feel the wildest and most inhuman
despair.

One night, when she was thus sunk and swallowed up in the maw
of miserable inward contemplation, a young man who was walking
by observed her. He was very young and eager, fresh from Cambridge, ardent after the mysteries and the subtleties of life, as is the
fashion of clever modern youth. The sight of this painted girl
leaning, motionless as some doll or puppet, against the iron shutters
of the vacant house, her head drooped, and her hands, as if the
strings to manipulate her had fallen loose from the grasp that guided
them, caught and eventually fascinated him. It was a late hour of
night. He passed on and returned, shooting each time a devouring,
analytical glance upon Cuckoo. Again he came back, walking a
little nearer to the houses. His heart beat quicker as he approached
the puppet. Its complete immobility was almost appalling, and each
time he came within view of it he examined it violently to see if a
limb was displaced. No, one might almost suppose that it was the
body of some one struck dead so suddenly against the shop that
she had not had time to fall, and so remained leaning thus.
With shorter and shorter revolutions, like a dog working itself up to
approach some motionless but strange object, the youth went by
Cuckoo, hesitating more and more each time he came in front of her
with strange feelings of one being vaguely criminal. He longed to
touch the puppet, to see if any quiver would convulse its limbs, any
light flicker into its eyes. And he was so fascinated and interested
that at last he did furtively stop precisely in front of it. For a
second both of them were motionless, he from contemplation of the
outward, she of the inward. Then Cuckoo's thoughtful jealousy
came to a ghastly crisis. Her imagination had shown her frightful
things and herself an utterly helpless and compelled spectator. The
puppet opened its red lips to utter a sob, lifted up its white and heavy
eyelids to let loose tears upon its unnaturally bright cheeks, stirred
its hanging hands to clasp them in a crude gesture of dull fury. The
youth started as at a corpse showing suddenly the pangs of life. His
movement shot Cuckoo like a bullet into her real world. Through
her tears she saw a man regarding her. In a flash old habit brought
to her a smile, a turned head of coquetry, an entreating hand, a
hackneyed phrase that reiteration rendered parrot-like in intonation.
The youth shrank back and fled away in the darkness. Long afterwards that incident haunted him as an epitome of all the horrors of
cruel London.

And Cuckoo, thus roused and deserted, put aside for the moment
her nightmare and started once more upon her promenade of the
night.

At last she began to fear that Julian would never come back, and, by a sudden impulse, she wrote to him, a short, very ill-spelt letter hoping he would come to tea with her on a certain afternoon. On the day mentioned she waited in an agony of expectation. She had put on his black dress, removed all traces of paint and powder from her face, remembering his former request and her experiment, tricked Jessie out in a bright yellow satin ribbon twisted into a bow almost larger than herself, and bought flowers—large ones, sun-flowers—to give to her dingy room an air of refinement and of gaiety. Amid all this brilliancy of yellow satin and yellow flowers she waited uneasily in her simple black gown. The day was dull, not wet, but brooding and severe, iron-grey, like a hard-featured Puritan, and still with the angry peace of coming thunder. The window was open to let in air, but no air seemed to enter, only the weariful and incessant street noises. Jessie wriggled about, biting sideways with animation to get at her yellow adornment, and pattering round the furniture seeking stray crumbs, which sometimes eluded her for a while and, lying in hidden nooks and corners, unexpectedly rewarded her desul-tory and impromptu search. Cuckoo leaned her arms across the table, glanced at the tea-things for two, and listened. A cab stopped presently. She twisted in her chair to face the window. It had drawn up next door, and she subsided again into her fever of atten-tion. Jessie found a crumb and swallowed it with as much action and large air of tasting it as if it had been a city dinner. The hands of the clock drew to the hour named in Cuckoo's note, touched it, passed it. A sickness of despair began to creep upon her like a thousand little biting insects. She shuffled in her seat, glanced this way and that, pressed her lips together and, taking her arms from the table, clasped her hands tightly in her lap. Then she sat straight up and counted the tickings of the clock, the spots on the tablecloth, the gold stars upon the wall-paper of the room. She counted and counted until her head began to swim. And all the time she waited, the lady of the feathers was learning wisdom. The lesson was harsh, as the lessons of time usually are, the lesson was bitter as Marah waters. And she thought the lesson was going to be a cross too heavy for her narrow shoulders to bear when the iron gate of the garden sang its invariable little note of protest on being opened. Cuckoo's head turned slowly to one side. Her haggard eyes swept the view of the path. Julian was walking up it.

She met him very quietly, almost seriously, and he shook hands with her as if they had been together quite recently and parted the best of friends. Only, as he held her hand, she noticed that he cast a hasty, and, as she fancied, a fearful glance into her eyes. Then he seemed reassured and they sat down to tea. Cuckoo supposed that he had for the moment dreaded what she called another row, and was satisfied by her expression of good temper. They drank their tea, and after a short interval of constraint began chattering together very much as usual. At first Cuckoo had hardly dared to look much at Julian lest he should see the joy she felt at his coming, but when she was pouring out his second cup she let her eyes rest fully on his face, and only then did she realise that a shadow lay upon it, a shadow from which it had been free before.

With a trembling hand she filled the cup and stared upon the shadow. She knew its brethren so well. In dead days she herself had helped to manufacture such shadows upon the faces of men. She had seen them come, thin, faint, delicate, impalpable as a veil of mist before morning. Only morning light never followed them. And she had seen them stay and grow and deepen and darken. Shadow over the eyes of the man, shadow round his lips, shadow like a cloud upon the forehead, shadow over the picture painted by the soul, working through the features, that we call expression. Many times had she seen the journey taken by a man's face to that haunted bourne, arrived at which it is scarcely any more a man's face but only a mask expressive of one, or of many, sins. Had Julian then definitely set foot upon that journey? As yet the shadow that lay over him was no more than the lightest film, suggestive of a slightly unnatural and forbidding fatigue. Yet Cuckoo shrank from it as from a ghost.

"Why, Cuckoo, how your hand is trembling!" Julian said.

"Oh I was out late last night," she answered, putting the teapot hastily down. And they talked on, pretending there were only two of them and no shadowy third.

Julian, having returned at last to the Marylebone Road, fell into his old habit of coming there often. And each time that he came the lady of the feathers counted a fresh step on his hideous journey towards the haunted bourne. Yet she never spoke of the dreary addition sum she was doing. She never reproached Julian, or wept or let him see that her heart was growing cold as a pilgrim who kneels, bare, in long prayers upon the steps of a shrine. For she had learnt wisdom, and hugged it in her arms. Valentine was scarcely ever mentioned between them, but once, and evidently by accident, Julian allowed an expression to escape him which implied that Valentine now objected to the intimacy with Cuckoo. Immediately the words were uttered Julian looked confused, and obviously would have wished to recall them, had it been possible.

"Oh, I know as he don't like me," Cuckoo said.

Julian answered nothing.

"Why d'you come then?" she continued, with a certain desperation. "There ain't nothin' here to bring you. I know that well enough."

She cast a comprehensive glance round over the badly furnished room.

"Nothin' at all," she added with a sigh.

While she spoke Julian began to wonder too why he came, why he liked to come there. As Cuckoo said, there was nothing at all to bring him so often. He liked her, he was sorry for her, he had even a deep running sympathy for her, but he did not love her. Yet he was fascinated to come to her, and there were sometimes moments when he seemed taken possession of, led by the hand, to that squalid room and that squalid presence in it. Why was that? What led him? He could not tell.

"I like coming here," he said, "and of course it's nothing to Valentine where I go."

Cuckoo glanced up hastily at the words. A little serpent of enmity surely hissed in them. Julian spoke as if he were a man with some rebel feeling at his heart. But the serpent glided and was gone as he added :

"I'm always with him when I'm not with you, for I haven't seen the doctor for ages."

"The doctor! Who's that then?" asked Cuckoo.

"Dr. Levillier. Surely you've heard me talk about him."

"No, dearie."

"Oh, he's a nerve doctor and a sort of little saint, lives for his work, and is a deuced religious chap, never does anything, you know."

Julian looked at her.

"Oh," she said.

"And believes in everything. He's a dear little chap, the kindest heart in the world, good to every one, no matter who it is. He's devoted to Valentine."

"Eh?" said Cuckoo, with a long-drawn intonation of astonishment.

"I say he's devoted to Valentine," Julian repeated rather irritably. His temper was much less certain and sunny lately than of old. "But I believe he's devoted to every one he can do any good to. We used to see him continually, but he's been abroad for weeks, looking after a bad case, a Russian Grand Duke in Italy, who would have him and pays him all the fees he'd be getting in London. He'll be coming back directly, I think."

"Where does he live?" said Cuckoo, ever so carelessly.

Julian gave the number in Harley Street rather abstractedly. Their conversation had led him to think of the little doctor. Would he be glad to see him again? And would Valentine? He tried to realise, and presently understood, and had a moment of shame at his own feeling. Soon afterwards he went away. That night, before she went to Piccadilly, Cuckoo walked round to Harley Street. She wandered slowly down the long thoroughfare and presently came to the doctor's house. There was a brass plate upon the door. The light from a gas lamp, just lit, flickered upon it and Cuckoo, stopping, bent downwards and slowly read the printed name, " Dr. Levillier." Did it look a nice name, a kind name? She considered that question childishly, standing there alone. Then, without making up her mind on the subject, she turned to go. As she did so she saw the tall figure of a man motionless under the gas lamp on the other side of the street. He was evidently regarding her, and Cuckoo felt a sudden thrill of terror as she recognised Valentine. They stood still on the two pavements for a minute, looking across at one another. Cuckoo could only see Valentine's face faintly, but she fancied it was angry and distorted, and her terror grew. She hesitated what to do, when he made what seemed to her a threatening gesture, and walked quickly away down the street.

CHAPTER VII

THE LADY OF THE FEATHERS BUCKLES ON HER ARMOUR

THAT evening Cuckoo remained in a condition of mingled terror and resolution. There was something about Valentine that filled her not merely with alarm but with a nameless horror, indescribable and inveterate. She felt that he was her deadly enemy and the enemy of Julian. But he had cast such a spell over Julian that the latter was blinded and ready to follow him anywhere, and not merely to follow him, but to defend every step he took. Cuckoo had a sense of entering upon a combat with Valentine. As she stood upon the doorstep in Harley Street and faced him under the gas lamp, were they not as antagonists definitely crossing swords for the first time ? It seemed so to her. And the impression upon her was so strong and so exciting, that for once she broke through her invariable routine. Instead of going to Piccadilly she went home to her lodgings. It was about half-past nine when she arrived and opened the door with her latch-key. Mrs. Brigg happened to be in the passage *en route* to the kitchen from some business in the upper regions. She stared upon Cuckoo with amazement.

" What ever," she began, her voice croaky with interrogation. " Are you ill ? What are you back for ? "

" I'm all right," said Cuckoo, crossly. " Leave me alone, do."

She turned into her sitting-room. Mrs. Brigg followed, open-mouthed.

" Ain't you a-goin' out agin ? "

" No ; oh do leave off starin'. What's the matter with you ? "

Mrs. Brigg heaved a thick sigh and shuffled round upon her heels, which made a noise upon the oilcloth like the boots of the comic man at a music-hall.

" Well," she said, with a sudden grimness, " I hope it'll be all right about the rent, that's all."

She vanished, shaking her head, on which a stray curl paper, bereft of its comrades of the morning, sat unique in a thin forest of iron grey wisps.

Cuckoo shut her door and sat down to think. But at first she had to receive the attentions of Jessie, who was even more surprised than Mrs. Brigg at her unexpected return, and who began to bark with shrill joy and run violently round the room with the speed of a rat emancipated from a cage. As she would not consent to repose herself again, Cuckoo at last put her into the next room on the bed, and shut the door on her. Then she returned, lit all the three gas burners and turned them full on, before she removed her hat, and definitely settled herself in for the evening. She was fearful, and dreaded darkness or even twilight. The pulse of London beat round her while she stretched herself on the hard sofa, let down her touzled yellow hair, and frowned slowly as the unlearned do when they know that they want to meditate.

Now and then she rose suddenly on her elbow, half turned her head towards the window and listened. She had thought she heard a step on the pavement pause, and the cry of the little iron gate. Then, reassured, she leaned back once more. She had taken off her boots, and her feet, in black stockings, gone a little white at the toes, were tilted up on the shoulder of the sofa. She fixed her eyes mechanically upon them while she began, all confusedly, and with the blurred vagueness of the illiterate, to plan out a campaign. Not that she said that word to herself. She did not know its meaning. All that she knew was that she wanted to put her back against the wall, or get into an angle, like a cornered animal, and use her teeth and claws against Valentine, that menacing figure with an angel's face. And what disgusted, and drove Cuckoo almost mad, as she lay there in the crude gaslight, was the abominable fact that she was desperately afraid of Valentine. There was something about him which filled her with intense horror, but with something worse than horror, intense fear. Why, she had all three gas burners alight because, having met him that night, and seen him watching her, she trembled at the faintest shadow, and must see things plainly, lest their dim outlines should appal her fancy by taking his form.

Only once had the lady of the feathers known such enfeebling terror as this, on the night when she fled from the hotel in the Euston Road and left Marr dying on the bed between the tall windows. More than once, in her thoughts, had she loosely linked Marr with Valentine, puzzled, scarcely knowing why she did so. And she repeated the mental operation now, more definitely. They had at least one thing in common, this extraordinary power of striking fear into her soul. And Cuckoo was not accustomed to sit with fear. Her life had bred in her a strong, tough-fibred restlessness. She was essentially a careless creature, ready to argue, quarrel, hold her own with anybody, proud, as a rule, of being a match for any man and well able to take care of herself. She had knocked about, and was utterly familiar with many horrors of the streets, and of nameless houses. She had heard many rows at night, had been in brawls, had been waked, in the dense hours, by sudden sharp cries for help, was accustomed to be alone with strangers, men of unknown history, of unknown deeds. And all these circumstances she met with absolute carelessness, with a devil-may-care laugh, or the sigh of one weary but not afraid. She was no more timid than the average English street boy. Only these two men, one dead, one alive, knew how to dress her in terror from head to foot, brain, heart and body. And so she joined them in a ghastly brotherhood.

But to-night she was making a conscious effort against the domination of Valentine, for the awakening of fear in her was counterbalanced by other feelings prompting her to fight. And once Cuckoo began to fight she felt that she would not lack courage. For she clung to action and hated thought, walking clearly in the one, but through a maze in the other.

Despite her fear of him something drove her to fight Valentine; only she did not know how to fight him. It was in a mood of doubt that she had wandered into Harley Street and bent to read the name on the door of Dr. Levillier. Julian's description of the doctor had appealed to her. The mention of his goodness, of his pure life, of his care for others had impressed her, she scarcely knew why, and brought into her mind a desire to see this little man. Yet he was devoted to Valentine. And then Cuckoo, lying back on the sofa, felt heart-sick, wondering at the power of this man whom she hated and feared, wondering how she could ever fight against his influence over Julian, wondering too a little why it was that she knew she must and certainly would fight it. For beyond the motive power of her love and jealousy, beyond the ordinary woman's desire to keep the man she admired from sinking to the level of the men she despised, there was another fiery and strong and urging insistent influence working upon her, working within her, crying to her like a voice to buckle on her armour and to do battle with the enemy. This influence came silently from without and spoke to the lady of the feathers when she was alone, and never more clearly and powerfully than to-night. It wrestled with her terror of Valentine and told her to put it away, to come into closer relations with him fearlessly, not to flee from him, but rather to watch him, dog him, learn what he was and what he was doing or trying to do. Yet fear fought this growing, stirring, strange warm influence that burned like a fire at Cuckoo's heart. She flushed and she paled as she lay there, with down-drawn brows and enlaced hands, her yellow hair falling over the hard, shiny horsehair of the sofa. She longed for some one to come to her who would give her counsel, help, courage, that she might fight for Julian who was too spell-bound to fight for himself, and who was falling so fast, so terribly fast, into the abyss where men crawl like insects and women are as poisonous weeds in the slime of the pit.

Oh, for some one!

Involuntarily she sat up and extended her thin arms almost as if in a beckoning gesture.

As she did so the front-door bell rang.

Cuckoo was startled and felt as if it rang for her. But that was unlikely; and there were other lodgers of her kind in the house. No doubt it was a visitor for one of them.

Mrs. Brigg went in weary procession along the passage and opened the door. A few words were indistinctly spoken in a man's voice. Then the street door shut, and almost simultaneously the door of Cuckoo's sitting-room opened very quietly and Valentine entered.

CHAPTER VIII

VALENTINE EXPOUNDS THE GOSPEL OF INFLUENCE TO THE LADY OF THE FEATHERS

VALENTINE closed the door behind him and stood by it, looking at Cuckoo gravely. She had pushed herself up on the sofa, using her elbows as a lever, and in an awkward attitude, half sitting, half lying down, stared at him with startled eyes. Her unshod feet were drawn in towards her body, and her dyed hair hung in a thick tangle round her face and on her shoulders. She said nothing.

Valentine put his hat down on the table and began to take off his gloves.

"I am glad to find you at home," he said politely.

Cuckoo shifted a little further back on the sofa. Now that she was actually shut up alone with Valentine, fear returned upon her and banished every other feeling, every desire except the desire to be away from him. She ran her tongue over her lips, which had suddenly become dry.

"What are you come for?" she asked, never taking her eyes from his.

"To see you. I have never yet returned your kind call upon me."

"Eh?"

Cuckoo spoke in the tone of one who had become deaf, and she felt as if the agitation of her mind actually clamoured within her like a crowd of human voices, deadening sounds from without. Valentine repeated his remark, adding :

"Won't you ask me to sit down?"

He put his hand on the back of a chair.

"May I?"

Cuckoo gave her body a jerk, which brought her feet down to the floor, so that she was sitting upright. She pushed out one of her hands as if in protest.

"You can't sit here," she murmured.

"I? Why not?"

"I can't have you here, nor I won't either,"

Her voice was growing louder and fiercer as the first paralysis of surprise died gradually away from her. After all she had not buckled on her armour only to run away from the enemy in it. The street Arab impudence was not quite killed in her by the strange influence of this man. The mere fact of having her feet firmly planted upon the floor gave Cuckoo a certain fillip of courage, and she tossed her head with that old vulgar gesture of hers which suggested the harridan. She pointed to the door.

" Out you go ! " she cried.

For her intrepidity had not risen to calm contemplation of an interview. She was only bracing herself up to the necessary momentary endurance of his presence, which followed upon Mrs. Brigg's admittance of him within the door.

Valentine heard the gentle hint unmoved, and replied to it by drawing a chair out from the table and sitting down upon it. A sort of rage, stirred by terror, ran over Cuckoo. She seized the back of his chair with both hands and shook it violently.

" No, you don't stay," she ejaculated ; " I won't have it ! "

It was characteristic of her to lose all sense of dignity at an instant, when dignity might have served her purpose. Her outburst might have been directed against a statue. Valentine neither moved nor looked in any way affected. Glancing at Cuckoo with a whimsical amusement, he said :

" What a child you are ! When will you learn wisdom ? "

Cuckoo took away her hands. A conviction pierced her that the weapons a woman may use with effect against an ordinary man could be of no service now, and with this man. She faded abruptly from anger and violence into fatigue, always closely accompanied by fear.

" I'm awful tired to-night," she said. " Please do go ! I'm home because I'm tired."

" The walk from Harley Street was too much for you. You shouldn't make such exertions."

For the first time a sinister note rang in his voice.

" I shall go where I like," Cuckoo answered, and this time with some real sturdiness of manner. " It ain't nothin' to you where I go, nor what I do."

" How can you tell that ? "

She laid her chin in the upturned palms of her two hands, planting her elbows on her knees.

" How can it be ? " she said. " I'm nothin' to you, nor I ain't goin⁴ to be either."

" That's what you say."

" And it's God's truth, too ! " she cried again with violence, as the sense of Valentine's inflexible power grew in her.

" I'm going to smoke if you will allow me," Valentine said.

Slowly he drew out and lit a cigarette, Cuckoo neither refusing
nor permitting it. With protruding lips he threw the light smoke
round him. Then speaking through it he said :
" Tell me why you go to Harley Street."
" I ain't goin' to talk to you."
" Tell me why. It lies out of your beat; it's a respectable
thoroughfare."
The words were said to sting. Cuckoo let them go by. She had
been stung too often, and repetition of cruelty sometimes kills what
it repeats. She had set her lips to silence, with a look of obstinacy
not impressive, but merely mulish and childish.
" Well ? " Valentine said.
She made no answer. He did not seem angry, but continued :
" You find few fish for your net there, I imagine. But perhaps
you don't go for fish. What was the name you read upon the door
while I watched you ? "
This time Cuckoo, changing her mind, as she often did, with all
the swiftness of a crude nature, answered him :
" You know well enough ! "
" It was Dr. Levillier, wasn't it ? "
She nodded her head silently.
" Why do you go to his door ? " What do you want with him ? "
Cuckoo's quick woman's instinct detected a suspicion of something
that was like anxiety in his voice as he said the words. In an
instant the warm impulse that, in her silent meditation, had led her
to buckle on her armour and to think, with a certain courage, that
she was to fight one day, stirred and glowed and leapt up, an impulse
greater than herself. The fear that had fallen upon her was
lessened, for she felt that this man too might, nay did, know fear.
" What's that to you ? "
She turned upon him boldly with the question, and he knew her
for the first time as an antagonist, who might actively attack as well
as passively hate. He leaned forward, and looked into her eyes
searchingly, with a sort of rapture of anxiety too. It recalled something to Cuckoo. She tried to remember what, but for a moment
could not. Then, as if reassured, he resigned his eager and nervous
posture of inquiry. That second movement brought the light that
Cuckoo's puzzled mind sought. It was Julian who had looked first
into her eyes with that strange watchfulness. These men echoed
one another in that glance which she could not understand. What
they sought in her eyes she could not tell. If it were the same
thing it could not be love. And it seemed to be a thing that they
feared to find.
" Dr. Levillier is a great friend of mine," Valentine said. " He
is a famous nerve doctor. Seeing you hovering about his door led

me to suppose you might be ill, and were going to consult him. I hope you are not ill."

"Not I!"

"Because he is away from home at present."

"Oh!"

"Do you want to see him?"

"I suppose I can see him like any one else, if I've a mind to."

"Well! He's—he doesn't see quite every one. His practice is only among the richest and smartest people in town. Some one else might answer your purpose better."

He spoke suavely, but the words he said cemented Cuckoo's previously vague thought, of trying, perhaps, to see Dr. Levillier, into a sudden strong determination. She divined that, for some reason, Valentine was anxious that she should not see him. That was enough. She would, at whatever cost, make his acquaintance.

"I'll see him if I like," she said hastily, lost to any appreciation of wisdom, through the desire of aiming an instant blow at Valentine.

"Of course! Why not?" was his reply.

"You don't want me to. I can see that," she went on still more unadvisedly. "You needn't think as you can get over me so easily."

Valentine's smile showed a certain contempt that angered her.

"I know you," she cried.

"Do you?" he said. "I wonder if you would like to know me? Do you remember Marr?"

The lady of the feathers turned cold.

"Marr!" she faltered; "what of him?"

"You have not forgotten him."

"He's dead!"

A pause.

"He's dead, I say."

"Exactly! As dead as a strong man who has lived long in the world ever can be."

"What d'you mean? I say he's dead and buried and done with." Her voice was rather noisy and shrill.

"That's just where you make a mistake," Valentine said quite gravely, rather like a philosopher about to embark upon an argument. "He is not done with. Suppose you fear a man, you hate him, you kill him, you put him under the ground, you have not done with him."

"I didn't kill him! I didn't, I didn't!" Cuckoo cried out, shrilly, half rising from the sofa. A wild suspicion suddenly came over her that Valentine was pursuing her as an avenger of blood under the mistaken idea that she had done Marr to death in the night.

"Hush! I know that. He died naturally, as a doctor would say, and he has been buried; and by now, probably he is a shell that can only contain the darkness of his grave. Yet, for all that, he's not done with, Miss Bright."

"He is! he is!" she persisted.

The mention of Marr always woke terror in her. She sat, her eyes fixed on Valentine, her memory fixed on Marr. Perhaps for this reason what her memory saw and what her eyes saw seemed gradually to float together, and fuse and mingle, till eyes and memory mingled, too, into one sense, observant of one being only, neither wholly Marr nor wholly Valentine, but both in one. She had linked them together vaguely before, but never as now. Yet even now the clouds were floating round her and the vapours. She might think she saw, but she could not understand, and what she saw was rather a phantom standing in a land of mirage than a man standing in the world of men.

"Some day, perhaps, I will prove to you that he is not," Valentine said.

"Eh, how?"

She had lost all self-consciousness now, and in her eagerness of fear, wonder and curiosity seemed tormented by the veil of yellow hair that was flopping in frizzy strands round her face and over her eyes. She seized it in her two hands, and with a few shooting gestures, in and out, wound it into a dishevelled lump, which she stuck to the back of her head with two or three pins. All the time she was looking at Valentine for an answer to her question.

"Perhaps I don't know how yet."

"Yes, you do though. I can see you do. What have you got to do with him, with Marr?"

"I never said I had anything to do with him."

"Ah! but you have. I always knew it!"

"Many men are linked together by thin, perhaps invisible threads, impalpable and impossible to define."

The lady of the feathers was out of her depth in this sentence, so she only tossed her head and murmured:

"Oh, I dessay!" with an effort after contempt.

But Valentine's mood seemed to change. An abstracted gaiety stole over him. If it was simulated, the simulation was very perfect and complete. Sitting back in his chair, the cigarette smoke curling lightly round him, his large blue eyes glancing gravely now at Cuckoo crumpled up on the horsehair sofa, now meditatively at some object in the little room, or at the ceiling, he spoke in a low, clear, level voice, as if uttering his thoughts aloud, careless or oblivious of any listener.

" Every man who lives, and who has a personality, has something to do with many men whom he has never seen, whom he will never see. Messengers go from him, as carrier pigeons go from a ship. He may live alone, as a ship is alone in mid-ocean, but the messengers are winged, and their wings are strong. They fly high and they fly far, and wherever they pause and rest, that man has left a mark, has stamped himself, has uttered himself, has planted a seed of his will. Have you a religion ? "

Valentine stopped abruptly after uttering this question, and waited for an answer. It was characteristic enough.

" What ? " said the lady of the feathers, staring wide-eyed.

" I say, have you a religion ? ",

" Not I. How can I when I don't go to no church ? "

" That is, no doubt, a convincing proof of heathendom. And yet I have a religion that never leads me to a church door. My religion is will, my gospel is the gospel of influence, and my god is power. Will binds the world into a net, whose strands are like iron. Will dies if it is weak, but if it is strong enough it becomes practically immortal. But, though it lives itself, it has the power to kill others. It can murder a soul in a man or a woman, and throw it into the grave to decay and go to dust, and in the man it can create a second soul diametrically opposite to the corpse, and the world will say the man is the same; but he is not the same. He is another man. Or if the will is not strong enough actually to kill a soul "—at this point Valentine spoke more slowly, and there was a certain note of uneasiness, even almost of agitation, in his voice—" it can yet expel it from the body in which it resides, and drive it, like a new Ishmael, into the desert, where it must hover, useless, hopeless, degraded and naked, because it has no body to work in. Yes ! yes ! that must be so ! The soul can have no power divorced from the body ! none ! none ! "

He got up from his chair, and began to pace the little room. Cuckoo watched him as a child might watch a wild animal in its cage. His face was hard and thin with deep thought, and hers was contorted under her yellow hair—contorted in a frantic effort to grasp and to understand what he was saying; for, stupid, ignorant as the lady of the feathers was, she had a sharp demon in her that often told her the truth, and this demon whispered now in her ear,

" Listen, and you may learn things that you long to know ! "

And she listened motionless, her eyes bright and eager, her lips shut together, her slim body a-quiver with intensity, mental and physical.

" How can it ? " Valentine went on. " What is a soul without a body ? You cannot see it. You cannot hear it, and if you think you can, that is a vile trick of the mind, an hallucination. For if one man can see it, why not another? Here, let me look into your eyes again."

As he said the last words, he stopped opposite to Cuckoo, suddenly caught her chin in his two hands, which felt hard and cold, and forcibly pushed up her face towards his. She was terrified, beginning now to think him mad, and to fear personal injury. Gazing hard and furtively into her eyes, he said:

"No; it's a lie! It is not there. It never was! It is dead and finished with, and I won't fear it."

As if struck by the fatigue of some sudden reaction, he sank down again into his chair, and went on with his apparently fantastic monologue:

"And if it was ever alive, what could it do? A soul can't work, except through a body; it must fasten on a body, and bend the body to its will—man is such a creature that he can only be influenced through flesh and blood, nerves, sinews, eyes, things he can see, things that he can hear. He is so grovelling that nothing more delicate than these really appeals to him."

Again, and this time with less abstraction, and with a sort of contemptuous humour, he turned to the lady of the feathers, and continued, as if once more aware of her presence:

"Are you imbibing my gospel, the gospel of will and of influence? I see you are by your pretty attitude and by the engaging face you are making at me. Well, don't get it wrong. A gospel gone wrong in a mind is dangerous and worse than no gospel at all. If you get this gospel wrong you may become conceited, and fancy yourself possessed of a power which you haven't a notion of. To use will, in any really effective way, you must train your body, and take care of it, not ruin it, and let it run to seed, or grow disfigured, or a ghastly tell-tale, a truth-teller, a town crier with a big bell going about and calling aloud all the silly or criminal things you do. Now you have forgotten this, or perhaps you never knew it, and so will could not work in you; not even, I believe, a malign will to do mischief. You have thrown your body to the wolves, and whoever looks upon you must see the marks of their teeth."

It was evident that he gloated on this idea that the body of the lady of the feathers was for ever useless for good, and even powerless to do much effective evil. He seemed to revel in the notion that she was simply a thing powerless, negative, and totally vain.

"I was mad ever to imagine the contrary," he said. Then, glancing away from personality, he exclaimed with more energy:

"But sometimes a will is so great, so trained, so watchful of opportunities, so acute and ready, that, instead of passing away practically on the passing away of the body in which it has been born and has lived, and merely living and working through the emanations of itself that have clung to men and women in many different places, instead—in fact—of being diffused—you understand me?" he broke out with an obvious delight in the grossness of her ignorance and the denseness of her bewilderment and misunderstanding of him—"which is a sort of death, it seizes, whole as a body with all all the members sound, upon another home. It commits, in effect, a great act of brigandage. It lives on complete, powerful—even more powerful than ever before, because to all its original powers it adds a glory of deception, and is a living life. If only you could understand me!"

Suddenly he burst into a peal of laughter that was a full stop to his philosophy. His cigarette had gone out. He threw it into the grate and stretched out his arms, still laughing. And Cuckoo gazing at him, as if fascinated, said silently to herself, "If only I could!"

For she felt as if Valentine were telling her a great secret, secure in the hideous knowledge that, though she heard it, it must remain a secret from her on account of her ignorance and of her stupidity. There was something in that feeling peculiarly maddening, yet Cuckoo displayed no irritation. The sharp little demon at her elbow whispered to her to be silent, told her that she might learn, might yet understand, if she would play a part, and be no more the wild cat, the foolishly impulsive lady of the feathers. Valentine struck his hand upon the table, and repeated:

"Why—why can't you understand?"

The piquancy of the situation evidently delighted his mind and his sense of mischief. He enjoyed playing the philosopher to a fool, and the more the fool became a fool the higher soared his philosophy and his appreciation of it. There is always something paradoxical in wisdom instructing folly, for, after all, folly can never really learn, can never really understand. Valentine hugged that thought.

"Go on," the lady of the feathers said, apparently in gaping wonderment.

"Why? do you mean to tell me you are interested?"

"I'm listenin'! It sounds wonderful!"

"It is wonderful!" Valentine cried. "Every living lie is wonderful. But you don't know yet much about will. My gospel is full of secrets and of subtleties, and only a few people are beginning to guess at its far-reaching power, and to aim at learning its truths and sounding its depths. And many unbelievers play with it, and never know that they are playing with fire. A man did this once. Shall I tell you about him?"

"Yes!" said Cuckoo.

And her soul cried to the darkness in which she imagined some vague power to dwell, cried aloud for understanding. This silent cry was so intense that she lay back upon the hard sofa, almost exhausted, and, as she lay there, something hot, like fire, seemed to make its nest in her heart, and to flame there, and to be alive, as a flame is alive, and to speak to her, but not aloud, as a flame speaks in the coals to the imagination of the watcher by the hearth. In that moment the lady of the feathers felt as if she were conscious of a new companion, a companion full of some intensity towards her, some anxiety about her, anxious and brilliant as a flame is, vital, keen, blazing, intense. Although she could not define her sensation thus, that lack of analytical power could not deprive her of it. She knew that her vision became clearer, that her mind became brighter, that a light illumined her, that she was, for the moment, greater than herself. But Valentine did not know it. He looked towards the sofa and saw spread upon it a thin, painted, haggard young creature, curled into a position at once passionate, languid and merely awkward, with relentless, thickly-tangled hair, staring eyes and half-opened lips, glowering in rouged stupidity and a coarseness of the gutter. He was a philosopher, with a beauty of the stars and of snows, with a refinement, white in its brilliance. She was an image of Regent Street, a ghastly idol of the town; and he was telling her strange things that she could never comprehend in a jargon that was to her as Greek or as Hebrew. It was too absurd. Yet he loved to tell her, and he could scarcely tell why he loved it.

" Go on," said the lady of the feathers.

" This man," Valentine said, assuming a devout earnestness to trick her more, and watching for the puzzled expression to grow and to deepen in her eyes, "this man had a holy nature, or I will say an unalterable will to do only things pure, reserved, refined, things that could not lead his body into difficulties, or his mind into quagmires. He was a saint without a religion. That is a possibility, I assure you, for a will can be amazingly independent. He had the peculiar grace that is said to belong to angels, a definite repugnance to sin. I know you understand me."

She nodded bluntly.

" I know—he couldn't go wrong, it was ever so," she ejaculated.

" If it was ever so—as the housemaids say—you put the position of this man in a nutshell, and if this strange will of his had never relented the transformation I am going to describe or—" he paused for a moment as if in doubt, then continued—" or rather to hint at, would never have taken place. But he grew dissatisfied with his will. It bored him ever so little. He fancied he would like to change it and to substitute for it the will of the world. And the will of the world, as you know well, my lady of the feathers, is to sin. For some time he longed, vaguely enough, to be different, to be, in fact, lower down in the scale than he was. But his longing to be able to desire sin did not lead him to desire it actually. One can force oneself to do a thing, you see, but one cannot force oneself to wish to do it, or to enjoy doing it. And this man, being a selfish saint—saints are very often very selfish—would not sin without desiring it. So it seemed that he must remain for ever as he was, a human piece of flawless porcelain, wishing to be cracked and common delft."

" Whatever did he wish it for ? " asked Cuckoo, with the surprise of a zany.

" Who can tell why one man wishes for one thing, another for another ? That, too, is a mystery. The point is that he did wish it, and that he did something more."

" What was that, eh ? "

" He deliberately tried to weaken and to deface his will, to alter it. And he chose curious means, acting under suggestion from another will or influence that was more powerful than his own, because it was utterly self-satisfied and desired only to be what it was. I don't think I will tell you what the means were. But his original dissatisfaction with his own goodness was the weapon that brought about his own destruction. His will did not change, as he believed, but what do you think actually happened to it ? I will tell you. It was expelled from his body. He lost it for ever. He lost, in fact, his identity. For will is personality, soul, the *ego*, the man himself. And this soul, if you choose to call it so, was driven into the air. It went away in the darkness like a bird. Do you see ? "

He waved his hand upward, and lifted his eyes, as if following with them the flight that he described.

" It flew away ! "

" Where did it go ? " ejaculated Cuckoo.

Valentine seemed suddenly to become fully aware of the depth of her interest.

" Ah ! even you are fascinated by my gospel, you who cannot understand it," he said. " But I cannot tell you where it went. I, too, have wondered."

He knit his brows rather moodily over this question of location. " I, too, have wondered. But I imagine that it died, that it ceased to be. Divorced from the body that was its home, degraded by dissatisfaction with itself, of what use could it be to any one ? Even if it still continues to be it is practically dead, for it can work neither harm nor good to any one, and the thing that cannot be good or evil, or turn others towards the one or the other, is dead. It is no more a will. It is no more an influence. It is a heart without a pulse in it ; in fact, it is nothing."

A sort of joy had leapt into his face as he dwelt on this idea of nothingness, and he added :

" It is something like your soul, my lady of the feathers. Do you hear me ? "

" Yes. I hear ! "

" But the will that ousted it gained in power by that triumph. Totally self-satisfied, desirous only of being that which it is, having no enemy of yearning disappointment with itself in its camp, it can do what will never did before. It can lead captive the soul that was formerly the captive of the soul that it drove away to die. Like an enemy it has seized its opponent's camp, and the slave dwelling in that camp is now its slave for ever."

As Valentine spoke he seemed to become almost intoxicated with the thoughts conjured up by his own words. His blue eyes blazed with a fury of shining excitement. His white cheeks were suffused with blood.

" I have made myself, my will, a God ! " he exclaimed passionately.

At the words the lady of the feathers moved suddenly forward on the sofa.

" What—*you !* " she said.

The last word was uttered with an intensity that could surely only spring from something near akin to comprehension, if not from actual comprehension itself. It certainly startled Valentine, or seemed to startle him. His face showed an amazement, like the amazement of a man raving to an image of wood, to whom, abruptly, the wood speaks with a tongue.

" What do you mean ? " he said, and his voice faltered from its note of triumph and of exultation.

Cuckoo resumed her former position.

" Only was you the will, or the man, or whatever it all is ? " she replied in the voice of one hopelessly muddled.

Valentine was reassured as to her stupidity.

" That has nothing to do with the story," he said.

" There was two of them, was there ? " she persisted, but still with the accent of a hopeless dullard.

" Oh yes. One will must always work upon another, or else there could be no story worth the telling."

" Oh, I see, that's it."

Valentine again broke into laughter.

" You see, do you ? " he said. " You see that, but do you see the truth of what I told you before about the connection of the will with the body ? Do you see why you have no power now, can never have power again ? Do you understand that the wreck of your body inevitably causes the wreck of your will, so that it really dies and ceases, because it can no more influence others ? Do you understand that ? I'll make you understand it now. Come here."

He got up from his chair and seized her two hands in his, dragging her almost violently up from the sofa. Her fear of him, always lurking near, came upon her with a rush at the contact of his hands and she hung back, moved by an irresistible repulsion. The slight and momentary struggle between them caused her hair, carelessly turned up and loosely pinned, to come down. It fell all round her in a loose shock of unnatural colour. Valentine's hands were strong and Cuckoo soon felt that resistance was useless. She let her body yield, and he drew her in front of the glass that stood over the mantelpiece. Pushing back the table behind them, he made her stand still in the unwinking glare of the three gas jets, which she had herself turned up earlier in the evening.

"Look there!" he cried, "look at yourself well! How can you have power over anybody?"

Their two faces, set close together as in a frame, stared at them from the mirror, and Cuckoo—forced to obedience—examined them as if, indeed, they were a picture. She saw the man's face, fair, beautiful, refined, triumphant, full of the courage that is based upon experience of itself and of its deeds and possibilities, full of a strange excitement that filled the face with amazingly vivid expression. She saw the bright blue eyes gazing at her, the red lips of the mouth curved in a smile. There was health in the face as well as thought. And there was power, which is greater than health, more beautiful even than beauty. And then she turned her eyes to the face's companion. Thin, sharp, faded, it met her eyes, half-shrouded in the thick, tumbled hair that shone in the mirror with the peculiar frigid glare that can only be imparted by a chemical dye, and can never be simulated by nature. One cheek was chalk white. The other, which had been pressed against the horsehair of the sofa, showed a harsh scarlet patch. All the varying haggard expressions of the world seemed crowding in the eyes of this scarecrow, and peering beneath the thickly blackened eyelashes that struck a violent discord against the yellow hair. The thin lips of the mouth were pressed together in an expression of pain, fear and weariness. Shadows slept under the eyes where the face had fallen into hollows. To-night there seemed no vestige of prettiness in those peaked features. Nothing of health, youth, gaiety or even girlhood was written in them, but only a terrible, a brutal record of spoliation and of wreckage, of plunder and of despair. And the gaslight, striking the flat surface of the mirror, made the record glitter with a thin, cheap sparkle, like the tinsel trappings of the life whose story the mirror revealed in its reflection.

How, indeed, could such a creature have power over fellow man or woman for good or for evil? If weakness can be written without words it seemed written in that wasted countenance, which Cuckoo examined with a creeping horror that numbed her like frost. As she did so, Valentine was watching the ungraciousness of her face in the glass deepen and glide, moment by moment, into greater ugliness, greater degradation. And as the little light there had ever been behind those unquiet eyes faded gradually away, in his reflected eyes the light leaped up into a fuller glare, sparkling to unbridled triumph. And his reflected lips smiled more defiantly, until the smile was no longer touched merely with triumph, but with something more vehement and more malign! Cuckoo did not see the change. She saw only herself, and her heart cried and wailed, What good—what good to love Julian? What good to hate Valentine? What good to fight for the man she loved against the man she loathed? As well set a doll to move its tense joints against an army, or a scarecrow to defy a god! Never before had she realised thoroughly the complete tragedy of her life. Hitherto she had assisted at it in fragments, coming in for a scene here, a scene there. Now she sat through the whole of the five acts, and the only thing she missed was the fall of the curtain. That remained up. But why? There was—there could be nothing more to come, unless a dreary recapitulation of such dreary events as had already been displayed. Such a cup could hold no wine that was not foul, thick and poisonous. And she had known herself so little as to imagine that she could really love, and that her love might fulfil itself in protection instead of in sensual gratification. Yes, vaguely she had believed that. She had even believed that she could put on armour and do battle against—and at this point in her desperate meditation the lady of the feathers shifted her eyes from her own face mirrored to the face beside it. As she did so, a sudden cry escaped from her lips. For a moment she thought she saw the face of the dead Marr, and the hallucination was so vivid that, when it was gone, and the mirror once more revealed the face of Valentine, Cuckoo had no thought but that she had really seen Marr. She turned sharply round and cast a glance behind her. Then:

"Did you see him?" she whispered to Valentine.

"Whom?"

"Him—Marr! He's not dead; he's here; he's here, I tell you. I see him in the glass!"

She shivered. The room seemed spinning round with her, and the two faces danced and sprang in the mirror, as if a hand shook it up and down, from side to side.

"If he is here," Valentine said, "it is not in the way you fancy. Your imagination has played you a trick."

"Didn't you—didn't you see him? Don't you see him now?"

"I see only you and myself."

As if for a joke he bent his head and peered closely at the mirror, like a man endeavouring to discern some very pale and dim reflection there.

"No, he's—he's not there!" he murmured, "but—— "

With a harsh exclamation he dashed his fist against the mirrored face of the lady of the feathers. The glass cracked and broke from top to bottom. Cuckoo cried out. Valentine's hand had blood upon it. He did not seem to know this, and swung round upon her with an almost savage fury.

"Don't—don't for God's sake," she cried, fearing an attack.

But he made no movement against her. On the contrary, an expression of relief chased the anger from his lips and eyes.

"Ah!" he said, "that's a lying mirror! It lied to you and to me. I smashed it. Well, I'll give you another that is more truthful, and more ornamental, too."

"What was it you saw?" she murmured.

"A silly vision, power where there is only weakness; a will, a soul, where there could not be one!"

"Eh? was it that you struck at?"

"Why do you ask?" he said with sudden suspicion.

"You struck where my face was," she said doggedly. "You did, you did!"

"Nonsense!"

"It ain't! Why did you do it then?"

A gleam of hope had shot into her eyes, lit by his weird attack upon her mirrored image. After all, despite his sneers at her faded body, his gibes at her faded and decaying soul, he struck at her as a man strikes at the thing he fears. In that faded soul a wild hope and courage leaped up, banishing all the sick despair which had preceded it. The lady of the feathers faced Valentine with a deathless resolution of glance and of attitude.

"You've been telling lies," she said, "you've been telling me damned lies!"

"What do you mean?"

"You said as I was—was done with."

A forced smile came like a hissing snake on Valentine's lips.

"So you are!"

"I ain't! I ain't! What's more you know it?"

"You have broken yourself to pieces as I have broken that mirror!"

He spoke with an effort after scathing contempt, but she detected a quiver of agitation in his voice.

"If I have, I'll break you yet!" she cried.

"Me? What are you talking about?"

"You know well enough."

"But do you know—do you know that I—I am Marr?"

He almost whispered the last words! A chill of awe fell over the lady of the feathers. She did not understand what he meant, and yet she felt as if he spoke the truth, as if this inexplicable mystery were yet indeed no fiction, no phantasy, but stern fact, and as if, strangely, she had at the back of her mind divined it, known it when she first knew Valentine, yet only realised it now that he himself told her. She did not speak. She only looked at him, turning white slowly as she looked.

"I am Marr," he repeated. "Now, do you understand my gospel? Understand it if you can, for you are bereft of the power that belongs of right only to the woman who is pure. Long ago, perhaps, you might have fought me. Who knows, you might even have conquered me? But you have thrown yourself to the wolves, and they have torn you till you are only a skeleton. And how can a soul dwell in a skeleton? Your soul, your will, is as useless as that vagrant soul of Valentine, which I expelled into the air and into the night. It can do nothing; you can do nothing either. If I have ever feared you, and hated you because I feared you, I have fooled myself. I have divined your thoughts. I have known your emnity against me and your love—*yours!*—for Julian. But if the soul and the will of Valentine could not save Julian from my possession, how can yours? You are an outcast of the streets! Go back to the streets. Live in them. Die in them! They are your past, your present, your future. They are your hell, your heaven. They are everything to you. I tell you that you are as much of them as are the stones of the pavement that the feet of such women as you tread night after night. And what soul can a street thing have? What can be the will of a creature who gives herself to every man who beckons, and who follows every voice that calls? I feared you. I might as well have feared a shadow, an echo, a sigh of the wind, or the fall of an autumn leaf. I might as well have feared that personal devil whom men raise up for themselves as a bogey. Will is God! Will is the devil! Will is everything! And you—you, having tossed your will away—are nothing."

He had spoken gravely, even sombrely. On the last word he was gone.

The lady of the feathers stood alone in the ugly little room, and heard the clock of the great church close by chime the hour of midnight. Her face was set and white under its rouge, in its frame of disordered canary-coloured hair. Her eyes were clouded with perplexity, with horror, and with awe. Yet she looked undaunted. Staring at the door through which the man men still called Valentine Cresswell had vanished, she whispered:

"It ain't true! It ain't! Nothin' does for a woman; not when she loves a man! Nothin'. Nothin'."

She fell down against the hard horse-hair sofa, and stretched her arms upon it, and laid her head against them, as if she prayed.

BOOK IV—DOCTOR LEVILLIER

CHAPTER I

THE LADY VISITS DOCTOR LEVILLIER

The Russian Grand Duke, whose malady was mainly composed of two ingredients, unlimited wealth and almost unlimited power, was slow in recovering, and slower still in making up his mind to part with the little nerve doctor whom he had summoned from England. And so London was beginning to fall into its misty autumn mood before Dr. Levillier was once more established in Harley Street. He had heard occasionally from both Valentine and Julian during his long absence, but their letters had not communicated much, and once or twice when he, in replying to them, had put one or two friendly questions as to their doings, those questions had remained unanswered. The doctor had been particularly reluctant to leave England at the time when the Grand Duke's summons reached him, as his interest and curiosity about Valentine had just been keenly and thoroughly roused. But fate fought for the moment against his curiosity. It remained entirely ungratified. He had not once seen Valentine since the afternoon in Victoria Street, when the lamentation of that thoroughfare's saint had struck consternation into the hearts of musical sinners. Nor had the doctor met any one who could give him news of the two youths over whose welfare his soul had learned to watch. Now, when he returned to London, he found that both Valentine and Julian were abroad. Only Rip, left in charge of Julian's servant, greeted him with joy; Rip, whose conduct had given the first strong impulse to his wonder and doubt about Valentine.

Dr. Levillier took up the threads of his long-forsaken practice, and gave himself to his work while autumn closed round London. One day he heard casually from a patient that Valentine and Julian had returned to town. He wondered that they had not let him know : the omission seemed curious and unfriendly.

During the day on which the news reached him he was, as usual busily engaged from morning till evening in the reception of patients His reputation was very great, and men and women thronged hi consulting-rooms. Although his rule was that nobody could ever gain admission to him without an appointment, it was a rule made to be broken. He never had the heart to turn any one from his door in distress, and so it frequently happened that his working day was prolonged by the admission of people who unexpectedly intruded themselves upon him. Great ladies more especially often came to him on the spur of the moment, prompted to seek his solace by sudden attacks of the nerves. A lover had used them ill, perhaps, or a husband had turned upon them and had rent a long dressmaker's bill into fragments, without paying it first. Or the *ennui* of an exquisite life of unbridled pleasure had suddenly sprung upon them like a grisly spectre, torn their hearts, shaken them into tears. Or—and this happened often—a fantastic recognition of the obvious fact that even butterflies must die, had abruptly started into their minds obtruding a skeleton head above the billowing *chiffons*, rattling its bones until the dismal sound outvied the *frou-frou* of silk, the burr of great waving fans, the click of high heels from Paris. Then, in terror, they drove to Dr. Levillier's door and begged to see him, if only for a moment.

There was no doctor in London so universally sought by the sane lunatics of society as Dr. Levillier. He was no mad doctor. He had no private asylum. He had never definitely aimed at becoming a famous specialist in lunacy. But the pretty lunatics came to him nevertheless ; the lunatics who live at afternoon parties, till the grave yawns at their feet, and they must go down the strange ways of another world, teacup in hand, scandal still fluttering upon their ashy lip ; the lunatics who live for themselves, until their eyes are hollow as tombs, and their mouths fall in from selfishness, and their cheeks are a greenish white from satiety, and lust's gratified flame, like beacons, on their drawn cheeks and along their crawling wrinkles ; the lunatics who seek to be what they can never be, the beauties of this world, the great Queens of the Sun, whose gaze shall glorify, whose smile shall crown and bless, whose touch shall call hearts to agony and to worship, whose word shall take a man from his plough and send him out to win renown, or snatch a leader from his ambition and set him creeping in the dust, like a white mouse prisoned by a scarlet silken thread ; the lunatics who dandle religions like dolls, and play with faiths as a boy plays with marbles, until the moment comes when the game is over, and the player is faced by the terror of a great lesson ; the lunatics who stare away their days behind prancing horses in the Park, who worship in the sacred groves of bonnets, who burn incense to rouged and powdered fashions, who turn literature into a "movement," and art into a cult, and humanity into a bogey, and love into an adulterous sensation; the lunatics who think that to "live" is only another word for to sin, that innocence is a prison and vice liberty; the lunatics who fill their boudoirs with false gods, and cry everlastingly: "Baal, hear us!" till the fire comes down from heaven, which is no painted ceiling presided over by a plaster god. These came to Dr. Levillier, day by day, overtaken by sad moments, by sudden, dreary crises of the soul, that set them impotently wailing, like Job among the potsherds. Many of them did not "curse God" only because they did not believe in Him.

It is not the fashion in London to believe in God just now.

Dr. Levillier had always, since he was a youth, walking hospitals and searching the terror of life for all its secrets, felt a deep care, a deep solicitude, for each duet, body and soul, that walked the world. He had never set them apart, never lost sight of one in turning his gaze upon the other. This fact, no doubt, accounted partially for the fact that many looked upon him as the greatest nerve doctor in London. For the nervous system is surely a network lacing the body to the soul, and *vice versâ*. Every *liaison* has it connecting links, the links that have brought it into being. One lust stretches forth a hook and finds an eye in another, and there is union. So with faiths, with longings, with fine aspirations, with sordid grovellings. There is ever the hook seeking the appropriate eye. The body has a hook, the soul an eye. They meet at birth and part only at death.

Dr. Levillier was constantly, and ignorantly, entreated to adjust the one comfortably in the other. It is a delicate business this adjustment, sometimes an impossible business. Half the Harley Street patients came saying, "Make me well." What they really meant was, "Make me happy." Yet the most of them would have resented a valuable mixed prescription, advice for the hook, and advice for the eye. Such prescriptions had to be very deftly, sometimes very furtively, made up. Often the doctor felt an intense exhaustion steal over him towards the close of day. This tremendous and eternal procession passing onwards through his life, filing before him like a march-past of sick soldiers, saluting him with cries, and with questions, and with entreaties; this never ceasing progress fatigued him. There were moments when he longed to hide his face, to turn away, to shut his ears to the murmuring voices, and his eyes to the pale, expressive faces, to put his great profession from him, as one puts a beggar into the night. But these were only moments, and they passed quickly. And the little doctor was always bitterly ashamed of them, as a brave man is ashamed of a secret tug of cowardice at his heart. For it seemed to him the greatest thing in all the world to help to make the unhappy rightly happier.

And this was, and had always been, his tireless endeavour. Upon this day one of these hated moments of mental and physical exhaustion had come upon him, and he struggled hard against his enemy. The procession of patients had been long, and more than once in the tiny interval between the exit of one and the entry of another, Dr. Levillier had peeped at his watch. His last appointment was at a quarter to five, then he would be free, and he said to himself that he would take a cab and drive down to Victoria Street. Valentine was often at home about six. The doctor put aside the little devil of pride that whispered " You have been badly treated," and resolved to make the advance to this friend, who seemed to have forgotten him. In times of fatigue and depression he had often sought Valentine in order to be solaced by his music. But this solace was at an end, unless, indeed, the strange burden of musical impotence had been lifted from Valentine, and his talent had been restored to him.

The last patient came to the doctor's door punctually and was punctually dismissed as the clock chimed the quarter of an hour after five. The last prescription was written. The doctor drew in a deep breath of relief. He touched the bell and his servant appeared.

" There is no one waiting ? " he asked.

" No, sir."

" I have made no other appointment for to-day, and I am going out almost immediately. If any patients should call casually tell them I cannot possibly see them to-day. Ask them to make an appointment. But I cannot see any one to-day under any circumstances."

" Yes, sir."

Dr. Levillier took his way upstairs, made a careful toilet, selected from his absurd array of boots a pair perfectly polished, put them on, took his hat and gloves, sighed once again heavily, almost as a dog sighs preparatory to its sleep, and turned to go downstairs. He forgot for the moment that he was prepared to watch Valentine. Perhaps, indeed, his long period of absence had dulled in his memory the recollection of any apparent change in his friend. For at this moment of fatigue he only recalled Valentine's expression of purity and high-souled health, and the atmosphere of lofty serenity in which he seemed habitually to dwell. The doctor wanted relief. How Valentine's presence would refresh him after this dreary array of patients, after the continuous murmurs of their plaintive voices ! As he opened his bedroom door he perceived his manservant mounting the stairs.

"Lawler, I can't see any one," he said more hastily than usual. "I told you so distinctly. I am going out immediately."

The man paused. He had been with the doctor for many years, and both adored and understood him. The doctor looked at him.

"It is a patient, I suppose?" he asked.

"Well, sir, I can't exactly say."

"A lady?"

"Yes, sir. At least, sir—well, no, sir."

"What do you mean?"

"A female, sir."

"What does she want?"

"To see you, sir. I can't get her to go. I asked her to, sir; then I told her to."

"Well?"

"She only gave me this and said she'd come to see you, and if you were in she'd wait."

He handed a card to his master. The doctor took it and read:

"Cuckoo Bright, 400 Marylebone Road."

The words conveyed nothing to his mind, for neither Julian nor Valentine had ever talked to him of the lady of the feathers.

"Cuckoo Bright," he said. "An odd name! And an odd person, I suppose, Lawler?"

Lawler pursed his lips rather primly.

"Very odd, sir. Not at all a usual sort of patient, sir."

"H'm. Go and ask her if she comes as a patient or on private business."

The man retreated and returned.

"The—lady says she's ill and must see you, sir, if only for a moment."

This was Cuckoo's ruse to get into the house, and was based upon Julian's long-ago remark that the doctor could never resist helping any one who was in trouble. Standing on the doorstep, she had histrionically simulated faintness for the special benefit of Lawler, who regarded her with deep suspicion.

"I suppose I must see her," the doctor said with a sigh. "Show her in, Lawler."

Lawler departed, disapprovingly, to do so, and, after a moment, the doctor followed him. He walked into his consulting-room, where he found the lady of the feathers standing by the writing-table. The autumn day was growing dark, and the street was full of deepening mist. Cuckoo was but a fantastic shadow in the room. Her dress rustled with an uneasy sound as the doctor came in. His first act was to turn on the electric light. In a flash the rustling shadow was converted into substance. Cuckoo and the doctor stood face to face and Cuckoo's tired eyes fastened with a hungry, almost a wolfish, scrutiny upon this stranger. She wanted so much of him. The look was so full of intense meaning that, coming in a flash with the electric flash, it startled the doctor. Yet he had seen something like it before in the eyes of those who suspected that they carried death within them, and came to ask him if it were true. He was surprised, too, by her appearance. The women of the streets did not come to him, although if they had been able to read the writing in his heart many of them would surely have come. He shook hands with Cuckoo, told her to sit down, and sat down himself opposite to her.

"What is the matter? Please tell me your symptoms," he said, gently.

"Eh?" was the reply, spoken in a thin and high voice.

"What has been troubling you?"

Cuckoo, who was wholly unaccustomed to answer a doctor's questions, started violently. She fancied from his words that he had divined the lie she had told when she said that she was ill, and knew that she came for a mental reason. Instinctively she connected the word "trouble" with the heart, in a way that was oddly and pathetically girlish. Acting upon this impulse she exclaimed:

"Then you know as I ain't ill?"

Dr. Levillier was still more surprised. Not understanding what was in her mind, he entirely failed to keep pace with its agility.

"Why do you come to me then?" he asked.

"Oh," she returned, with a quickly gathering hesitation, "I thought as perhaps you knew."

"I! But we have never met before."

The doctor bent his eyes on her searchingly. For a moment he began to wonder whether his visitor was quite right in her head. Cuckoo shuffled under his gaze. The very kindliness of his face and gentleness of his voice made her feel hot and abashed. A prickly sensation ran over her body, as she cleared her throat and said, monosyllabically:

"No."

The doctor waited.

"What is it?" he said at length. "Tell me why you have called. If you are not ill, what is it you want of me?"

"You'll laugh, p'raps."

"Laugh? Is it something funny, then?"

"Funny! Not it!"

The sound of her voice seemed to give her some courage, for she went on with more hardy resolution:

"Look here, you can see what I am—oh yes you can—and you wonder what I'm doin' here. Well, if I tell you, will you promise as you won't laugh at me?"

This was Cuckoo's way of delicately sounding the doctor's depths. She thought it decidedly subtle.

"Yes, I'll promise that," the doctor said.

He looked at her faded young face and felt no inclination to laugh.

"Well then," Cuckoo said, more excitedly, "you know Ju— Mr. Addison, don't you?"

The doctor began to see a ray of light.

"Certainly I do," he said.

"And Mr. Cresswell?"

"He is one of my most intimate friends."

The words were spoken with an unconscious warmth that chilled Cuckoo. For surely the man who spoke thus of the man she hated must be her enemy. She faltered visibly, and a despairing expression crept into her eyes.

"I don't know as it's any use my sayin' it," she began as if half to herself.

The doctor saw that she was much troubled and the kindness of his nature was roused.

"Don't be afraid of me," he said. "You have come here to tell me something, tell it frankly. I am a friend of both the people you mention."

"You can't be that," she suddenly cried. "Nobody can't be that!"

"Why not?"

"You ought to know."

She said it fiercely. All her self-consciousness was suddenly gone, swept away by the flood of thought and of remembrance that was surging through her mind.

"Why can't you see what he is," she exclaimed, "any more than he can, than Julian—Mr. Addison, I mean? Any one'd think you was all mad, they would."

Dr. Levillier was glad he had admitted the lady of the feathers to his presence. Interest sprang up in him, alive and searching.

"Tell me what you mean," he said. "Are you talking about Mr. Cresswell?"

"Yes, I am; and I say of all the beasts in London he's the greatest."

Cuckoo did not choose her words carefully. She was highly excited and she wanted to be impressive. It seemed to her that to use strong language was the only way to be impressive. So she used it. The doctor's face grew graver.

"Surely you hardly know what you're saying," he said very quietly.

But his thoughts flew to that summer night when his mastiffs howled against Valentine, and he felt as if a mystery were deepening round him as the autumn mist of evening deepened in the street outside.

"I do," she reiterated. "I do. But nobody won't see it. And it's no use what I see. How can it be?"

The words were almost a wail.

"Tell me what you see."

Cuckoo looked into the doctor's sincere eyes, and a sudden rush of hope came to her.

"That's what I want to. But if you like him you'll only be angry."

"No, I shall not."

"Well, then. I see as he's ruinin' his friend."

"Ruining Mr. Addison?"

"Yes."

It struck the doctor as very strange that such a girl as Cuckoo obviously was should cry out in such a passionate way against the ruin of any young man. Was it not her fate to ruin others as she herself had been ruined? He wondered what her connection with the two youths was, and perhaps his face showed something of his wonder, for Cuckoo added, after a long glance at him:

"It's true, yes it is," as if she read his doubts.

"How do you come to know it?" the doctor said, not at all unkindly, but as if anxious to elucidate matters.

"Why, I tell you I can see it plain. Besides," and here she dropped her voice, "Valentine, as he calls himself—though he ain't —as good as told me. He did tell me, only I couldn't understand. He knew I couldn't—d'you see? That's why he told me. Oh, if he'd only tell you!"

Fragments of Valentine's exposition of his deeds and of his strange gospel were floating through Cuckoo's mind as fragments of broken wood float by on a stream, fragments of broken wood that were part of a puzzle, that should be rescued by some strong hand from the stream, and fitted together into a perfect whole.

"Valentine! You say he told you that he was ruining Julian?"

Unconsciously the doctor used the Christian names. His doing so set Cuckoo more at her ease.

"Yes. Not like that. But he told me. He ain't what you think, nor what Julian thinks. He's somebody else, and you can't tell it. He's laughing at you all."

Thus the gospel came forth from the painted lips of Cuckoo, crude and garbled, yet true gospel. The doctor was completely puzzled. All he gathered from this announcement was that Valentine seemed in some way to have been confiding in this girl of the streets. Such a fact was sufficiently astounding. That they should ever have been associated together in any way was almost incredible to any one who knew Valentine. Yet it was quite obvious that they did know each other, and in no ordinary manner.

"Do you know Mr. Cresswell well?" the doctor said.

He saw that he could only make the tangle clear by being to some extent judicial. Humanity merely excited Cuckoo to something that was violently involved, passionate, and almost hysterical.

"Well enough."

"And Mr. Addison?"

Cuckoo flushed slowly.

"Yes, I know him—quite well."

An almost similar answer, but given with such a change of manner as would be only possible in a woman. It told the doctor much of the truth and gave him the first page of a true reading of Cuckoo's character. But he went on with apparently unconscious quietude:

"And you came here to tell me, who know and like them both, that the one is ruining the other. What made you come to me?"

"Why, somethin' Julian said once. He thinks a lot of you. I was afraid to come, but I—I thought I would. It's seein' them—at least Julian—since they got back made me come."

"I haven't seen them yet," the doctor said, and there was an interrogation in the accent with which he spoke. Something in Cuckoo's intense manner roused both wonder and alarm in him. She evidently spoke, driven by a tremendous impulse. What vision had given that impulse life?

"Ah!" she said, and fell suddenly into a dense silence, touching her left cheek mechanically with her hand, which was covered by a long black silk glove. She alternately pressed the fingers of it against the cheek bone and withdrew them, as one who marks the progress of a tune, hummed or played on some instrument. Her eyes were staring downwards upon the carpet. The doctor watched her, and the wonder and fear grew in him.

"Have you nothing more to tell me?" he said at last.

"Eh?"

She put down her hand slowly and turned her eyes on him.

"What do you wish me to do?" he said. "I do not know yet what may——" he checked himself and substituted, "I must go and see my friends."

"Yes, go."

She nodded her head slowly, and then she shivered as she sat in the chair.

"Go, and do somethin'," she said. "I would—I want to—but I can't. It's true, I suppose, what he said. I'm nearly done with, I'm spoilt. I say, you're a doctor, aren't you? You know things? Tell me then, do, what's the good of goin' on being able to feel—

I mean to feel just like anybody, anybody as hasn't gone down, you know—if you can't do anythin' the same as they can, get round anybody to make 'em go right? I could send him right, I could, as well as any girl, if feelin' 'd only do it. But feelin' ain't a bit of good. It's looks, I suppose. Everythin' 's looks."

" No, not everything," the doctor said.

Cuckoo's speech both interested and touched him. Its confused wistfulness came straight from the heart. And then it recalled to the doctor a conversation he had had with Valentine, when they talked over the extraordinary influence that the mere appearance—will working through features—of one man or woman can have over another. The doctor could only at present rather dimly apprehend the feeling entertained for Julian by Cuckoo. But as he glanced at her, he understood very well the pathos of the contest at present raging between her heart and the painted shell which held it.

" Nobody who feels goodness is utterly bereft of the power of bringing good to another," he said. " For we can seldom really feel what we can never really be."

Light shone through the shadows of the tired face at the words.

" He said different from that," she exclaimed.

" He—who ? "

" Him as you call Valentine. That's why he told me all about it, because he knew as I shouldn't understand, and because he thinks I can't do nothin' for any one. But I say, you do somethin' for Julian, will you, will you ? "

There was a passion of pleading in her voice. She had lost her fear of him, and, stretching out her hand, touched the sleeve of his coat.

" I don't understand it all," the doctor said. " I don't like to accept what you say about Mr. Cresswell even in thought. But I will go and see him, and Julian. The dogs," he added in a low and secret voice to himself. " There is something terribly strange in all this."

He fell into a silence of consideration that lasted longer than he knew. The lady of the feathers began to fidget in it uneasily. She felt that her mission was perhaps accomplished and that she ought to go. She looked across at the doctor, pulled her silk gloves up on her thin arms, and kicked one foot against the other. He did not seem to notice. She glanced towards the window. The fog was pressing its face against the glass like a dreary and terrible person looking in upon them with haggard eyes. It was time, she supposed, for her to drift out into the arms that belonged to that dreary and terrible face. She got up.

" I'll go now," she said.

The doctor did not hear.

" I'll go now, please," she repeated.

This time he heard and got up. He looked at her and said, "I have your address. I will see you again."

If misery chanced to stand once in his path, he seldom lost sight of it till he had at least tried to bring a smile to its lips, a ray of hope to its eyes. But in the instance of Cuckoo he had other reasons, or might have other reasons, for seeing her in the future.

" You are sure you have nothing more to say to me ? " he asked.

She shook her head.

" No, I don't think," she murmured.

" Then good-bye."

He held out his hand. She put hers in it, with an action that was oddly ladylike for Cuckoo. Then she went out, rather awkwardly, in a reaction, to the hall, the doctor following. He opened the door for her, and the mist crawled instantly in.

" It's a gloomy night," he said. " Very autumnal."

" Yes, ain't it ? I do hate the nights."

She spoke the words with an accent that was venomous.

" O-r-r ! " she said.

And with that ejaculation, half an uttered shiver, half a muttered curse, she gave herself to the fog, and was gone.

Dr. Levillier stood for a moment looking into the vague and dreamy darkness. Then he put on his coat and hat, caught up a cab whistle, and, with a breath, sent a shrill and piercing note into the night. Long and mournfully it sounded. And only the moist silence answered like that paradox—a voice that is dumb. Again and again the cry went forth, and at last there was an answering rattle. Two bright eyes advanced in the fog very slowly, looking for the sound, it seemed, as for a thing visible. The doctor got into the cab, and set forth in the fog to visit Valentine.

CHAPTER II

THE VOICE IN THE EMPTY ROOM

WHEN the doctor arrived at the Victoria Street flat Valentine's man answered his ring. Wade had been with Valentine for many years and was always famous for his great devotion to, and admiration of his master. Wade was also especially partial—as he would have expressed himself—to Dr. Levillier, and when he saw who the visitor was, his face relaxed into contentment that strongly suggested a smile.

" Back at last Wade, you see," the doctor said, cheerfully. " Is Mr. Cresswell in ? "

" No sir. But I expect him every minute to dress for dinner. He's dining out, and it's near seven now. Will you come in and wait ? "

" Yes."

The doctor entered and walked into the drawing-room, preceded by Wade, who turned on the light.

" Why ! what have you been doing to the room ? " the doctor said, looking round in some surprise. " Dear me. It's very much altered."

In truth, the change in it was marked. The grand piano had vanished, and in its place stood an enormous cabinet made of wood, stained black, and covered with grotesque gold figures, whose unnatural faces were twisted ·into the expressions of all the vices. Some of these faces smiled, others scowled, others protruded forked tongues like snakes and seemed to hiss along the blackness of the background. The shapes of the figures were voluptuous and yet suggested, rather than fully revealed, deformity, as if the minds of these monsters sought to reveal their distortion by the very lines of their curved and wanton limbs. Upon the top of this cabinet stood a gigantic rose-coloured jar filled with orchids, the Messalinas of the hothouse, whose mauve corruption and spotted faces leered down to greet the gold goblins beneath. It was easy to imagine them whispering to each other soft histories of unknown sins, and jeering at the corrupt respectabilities of London, as they clustered together

and leaned above the ruddy ramparts of the china, wild flowers as
no hedgerow violet, or pale smirking primrose, is ever wild in the
farthest wood.

Glancing from this cabinet, and those that stood upon it, the
doctor was aware of a deep and dusty note of red in the room,
sounding from carpet and walls, tingling drowsily in the window
curtains and in the cushions that lay upon the couches. This was
not the crude and cheerful sealing-wax red with which the festive
Philistine loves to dye the whiteness of his dining-room walls, cooling
its chubby absurdity with panels of that old oak which is for ever
new. It was a dim and deep colour, such as a dust-filmed ruby
might emit if illuminated by a soft light. And Valentine had
shrouded it so adroitly, that though it pervaded the entire room it
always seemed distant and remote, a background, vast perhaps, but
clouded and shadowed by nearer things. These nearer things were
many, for Valentine's original asceticism, which had displayed itself
essentially in the slight bareness of his principal sitting-room, had
apparently been swept away by a tumultuous greed for ornaments.
The room was crowded with furniture, chairs and sofas of the most
peculiar shapes, divans and tables, book-stands and settees. One
couch was made of wood carved and painted into the semblance of a
woman, between whose outstretched arms was placed the pillow to
receive the head of one resting there. Another lay on the bent backs
of two grinning Indian boys, whose crouching limbs seemed twined
into a knot. Upon the tables and cabinets stood a thousand ornaments, many of them silver toys, sweetmeat boxes, tiny ivory figures,
and wriggling atrocities from the East. But what struck the doctor
most in the transformation of the room was the panorama presented
upon its walls. The pictures that he remembered so well were all
gone. The classical figures, the landscapes full of atmosphere and of
delicacy had vanished. And from their places leered down jockeys
and street-women painted by Jan Van Beers and Dégas, Chaplin
and Gustave Courbet, while above the mantelpiece, where once had
hung "The Merciful Knight," a Cocotte by Leibl smoked a pipe
into the room. It seemed incredible that Valentine could be at rest
in such a livid chamber, and not even the vague communications of
Cuckoo woke in the doctor such a definite and alive sensation of discomfort as this vision of outward change that must surely betoken
an inward transformation of the most vivid and unusual kind. And
everywhere, as a deep and monotonous bell ringing relentlessly
through a symphony of discordant and crying passions, there sounded
that sinister note of deep and dusty red. Despite his own complete
health of mind, and the frantic disquisitions of the morbid Nordau,
the little doctor felt as if he heard the colour, as if it spoke from
beneath his very feet, as if it sang under his fingers when he laid

them on the brocade of a couch, as if the room palpitated with heavy music which murmured drowsily in his ears a monotonou song of dull and weary change. No silence had ever before spoke to him so powerfully. He was greatly affected, and did not scrupl to show his discomfort to Wade, who waited respectfully by th door.

"What an alteration!" he said again, but in a lower and mor withdrawn voice. "I cannot recognise the room I once knew—an loved."

"Mr. Valentine has been doing it up, sir."

"But why, Wade, why?"

"I don't know, sir. A fancy, I suppose, sir."

"An evil one," the doctor murmured to himself.

He glanced at Wade. It struck him that the man's mind migh possibly march with Cuckoo's in detection of his master's transforma tion, if transformation there were. Wade returned the doctor' glance with calm good breeding.

"Mr. Valentine is well, I hope, Wade?" he said.

"Very well, sir, I believe."

"And Mr. Addison?"

"I couldn't quite say, sir, as to that."

"Do you mean that he looks ill?"

"I couldn't say, sir. Mr. Julian don't look quite what he was, t my view, sir."

"Oh."

The butler's level voice mingled with the clouded red of the room and again a prophetic chord of change was struck.

"Thank you, Wade," said the doctor.

The man retired, and the doctor was left alone in the empt room.

*   *   *   *   *

Although he was intensely sensitive, Dr. Levillier was not a mar whose nerves played him tricks. He was above all things sane, botl in mind and in body, full of a lively calm and a bright power o observation. Indeed, having made the nervous system his specia life-study he was perhaps less liable than most other human being to be carried away by the fancies that many people tabulate a realities, or to be governed by the beings that have no real existence and are merely projected by the action of the imagination. Half at least of his great success in life had been owing to his self-possession which never verged on hardness, or fused itself with its near relation stolidity. No man, in fact, was less likely to be upset by the creature of his mind than he. Yet when Wade had gently closed the drawing-room door, and retreated into his private region, the doctor allowed himself to become the possession of an influence which, to the end of his life, he believed to proceed from the empty room in which he sat, not from his mind who sat there. The electric light shone softly beneath the shades that shrouded it, and revealed delicately but clearly every smallest detail of the crowded chamber.

The hour was quiet. No fire danced in the grate. Dr. Levillier leaned back in his low chair with the intention of composedly awaiting Valentine's return. But the composure which had already been slightly shaken by the visit of the lady of the feathers, and by the words of Wade, was destined to be curiously upset by the motionless vision of the empty room.

Sitting thus in it alone the doctor examined it with more detail, and with a more definite remembrance of Valentine's habit of mind than before. And he found himself increasingly amazed and confounded. For not only was the change great, but it was not governed and directed by good taste, or even by any definite taste, either good or bad. A number of people might have devised the arrangement and selection of the mass of furniture and ornaments, and have thrown things down here and there in sheer defiance of each other's predilections. Only in the setting, the red setting of the picture, was there evidence of the presence of a presiding genius. In that red setting the doctor supposed that he was to read Valentine. He could read nobody in the rest of the room, or perhaps everybody whose taste refused purity and calm as foolish Dead Sea growths. Some of the silver ornaments might have assembled in the garish boudoir of a Parisian *fille de joie* as the carved woman might have been the couch to which Thaïs tempted Paphnuce, and the Indian boys the lifeless slaves of Aphrodite. The jockeys on the wall would have been at home on the lid of a cigar-box belonging to any average member of the *jeunesse dorée* of any Continental city, while an etching of Felicien Rops that lounged upon a side-table would have been eminently suitable to the house of a certain celebrity nicknamed the "Queen of Diamonds." The golden figures that sprawled over the huge cabinet must have delighted certain modern artists, whose rickety fingers can only portray in line a fanciful corruption totally devoid of relation to humanity, but such frail spectres would have shrunk with horror from certain robust works of art, over which the most healthy of the beefy brigade might have smacked large lips for hours. The room was in fact one quarrel between the masculine and feminine, the corrupt "modern" and the flagrant Philistine, the vaguely suggestive nineteenth-century Athenian and the larky and unbridled schoolboy. A neurotic woman seemed to have been at work here, a sordid youth there. On a side-table the hysterical man of our civilisation fought a duel in taste with some Amazon whose kept vow had evidently wrought a cancer in her mind. In every corner there was

R

the clash of civil war. Yet there was always the cloudy red, visible through the lattice-work of decoration, as the blue sky is visible through the lattice-work of a Tadema interior. In that clouded red the doctor felt himself reading a new yet powerful Valentine, and in the grotesque orchids leaning their mis-shapen chins upon the rosy rim of their vase. Those flowers had evil faces, and they seemed strangely at home in the silent room where no clock ticked and no caged bird twittered. Only the red cloud spoke like a dull voice, and Dr. Levillier sat and listened to it, until he felt as if he began to know a new Valentine. There is an influence that emanates from lifeless things, strong, subtle, and penetrating; an influence in form, in colour, in scent, even in juxtaposition. And such influence is like a voice speaking to the soul. There was a voice in that empty room; and the words it uttered stirred the doctor to a greater surprise, a greater dread than the words of Cuckoo. Her painted lips related that which might well be a legend of her fancy or of her hate. This voice related a reality and no legend.

As the doctor sat there he conversed of many strange and evil matters, of many discomforting affairs. He was the interrogator, the perpetual anxious questioner, and the voice in the empty room gave vague and sinister answers. That was a terrible catechism, a catechism of the devil, not of God. Question and answer flowed on, and in the doctor's soul the anxiety and the distress ever deepened. Nor could he control their development, although at moments his common sense broke into the catechism like a cool voice from without, and sought to interrupt it finally. But the twig could not stay the torrent. And the darkness deepened, darkness in which there was a vision of fire, the vision of a man, fantastic and menacing. He was the genius of this room. This room sang of him. Yes, even now the twisted silver goblins, the curved monstrosities on the cabinet, the crouched Indian boys, the leering pictures, and always the dull red cloud on wall and carpet, cushion and hanging. And then a strange deception overtook the doctor and shook his usually steady nerves. The red cloud seemed to his observing eyes to tremble, like a flame shaken in a breath of wind, and to glow all around him. He looked again, endeavouring to laugh at his delusion. But the glow deepened and there was surely distinct movement. Everywhere on walls, floor, hangings, couches, faint, thin shadows took shape, grew more definite. He watched them and saw that they were tiny flames, glowing red relieved against the red. It was as if he sat in the midst of a ghostly furnace; for these flames had no pleasant crackling voices. Silently they burned, and fluttered upward noiselessly. He saw them move this way and that. Some leaped up; others bent sideways; others wavered uncertainly, as if their desire were incomplete, and their intention undecided. The doctor stared upon them, and listened for the chorus that fires sing to tremble and to murmur from their lips. Yet they sang no chorus, but always, in a ghostly silence, aspired around him. He knew himself to be the victim of a delusion. He knew what he would have said to a patient seeking his aid against such a deception of the senses. In his common sense he knew this, and yet he gradually lost the notion that he was being deceived, and allowed himself to drift, as he had seen others drift, into the fancy that he was holding strange intercourse with the actual. These flames were real. They had forms. They moved. They enclosed him in a circle. They embraced him. As he watched them he fancied that they longed to be near to him, and—and—yes—so ran his thoughts—to communicate something to him, to sigh out their fiery hearts on his. They trembled as if convulsed with emotion, with desire. They tried to escape from the sinister red background that held them in its grasp as in a leash. The doctor was impelled ardently to believe that they yearned to find voices and to utter some word. And then, on a sudden, he recalled Julian's declaration on the night of Valentine's trance that he had seen a flame shine from his friend's lips and fade away in the darkness. He recalled, too, Julian's question about death-beds. Was the soul of man a flame? And, if so, were these flames many souls, or one soul reproduced on all sides by his excitement, and by the intensity of his gaze after them?

They burned more clearly. Their forms were more defined. Then suddenly they grew vague, blurred, faint all around him. They faded. They died into the red of the room. And once more the doctor sat alone.

He listened and heard the click of a key in the front door. And then suddenly the horror that he had felt long ago, on the night when he was followed in Regent Street, once more possessed him. He got on his feet to face it, and, as the drawing-room door was pushed slowly open, faced Valentine.

CHAPTER III

THE DOCTOR MEETS TWO STRANGERS

Upon seeing the doctor Valentine paused on the threshold of the door, and, as he paused, the doctor's horror fled.

"Valentine," he said, holding out his hand.

"Doctor."

Their hands met and their eyes. And then Levillier had an instant sensation that he shook hands with a stranger. He looked upon the face of Valentine certainly, but he was aware of a subtle, yet large, change in it. All the features were surely coarser, heavier. There was a line or two near the eyes, a loose fulness about the mouth. Yet, as he looked again, he could not be certain if it were so, or if his memory were at fault, groping after a transformation that was not there. The words he now said truthfully expressed his real feeling in the matter.

"You are quite a stranger to me," he said.

Valentine accepted the remark in the conventional sense.

"Yes, quite a stranger. We have not met for an age."

The voice was cool and careless.

"I have been waiting for you," the doctor went on, still unable to feel at his ease. "By the way, how you have changed your room."

"Yes. Do you like it?"

"Well, frankly, no."

"I am sorry for that," Valentine replied, drawing off his gloves. "Julian chose a great many of the things in it."

"Julian! Did he devise the colour scheme?"

"That curious red? No, that was my idea. But he had a great deal to do with the new furniture and the ornaments."

"I should have supposed many minds had been at work here."

Valentine smiled, and the doctor was convinced that both his mouth and eyes had altered in expression.

"That's true in a way," he answered. "Julian has had various advisers—of the feminine gender. The love of the moment is visible all over this room. That is why it amuses me. Those silver ornaments were chosen by a pretty Circassian. A Parisian picked out that black cabinet in a warehouse of Boulogne. A little Italian insisted upon that vulgar painted sofa—and so on."

" Why do you allow such people to have any intercourse with a room of yours ? "

" Oh, it amused Julian, and I was tired of my room as it was. After 'The Merciful Knight' went to be cleaned, I resolved on a change."

" For the worse."

" Is it for the worse ? "

" Surely."

The eyes of the two men challenged each other. Valentine's glance was carelessly impudent and hardy. The deference which he had always given to the doctor was gone. If it had been genuine it was dead. If it had only been a mask it had apparently served its purpose and was now contemptuously thrown aside. Dr. Levillier was deeply moved by the transformation. His friend had become a stranger during the interval of his absence. The man he admired was less admirable than of old. He recognised that, although he was not yet fully aware of the transformation of Valentine. Before he left England he vaguely suspected a change. Now the change hit him full in the heart. So acute was it that, in an age of miracles, he could well have believed Cuckoo Bright's disjointed statement. Valentine was, to his mind, even in some strange way to his eye, at this moment no longer Valentine. He was talking with a man whose features he knew certainly, but whose mind he did not know, had never known. And his former resolution to watch Valentine closely was consolidated. It became a passion. The doctor woke in the man. Nor was the old friend and lover of humanity lulled to sleep.

" How is Julian ? " the doctor asked, dropping his eyes.

" Very well, I think. He will be here directly. He's coming to fetch me. We are dining at the Prince's in Piccadilly in the same party. That reminds me, I must dress. But do stay, and have some coffee."

" No coffee, thank you."

" But you will stay and see Julian. I daresay he will be here early."

" Yes, I will stay. I should like to meet him."

After a word or two more, Valentine vanished to dress, and the doctor was once more alone. He was much perplexed and saddened, but keenly interested too, and, getting up from the chair in which he had been sitting, he moved about the grotesque and vulgar room, threading his way through the graceless furniture with a silent and gentle caution. And as he walked meditatively he remembered a conversation he had held with Valentine long ago, when the latter

had spoken complainingly of the tyranny of an instinctive purity.
The very words he had used came back to him now :

"The minds of men are often very carefully, very deftly poised,
and a little push can send them one way or the other. Remember
if you lose heaven, the space once filled by heaven will not be left
empty."

Had not the little push been given? Had not heaven been lost?
That was the problem. But Dr. Levillier, if he saw a little way
into effect, was quite at a loss as to cause. And already he had a
suspicion that the change in Valentine was not quite on the lines of
one of those strange and dreadful human changes familiar to any
observant man. This suspicion, already latent, and roused, perhaps,
in the first instance long ago by the mystery of Rip's avoidance of
his master, and by the shattering of Valentine's musical powers,
was confirmed in the strongest way when Julian appeared a few
minutes later. Yet the change in Julian would have seemed to
most people far more remarkable.

He came into the drawing-room rather hastily, in evening dress
with a coat over it. Wade had forewarned him of the doctor's
presence, and he entered speaking loud words of welcome, and
holding out a greeting hand. The too ready voice and almost
premature hand betokened his latent uneasiness. Vice makes some
people unconscious, some self-conscious. Julian belonged at present to
the latter tribe. Whether he was thoroughly aware of self-alteration
or not, he evidently stirred uneasily under an expectation of the
doctor's surprise. This drove his voice to loud notes and his manner
to a boisterous heartiness, belied by the shifting glance of his brown
eyes.

The doctor was astounded as he looked at him. Yet the change
here was far less inexplicable than that other change in Valentine.
Its mystery was the familiar mystery of humanity. Its horror was
the horror that we all accept as one of the elements of life. Deterioration, however rapid, however complete, does not come upon us
like a ghost in the night to puzzle us absolutely. It is not altogether out of the range of our experience. Most men have seen a
man crumble gradually, through the action of some vice, as a wall
crumbles through the action of time, fall into dust and decay, filter
away into the weed-choked ditches of utter ruin and degradation.
Most women have watched some woman slip from the purity and
hope and innocence of girlhood into the faded hunger and painted
and wrinkled energies of animalism. Such tragedies are no more
unfamiliar to us than are the tragedies of Shakespeare. And such
a tragedy—not complete yet, but at a third-act point, perhaps—now
faced Dr. Levillier in Julian. The wall that had been so straight
and trim, so finely built and carefully preserved, was crumbling fast

to decay. A ragged youth slunk in the face, beggared of virtue, of true cheerfulness, of all lofty aspiration and high intent. It was youth still, for nothing can entirely massacre that gift of the gods, except inevitable Time. But it was youth sadder than age, because it had run forward to meet the wearinesses that dog the steps of age but that should never be at home with age's enemy. Julian had been the leaping child of healthy energy. He was now quite obviously the servant of lassitude. His foot left the ground as if with a tired reluctance, and his hands were fidgety yet nerveless. The eyes, that looked at the doctor and looked away by swift turns, burned with a haggard eagerness unutterably different from their former bright vivacity. Beneath them wrinkles crept on the puffy white face as worms about a corpse. Busy and tell-tale, they did not try to conceal the story of the body into which they had prematurely cut themselves. Nor did Julian's features choose to back up any reserve his mind might possibly feel about acknowledging the consummate alteration of his life. They proclaimed, as from a watch tower, the arrival of enemies. The cheeks were no longer firm, but heavy and flaccid. The mouth was deformed by the down-drawn looseness of the sensualist, and the complexion beaconed with an unnatural scarlet that was a story to be read by every street boy.

Yet, even so, the doctor, as he looked pitifully and with a gnawing grief upon Julian, felt not the mysterious thrill communicated to him by Valentine. These two men, these old-time friends of his, were both in a sense strangers. But it was as if he had at least heard much of Julian, knew much of him, understood him, comprehended exactly why he was a stranger. Valentine was the total stranger, the unknown, the undivined.

Long ago the doctor had foreseen the possibility of the Julian who now stood before him. He had never foreseen the possibility of the new Valentine. The one change was summed up in an instant. The other walked in utter mystery. The doctor had been swift to notice Julian's furtive glance, and was equally swift in banishing all trace of surprise from his own manner. So they met with a fair show of cordiality, and Julian developed a little of his old cheerfulness.

" Val's dressing," he said. " Well, there's plenty of time. By the way, how's your Russian, Doctor ? "

" Better."

" You've cured him ! Bravo ! "

" I hope I have persuaded him to cure himself."

Julian looked up hastily.

" Oh, that sort of complaint, was it ? "

He laughed, not without a tinge of bitterness.

" Perhaps he doesn't want to be cured."

" I have persuaded him to want to be, I think."

" Isn't that rather a priest's office ? " Julian asked.

The doctor noticed that a very faint hostility had crept into his manner.

" Why ? "

" Oh, I don't know. Such an illness is a matter of temperament, I daresay, and the clergy tinker at our temperaments, don't they, while you doctors tinker at our bodies."

" A nerve doctor has as much to do with mind as body, and no doctor can possibly do much good if he entirely ignores the mind. But you know my theories."

" Yes. They make you clergyman and doctor in one, a dangerous man."

And he laughed again, jarringly, and shifted in his seat, looking around him with quick eyes.

" What do you think of the room ? " he said abruptly.

" I think it entirely spoilt and ruined," the doctor answered, gravely.

" It's altered, certainly."

" Yes, for the worse. It was a beautiful room, one of the most beautiful in London."

A momentary change came over Julian. He dropped his hard manner, which seemed an assumption to cover inward discomfort or shame.

" Yes," he said almost regretfully. " I suppose it was. But it's gayer now, got more things in it. Full of memories this room is."

The last remark was evidently put forth as a feeler, to find out what Valentine had been talking about Dr. Levillier was habitually truthful, although he could be very reserved if occasion seemed to require it. At present he preferred to be frank.

" Memories of women," he remarked.

" Oh, you've heard ? "

" That several tastes helped to make this room the pandemonium which it is. Yes."

" You're severe, Doctor."

" Perhaps you like the room for its memories, Addison."

Julian looked doubtful.

" I don't know. I suppose so," he hesitated.

" By the way, is there among these vagrant memories of Circassians, Greeks, and Italians anything chosen by Cuckoo Bright ? "

Julian started violently.

" Cuckoo Bright," he exclaimed, " what do you know of her ? "

As he spoke Valentine strolled into the room dressed for dinner. He was drawing on a pair of lavender gloves, and looked down sideways at his coat to see if his buttonhole of three very pale and very perfectly matched pink roses was quite straight.

" Cuckoo Bright ? " he echoed. " Does everybody know her, then ? How came she into your strict life, Doctor ? "

Dr. Levillier noticed that Valentine, like Julian, carefully set him aside as a being in some different sphere, much as a great many people insist on setting clergymen. This fact alone showed that he was talking with two strangers, and seemed to give the lie to long years of the most friendly and almost brotherly intercourse.

" Is my life so strict, then ? " he asked gently.

" I think little Cuckoo would call it so, eh, Julian ? "

He glanced at Julian and laughed softly, still drawing on his gloves. In evening dress he looked curiously young and handsome and facially less altered than the doctor had at first supposed him to be. Still there was a difference even in the face ; but it was so slight that only a keen observer would have noticed it. The almost frigid and glacial purity had floated away from it like a lovely cloud. Now it was unveiled, and there was something hard and staring about it. The features were still beautiful, but their ivory lustre was gone. A line was pencilled, too, here and there. Yet the doctor could understand that even Valentine's own man might not appreciate the difference. The manner, however, was more violently altered. It was that which made the doctor think again and intensely of Cuckoo's vague yet startling statement.

" Where did you meet Cuckoo, Doctor ? "

It was Julian who spoke, and the words were uttered with some excitement.

" I have met her," Levillier replied.

It was sufficiently evident that he did not intend to say where. But Valentine broke in :

" She has called on you again, then, and this time found you at home. I scarcely thought she would take the trouble."

" Again ! " the doctor said.

" Yes. One evening when you were away I saw her at your door and ventured to give her a piece of advice."

" And that was ? "

" Not to trouble you. I told her your patients were of a different class."

" In that case I fear you misrepresented me, Cresswell. I do not choose my patients. But Cuckoo Bright is no patient of mine."

" If she's not ill," Julian said, " why should she go to you ? "

" That is her affair, and mine," the doctor answered, in his quietest and most finishing tone.

Julian accepted the delicate little snub quietly, but Valentine sneered.

" Perhaps she went to seek you in your capacity of a doctor of the mind rather than of the body. Perhaps, after all, she sought your aid."

As he spoke the doctor could not help having driven into him the conviction that the words were spoken with meaning, that Valentine knew the nature of Cuckoo's mission to Harley Street. There rose in him suddenly a violent sensation of enmity against Valentine. He strove to beat it down, but he could not. Never had he felt such enmity against any man. It was like the fury so obviously felt by Cuckoo. The doctor was ashamed to be so unreasonable, and believed for a moment that the poor street girl had absolutely swayed him, and predisposed him to this animus that surged up over his normal charity and good, clear impulses of tenderness for all that lived.

" My aid," he said—and the turmoil within him caused him to speak with unusual sternness. " And if she did, what then ? "

" Poor Cuckoo ! " Julian said, and there was a touch of real tenderness in his voice.

" Oh, I have nothing to say against it," Valentine replied, buttoning slowly and carefully the last button of the second glove. " Only, Cuckoo Bright is beyond aid. She can neither help herself nor any one else."

" How do you know, Cresswell ? "

" Because I have observed, Doctor. Once I, too, thought that even Cuckoo might—might—well, have some fight in her. I know now that she has not. Her corruption of body has led to worse than corruption of mind, to corruption of will. Cuckoo Bright is as helpless as is a seabird with a shot through its wings upon the sea. She can only drift in the present—die in the future."

The doctor listened silently. But Julian said again :

" Poor, poor Cuckoo ! "

The exclamation seemed to irritate Valentine, for he caught up his cloak and cried :

" Bah ! Let's forget her. Doctor, we must say good-night. We are due at the Prince's. It has been good to meet you again."

The last words sounded like the bitterest sarcasm.

CHAPTER IV

THE DEATH OF RIP

ALTHOUGH Dr. Levillier's visit to Victoria Street had been such a painful one he had no intention whatever of letting the two young men drift away out of his acquaintance. He wanted especially to be with them in public places, and to see for himself, if possible, whether Cuckoo's accusation against Valentine were true. That a frightful change had taken place in Julian's life, and that he was rapidly sinking in a slough of wholly inordinate dissipation was clear enough. But did Valentine, this new strange Valentine, lead him or merely go with him, or stand aloof smiling at him and letting him take his own way like a foolish boy? That question the doctor must decide for himself. He could only decide it satisfactorily by ignoring Valentine's impertinence to himself, and endeavouring to resume his former relations of intimacy with these old friends who were strangers. He began by asking them both to dinner. Rather to his surprise they accepted and came. The mastiffs were shut close in their den below lest they should repeat their performance of the summer. The dinner passed off with some apparent cheerfulness, but it served to show the doctor the gulf that was now fixed between him and his former dear associates. He was on one shore, they on another. Their faces were altered as if by the desolate influence of distance. Even their voices sounded strange and far away. Great spaces had widened between their minds and his. He endeavoured at first to cover those spaces, to bridge that gulf; but he soon came to learn the vanity of such an attempt. He could not go to them nor would they return to him. He could only pretend to bridge the gulf by the exercise of a suave diplomacy, and by carefully banishing from his manner every trace of that dispraising elderliness which seems to the young the essence of prudery arising, like an appalling Phœnix, from the ashes of past imprudence. In this way he drew a little nearer to Julian, who obviously feared at first to suffer condemnation at his hands, but, finding only geniality, lost his uneasiness and suffered himself to become more natural.

But this thawing of Julian, the quick response of humanity to the adroit treatment of it, only threw into harsher relief the immobility of Valentine, and to him the doctor drew no nearer, but seemed, with each moment, more distant, more absolutely divided from him. And the gulf between them was full of icebergs, which filled the atmosphere with the breath of a deadly frost. This was what the doctor felt. What Valentine, the new Valentine, felt could not be ascertained. He wore a brilliant mask, on whose gay mouth the society smile was singularly well painted. He wore a manner edged with tinkling bells of brilliancy. Happiness and ease beamed in his eyes. Yet his look, his voice, his smile, his gaiety chilled the doctor and set him mentally shivering. And with each bright saying and merry laugh he struck a blow upon the former friendship. The doctor fancied he could actually hear the sound of the hammer at its work.

The simile of the hammer was peculiarly consonant with his present view of the new Valentine, for, despite the latter's gaiety, ease, and self-possession, his smiling sociability and expansiveness, the doctor was perpetually conscious of a lurking violence, an incessant and forcible exigence in him. It might be a fancy, but the doctor was not as a rule the prey of fancies. Yet Valentine gave no outward hint of inward turmoil. Rather did the doctor divine it as by a curious intuition that guided him to that which lay in hiding. And it was this apprehension of a deep violence and peculiar, excessive animation in Valentine that woke the doctor's deepest wonder, and set that gulf between them so widely. For all violence had once been so specially abhorred by Valentine. He had so loved and sought all calm. The calm, he had often said, were the true aristocrats of life. Fury and any wild movements of the passions were of the gutter.

That dinner was returned. The doctor dined with Valentine and Julian more than once, and accompanied them to the theatre. But he was unable to make certain of Valentine's precise attitude towards Julian, although he saw easily that the influence of the one over the other had rather waxed than waned. This being so, it followed that Julian, having completely changed, the influence that guided him must have completely changed also. The pendulum had swung back. That often happened in the record of men's lives. But not in such a way as this. The doctor, like Cuckoo, recognised the existence of a mystery. But he was by no means prepared to accept her fantastic and ignorantly vague explanation of it. That was a wild fable, a fairy tale for a child, not a reasonable elucidation for a man and a doctor. The most curious thing of all was that she declared that Valentine had actually told her the truth about the matter, knowing that she could not understand it. The doctor resolved to see her later, and to question her more minutely on this point. Meanwhile he began to watch Valentine carefully, and with the most sedulous attention to every detail and *nuance* of manner, look, and word. He understood Julian. His sad case was to an extent due to his long happiness and freedom from the bondage in which so many men move wearily. It was as if his passions had been dammed up by the original influence of Valentine. Through the years, behind the height of the dam, the waters had been rising, accumulating, pressing. Suddenly the dam was removed, and a devastating flood swept forth, uncontrollable, headlong, and furious. Julian needed rescue, but the only way to rescue seemed to lie through Valentine, within whose circle of influence he was so closely bound. The mystery of Valentine must be laid bare.

And so the doctor watched and wondered, bringing all his knowledge of the world and of the minds and bodies of men to help him.

And meanwhile the lady of the feathers was seen nightly in Piccadilly.

And Julian went his way steadily downwards.

* * * * * * *

One night there was a flicker of snow over London, and the air was chill with the breath of coming winter. The dreary light of snow illumined the faces of all who walked in the streets, painting the brightest cheeks with a murky grey pigment, and making the sweetest eyes hollow and expressive of depression. Heavily the afternoon went by and the evening came sharply, like a blow.

Dr. Levillier was engaged to dine with Julian and Valentine at the former's room in Mayfair. Of late Valentine had seemed to seek him out, and especially to enjoy seeing him in the company of Julian. And the doctor fancied he detected something of a triumph that was almost blatant in Valentine's manner when they three were together, and when the doctor's eyes rested sorrowfully upon that crumbling wall, which had once been so fair and strong. Of late, too, the doctor, ever watching for the signs of change in Valentine, had grown more and more aware that he was an utterly, through and through, different man from the youth men had called the Saint of Victoria Street. He felt the transformation to be inhuman, and, by slow and reluctant degrees, he was beginning to form an opinion. It was only in embryo as yet, a shadow hesitating in the background of his mind. He shrank from holding it. He shuddered at its coming. Yet, if it were right, it might explain everything, might make what was otherwise incredible clear and comprehensible.

Was this vile change in his friend caused by a radical distortion of mind? Was Valentine a madman?

Lunacy turns temperaments upside down, transforms the lamb into the tiger, the saint into the murderer.

Was Valentine then mad, and was the monstrous distortion of his brain playing upon the life of Julian, who, like the rest of the world, believed him sane ?

The thought came to the doctor, and once it had been born it was often near to him. Yet he would not encourage it unless he could rest it upon facts. That a man should change was not a proof of his madness, however unaccountable the change might seem. The doctor watched Valentine, and was compelled to admit to himself that in every way Valentine seemed perfectly sane. His cynicism, his love of ordinary life, his toleration of common and wretched people, might seem amazing to one who had known him well years ago, but there were many perfectly sane men of the same habits and opinions, of the same modes of speech and of action. If the doctor's strange thought were to become a definite belief, much more was needed, something at least of proof, something that would carry conviction not merely to the imagination, but to the cool and searching intellect.

On this night of the first snow the doctor's thought moved a step forward towards conviction.

When he arrived at Julian's rooms, he was greeted by Valentine alone.

" Our host has deserted us," he said, leading the doctor in to the fire.

" What, is he ill ? "

" He has not returned. He went away last night—on a quest of a certain pleasure. This afternoon he wired asking me to entertain you. He was unavoidably detained, but hoped to arrive in time for dessert. His present love's arms are very strong. They keep him."

" Oh ! " the doctor said, slipping out of his cloak, " we dine here then ? "

" We do, alone. I don't think we've dined alone since Julian and I came back from abroad, and you deserted your Russian."

" No. I will consider myself your guest."

It struck the doctor that here was an excellent opportunity for confirming or abandoning his dreary suspicion. Alone with Valentine he would be able to lead the conversation in any direction he chose. He was glad that Julian had not returned, and resolved to use this opportunity.

They went into the dining-room and sat down to dinner. Valentine was apparently rather amused at playing the host in another man's house. It was novel and entertained him. He was obviously in splendid spirits, ate with good appetite and drank the champagne with an elation not unlike the elation of the dancing wine. More than once, too, he alluded to Julian's absence and probable occupation, as if both the one and the other were bouquets in his cap, or laurels in some crown which he alone could wear. Dr. Levillier noticed it and sought to draw him on in that direction, and to lead him to some open acknowledgment of his share in Julian's rapidly proceeding ruin. But Valentine changed the conversation into another channel without apparently observing his companion's intention, or deliberately frustrating it. He chattered of a thousand things, mostly of topics that are the common converse of London dinner tables. The doctor joined in. To a listening stranger the two men would have seemed old friends, pleasantly at ease and secure with one another. Yet the doctor was doing detective duty all the time. And Valentine! was he not secretly revelling in that destruction of a human soul that was galloping apace?

Course succeeded course. At last dessert was placed upon the table. Valentine raised his glass with a smile:

"Let us drink the health of Julian's absence," he said. "For you and I get on so perfectly together."

"Rather a cruel toast in Julian's own rooms," said the doctor.

"Ah, but he's happy enough where he is."

"You know where that is?"

"No—I only suspect," Valentine cried gaily. "In the wilds of South Kensington, in a tiny house, all Morris tapestry and Burne-Jones stained glass, dwells the latest siren who has been calling to our Ulysses. He is there, I suspect. Wait a moment though. His telegram might tell us. Where was it sent from?"

He sprang up, went to the writing-table near the window, and caught up the crumpled thin paper that he had flung down there. Smoothing it out, he read, holding the paper close to a wax candle:

"Handed in at the Marylebone Road office at 5.50."

His brow clouded.

"Marylebone Road," he repeated, looking at the doctor. "Why should he be there?"

His words immediately set the doctor on the track.

"Does not Cuckoo Bright live there?" he said.

"Yes, she does."

"May he not be with her?"

Valentine had dropped the telegram. He was standing at the table, and he pressed his two fists, clenched, upon the white cloth.

"I have told him he must give Cuckoo up," he said, almost in a snarl.

The doctor glanced at him quickly.

"You have told him?"

"Advised him, I mean."

"You dislike her?"

"I! No. How can one dislike a painted rag?. How can one dislike a pink and white shell that holds nothing?"

"Every body holds a soul. Every human shell holds its murmur of the great sea."

"The body of Cuckoo then contains a soul that's cankered with disease, moth-eaten with corruption, worn away to an atom not bigger than a grain of dust. I would not call it a soul at all."

He spoke with more than a shade of excitement, and the gay expression of his face had changed to an uneasy anger. The doctor observed it, and rejoined quietly :

"How can you answer for another person's soul? We see tho body, it is true. But are we to divine the soul from that—wholly and solely?"

"The soul! Let us call it the will."

"Why?"

"The will of man is the soul of man. It is possible to judge the will by the body. The will of such a woman as Cuckoo Bright is a negative quantity. Her body is the word ' weakness,' written in flesh and blood for all to read."

"Ah, you speak of her will for herself," the doctor said, thinking of Cuckoo's broken wail to him, as she sat on that autumn evening in his consulting-room. "But what of her will for another, her soul for another?"

He had spoken partly at random, partly led by the thought, the suspicion that Cuckoo's abandoned body held a fine love for Julian. He was by no means prepared for the striking effect his remark had upon Valentine. No sooner were the words spoken than a strong expression of fear was visible in Valentine's face, of terror so keen that it killed the anger which had preceded it. He trembled as he stood, till the table shook; and, apparently noticing this, and wishing to conceal so extreme an exhibition of emotion, he slid hastily into a seat.

"Her will for another," he repeated, "for another. What do you mean by that? where's the other then? who is it?"

The doctor looked upon him keenly.

"Anybody for whom she has any desire, any solicitude, or any love—you, myself, or—Julian."

"Julian!" Valentine repeated unsteadily. "Julian! you mean to say you——"

He pulled himself together abruptly.

"Doctor," he said, "forgive me for saying that you are scarcely talking sense when you assume that such a creature as Cuckoo Bright can really love anybody. And even if she did, Julian's the last man—oh, but the whole thing is absurd. Why should you and I talk about a street girl, a drab whose life begins and ends in the gutter? Julian will be here directly. Meanwhile let us have coffee."

He pushed his cigarette case over to the doctor, and touched the bell.

" Coffee ! " he said when Julian's man answered it.

The door stood open, and as the man murmured, " Yes, sir," a dog close by howled shrilly.

The noise diverted Valentine's attention, and roused him from the agitation into which he had fallen. He glanced at the doctor.

" Rip," he said.

" Howling for his master," said the doctor.

" Wait a moment," Valentine said to the man, who was preparing to leave the room. Then, to the doctor :

" I am his master."

" To be sure," rejoined the doctor, who had in truth for the moment forgotten the fact.

So long a time had elapsed since the little dog took up his residence with Julian.

" You think he's howling for me ? " Valentine said.

" I was thinking of Julian at the moment."

" And what do you say now ? Still that he is howling for his master ? "

The dog's voice was heard again. It sounded almost like a shriek of fear.

" No," the doctor replied, wondering what intention was growing in Valentine's face.

" Oh ! " Valentine said curtly.

He turned to the man.

" Bateman, bring Rip in here to us."

The man hesitated.

" I don't think he'll come, sir."

" I said, bring him to us."

The man went out, as if with reluctance. Valentine turned to the doctor.

" We spoke about soul, that is will, just now," he said. " To deny the will is death, despite Schopenhauer. Death ? Worse than death —cowardice. To assert the will is life and victory. With each assertion a man steps nearer to a god. With each conquest of another will a man mounts, and if any man wants to enjoy an eternity he must create it for himself, by feeding his will or soul with conquest till it is so strong that it cannot die."

His eyes shone with excitement. It seemed to the doctor that he was caught in the whirlpool of a violent reaction. He had shown fear, weakness ; he was aware of it and determined to reassert himself. The doctor answered nothing, neither agreeing with his fantastic philosophy, nor striving to controvert it. And at this moment there was the sound of a struggle and of whining outside.

s

The door was pushed open, and Julian's man appeared, hauling Rip along by the collar. The little dog was hanging back with all its force, and striving to get away. Having succeeded in getting it into the room the man quickly retreated, shutting the door hastily behind him. The little dog was left with Valentine and the doctor. It remained shrinking up against the door in a posture that denoted abject fear, its pretty head turned in the direction of Valentine, its eyes glaring, its teeth snapping at the air. The doctor looked at it and at Valentine. His pity for the dog's condition was held in check by a strange fascination of curiosity. He leaned his arms on the table and his eyes were fixed upon Valentine, who got up slowly from his chair.

"I have let Rip be the prey of his absurd fancies long enough, Doctor," he said. "To-night I will make him like me as he used to, or at least come to me."

And he whistled to the dog and called Rip, standing by the table. Rip howled and trembled in reply, and snapped more fiercely in the direction of Valentine.

"Do you see that, Doctor? But he shall come. I will make him."

He shut his lips firmly and stared upon the animal. It was very evident that he was exerting himself strongly in some way. Indeed he looked like a man performing some tremendous physical feat. Yet all his limbs were still. The violence of his mind created the illusion. Rip wavered against the door. There was foam on his jaws and his white legs trembled. Valentine snapped his fingers as one summoning or coaxing a dog. The doctor started at the sound and leaned further forward along the table to see the upshot of this strange fight between a man's desire and an animal's fear. Rip scarcely whined now, but turning his head rapidly from one side to the other, with a motion that seemed to become merely mechanical, he made a hoarse noise that was like a terrified and distressed growl half strangled in his throat. But though he wavered against the door he did not obey Valentine and go to him, and the doctor was conscious of a sudden thrill of joy in the dog's obstinacy. This obstinacy angered Valentine greatly. His face clouded. He bent forward. He put out his hands as if to seize Rip. The dog snapped at him frantically, wildly. But Valentine did not recoil. On the contrary, he advanced, bending down over the wretched little creature. Then Rip shrank down on all fours by the door. To the doctor's watching eyes he seemed to wane visibly smaller. He dropped his head. Valentine bent lower. Rip lay right down, pressing himself upon the floor. As Valentine's hand touched him a quiver ran over him, succeeded by a surprising stillness.

The doctor made a slight sound. He knew that Rip was dead. Valentine took the little dog by the scruff of its neck and lifted it up. Then he, too, saw what he held. He glanced at the doctor, and there was a glare of defeat in his eyes. Then he passed across the room to the window, still holding the dog, pulled aside the curtain and thrust up the window. The ground was white and the snow was falling. With an angry gesture he flung the body out. It dropped with a soft noise in the snow and lay there.

Valentine closed the window, but the doctor felt as if he still saw the poor little corpse in the snow. And he shuddered.

A moment afterwards there was a step in the passage, and Julian entered. He was looking haggard and excited, and ill with dissipation. His eyes shone in deep hollows that seemed to have been painted with indigo, and his lips were parched and feverish.

" Where have you been, Julian ?" said Valentine.

" Oh, with her—with Molly, of course," he replied.

" What ? Till now ? "

Julian seemed uneasy under his scrutiny.

" Till this morning," he replied, almost suddenly.

" Well, but since then ? "

" With Cuckoo. Oh ! don't bother me."

He went over towards the window.

" Oh, how hot it is here," he said.

He glanced at the bright fire.

" Intolerably ! " he murmured.

And he opened the window to the drifting snow.

" Am I mad ? " he suddenly cried to them. " I saw the flame in her eyes again to-day, in Cuckoo's eyes. It held me with her. I'll swear it held me. It wouldn't let me go—wouldn't let me— till now ! "

He sank down in a chair by the window, and, turning his back on them, pushed his head out to get air.

" I say," he suddenly called. " What's that, that lying there ? "

Valentine and the doctor joined him. He was pointing to the body of Rip, which was already almost covered by the snow.

" That," Valentine said ; " that is——"

" The body of a creature that died fighting," the doctor interrupted. " A fine fashion of dying. Look at it, Julian. Its soul was indomitable to the last, and so it won the battle it fought. It won by its very death even. Nature is at work on its winding-sheet."

Valentine said nothing.

CHAPTER V

DOCTOR LEVILLIER VISITS THE LADY OF THE FEATHERS

JULIAN'S utterance about the flame that held him with the lady of the feathers struck Dr. Levillier forcibly at the time it was made, and remained in his mind. He could not fail to connect it with his own experience in Valentine's empty room and, going further back, with the last sitting of the two young men which was succeeded by the long trance of Valentine. And as he thought of these things, it suddenly occurred to him that the ghastly change which had taken place in Valentine might well date from that night. Since the death of Rip the doctor had formed the opinion that Valentine was no longer perfectly sane. His excitement, the fury of his eyes when he spoke of the triumphs of will, seemed to give the clue to his transformation. The insane perpetually glorify themselves, and are transcendent egoists. Surely the egoism of insanity had peeped out in Valentine's diatribe upon the eternity of a strong man's individual will. The night of the trance had been a strange crisis of his life. He had seemed to recover from it, to come back from that wonderful simulation of death, healthy, calm, reasonable as before. This might have been only seeming. In that sleep the sane and beautiful Valentine might have died, the insane and unbeautiful Valentine have been born. There are many instances of a sudden and acute shock to the nervous system leaving an indelible and dreary writing upon the nature. If Valentine had thus been tossed to madness it was very possible that his dog, an instinctive creature, should recognise the change with terror. It was even possible that other instinctive creatures should divine the hideous mind of a maniac hidden in the beautiful body of an apparently normal man. And Cuckoo, she too was instinctive, a girl without education, culture, the reading that opens the mind and sometimes shuts the eyes. Cuckoo Bright, she had divined the evil of Valentine. To her he had made confession. In her eyes Julian had seen the mysterious flame. Some influence from her had kept him from his invited guests and from his house. Yes, Cuckoo, the lady of the feathers, the blessed damozel of Regent Street and Piccadilly Circus, the painted and possessed, faded and degraded wanderer of the pavements, seemed to become the centre of this wheel of circumstance, as Dr. Levillier reflected upon her.

It was time for him to go to Cuckoo. Julian's descent must be stayed, before he went down, like a new Orpheus without a mission, into Hades. Valentine's influence, whether mad or sane, must be fought. It was to be a struggle, a battle of wills, of what Valentine chose to consider souls. And some prompting led the doctor to think of Cuckoo as a possible weapon. Why? Because she had even once held Julian against his will, against the intention of his soul.

So the doctor at length sought the lady of the feathers. She had been passing through a period of great and benumbing desolation, believing that her last appeal, her great effort for Julian had been a failure. For the doctor had not come to her, and Cuckoo could not tell that he was making observations for himself and that she was often in his mind. She supposed, that he, like all others, laughed at her pretensions to gravity, swept her exhibition of real and honest emotion away from his memory with a sneer, considered her despair over another's ruin a vile travesty, a grinning absurdity and trick. Never had Cuckoo felt more lonely than in these days, though a vast loneliness is the constant companion of her large sisterhood. Even Jessie failed to comfort her, and she could find little courage within herself. And yet there were moments when the vigour that had led her once to defy Valentine, when the fire that had sprung up in her, as a flame may burst forth in a swamp, seemed to be near to her again. She felt a new possibility within her, stirring, striving. It was at such moments that she longed to see the doctor, and could have cursed him for not coming to her. For at such moments she seemed only waiting for a touch of sympathy, a word of encouragement, to perform some great action, some momentous deed. But the touch, the word, were lacking, and her life and experience of constant and monotonous degradation dulled the impulse, stifled the enthusiasm that she could not understand. And she fell again to brooding, and to an ignorant and vague consciousness of impotence.

She bought a new hair dye, painted her thin cheeks more heavily than ever before, and sought, almost with a wild exultation that swiftly fled away, to sink lower.

The monotony of sin is one of the scourges of sin. In those days Cuckoo suffered many stripes. Her eyes grew more weary, her smile in Piccadilly more mechanical, her walk more puppet-like than ever. Life was like a moving dream of horror. And yet no day passed without a gleam of that strange sensation of ignorant power, fluttering upward, fading away, pausing, passing, dead.

She did not know what it meant. She could not keep it nor use it. She could not unravel its message nor rest upon its strength. It was gone almost while it came, but it did something for the lady of the feathers. It gave to her the little seed of expectation that, quite alone in a weary desert, yet makes of that desert the plot men call a garden. Like a thread of steel it held up this girl from the uttermost abyss, until at last the doctor's hand struck upon her door.

Julian's occasional visits were as the scourgings of God, giving to Cuckoo a vision of shifting ruin, in which she—so she told herself, thinking of the dance of the hours—had been the first to have a share.

It was a wintry afternoon when the doctor came. Frost clung stealthily round the grimy black trees, outlining their naked boughs with meagre lines of white sewn with smuts. Above the frost hung the fog as if in charge of the town, a despondent and gloomy sentinel. During the morning the sun had lain in the fog like a faint blood-red jewel in a thick and awkward sulphur setting, but with the afternoon the jewel faded to a distant dim phantom, from that to blank nothingness. As if satisfied with this piteous exit, the fog drew closer, keeping especially heavy watch upon the long and bleak line of the Marylebone Road, and taking the high and narrow house in which Cuckoo dwelt under its severest protection. Twilight wanted to come as the afternoon drew on, but it had been forestalled and was practically already there. Doubtless it did come, but no one was much the wiser. The lamps had been alight all day, and no procession of gloomy things, advancing from whithersoever, could have added much to the volume of the crowding darkness, or have appreciably increased its density. In the darkness the cold gathered, and the frost began to take a harder grip of everything, of desolate, solitary pumps in tiny and squalid back-yards, of pipes that crawled like liver-coloured snakes over the unpresentable sides of houses, of pools thick with orange-brown mud, and vagrant bushes creaking above the grimy earth in places that children named gardens.

Fog and frost had taken a strong grip, too, upon the heart of the lady of the feathers. Somewhere about eleven o'clock in the morning she had stirred wearily in her bed, had stretched out her arms to the stagnant air of the room, and crouched up on her pillow in a grotesque hump. For awhile the hump remained motionless. Then Cuckoo rolled round and extended a bare thin leg to test the atmosphere. The leg was quickly withdrawn, the atmosphere having been evidently tried in the balance and found wanting. Cuckoo's bell rang and Mrs. Brigg was called for tea and toast, while once more the hump decorated the upper part of the disordered bed. Jessie, awakened in her basket at the foot of the bed, joined the hump, whining a greeting,

and wriggling furiously in an effort to tunnel her way to the ultimate depths of sheets and blankets. Then Mrs. Brigg, of yellowish
and bleak aspect, beneath a tumbled appurtenance that she called a
cap, appeared with a tray.

"Going to stop abed?" she asked, in a husky voice, in which the
smuts seemed floating.

"Yes. What's there to get up for?" Cuckoo groaned.

"Nothun' as I know of."

And Mrs. Brigg was gone about her business.

All the morning Cuckoo lay staring at the blank square of the
window, and Jessie snored under the blankets. The tea was drunk,
the toast lay about in fragments. One bit, hard and many cornered
as it seemed, somehow gained entrance to the bed, and greeted
Cuckoo's every movement with uncompromising grittiness. No
shaking of coverlet and sheet, no beating of pillow, no kicks and
scufflings could expel it. The bed seemed full of hard bits of toast,
and Cuckoo felt as if an additional burden were laid upon her by
this slight evil. But, indeed, the horror of her existence reached a
culminating point to-day, a point of loneliness, vacant dreariness,
squalor and degradation that could not be surpassed. The preceding
night had been peculiarly horrible, and, as Cuckoo now lay on the
tumbled bed, in the dim, cold room, with the fog gazing in, the
leaden hours of winter crawling by, she felt as if she could bear no
more. She could bear no more addition to her sick weariness; no
more addition to her useless hunger of love for Julian, that could
never be crowned with anything but despair; no more addition to
her bodily fatigue, born of tramping monotony succeeded by yet
more enervating weariness of the flesh. She could bear no more.
Yes, but she must bear more. For Cuckoo knew that she was not
dying, was not even ill. She was only tired in body, prostrate in heart,
deserted in life, and forced to witness the quick and running ruin of
the man she had the farcical absurdity to love. Imaginative, for
once, in her morbid fatigue, she began to wish that she could fade
away and become part of the fog that lay about London, be drawn
into its murkiness, with all her murky recollections, her fiendish
knowledge, her mechanical wiles of the streets, her thin and ghostly
despairs and desires. For they seemed thin and ghostly, they too,
to-day, fit food for the fog, as indeed the whole of her was. How
could such as she evaporate into sweet air, a clear heaven?

She caught at the hand-glass, leaning far out on the bed, as the
blessed damozel o'er the bright bar of heaven, and tried to see,
with staring eyes, how the new hair dye that she was now using
became her. Her mind was vagrant, coming and going miserably,
from that love of hers which was strangely strong and subtle, to the
powder-box with its arsenic green lid, or the rouge-pot of dirty

white china. And by each event it paused and sank, as if benumbed by the increasing frost. Leaning again to put back the hand-glass she fell over too far and dropped it. The glass fell face downwards and was smashed. Cuckoo laughed aloud, revelling feebly in the additional misery a superstitious mind now began to promise her. The fragments of broken glass actually pleased her, and, on a sudden, she resolved to set her feet in them, that she might be cut and wounded, that she might bleed outwardly as she had been bleeding inwardly for so long. She swung her legs over the breadth of the bed, disorganising Jessie, planted her feet in the array of glass and stood up. As she did so the doctor mounted her doorstep, plied the knocker and rang the bell. Cuckoo stood listening. A fragment of glass had really penetrated the bare sole of her foot, which bled a little gently on the carpet. But she scarcely knew it. She heard Mrs. Brigg go by, and then steps sounding in the passage. Then there came to her ears a quiet voice with a very characteristic note of bright calmness in it. Standing in her frilled night-dress among the bits of glass, Cuckoo flushed scarlet all over her face and neck. She knew who the visitor was. With one dart she reached the wash-stand. Sponges, brushes, combs, all her weapons of the toilet were immediately in commotion, and when Mrs. Brigg opened her door, the room was a whirlpool of quick activities, in the midst of which, as on a frowsy throne, Jessie stood upon the bed barking excitedly. Mrs. Brigg came in and closed the door. Her thin lips were pursed.

"Light the fire!" Cuckoo called at her from the basin.

"What do you want the doctor for?"

Mrs. Brigg uttered the words with some suspicion.

"Hurry up and light the fire?"

Cuckoo turned round, her hands darting in her hair, and actually laughed with a touch of merriment.

"You old owl! He's not come to doctor me, only to see me."

Mrs. Brigg looked relieved, but still surprised.

"Oh," she said. "That's it, is it?"

She paused as if in consideration.

Suddenly Cuckoo sprang on her, twisted her round, and spun her out into the cold passage. "Light the fire I tell you!"

She banged the bedroom door and went on with her rapid toilet.

When she came into the sitting-room an uneasy fire was sputtering in the grate, one gas jet flared, and Dr. Levillier was standing by the window looking out at the fog. He turned to greet her.

"I thought you'd forgotten—or didn't mean to come," Cuckoo said; "they often do—people that say they will to me, I mean."

The doctor held out his hand with a smile.

"No. Am I interrupting you?"

"Me!" said Cuckoo, in amazement, thinking of her empty days. "Lord no."

Her accent was convincing. The little doctor sat down by the fire and put his hat and gloves on the table.

"Mrs. Brigg thought I was ill—you bein' a doctor," Cuckoo said, with an attempt at a laugh. She felt nervous now, and was not sustained to-day by the strung-up enthusiasm which had supported her in Harley Street. "Funny there bein' a fog again this time, ain't it?"

"Yes. I hope we shall meet some day in clear weather."

As the doctor said that, following a tender thought of the girl, he glanced round the room and at Cuckoo. "I hope so," he repeated. Then, rather abruptly:

"Two or three nights ago I went to dine with Mr. Addison. He was out. He was here with you."

Cuckoo got red. She could still be very sensitive with a few people, and perhaps Mrs. Brigg and her kind had trained her into irritable suspicion of suspicion in others.

"Only for a friendly visit," she said hastily. "Nothin' else. He would stop."

"I understand perfectly," the doctor said gently. Cuckoo was reassured.

"Did he say as he'd been?"

"Yes."

Cuckoo looked at the doctor and a world of reproach dawned in her eyes.

"I say," she said, "you haven't done nothin'. He's worse than ever. He's gettin'—oh, he's gettin' cruel bad."

Tears came up over the world of reproach.

"It's all him, all Valentine," she said.

And Dr. Levillier was moved to cast reticence, the usual loyalty of one man to another who has been his friend, away. Somehow the dead body of Rip lying in the snow put that old friendship far off. And also an inward thrill caught him near to Cuckoo. An impulse, swift and vital, thrust his mind to hers.

"You are right," he answered. "I believe that it is all Valentine."

"There! Didn't I tell you?" Cuckoo cried with eyes of triumph. "It's been him from the first. Oh, get him—get Julian away."

The doctor laid his hand upon Cuckoo's, which was stretched upon the tablecloth, very gently, almost abstractedly.

"Will you tell me something?" he said.

"What's it?"

"You love Julian?"

"Me!" the lady of the feathers said.

Her voice trembled over the word. She stole a hasty, hunted glance at the doctor. Was he too going to jeer at her? Would no one allow her to have a clean corner in her heart?

"You're laughin' at me. What's the good of such as me doin' a thing like that—lovin' a man?"

"I think you must love Julian. If you do, perhaps you are meant to protect and save him."

A secret voice prompted the doctor with the words he spoke, gave them to him, bent him irresistibly to repeat them. Never before had he felt what it is to be between the strong hands of destiny.

"Me! Me save any one!" Cuckoo said, trembling.

"Yes, you. There is something in you—I feel it and I can't tell you why, nor what it is—something that has hold of Julian. He told us so the other night. Don't you know what it is?"

"Eh?"

"Perhaps he feels that you love him—purely, cleanly."

"I do—oh! I do that!" Cuckoo cried.

A wonder as to the relations between Julian and this girl shot through the doctor. He was the last man in the world to think evil of any one, but, just then, as Cuckoo moved, the gas light struck fully on her. The dye on her hair shone crudely. The red and white of her face burned as on the face of a clown. And then even the doctor's good heart wondered. Cuckoo knew it in an instant, and her face hardened and looked older.

"Oh, go on," she said rudely. "Think as the others do. Damn you men! Damn you! Damn you!"

And, without warning, she put her head down on the table and broke into a wild passion of tears. She sobbed, and, as she sobbed, she cursed and clenched her hands. She lost herself in fury and in despair. The Fates had stung her too hard this time, and she must blaspheme against them, with her voice of the streets, her language of the streets, her poor heart—not quite of the streets. The Fates had stung her too hard, for they had put a flaw even in this one self-respect of hers. That one night accused her whenever she thought of Julian, whenever she saw the dissipation deepen round his eyes. She was not to have even one thing that she could be quite proud of, not one thing of which she could say, "This has been always pure." And then she turned on the doctor and cried:

"Go on—think it—think it! Think what you like! But I'll tell you the truth. There was only once I did him any harm and that wasn't my fault. I never wanted to. I hated it. I told him I hated it. I didn't want him to be that, like the others. And that was Valentine too. And now—just because of that I'm no use. And you'd said I might be, you'd said I might be."

"And I say you shall be."

The wail died in Cuckoo's throat. The tears were arrested as by a spell. Dr. Levillier had got upon his feet. All the truth and tenderness of his heart was roused and quickened. He knew real passion, real grief, and from that moment he knew and trusted the lady of the feathers. And by the strength of her bitterness, even by the broken curses that would have shocked so many of the elect of this world, he measured the width and the depth of her possibilities. She had sent to damnation—what? The vile cruelty, the loathsome, unspeakable, dastardly mercilessness of the world. To damnation with it! That was the loud echo in his man's heart.

"That one night is nothing," he said. "Or rather it is something that you must redeem. It is good to have to pay for a thing. It is that makes one work. There is a work for you to do, a work which I believe no one else can do. You love Julian. Love him more. Make him love you. My will cannot fight the will of Valentine over him. No man's will can. A woman's may. Yours may, shall."

His pale, small, delicate face flamed with excitement as he spoke. Few of his patients looking upon him just then would have known their calm little doctor. But Cuckoo had cried to him out of the very depths, and out of the very depths he answered her, still prompted—though now he knew it not—by that secret voice which sometimes rules a man, at which he wonders ignorantly, the voice of some soul, some great influence, hidden from him in the spaces of the air, the voice of a flame, warm, keen, alive, and power prompting.

And Cuckoo, as she listened to the doctor, had once again a hint of her own strength, a thrill of hope, a sense that she, even she, was not broken quite in pieces upon the cruel wheel of the world.

"Whatever can I do?" she said, "Valentine's got him."

As she spoke, the doctor, restless, as men are in excitement, had moved over to the mantelpiece, and stood with one foot upon the edge of the fender. Thinking deeply, he glanced over the photographs of Cuckoo's acquaintance, without actually seeing them. But presently one, at which he had looked long and fixedly, dawned upon him, cruelly, powerfully. It was the face of Marr.

"Who is that?" he said abruptly to Cuckoo.

"That?" She too got up and came near to him, lowering her voice almost to a whisper. "That's really *him.*"

"Him?"

"Valentine."

The doctor looked at her in blank astonishment.

"Yes, it is," Cuckoo reiterated, and nodding her head with the obstinacy of a child.

"That—Valentine! It has no resemblance to him."

The doctor took up the photograph, and examined it closely. "This is not Valentine."

"He told me it was. It's Marr—and somehow it's him now."

"Marr," said the doctor, sharply. "Why, he is dead. Julian told me so. He died—he died in the Euston Road on the night of Valentine's trance. Ah, but you know nothing about that. Did you know Marr, then?"

"Yes, I knew him."

Cuckoo hesitated. But something taught her to be perfectly frank with the doctor. So she added:

"I'd been with him at that hotel the night he died."

"You were the woman! But then how can you say that this (he touched the photograph with his finger) is Valentine?"

"He says he's really Marr."

Cuckoo spoke in the most mulish manner, following her habit when she was completely puzzled, but sticking to what she believed to be the truth.

"Marr and Valentine one man! He told you that?"

"He says to me—I'm Marr."

Cuckoo repeated the words steadily, but like a parrot. The doctor said nothing, only looked at her and at the photograph. He was thinking now of his suspicion as to Valentine's sanity. Had he, perhaps in his madness, been playing on the ignorance of the lady of the feathers? She went on:

"It was on the night he told me all that. I couldn't understand what he is and what he's doin'. And he said that the real Valentine had gone. And then he said—I am Marr."

"The real Valentine gone. Yes," said the doctor, gravely, "that is true. Does he then know that he is——?" Mad was on his lips, but he checked himself.

"What else did he say that night?" he asked. "Can you remember? Can you tell me? Try to remember. If you succeed, you may help Julian."

Cuckoo frowned till her long, broad eyebrows nearly met. The grimace gave her the aspect of a sinister boy, bold and audacious. For she protruded her under lip, too, and the graces of ardent feeling, of pain and of passion, died out of her eyes. But this abrupt and hard mask was only caused by the effort she was making after thought, after understanding. She pressed her feet upon the ground, and the toes inside her worn shoes curved themselves inwards. What had Valentine said? What—what? She stared dully at the doctor under her corrugated brows.

"What did he say?" she murmured, in an inward voice, "Well—he didn't want me to see you. He came here about that—my seein' you."

" Yes."

" And—and Marr's not dead, he says, at least not done with Yes, that was it—he says as no strong man who's lived long's done with when he's put away. See ! "

Her face lighted up a little. She was beginning to trust her memory.

" The influence of men lives after them," the doctor said. " Marr's too. Yes. He said that ? "

She nodded. Then with a flash of understanding, a flash of that smouldering power which she had felt in loneliness and longed to tear out from its prison, she cried :

" That's it. That's how he's Marr then."

She hesitated.

" Isn't it ? " she said, flushing with the thought that she might be showing herself a fool. For she scarcely understood what she really meant.

" Valentine, no longer himself but endowed with the influence of Marr," the doctor muttered. " She means that he told her something like that. The phantasy of an unsteady brain." " Go on," he added to her.

But Cuckoo was relapsing into confusion already.

" And then he talked a lot about will, as he called it. Can't remember what he said."

" Try to."

She was silent, knitting her brows.

" It's no use. I can't," she said despairingly. " But I know he says that he's really Marr and that he's killed Valentine. He said that ; I know he did."

She glanced eagerly at the doctor, in the obvious hope that his cleverness, which she believed to be unlimited and profound, would in a flash divine all the strange secret from this exposition of her disjointed recollection. With each word she spoke, however, the doctor became more and more convinced that Valentine had only been cruelly amusing himself with her, or weaving for her benefit some intricate web of vain madness. And Cuckoo, noticing this now, and recollecting the momentary clearness of comprehension which had seized her at one point in Valentine's wild sermon to her, was mad with herself for not being able to seize again that current of inspiration, almost mad with the doctor for not unravelling the mystery. This excess of feeling finally drowned and swept away as a corpse the memory of the gospel of influence.

" I can't remember no more," she said stolidly. " There was ever such a lot about—about some one as was good and didn't want to be good any more, and so it was driven away—I don't know. P'raps he was only gamin' me."

She stared moodily at her feet, which she had stuck out from under her dress. The doctor said nothing, but at her last speech his face had lit up with a sort of excitement. For had she not described in those few ill chosen words the very mental position of the former Valentine? A saint at first with his will, a saint at last against his will—and now a saint no more. That was, perhaps, the key to the whole matter. A good man prays to be no longer good. His prayer is granted. His grievous desire is fulfilled. And then he may pray in vain for ever to be as he once was. Yet the change in Valentine was more even than this, more than the gliding from white purity to black sin. There was something.

As Cuckoo and the doctor sat in silence, she staring vacantly and empty of thought, being now utterly and chaotically puzzled, he thinking deeply, the door bell rang. In a moment Mrs. Briggs appeared, went to Cuckoo and muttered in her ear:

"Mr. Haddison wants to come in. I told him you was busy."

"Oh," said Cuckoo, "I say—wait," and then to the doctor, "It's him. It's Julian."

"Let him in," the doctor said quickly.

To see Cuckoo and Julian together might tell him much.

Julian came in, stumbling rather heavily at the entrance of the room.

CHAPTER VI

CLEAR WEATHER

"DAMN that mat!" he exclaimed. "I say Cuckoo, who the——?" The question faded on his lips as he saw Dr. Levillier, on whom he gazed with a vacant surprise that, added to the unsteadiness of his movement upon them, spoke his condition very plainly.

"You, doctor! Well, I'm damned! What are you here for?"

"To see Miss Bright," the doctor said coolly.

He had pushed forward a chair quickly with his foot. Julian collapsed in it by the table. Beads of the fog lay all over his long greatcoat and upon his hat, which he had not yet taken off. His face was flushed and dull.

"It's an infernal evening," he said. "You doctoring Cuckoo, eh?"

"I have been talking to Miss Bright."

"Oh, all right. I don't mind. Cuckoo, help me off with this coat. There's a good girl."

She obeyed without a word. When the coat was off Julian threw himself back in the chair and heaved a long sigh. His hat fell on to the floor with a bang, but he did not seem to notice it. His face was moody and miserable.

"Molly's thrown me over," he said.

Cuckoo caught her breath sharply and stole a glance at the doctor.

"Have some tea?" she said.

"No; a brandy and soda."

"Haven't got it. You must do with tea."

She rang the bell and ordered it despite his grumblings. Mrs. Brigg made no difficulty. Julian had long ago soothed her delicate susceptibilities with gold.

So, Cuckoo, oddly shy and excited, made tea for the doctor and Julian. The tea cleared the latter's fogged brain a little, but he was still morose and self-centred. He had evidently come to pour some woes out to Cuckoo, and was restrained by the presence of the doctor, at whom he looked from time to time with an expression that was near to disfavour. But the doctor began to chat easily and cordially, and Julian gradually thawed.

"I suppose you know Rip's dead," he said presently. "Went out the other night and got frozen in the snow. Poor little beggar. Val's awfully cut up about it."

"Is he?" said the doctor.

"Yes. Dear old Val. Dev'lish hard Rip's never making it up with him again, wasn't it? Rip didn't know a good fellow did he, Doctor?"

"He was devoted to Valentine once," the doctor said.

"Ah, but he changed. Dogs are just like women, just like women, never the same two days together. Curse them."

He appeared to have forgotten Cuckoo's presence, and she sat listening eagerly, quite unmoved by the dagger thrust at her sex.

"Dogs don't usually change. Their faithfulness bears everything without breaking."

"Except a trance then," Julian said, still with a wavering in-and-out stolidity, at the same time mournful and almost ludicrous.

"That trance did for Rip, did for him I tell you. He never knew poor old Val again. As if he thought him another man after that, another man."

The doctor's eyes met Cuckoo's. She had a teacup at her rouged lips, and had paused in the act of drinking, fascinated by the words that wound so naturally into the legend of change which she knew and knew not.

"As if Val wasn't just the same," Julian pursued, shaking his head slowly. "Just the same."

"You think so?" the doctor said, quickly.

"Eh?"

"You think that trance made no difference to him?"

"Why; how should it?"

Cuckoo drank her tea hastily and put the cup down.

"How should it?" Julian repeated, as if with a heavy challenge.

"It might in many ways, to his health——"

"He's stronger than ever he was."

"Or to his mind, his nature. You see no change there that might have frightened Rip?"

"Not I. He's more of a man, good old Val, even than he was."

"Ah! You acknowledge there is a change."

"Give me some more tea, Cuckoo," Julian said, thrusting his cup towards her. "Make it strong. It's picking me up." He sat forward in his chair, and began to light a cigar, keeping his eyes on the doctor.

"Well, if you call that a change; to get like other men. Old Val was a saint. I loved him then, but I love him ten times more now he's—a—the other thing, you know. Ten times more. He knows the world now and his advice is worth having. I'd follow him anywhere. He can't go wrong. Takes care of himself and of me too. I might have been anything—anything, but for him. Instead of what I am——"

He drew himself up with some pride, and pulled at the cup which Cuckoo pushed towards him.

"I'm just what Val makes me; just what he makes me," he said, taking obvious joy in the thought. "Val can make me do anything. You know that, Doctor?"

"Yes. Then you have changed with him, become more of a man, as you call it, with him. Is that so Julian?"

"I suppose so."

Julian was drinking his tea, which had become very strong from standing.

"And are you happier than you were before?"

The doctor spoke insistently and gravely. Cuckoo had taken Jessie on to her lap and now stroked the little dog quickly and softly with a thin, fluttering hand. Julian seemed trying to think, to dive into his mind and discover its real feelings.

"I suppose so," he said presently. "But who's happy? I should like to know. Cuckoo isn't. Are you, Cuckoo?"

It seemed a cruel question, addressed to that spectre of girlhood.

"I dunno," she answered swiftly. "It don't matter much either way."

"She may be," the doctor said. "And you were happy, Julian."

The tea had certainly cleared the boy's brain. His manner was more sensible, and the heavy sensuality had gone from his eyes. Though he still looked haggard and wretched, he was no longer the mere wreck of vice he had seemed when he drifted into the little room out of the fog.

"Was I?" he said slowly. "It seems a devil of a time ago."

The doctor's heart warmed to these two young creatures, children to him, yet who had seen so much, gone so far down into the depths that lie beneath the feet of life. He thought in that moment that he could willingly give up all his own peace of mind, success, fame, restfulness of heart, to set them straight up, face to face with strength and purity once more. One was well born, educated, still handsome, the other a so-called lost woman, and originally only a very poor and hopelessly ignorant girl. Yet their community of misery and sorrow put them side by side, like two children who gather violets in a lane together, or drown together in some strong, sad river.

"It is not so long, Julian," he said. "Only before Valentine's trance."

Julian caught him up quickly.

T

" Why d'you say that, Doctor ? "

" Why ?   Simply because it is truth."

" You're always at that trance. I believe it's just because you told us not to sit again. But there was no harm done."

" You are sure of that ? "

As he put the question the doctor's mind was on a hunt round that sleep and waking. He had gradually come to think that night a night of some strange crisis, through which Valentine had passed from what he had been to what he was. Yet his knowledge could not set at the door of that unnatural slumber the blame of all that followed it. His imagination might, but not his knowledge. He wondered whether Julian might not help him to elucidation.

" Sure ? of course ! Why not ? Valentine's all right. I'm all right. Rip's the only one gone. And if he'd only stayed in the house that night he'd be all right too."

" No, Addison."

Julian stared at this flat contradiction.

" Not ? "

" Rip never went out of the house."

" But he died in the snow."

" No," the doctor said quietly. " He died in your dining-room of fear—fear of his old master, Valentine."

" What ? " said Julian, gripping the table with his right hand " Val had been at him ? "

In two or three simple, straightforward words, the doctor described the death of Rip. When he had finished Cuckoo gave a little cry and clasped the astonished and squirming Jessie close in her arms Julian's brow clouded.

" He might have left Rip alone," he said. " It's odd dogs can't bear Val now."

" Again since that trance," the doctor said.

Julian looked at him with acute irritation, but said nothing Then, turning his eyes on Cuckoo, who was still hugging Jessie, he snapped his fingers at the little dog and called its name. Cuckoo extended her arms, holding Jessie, to Julian, and he took the small creature gently. And, as he took her, he bent forward and gazed long and deeply into Cuckoo's eyes. She trembled and flushed, half with pleasure, half with a nervous consciousness of the doctor's presence.

" Oh, why do you ? " she murmured, turning her head away. The action seemed to make Julian aware that perhaps his manner was odd, and his subsequent glance at the doctor was very plainly, and even rudely, explanatory of a wish to be alone with Cuckoo. The doctor read its meaning and resolved to go away. With the quick observation and knowledge of men which long years of training had given to him, he saw that, strangely enough, the only creature whose influence could in any way cope with the influence of Valentine was not himself, who once had been as a seer to the two young men, but the thin, spectral, weary, painted Cuckoo. There, in that small room, with the long murmur of London outside, sat these two human beings, desolate woman, vice-ridden man, both fallen down in the deep mire, both almost whelmed in the flood of Fate. And he stood strong, faithful, clean-souled, brave-hearted, yet impotent, regarding them. For some power willed it that misery alone could hold out a helping hand to misery, that vice and degradation must rise to thrust back vice and degradation. The fallen creature was to be the protector, the unredeemed to be the redeemer. Dr. Levillier knew this when he saw Julian's long glance into the hollow eyes of Cuckoo. And he thrilled with the knowledge. It seemed to him a great demonstration of the root, the core, of divine pity which he believed to be the centre of the scheme of the world. Round this centre revolved wheels within wheels of cruelty, of agony, of ruthless passions and of lawless bitterness. Yet they radiated from pity. They radiated from love. How it was so he could not tell, and there the pessimist had him by the throat. But that it was so he felt in his inmost heart, and never more than now, when the tired boy sneered at him, who was an old friend, clean of life, gentle of nature, and turned to this girl, this thing that loathsome men played with and scorned. Cuckoo flushed and trembled; this divine pity outpainted her rouge, and shook that body which had so often betrayed itself to destroyers. This divine pity gave to her, who had lost all the power to find freedom for another soul that lay in bondage.

The doctor gazed for an instant at the boy and girl, and was deeply moved. His lips breathed a word that was a prayer, for Julian, for the lady of the feathers.

Then he got up.

" I have to go," he said.

Julian said nothing ; Cuckoo flushed again, and accompanied the doctor to the hall door. When she had opened it, and they looked out, it was very cold, but the fog had lifted, and was floating away to reveal a sky full of stars, which always seem to shine more brightly upon frost. The doctor took the girl's hand.

" I see you in clear weather," he said.

" You don't—you don't think as he'll—as I'll——" stammered Cuckoo, glancing awkwardly towards the lighted doorway of the little sitting-room, and then at the doctor. The church clock striking 7.30, pointed the application of the hesitating murmur. It was unconventionally late for an afternoon call.

" It'll be all right, you know that ? " said the lady of the feathers.

" Yes, I know that," he answered. " You have to fight, I feel that ; only you can do it. You have to fight this—this——" and here the doctor's loyalty spoke, for he could not betray even this new Valentine, " this strange madness of Valentine's. Pit your will against his, and conquer for Julian's sake."

" Will," said Cuckoo.   " That's what he says I can't have."

" Won't you pray to have it given you ? " said the little doctor.

Cuckoo looked at him wondering.   Then she said :

" I believe I could fight better'n pray."

" Sometimes battle is the greatest of all prayers," said the doctor.

The iron gate clicked. He was gone. Cuckoo cast an oblique glance up at the stars before she shut the door, and retraced her steps down the passage.

CHAPTER VII

BATTLE ARRAY

WHEN Julian left the Marylebone Road that night it was nearly ten o'clock. He was quite sober and looked preternaturally grave as he opened the little gate and stepped out into the frost-bound street. In the lighted aperture of the doorway behind him Cuckoo stood like a shadow half revealed peeping after him, and he turned and waved his hand to her. Then he walked away slowly, meditating. That night the fight for the possession of his will, his soul, had begun in deadly earnest. He did not know it, yet he was vaguely aware that he began to move in the midst of unwonted circumstances. Cuckoo had not been able wholly to conceal from him her strong mental excitement. Since her conversation with the doctor she had become a different woman. For the one word had been spoken which could change weakness into strength, utter self-distrust into something that at least resembled self-reliance. The doctor had broken Valentine's spell over Cuckoo with that word. He believed in her. He told her to fight. He assumed that she had some power, even more power for Julian than he had. "Only you can do it," he had said. The sentence armed her from head to foot, put weapons in her hands, light in her hollow eyes, a leaping exultation in her heart. The flickering power that she had marvelled at, and then despaired of, burnt up at last into a strong flame. That evening it had dazzled Julian's eyes. He seemed to see a new Cuckoo, and he was thinking of her as he walked along now in the frost under the stars. His meditation was not very intellectual or very profound, for since the change in his life Julian had put his old intellectualities away from him. Passion, so long guarded, so bravely repressed, once it had broken loose stormed all the heights of his nature and drove every sentiment that tried to oppose it into exile. The animalism that is so generally present in a boy physically strong took possession of him, and would not tolerate any divided allegiance. It declined to permit his life to be a thing of mingled enjoyments, now rejoicing in the leaping desires of the body, now disregarding them for the aspirations and clear contentments of the mind. It seemed revengeful, like a man long kept fasting against his will, and, having at last come into its empire made that empire an autocracy, a tyranny. Julian had passed at a step from one extreme to another, and had already so lost the habit of following any mental process to a conclusion that he could no longer think clearly with ease, or observe himself with any acuteness. He was for the time all body, knew his muscles, his flesh, his limbs, like intimates; his mind only distantly, like a stranger. With passion, with greed, he had seized on all those pleasures which he had previously feared and shunned, until his brain was heavy as is the brain of a glutton and a drunkard, and his mind stepped in any direction with a languid lethargy. So to-night he had the face of a man puzzled as he walked in the frost under the stars.

Once the hint of some power lurking in Cuckoo had thrilled and awed him, as only a certain clearness—a certain receptive, appreciative clearness—can be thrilled and awed. Now the abrupt development of that power almost distressed, because it confused him. He had gone down lower in the interval between the two possibilities of sensation.

" What the devil's come over Cuckoo ? " so ran his thought with a schoolboy gait. That something had come over her he recognised. She was no longer the girl he had stared at in Piccadilly, the creature he had pitied in the twilight hour of their first friendly interview. Nor was she the woman whose soul he had injured by his cruel whim, the woman who had beaten him with reproaches, and made him for an instant almost ashamed of his lusts. All these humanities, perhaps, slept, or woke, in her still. Yet it was not they which heavily concerned him on his way to the Marble Arch. There is a vitality about power of whatever kind, that makes itself instantly felt, even when it is not understood, even when it is neither beloved nor appreciated. Julian was confused by his dull and sudden recognition of power in Cuckoo. No longer did it flash upon him, a mystery of flame in her eyes, moving him to the awe and the constraint that a man may feel at sight of an unearthly thing, a phantom, or a vision of the night. (He had looked for the flame in her eyes, and he had not found it.) But it glowed upon him more steadily, with a warmth of humanity, of something inherent, rooted, not detached and merely for the moment and as if by chance, prisoned in some particular place, from which at a breath it might escape. It drew him to Cuckoo, and, at the same time, it slightly repelled him, the latter—though Julian did not know it—by the sharp abruptness of its novelty. For the doctor had lit a blaze of strength in the girl by a word. Julian's eyes were dazzled by the blaze. Custom might teach them to face it more calmly. At present he could look at the stars with greater ease. Indeed, as he walked, he did look at them, and thought of the eyes of Cuckoo, and then of the eyes of all women, and of their strange intensities of suggestion and of realisation, of their language of the devil and of the clouds, of their kindling vigours. But the eyes of Cuckoo were no longer as the eyes of any other woman. Julian glanced at a girl who watched him from the corner of the street. He knew that Cuckoo looked each night at men as that girl looked at him. He knew it, yet he felt that he did not believe it. For to him she was dressed, already, in the fillet of some priestess, in the robes of one tending some strange and unnamed altar. She woke in him a little of the uneasy fear and uneasy attraction that a creature whom a man feels to be greater than himself often wakes in him. That evening, while Julian sat with her, he had been seized with curious conflicting desires to fall before her or to strike her, to draw her close or to fend her off from him, all dull, too, and vague as in heaviness of dreaming. Those feelings, vague in the house, were scarcely clearer in the cold and in the open spaces of the night, and Julian was conscious of a sense of irritation, of anger against himself. He felt as if he were an oaf, a lout. Was it, could it be Cuckoo who had made him feel so? After all, what was she? Julian tried to hug and soothe himself in the unworthy remembrance of Cuckoo's monotonous life and piteous deeds, to reinstate himself in contented animalism by thoughts of the animalism of this priestess! He laughed aloud under the stars, but the laugh rang hollow. He could not reinstate himself. He could only wearily repeat, " What the devil's come over Cuckoo ? " with an iteration of dull, moody petulance.

A hansom suddenly pulled up beside him and a voice called :
" Julian ! Julian, where are you coming from ? "
It was Valentine. He was muffled in a fur coat, and stretched himself over the wooden apron to attract his friend's attention.
" I have been to your rooms," he continued. " Don't you remember we had arranged to dine together ? "
Julian looked at him without animation.
" I had forgotten it," he answered.
" Your memory is becoming very treacherous," Valentine said. " Where are you off to ? Get in. I will drive you."
" I hadn't any plan," Julian said, getting into the cab.
" Drive to the Savoy," Valentine called to the cabman. " I want some supper," he added.
" I can't come in. I'm not dressed."
" We will have a private room then. Have you dined ? "
" I ? No."
Valentine looked at him narrowly.
" Have you been in the Marylebone Road again ? " he asked.
" Yes."

" Why ? "

" I don't know."

The answer was the bald truth. In making it Julian experienced a slight feeling of relief. He was putting into words the vagueness that perplexed him. He wondered why he did go to see Cuckoo.

" But you must know. You must have a reason," said Valentine.

" If I have I don't know what it is. I wish you would tell me, old fellow."

" I can't supply you with reasons for all your actions."

" And I can't supply myself with reasons for any of them," Julian said slowly. The words were leading him to a dawning wonder at his own way of life, a dawning desire to know if there were really any reasons for the things he did. But Valentine did not accept the reply as satisfactory. On the contrary, it evidently irritated him still more, for he said with unusual warmth :

" Your reason for dropping your engagements, throwing me over and wasting my evenings is quite obvious. The blessed damozel of the feathers is attractive to you. Her freshness captivates you. Her brilliant conversation entertains you. She is the powdered and painted reason of these irrelevant escapades."

" Don't sneer at her, Val."

The words came quickly, like a bolt. Valentine frowned, and a deepening suspicion flashed in his eyes.

" I did not think you were so easily flattered," he continued.

" Flattered ? "

" Yes. Cuckoo Bright admires you, and you go to No. 400 to smell the rather rank fumes of the incense which she burns at your shrine."

" Nonsense," Julian cried warmly.

" What other reason can you have ? She has no beauty ; she has no conversation, no gaiety, no distinction, no manners—she has nothing. She is nothing."

" Ah, it's there you're wrong."

" Wrong ! "

" When you say she is nothing."

" I say it again," Valentine reiterated almost fiercely. " The lady of the feathers is nothing, nothing at all. God and the devil—they have both completely forgotten her. A creature like that is neither good, nor would I call her really evil, for she is evil merely that she may go on living, not because she has a fine pleasure in sin. But if you sell your will for bread and butter you slip out of the world, the world that must be reckoned with. I say Cuckoo Bright is nothing."

" And I tell you she is something extraordinary."

As Julian spoke the words the cab stopped at the Savoy. Valentine sprang out and paid the man. His face was flushed as if with heat, despite the piercing cold of the night.

" A private room and supper for two," he said to the man in the vestibule. " Take my coat," and he drew himself with obvious relief from the embrace of his huge coat. Julian and he said nothing more until they were sitting opposite to one another at a small oval table in a small and strongly decorated room, whose windows faced the Thames Embankment. The waiter uncorked a bottle of champagne with the air of one performing a religious rite. The electric light gleamed and a fire chased the frost from recollection. Julian had already forgotten what they had been talking about in the cab. The first sip of champagne swept the heavy meditativeness from him. But Valentine, unfolding his napkin slowly, and with his eyes on the *menu*, said :

" In what way is she something extraordinary ? "

" H'm ? " Julian muttered.

" Surely you can define it ? "

" What, Val ? "

" The peculiarity of Cuckoo Bright that you laid so much stress on just now."

" Oh, yes, now I remember. No, I can't define it. How good this soup is. The soup here——"

" Yes, yes ; our coming here again and again to eat it proves our appreciation. Julian, do endeavour to answer my question. I am really interested to know exactly what it is that has taken you again to Marylebone Road."

Julian drank some more champagne. His eyes began to sparkle.

" Can you give a reason for everything that you do ? " he asked.

" I think I certainly could for every act that I reiterate."

" Then you're built differently from me. But I've told you all I can. I like Cuckoo. She's a damned nice girl."

Valentine's lip curled.

" I can't agree with you, Julian."

" You don't know her as I do."

" Not quite."

Julian reddened.

" Come now," he began, and then checked himself and laughed good-naturedly. " You can't play the saint any more, you know, Val," he said.

" I have no wish to. I discovered long ago that a saint is only the corpse of a man, not a living man at all. But we are talking about this corpse of a woman."

" Cuckoo's no corpse. By Jove, no. I believe she's got a power that no other woman has."

" How so ? You haven't been imagining that absurd flame in her eyes again ? "

Valentine spoke with furtive uneasiness. He was scarcely eating or drinking, but Julian was doing ample justice to the wine and displayed a very tolerable appetite. He lifted his glass to his lips and put it down before he answered:

"No. It's gone."

Valentine seemed relieved

"Of course. I knew it was an hallucination. You went to satisfy yourself, I suppose. And now——"

"Since it's gone Cuckoo seems to me—I don't know—changed somehow. Val, there must be a few people in the world with great power over others. You are one. Marr was another, and——" he paused.

"And what?" Valentine said rather loudly.

"Well," Julian paused again, as if conscious that he was about to say something that would seem ridiculous, "Cuckoo——"

"Is a third! You think it reasonable to bracket me with a woman like that, to compare my will, mine, who have lived the life of thought as well as the life of action, who have trained my powers to the highest point, and offered up sacrifices—yes, sacrifices—to my will, to that degraded, powerless creature! Julian!"

He stopped, clenching his hand as it lay upon the table. Never before had Julian seen him so profoundly moved. All his normal calm and self-possession seemed deserting him. His lips worked like those of a man in the very extremity of rage, and the red glow in his cheeks faded into the grey of suppressed passion. Julian was utterly taken aback by such an exhibition of feeling.

"My dear fellow," he stammered, "I didn't mean—I had no idea——"

"You did mean that. You do. And I—I have been fool enough to believe that you relied upon me, on my judgment, that you looked up to me—that—good God, how absurd!"

He lay back in his chair and burst into a paroxysm of loud and mirthless laughter, while Julian, holding his champagne glass between his fingers, and twisting it stealthily round and round, regarded him with a blank stare of utter confusion and perplexity. Valentine continued to laugh so long that it seemed as if he were seized in the grip of a horrible hysteria. But just as the situation was becoming actually intolerable, he suddenly controlled himself with an obvious and painful effort. After remaining perfectly silent for two or three minutes, he said, in a voice that struggled to be calm, and succeeded in being icy:

"Julian, you have torn the veil of the Holy of Holies from the top to the bottom with a vengeance. But why have you kept up the deception so long, when, after all, there was nothing behind the veil? That was surely unnecessary."

"What is the matter with you, Val? I don't understand you."

" Nor I you. And yet we say that we are intimate friends. There's an irony."

At this point the waiter came in with an omelette and the conversation ceased, checked by his peripatetic presence. As soon as he had retreated, with all the hushed activity of a mute rolling on castors, Julian exclaimed :

" It's not an irony. You choose to make it so. You're not yourself to-night, Valentine. I do not compare you with poor Cuckoo. How could I ? She's down in the dirt and you are far away from the dirt. And of course your power over any one must be a thousand times greater than hers."

" If it came to a battle ? If it came to a battle ? " interrupted Valentine, " You say that, Julian ? "

" A battle ! of what ? "

" Of wills, naturally, Cuckoo Bright's will against mine ? "

" But what a strange idea——"

" You haven't answered my question."

" Because I don't see the force of it."

" Answer it nevertheless."

" Then Cuckoo would be beaten at once," Julian said. But there was no ring of conviction in his voice, and he fell at once into silence after he had spoken the words. Valentine saw by his frowning face and puckered forehead that the idea of such a battle had set in motion a train of thought in his mind.

" You are wondering, Julian," Valentine said.

Julian looked up.

" Who doesn't wonder in this beastly world ? " he said morosely.

" I never do. I prefer to act. Drink some more champagne."

He pushed the bottle over and went on :

" You are wondering why I spoke of a battle between Cuckoo Bright and me. Well, I'll tell you. I spoke because I see that there is to be such a battle."

Julian drank his champagne and looked definitely and increasingly astonished, as Valentine continued :

" There is to be such a battle. I have seen it for a long time. Julian, you may think you know women. You don't. I said just now that a woman like Cuckoo Bright is nothing, but I said it for the sake of uttering a paradox. No woman is ever nothing in a world that is full of the things called men. No woman is ever nothing so long as there is a bottle of hair-dye, a rouge pot, a dressmaker, and—a man within reach. She may be in the very gutter. That doesn't matter. For from the very gutter she can see—not the stars, but the twinkling vanities of men, and they will light her on her way to Mayfair drawing-rooms, even perhaps to Court. Who knows ? And God—or the devil—has given to every woman the knowledge of her possibilities. Men have only the ignorance of theirs."

"What has this to do with Cuckoo and me?" Julian said. "This bottle is empty, Valentine."

Valentine rang hastily for another.

"And what on earth has it got to do with a battle between you and Cuckoo?"

"Everything. She hates me. She has told you so again and again."

Julian looked expressively uncomfortable. ·

"I've always stood up for you," he began.

"I believe it. She hates me not because I am myself, but simply because I am your closest friend. Hush, Julian. It's much better all this should be said once for all. Many women are intensely jealous of the men friends of men whom they either love, or who they mean shall love them. Look at the wives who drive their husband's old chums from intimacy into the outer darkness of acquaintanceship. Wedding-days break, as well as bind, faith. And you have had your wedding-day with Cuckoo."

"That was an accident. She loathes to think of it."

"She may say so. But it puts a fine edge on her hatred of me nevertheless."

"No, Valentine, no. Her dislike of you is simply silly—instinctive."

"She tells you so. Ah! I was wrong to call her nothing. But it is her hatred of me that must bring us to battle unless——"

"Unless what?"

"You give her up now, once and for all."

"Give Cuckoo up!"

The words came slowly, and the voice that uttered them sounded startled and even shocked. Valentine began to gauge the new power of the lady of the feathers from that moment.

"That's a—a strong thing to do, Val."

"It won't hurt you to do a strong thing for once in your life."

"Even if it didn't hurt me I think it would hurt her very much. For, Valentine, I believe you said truth when you said to me once 'That girl loves you.' Do you remember?"

"Perfectly. Loves you, your birth, your position, your money, your good looks, perhaps your standpoint above the gutter. I can well believe that Miss Bright, like all her sisterhood, loves with undying love that combination of flesh-pots, her notion of the ego of a man."

"She has never accepted a halfpenny from me."

"Because she means eventually to have twenty-one shillings in the pound. Have some more champagne."

" Yes. You are wrong, Val, utterly wrong. Cuckoo's not mercenary. If such a girl could be good, she is good."

There was just a touch of the maudlin in Julian's voice. He went on, very earnestly, and nodding his head emphatically over even his conjunctions.

" And if she were what you say, she would have no influence over me, and I should hate her. But to me she is just what a good girl might be. Why, even the doctor—— "

" Was he there to-night ? " Valentine cried, with a sudden inspiration.

" Of course he was. And you know what a particular little chap he is."

" Why was he there ? "

" Just to see Cuckoo, you know, in a friendly way."

Valentine realised then that the battle had begun. He divined the meaning of the doctor's visit. He guessed what it had done for the lady of the feathers. And he sat silent while Julian went on drinking more champagne.

" I believe he likes Cuckoo, Val. I am sure he does. And he behaved quite as if—quite as if he—you know—respected her. And it's all nonsense her hating you, and having a battle, and all that kind of thing, with you. She's only fanciful. She's not—— "

" Would you give her up if I asked you to ? Mind, Julian, I don't say I ever shall ask you. But if I do ? "

" Don't ask me to, don't ask me. Poor Cuckoo, poor girl, she's got no friends, money, or—or anything. Poor Cuckoo. Poor Cuck—Cuck—— "

He fell back in his chair, nodding his head, and reiterating his commiseration for the lady of the feathers in a faint and recurring hiccough. Valentine got up and rang the bell.

" The bill, please, waiter."

" Yes, sir."

The man glanced at Julian with the shadow of a pleasing, and apparently also pleased, smile and withdrew. Valentine stood for a moment looking at the leaning figure on the chair, relaxed in the first throes of a drunken slumber. His anger and almost unbridled emotion completely died away as he looked.

" Can it be called a battle after all ? " he said to himself. " They may not know it, but it is practically won already."

The waiter re-entered. Valentine paid the bill, and the breath of the frost shortly revived Julian into an attempt at conversation.

" Don't ask me to give her up, Val, don't, don't ask me. Poor girl. Poor, poor Cuck—Cuck."

The name of the lady of the feathers seemed a good one for a tipsy tongue to play with.

CHAPTER VIII

THE DOCTOR RECEIVES A VISIT FROM MRS. WILSON

DR. LEVILLIER grew more puzzled day by day. His observation of Valentine taught him only one thing certainly, and beyond possibility of doubt, and that was the death of the youth he had once loved, the living presence of a youth whom he could not love, whom he could only shrink from and even fear. He held to the theory that this radical and ghastly change must be caused by some obscure dementia, some secret overturning of the mind ; but he was obliged to confess to himself that he held to it only because, otherwise, he would be floating helpless, and without a spar, upon a tide of perplexity and confusion. He could not honestly say that he was able to put his finger upon any definite signs of madness exhibited by Valentine, any that would satisfy a mad doctor. He could only say that Valentine's character had been strangely beautiful and was now strangely evil, and that the soul of Julian was following rapidly the soul of Valentine. The more closely he watched Valentine the more astounded did he become and the more eager to detach Julian from him. But the strangest thing of all, as the doctor allowed in one of his frequent self-communings—was that though formerly he had loved Valentine better than Julian it never occurred to him that the work of rescue might be undertaken on behalf of the former. His mind dismissed the new Valentine into a region that was beyond his scope and power. He felt instinctively that here was a soul, a will, that his soul could not turn from its ends or detach from its pursuits. The new Valentine was a law to himself. What moved the doctor to such horror was that the new Valentine was a law to Julian. And there was something peculiarly dreadful in the idea which he held, that Julian, once under the beautiful influence of Valentine's sanity, was now under the baneful influence of his insanity. The doctor had gone the length of deciding, in his own mind, that Valentine's sane period of life and insane period lay one on each side of a fixed gulf, and that fixed gulf was his long trance succeeding the final sitting of the two young men. This conclusion was arrived at with ease, once the theory of a subtle lunacy was accepted as a fact. For, on sending his mind back along the ways of recollection, the doctor was able to recall hints of the new Valentine dating from that very night, but never before it. The first hint was Rip's manifested fear, and this led on to others which have been already mentioned. Having made up his mind that this trance was the motive-power of Valentine's supposed madness, the doctor sought in every direction to increase his knowledge on the subject of simulations of death by the human body. He looked up again the cases of innumerable hysterical patients whom he had himself treated, sometimes with success, sometimes with failure. He consulted other doctors, of course without mentioning the object of his research. He endeavoured to apply to Valentine's case standards by which he was quickly able to form a satisfactory opinion on the cases of others. He even went so far as to examine as closely as possible into the history of table-turning, the uses ascribed to it by its votaries, and the results obtained from it by credible—as opposed to merely credulous—witnesses. But he found no case that seemed in any way analogous to the strange case of Valentine. As was only natural, the doctor did not forget the possibility of hypnotism, which had struck him during his second conversation with the lady of the feathers. Her confused declarations on the subject of Valentine and Marr being one person, if they were really a true account of what Valentine had said to her—which seemed very doubtful—could only be made clear by accepting as a fact that the dead Marr had laid a hypnotic spell upon Valentine, which continued to exist actively long after its weaver slept in the grave. But Marr and Valentine had never met. This fact seemed fully established. Valentine had always denied any knowledge of him before the trance. Julian had always assumed that only he of the two friends had any acquaintance with Marr. And again, when the doctor one day, quite casually, said to Valentine, "By the way, you never did meet Marr, did you?" Valentine replied, "Never, till I saw him lying dead in the Euston Road."

The doctor could see no ray of light in the darkness that could guide him to the clue of the mystery. He could only say to himself, "It must be, it must be an obscure and horrible madness," and keep his theory to himself. Sometimes, as he sat pondering over the whole affair, he smiled, half sadly, half sarcastically. For the event brought home to his ready modesty the sublime ignorance of all clever and instructed men, and taught him to wonder as he had often wondered, that there exists in such a world as ours such a fantastic growth as the flourishing weed, conceit.

Another matter that puzzled him greatly was this. As the days went on, and as Valentine grew—and he did grow—more certain of his own power for evil over Julian, and as, consequently, he took less and less pains to hide the truth of his personality from the knowledge of the doctor, the latter was frequently seized with the appalled sensation which had long ago overtaken him when he was followed in Regent Street and in Vere Street. This recurrence of sensation and the certainty forced gradually upon the doctor that it was caused by the presence of Valentine, naturally led him to wonder whether it were possible that the man who had dogged his steps, and eventually fled from him, could have been Valentine himself. If that were indeed so, then this madness—if it did exist—must surely have come upon Valentine before the trance. Nothing but a madness could have led him thus in the night hours to steal out in pursuit of the friend who had but just left his house and company. But the doctor knew of no means by which he could satisfy himself of Valentine's movements on the night in question. To ask Valentine himself would be to court a lie. Once the doctor thought for a moment of having recourse to Wade. But then he remembered that the butler did not sleep in the flat, and had no doubt long gone home before the event of the night in question. So, again, he was confronted with a dead wall, beyond which he could see no clear view or comprehensible country.

About this time there happened an event which struck strongly upon the doctor's mind. He was one day as usual in his consulting-room, receiving a multitude of patients, when his man-servant entered with a card on a salver.

" A lady, sir, who wishes to see you. She has no appointment."

The doctor took the card. On it was printed merely " Mrs. Wilson."

" I cannot see the lady to-day," he said, " unless she can call again after five o'clock. But I can see her then, or to-morrow morning at ten. Ask her which she would prefer."

After a moment's absence Lawler returned.

" The lady will come at five o'clock this evening, sir."

" Very well."

And the doctor bent his mind once more steadily upon his work.

At five o'clock the door opened, and a tall, square, and strong looking woman, dressed in black, walked quietly into the room. She bowed to the doctor and sat down.

"I am glad you could see me to-day," she said. I leave London early to-morrow morning. I hate London."

She spoke in a full and rather rich voice, with a slightly burring accent, and looked the doctor full in the face with a pair of large and sensible grey eyes. Nature had certainly built her to be one of those towers of women, strong for themselves, for their sex, and often for men also, who possess a peculiar power, given in quite full measure to no male creature, of large sympathy and lofty composure.

But the doctor saw at a glance that some adverse fate had disagreed with the intentions of nature, and fought against them with success. Circumstances must have arisen in this woman's life to break down her unusual equipment of courage and resolution, or, if not to break it down, to dint and batter the shield she carried over her heart and life. For her fine face was lined with care, her naturally firm mouth was tormented by an apparently irresistible quivering, that, once prompted by long and painful emotion, had now become habitual and mechanical, and her eyes, although they met the eyes of the doctor with a peculiar large reception and return of scrutiny, held in their depths that hunted expression which is only developed by long agony, either physical or mental. So much the doctor read in a glance before his patient began to detail her symptoms. She detailed them with a certain obvious shame and a slow conquering of reticence that made her speak very deliberately.

She began by saying, in no insulting manner, that she had kept clear of doctors during almost the whole of her life, that she had meant to keep clear of them till her death.

" For I was born with a constitution of iron," she said, " and I have always lived on the most sanitary principles, and with the utmost simplicity. So I hoped to go to my grave without much suffering. Certainly I never expected to have to consult any one on the ground of nervous breakdown. Yet that is exactly why I am here with you at this moment. The circumstances of my life have been too much for me, I suppose."

There was a grave pathos in her voice as she uttered the last words.

" At any rate," she continued, after a pause, " I would like you to help me if you can. The cause of my breakdown is remote enough, several years old. I had a tremendous burden to bear then, and I bore it, as I thought bravely, for a long time. At last it grew intolerable, and then I succeeded at last in getting it removed, in getting rid of it, you understand, altogether. The odd thing is that while I was bearing my burden my strength did not fail me, my courage did not utterly give way. Only when the burden was removed did I faint because of it. My trouble was partially physical —I had to endure grave physical cruelty at that time—but chiefly mental. My agony of mind ran a race with my agony of body, and won easily. It's generally so with women, I believe ? "

She waited as if for a reply.

" Yes, it is often so," Dr. Levillier answered.

" Ever since the burden was lifted from my shoulders," she continued, " I have been getting steadily worse. Each month, each year, I become more and more degraded in my cowardice, my fear of trifles, even of things which have no existence at all. All this is perhaps—perhaps—peculiarly painful to me because I am naturally,

U

you must understand, what sane people call a strong-minded woman. I had originally complete physical courage, didn't know the meaning of the word fear, despised those who did, I am afraid. So you see this. is very bad for me; it cuts so deep into my mind, you see. It makes me hate and loathe myself so. I sleep badly, and have the usual symptoms of nervous collapse, I believe. I'm strong one moment, feeble, no good at all, the next. My appetite has long been bad, and so on. But it isn't that sort of thing I mind. I could fight with that well enough. It's my horrible deterioration of mind that troubles me, that has brought me here, to you, in spite of my hatred of London, of every city. It was in a city, though not in London, that I bore that burden I told you of. It doesn't seem possible to me, but I'm told, and I read, that my mind diseased may be an effect, and that the cause may lie in my body. That's why I come to you. Doctor Levillier, root out the disease if you can."

She ended speaking almost with passion, her lips trembling all the time and her eyes never leaving his face. Then she added, with a curious, characteristic abruptness:

"I will tell you that I've plenty of money. Lack of funds is no weapon against my return to health—if my return is in any way possible.

Dr. Levillier smiled slightly.

"You are anticipating the usual 'long sea voyage' formula, I see," he said.

"Possibly."

"I should not prescribe it for you off-hand," he said. "Sea air is not a specific for all nervous complaints, as some people seem to think. You have no bodily pain?"

"No. I often wish I had."

"What you tell me about your gradual collapse coming on after the crisis of your troubles was over, and not during it, does not surprise me. Nor am I puzzled by your malady increasing if, as I suppose, you are living idly"

"I am. I have no courage to do anything or see anybody."

"Exactly. You live in a sort of hiding."

"Why—yes. You see, once I was well-known to a good many people. My troubles became known to them, too. I could not get rid of that burden I told you of except by blazoning them abroad. I shrink from meeting any people now. Therefore I live very quietly. I——"

Suddenly she seemed to grow tired of the half-measures in frankness that had so far governed her communications. She spread forth her hands with a very characteristic, ample gesture of sudden confidence.

" I think I'll tell you exactly what it was," she said. " You may have read of me. Long ago, some years at least, I was obliged to take action against my husband, a Mr. Wilson, who afterwards assumed the name of Marr. I charged him with cruelty, won my case, and obtained a judicial separation."

Then Dr. Levillier knew that he looked on the former wife of the strange, cruel, dead man, whose influence had entered into the lives of his two friends.

" You may have heard of my case ? " Mrs. Wilson said.

" Certainly I have."

" It was bad even from a newspaper point of view, I believe. People congratulated me on getting rid of a brute, and thought I was all right and ought to be happy. But the newspapers and the world never knew what I had gone through, the real horrors, before I insisted on release. You started when I called my husband a brute just now, Doctor Levillier; I noticed it. The phrase hurt you, coming from any wife about any husband. I know why. A boy once told me that his mother was always drunk. He hurt me then into hating him for the rest of my days. But I called a stranger a brute, not the man I loved and married, not the man I loved after I married him. Doctor Levillier, do you believe in possessions ? "

She had been gradually getting excited while she spoke, and, on the last words, she leaned forward in her chair and struck her hand down in her lap.

" Do you mean possession by the devil ? " said the doctor, very quietly, opposing a strong calm to her intensity.

" Yes. I do. My experience obliges me to. I knew, for a year before I married him, I married, I lived for two years after I married him, with a man who was my conception of what a man should be, strong, gentle, tender, brave, a hero to me. I got rid of a devil, after I had endured two years of torture at his hands. It is no use to tell me those two distinct men I knew were one and the same man. My soul, my heart, declare that it's a lie. There were such differences. My husband loved music ; this man hated it, yet had the power to use it as a means of tormenting me. But I needn't dwell on the evidences of change. Suffice it to say that the thing that crushed me, the thing that has brought me down into the dust where I am, dust of cowardice, and weakness, and impotence to do or to be anything, was the horror of awakening to a knowledge of that change, of having to live as wife with this devil, whom I knew not, who was a stranger to me. Only the features were my husband's, nothing else. I got rid of a stranger. The man found dead in the Euston Road was a stranger whom I hated, nothing more to me than that."

As she spoke, in a deep, resonant voice that pulsated through the room, Dr. Levillier recalled, almost with a thrill, Julian's words to him in Harley Street, on the night of the *fracas* with the mastiffs, words spoken about the dead Marr : "His face dead was the most absolutely direct contradiction possible to his face alive. He was not the same man." He recalled these words and the thought shot through his mind, "Did the man this woman loved return at the moment of death ?"

And that change in Valentine !

He said to Mrs. Wilson, betraying none of the excitement that he really felt:

" You spoke of cruelty. You had to endure physical cruelty ? "

" Worse ; to see it endured by others, dumb, helpless creatures, by my own dog."

A great shudder ran through her.

" I can't talk of it," she said. " But it made me what I am. Can you do anything for me ? Why do you look at me like that ?"

For, at her word about the dog, the doctor had fallen into a tense reverie, looking steadily upon her, yet as one who sees little or nothing. He roused himself quickly.

" Tell me something of the symptoms of your mental malady," he said. " These fancies that distress you ; of what nature are they ? "

She told him. Many of them were symptoms well known to all those who have suffered acutely after some great shock, imagined sounds, movements, and so forth. The doctor listened. He had heard such a story many times before.

" I, *I* am full of these ghastly, these degrading fancies," Mrs. Wilson cried, with a sort of large indignation against herself, and yet an uncertain terror. " Is it not——? "

She suddenly stopped speaking.

" There's some one at your door," she said, after a second or two of apparent attention to some sound without.

" I daresay. A patient."

At this moment a voice, which Dr. Levillier immediately recognised as the voice of Valentine, was audible in the hall.

Mrs. Wilson turned suddenly very pale, and began to tremble and gnaw her nether lip with her teeth in an access of nervous disturbance.

" In God's name tell me who that is," she whispered, turning her head in the direction of the door. " It can't be—it can't be——" Valentine's voice rose a little louder. " It *is* his voice."

" Fancy ! " the doctor said firmly. " It is the voice of a friend of mine, Mr. Valentine Cresswell."

Mrs. Wilson said nothing. She was trying to force herself to believe the evidence of another's sense against her own. Such a task is always difficult. At last she looked up and said :

"There, doctor, there you have an exhibition of my illness. It's horrible to me. Can you cure it ? "

" I will try," the doctor answered.

But he found it very difficult just at that moment to say the three words quietly, to let Valentine go after leaving his message, without confronting him with this haggard patient who was entering the pool of Bethesda.

CHAPTER IX

A SHADOW ON FIRE

WHEN a naturally calm, clear and courageous mind finds itself besieged by what seem hysterical fancies it is troubled and perplexed, and is inclined to take drastic measures to restore itself to its normal condition. Dr. Levillier found himself the prey of such fancies after his interview with Mrs. Wilson. He had prescribed for her. He had very carefully considered what way of life would be likely to restore her to health, and to banish the demons which had brought her strength and unusual self-reliance so low. He had received her gratitude, and had dismissed her to the following of his plans for her benefit. All this he had done with calm deliberation, the very cheerful composure which he always practised towards the victims of nervous complaints. But even while he did this his own mind was in a turmoil. For this woman had let fall statements with regard to her dead husband which most curiously bolstered up Cuckoo's fantastic assertion that Valentine and Marr were the same man. Marr had been cruel to animals, to dogs, had evidently taken a keen enjoyment in torturing them, and, on hearing Valentine's voice, she had turned pale and declared that it was the voice of her husband. Then her strange declaration about her husband's use of music as a mode of cruelty! These circumstances appealed powerfully to the doctor's mind, or at least to that unscientific side of it which inclined him to romance, and to a certain sympathy with the mysteries of the world. Many Europeans who go to India return to their own continent imbued with a belief in miracles, modern miracles, which no argument, no sarcasm, can shake. But there are miracles in Europe, too. The magicians of the East work wonders in the strange atmosphere of that strange country whose very air is heavy with magic. Yet England, too, has her magicians. London holds in the arms of its yellow fogs and dust-laden clouds miracles. Dr. Levillier found himself assailed by ideas like these as he thought of that transformed Marr, "possessed," as the pale, strongly-built wreck of a grand, powerful woman had named it, as he thought of the transformed Valentine, the hour of whose transformation coincided with the hour of Marr's death. Why had this new, horrible, yet beautiful creature, risen out of the ashes of the trance that was practically a death ; why had he such amazing points of resemblance to Marr ? Why had the influence of Marr been deliberately intruded into the calm, happy, and safe lives of Julian and Valentine ? Marr was cruel to dogs, and dogs showed rage and terror when the new Valentine approached them. Marr had a hatred, yet a knowledge of music. The new Valentine, when forced to sing, sang like some wild, desolate thing, with reluctant and terrible voice. And at this point the doctor used the curb suddenly and pulled himself up sharply. He felt that it was useless, that it was unworthy to plunge himself thus in romance, and to hang veils of mystery around these facts which he had to accept and to deal with. A touch of humanity is worth all the unhuman romance in the world. Humanity lay at the doctor's gate, sore distressed, sinking to something that was beyond distress. So, putting his fancies resolutely behind him, Dr. Levillier resolved to fight through that frail weapon, the lady of the feathers, the battle of Julian's will against the will—which he now fully and once for all recognised as malign—of the man he must still call Valentine. Valentine had said to Julian, at the Savoy, " If it came to a battle— Cuckoo Bright's will against mine ! " The doctor had not heard those words. Yet, under the stars on the doorstep of Cuckoo's dwelling he, too, had spoken to the girl of a fight. Thus he had poured a great ardour into her heart. The three souls, Cuckoo's, Dr. Levillier's, Valentine's were thus set in battle array. They understood what they faced, or at least that they faced warfare. Only Julian did not understand—yet. He was besotted by the spell of the one he called friend laid upon him, and by the vices in which he had been taught to wallow. His brain was clouded and his eyes were dim, as the brains and eyes of the *malades imaginaires* who carry on the scheme of sin and of sorrow in the world, and prolong by their deeds the long travail of their race. Julian did not understand. For now he seldom thought sincerely. Sincere thoughts and the incessant and violent acts of passion do not often dwell together.

The progress of Julian towards degradation had now become so rapid that his many acquaintances talked of him openly as of one who had practically " gone under." Not that he had ever done any of those few things at which society, whose door is generally ajar, with Mrs. Grundy's large ear glued to the keyhole, resolutely shuts the door. He had not forged, or stolen a watch, or killed anybody, or married a grocer's widow, or anything of that kind. But he had thrown his life to the pleasures of the body, and made no secret of the fact. And the pleasures of the body, like eager rats, had gnawed away his power of self-control until he could resist nothing, no wish of the moment, no desire born illegitimately of passing excitement or the prompting of wine. So he committed many follies, and his follies had loud voices. They shrieked and shouted. And society heard their cries, held the door a little more ajar, and listened with that passion of attention which virtue accords to vice. But society, having heard a good deal, shook its head over Julian. He had acquired such a taste for low company that he ought to have been born a peer. Certainly he had money. That made his errors chink rather pleasantly, and filled the bosoms of many mothers with an expansive charity towards him. Still the general opinion was that he was sinking very low. In fact, the legend of Julian's shame was now written on his face in such legible and vital characters that the most short-sighted eyes could not fail to read it. The eager beauty of untarnished youth had faded into the dull, and often sulky, languors of the utterly indulged body. Julian was often exhausted and passing through those leaden-footed dreams that fitfully entrance the vicious, those dreams that are colourless and sombre, that press upon all the faculties and yet have no real meaning, that stifle all intentions, and put an end, for the moment, to all active desires. People talk of the vicious as " living," but half their time they are curiously dead, for their sins blunt their energies and lull them into a condition that resembles rather paralysis than slumber.

Since the night on which he had supped with Valentine at the Savoy, Julian had given himself up to the company and influence of his friend more than ever, and London, which had once nicknamed Valentine the Saint of Victoria Street, began to dub him with quite another name. For it gradually became apparent to those who only knew the two young men slightly that Valentine exerted an extraordinarily powerful influence over Julian, and that the influence was imperatively evil. At first many were deceived by the clear beauty of Valentine's face, but that was beginning to fade. A thin line, pencilled here and there with a fairylike delicacy, a slight puffiness beneath the blue eyes, a looseness of the cheeks, a droop of the lips, all very demure, as it were, and furtive, shed alteration upon his fair beauty. He himself noticed it, as he looked in a mirror one night, and silently cursed the inevitable effect which mind produces upon matter. No man's face can for ever remain an entirely deceptive mask. The saintly expression of Valentine's was rapidly becoming a thing of the past. He wondered whether Julian noticed it. But Julian was too much preoccupied with his own energies of dreary action and lacerating fatigues of subsequent thought, or it would be truer to say moodiness, to notice anything. He was self-centred, as are all sinners, immersed in his own downfall like a man in an ocean. He was unconscious that he was the subject of battle, that four wills were to contend for his soul's sake. Four wills, yet one expressed itself in no outward form. It was in exile, till the day of its redemption should dawn.

   *   *   *   *   *

On the night when Valentine heard Julian babble incoherently the name of the lady of the feathers he said to himself that the battle should be his, and he leaned upon his will to feel its power and its glory. That night he forgot his fury, the intense emotion that had overtaken him at the supper table as he gauged, or strove to gauge, the influence that Cuckoo was obtaining over Julian. He forgot Dr. Levillier. He remembered only himself and his own strength, which he was now to test to its foundations. And when he woke again to thoughts of others it was only to laugh at the force arrayed against him. The lady of the feathers moved, to his fancy, like the most piteous of puppets, a jeering fate manipulating the strings. This manipulator had kept her long to one set of motions, stiff pleading arm, anxious head, interrogative joints, and a strut of wolfish eagerness and hunger. But such a game was now to be abandoned. And behold the puppet a warrior forsooth, a very Amazon, hounded to fight by the doctor's voice, the doctor's word of encouragement, battling with the stiff arms that had abandoned the pleading gesture, stern in a wooden attitude of defiance. And Fate, in fits of laughter at the string holding! Then Valentine lost his fear, and could have been angry that such a scarecrow was the creature selected by Fate to draw a sword against him. He chose to forget the vision in the mirror when he struck at the staring reflection of the lady of the feathers and shivered under the influence of a cold terror. He chose to remember only the thin and fearful woman who had given her body to the world, and so had surely given her soul to a mill that had long ago ground it to powder.

There is nothing so terrible to one screwed up to the highest pitch of action as a monotony of waiting. Scourging were better, the hemp or the fire. The lady of the feathers had been stirred to a strange enthusiasm, and to a belief in herself, a faith more wonderful to some, more unaccustomed and remote, than any faith in God or devil. A flood of energy flowed over her, warm as blood, strong as love, keen with the salt of beautiful novelty, turbulent as the seas when the great tides take hold on them. It was to her as if for the moment the world's centre was just there, where she was, in the winter and in the Marylebone Road, within sound of the great church clock, the great church bells, the cries of the street, the very steam panting up from the Baker Street Station. Cuckoo was in the core of things, and the core of things is fierce and hot and action prompting. That half revealed shadow waving good-bye to

Julian as he stepped into the frosty night was a shadow on fire.
Yet he had scarcely looked back at it. But Cuckoo was to learn to
the last word the lesson of patience. Inspired by the sympathy of
the doctor and by something deep in her own heart, she was, for the
moment, all courage, all flame. She was ready to fight. She was
ready to do supreme things, to touch the stars. The stars went out
and she had not touched them. The morning dawned very chilly,
very dark, the morning that brought Mrs. Brigg to her room yellow
and complaining. Still Cuckoo was conscious of a high beating
courage that made summer in that winter day. She astonished the
old keeper of that weary house by the vivacity of her manner, the
brightness of her look. For Mrs. Brigg was well accustomed to sad
morning moods, to petulant lassitude, and dull grimness of unpainted
and unpowdered fatigue, but had long been a stranger to early
moods of hope or of gaiety. Mornings, in houses such as hers, are
recurring tragedies, desolating pulses of Time, shaking human hearts
with each beat nearer and nearer to the ultimatum of sorrow. She
knew not what to make of this new morning mood of Cuckoo, and
wagged a heavily pensive head over it, unresponsive and muttering.
Jessie, too, was astonished but more pleasantly. The little dog,
dwelling ignorantly in the midst of degradation, had learned
quickly the swing of its beloved mistress's moods. In the dim
morning it was ever the comforter of misery it could not rightly
understand, not the playfellow of happiness that stirred it to
leaps and barks of wonder and excitement. In the mornings
Cuckoo held it long against her thin bosom, sometimes crushed
it nearly breathless, pushing its little head down in the nest
of her arms and telling it a tale of the world's woe, that sent
long and thin whimpers twittering through its body. The fluttering whisper of morning misery, or the silence of vacant
fatigue, these were accustomed things to Jessie. Even if she did
not thoroughly understand them she was ready for them, and eagerly
responsive as dogs are to emotions along whose verges they tread
with the soft feet of sympathy, the sweeter for the ignorance that
paints their generosity in such tender colours. But Jessie was
bouleversée by this passionate, eager Cuckoo, this shadow on fire, who
was alive almost ere London was alive, instead of half dead until
half London slept. The shadow on fire snatched her out of her
sleep, tossed her in air, spoke to her with a voice that thrilled her
to quick barking excitement, played with her till the little dog's
flux of emotions threatened to consummate in a canine apoplexy and
Mrs. Brigg battered at the door with a shrill, "Keep that beast
quiet, can't yer?" All this was Cuckoo fighting; battle in the bed-
clothes, battle with soap and water, curling-pins, corset, shoes.
Each little act was performed with an energy it did not demand.

The sponge was squeezed dry like a live thing being strangled; the tooth-brush played as Maxim guns on an enemy; buttons went into button-holes with a manner of ramrods going into muskets; hooks met eyes as one army meets another. Battle in all that morning's common tasks, setting them high, dressing them with chivalry and strong endeavour. Cuckoo went into her sitting-room swiftly, with glowing cheeks and flaming eyes, as one ardently expectant. And then——? Mrs. Brigg had lit the fire, but it had spluttered out into a mass of blackened, ghostly paper and skeleton sticks. A little more battle in the relighting of it. But then—the blank day of the girl of the streets. Cuckoo sat down, watched the growing fire, and wondered what she had expected. She was conscious that she had expected something, and something not small. Her mood had demanded it. But our moods are often like disappointed brigands who, having waylaid a pauper, demand with levelled pistols that which the pauper has so vainly prayed for all his life. Moods come from within. They are not evoked to dance valses with suitable partners from without. And so Cuckoo's strong excitement and energy found nothing to dance with. She sat there growing gradually less alive, and wondering why she had hastened to get up, why she was fully dressed, instead of wrapped in the usual staring pink dressing-gown with the chiffon cascades down the front. Mornings were of no use to her, never had been. God might as well never have included them in the scheme of His days, so far as she was concerned. But this morning she had thought, had felt—it seemed impossible that she should feel so unusual and that nothing should happen. She was ready, but Fate was in bed and asleep. That was really the gist of the feeling that came over her. She thought of Dr. Levillier, the man who had set a torch at last to her nature and fired it with new ardour. He was at his work in the morning, seeing, speaking to, that passing line of strangers who walked on for ever through his life. His energies were employed. Perhaps he had forgotten Cuckoo and her empty mornings. Almost for the first time in her life the lady of the feathers definitely longed for a legitimate occupation. How she could have flown at it to-day. But already the bright mood was fading. It could not last in such an atmosphere. As Cuckoo had said, she could fight better than she could pray. But it seemed to her, after a while, that there was only room in this cheerless, dark house to pray, no room at all to fight. She tried reading yesterday's evening paper left on the horsehair sofa by Julian. But reading had never been a favourite occupation of hers, and to-day she wanted to save Julian, to make him love her and so to win him from Valentine. She did not want to sit in the twilight of a winter's day reading about people she had never seen, things she did not understand. And she threw the paper down.

. To make Julian love her. Cuckoo flushed, yes, even sitting there quite alone, for Jessie had retired to the warmth of the bedroom blankets, as she said it in her mind. The doctor had told her to do it. Her heart had told her to try to do it long ago. But she trusted the doctor and she did not trust her heart. And how could she trust her power to make Julian love her? Cuckoo had once known very well how to make a man desire her. In the very early days of her career she had been a very pretty girl. Her old mother, who believed her dead, had often cried and said to the neighbours that her beauty had been Cuckoo's undoing. Thus do we lay blame on the few fine gifts that should gild our lives. But Cuckoo had been very pretty and had soon learnt the first foul lesson of her *métier*, to wake swift desire. As time went on and she wasted her gift of beauty along the pavements of London, she found this poor power failing in strength and in certainty. As to the power of wakening that slower, deeper, kindred, yet opposed desire of love, Cuckoo had never known whether she possessed it. She had had many lovers but nobody to love her really, and this in days of her beauty, or at any rate her gracious prettiness. No wonder then that now a chill ran over her at the thought of the task that lay before her if she was to gain her battle. To break Valentine's influence she had to make Julian love her. How? Instinctively, and with a sense of horror, she knew that her usual practised arts, instead of helping almost fatally handicapped her now. She loved Julian purely, so purely that she could not endure that he should meet her degradation as he had met it on that one night she never thought of but with repentance. Yet to her ignorance, to her, rising towards purity now, yet ever steeped in the coarsest knowledge, it seemed that the thing called love could hardly utter itself save by some threadbare blandishment, or parrot combination of words, used each night by a hundred women of the town. Cuckoo knew no language of love that was not, so to say, bad language, inasmuch as it was used by those whom she hated. And hitherto she had been content to keep her love for Julian a silent love, except on the few occasions when she had obliquely shown it by the anger of jealousy or of reproach. She wished nothing bodily from him, or, if she did, stifled the wish in the mutely repeated record of her own unworthiness. But now, if she was to draw his soul to hers, she must move forward, she must surely commit some sacrifice, perform some deed. What deed could she perform? What sacrifice could she make that would win upon him, that would alter his relation towards her from one of eccentric friendship to one of affection that might even be governed?

The lady of the feathers did not reason this all out in her mind as she sat before the spluttering fire, but she felt it, a tangled mass of thoughts, catching her brain as in a net, catching her life as in a net, too. How could she make Julian love her? What could she do? And all the time, as she asked herself passionately that question, the hours were gliding by towards the evening refrain of her life. Cuckoo began to consider this evening refrain as she had never considered it before, as it might affect another if he loved her. If she made Julian love her, if she succeeded in this attempt that seemed as if it must be impossible, what of her evening refrain then? And what would be the conclusion of such a love? She could not tell, she could only wonder. The strange thing about the lady of the feathers, and about many of her kind, was that she never dreamed of such a thing as owing a duty to herself, to her own body, her own soul or nature. Cuckoo knew not the meaning of self-respect. Had you told her that her body was a temple—not of the Holy Ghost, but of a wonderful, exquisite thing called womanhood, and for that reason should not be defiled, she would have stared at you under drawn eye-brows, like a fierce boy, and wondered what in heaven or earth you were talking jargon about. To get at her sympathy you must talk to her of duty to another; and if she had a soft feeling for that other, then she understood you, and then alone. It was the cause of Julian and his safety that made her now consider this evening refrain of her life as she sat there. And her mind ran back to Julian's first visit to her and to his first request. He asked her to stay at home just for one night with Jessie. And she refused. If she had not refused. If she had stayed at home. If she had at that moment, from that moment, given up her life of the street, would Julian have loved her then? Would she have been able to do something for him? For hours Cuckoo sat there pondering in her vague, desolate way over questions such as these. But she could give no answer to them. And then she thought of that horrible night when the hours danced to the music of the devil, when she gave Julian that first little impetus which started him on his journey to the abyss. And at that thought she grew white, and she grew hot, and she wondered why she had been born to be the lady of the feathers and the wrecker, not of men's lives—she never thought of men tenderly in the mass—but of this one life, of this one man, whom she loved in a strange, wild, good-woman way.

"C-r-r-r!" she said, her tongue flickering against her teeth. Jessie stirred in the blankets, came to the floor with a "t'bb" and ran into the room with curved attitudes of submission. But Cuckoo would not notice the little dog. She stared at the fire and looked so old, and almost intellectual. But there was nobody to see her. What a long, empty day it had been, this day for which she had risen eagerly as to a day of battle! What a long, empty day and no deed done in it. And now the hour of the evening refrain was come. Cuckoo had wanted this day to be a special day, for it was the first of those new days which were to come after the doctor's word of hope. And nothing had happened in it. Nobody had come. The doctor was with his patients. Julian was—ah surely—with Valentine. And she, Cuckoo, this poor, pale girl, who wanted to fight and to do battle, was alone. And she had been so eager in the morning. And now the night was falling and she had not struck a blow. The hour chimed. It was the hour of the evening refrain.

Suddenly Cuckoo got up. She went over to the window and pulled down the blind so sharply that she nearly broke it. She struck a match violently, and lit the gas. She ran into the bedroom, caught her hat, which lay ready for service on the top of the chest of drawers, and cast it with a crash into a cardboard box, jamming the lid down on it. She seized her jacket, which lay on the bed, and strung it up on a hook, as if she were hanging a criminal. Then she came back into the sitting-room, sat down in the chair, took up the evening paper of yesterday, and began to read, with eyes that gleamed under frowning brows, about "Foreign Affairs" and "Bimetallism."

And that night the evening refrain of Cuckoo's life did not follow the verse of her day.

She sat there all alone.

It was her way—the only way she could devise—of beginning to fight the battle for Julian.

She did not stay at home with any thought of purifying herself by the action. Another day she might go out as usual. But Julian had once asked her not to go. She had gone then. Now she obeyed him, and the obedience seemed to bring him a little nearer to her.

CHAPTER X

THE DOCTOR DRIVES OUT WITH THE LADY
OF THE FEATHERS

Some days later Cuckoo received a telegram from Harley Street. It came in the morning, and ran as follows :

"Call here to-day if possible. Important. Levillier." Cuckoo read it, trembling. In her early days telegrams came often to her door—" Meet me at Verrey's, four-thirty"; " Piccadilly Circus, five o'clock to-day." Such messages flickered through her youth, forming gradually a legend of her life. But this summons from the doctor at the same time frightened her and braced her heart. It might mean that Julian was ill, in danger—she knew not what. But, at least, it broke through the appalling inaction, the dreary stagnation, of her days. The lady of the feathers had fought, indeed, of late that worst enemy, mental despair, bred of grim patience at last grown weary. That was not the battle she had been inspired to expect, to prepare for. The doctor's telegram at least swept the unforeseen foe from the field, and seemed to set the real enemy full in view.

"There arn't any answer," the lady of the feathers said to Mrs. Brigg, who waited in an attitude expressive of greedy curiosity.

"Which of 'em is it ? " demanded that functionary.

"Shan't tell you," Cuckoo hissed at her.

The filthy groove in which the landlady's mind for ever ran began to rouse her to an intense animosity.

"Well, it's all one to me so long as I'm paid regular," muttered Mrs. Brigg, with a swing of her dusty skirts and a toss of her grey head, governed by pomade, since it was a Saturday. Mrs. Brigg must once have held Christian principles, as she always prepared the ground for certain Sabbath curls the day before.

Cuckoo ran to dress herself. It was seldom indeed that she stirred out in the morning, so seldom that that alone was an experience. Arrived in the bedroom, she pounced mechanically on rouge and powder, and was about to decorate herself when she suddenly paused with outstretched hands. She was going out into the bright wintry sunlight, and she was going to the doctor's house, full, perhaps, of those smart patients of whom Valentine had once spoken to her. What sort of an apparition would she be among them? She dropped her hands hesitating. Then she turned to a cupboard, drew out the one famous black gown and put it on. She crowned her head with Julian's hat, hid her hands in black silk gloves, pulled down her veil and seized an umbrella. Somehow Cuckoo vaguely connected respectability with umbrellas, although even the most vicious are fain to carry them in showery London. Then she looked at herself in the glass and wondered if her appearance were deceptive enough to trick the sharp eyes of the patients. The glance reassured her. She seemed to herself an epitome of black propriety, and she set forth with a more easy heart. As she walked her mind ran on before, seeking what this summons meant and debating possibilities without arriving at conclusions. At the end of Harley Street her walk, which had been rapid, achieved a *ritardando* and nearly came to a full close before she gained the doctor's door. Cuckoo could be a brazen hussy. A year ago she could scarcely be anything else. But that love of hers for Julian had, it seemed, a strange power of undermining old habits. It laid hands upon so many perceptions, so many emotions with which it should surely have had nothing to do, and made subtle inroads upon every dark corner of the girl's nature. From it came this *ritardando*. For Cuckoo was filled with a very human dread of exposing Dr. Levillier to misconception by her appearance in the midst of his patients. Had it been late afternoon instead of morning her fortitude would certainly have been greater, and might even have drawn near to impudence. But the clear light of approaching noontide set her mind blinking with rapid eyelids, and when she actually gained the street door her discomfort was acute.

As she put up her hand to touch the bell the door opened softly and a stout Duchess issued forth. Cuckoo didn't know she was a Duchess, but she quailed before the plethoric glance cast upon her, and her voice was uneven as she asked for the doctor.

" Have you an appointment, ma'am ? " asked Lawler, who did not recognise her behind her black veil.

" I was asked to come," Cuckoo murmured.

" What name, ma'am ? "

" Cuck—Miss Bright."

She was admitted. The doctor, in the hurry of business, had omitted to give Lawler any instructions in the event of Cuckoo's prompt response to his telegram. So she was shown into the waiting-room, in which three or four people were turning over illustrated papers with an air of watchful idleness and attentive leisure. Cuckoo sat down in a corner as quietly as possible, and Lawler vanished.

The leaves of the illustrated papers rustled in the air with a dry sound. To Cuckoo they seemed to be crackling personal remarks about her, and to be impregnated with condemnation. She cast a furtive glance upon the square room and perceived that they were turned by four ladies, and that three of these ladies were looking straight at her. The eight eyes met in a glance of inquiry and were instantly cast down. Again the leaves of the illustrateds rustled, this time, Cuckoo felt convinced, more fiercely than before. The *frou-frou* of the skirts of one of the ladies joined in the chorus, which was far from crying "Hallelujah!" Cuckoo began to feel a growing certainty that, despite the black veil and the neat umbrella, feminine instinct had divined her. She was totally unaccustomed to such an atmosphere as that which prevailed in this room, and began to be the victim of an odd, prickly sensation, which she believed to be physical, but which was certainly more than half moral. A wave of heat ran over her body. It was like the heat which follows on a received slap. One of the illustrateds deleted its voice from the general chorus. Cuckoo was aware of this, and looked up again to find two eyes fixed upon her with an expression of thin distaste that was incapable of misinterpretation. A second illustrated ceased to sing, two heads were inclined towards one another, and the " t'p, t'p, t'p " of a low whisper set the remaining two ladies at their posts as sentinels on the lady of the feathers.

Cuckoo put her hand to her face to pull her veil a little lower down. By accident she tugged too hard, or it had been badly fastened to her hat, for one side got loose instantly and fell down, revealing her face frankly.

The " t'p, t'p, t'p " sounded again, multiplied by two. Cuckoo, thrown into confusion by the malign behaviour of her veil, caught awkwardly at the dropped end with an intention of readjusting it, but something in the sound of the whispering suddenly moved her to a different action. She snatched the veil quite off, set her feet firmly against the thick Turkey carpet, raised her eyes and stared with all her might at the four ladies, hurling, as a man hurls a bomb, an expression of savage defiance into her gaze. The whispers stopped ; a thin and repeated cough, dry as Sahara, attacked the silence, and eight eyes were vehemently cast down. Cuckoo continued staring, folding her hands in her lap. The prickly sensation increased, but she considered it now as a thing to be jumped on. Recognising that she was recognised, she was instantly moved to play up to her part, and she longed to stare the four women out into Harley Street. If the energy of a gaze could have achieved that object they must have backed through the doctor's plate glass into the area forthwith. They were in fact most obviously moved, and their attitudes expressed, by a community of lines, virtue rampant and agitation gules. A shattering silence endured till Lawler appeared to bid two of these virgins with lit lamps of self-righteousness to the consulting-room. As they rose the two other ladies rose also and followed in their wake. Lawler politely protested, but they were now to proclaim their beauty of character.

"We should prefer to wait in another room," said the lady who had coughed as a communication with heaven.

"Yes, another room," added the other, and, as she spoke, she half turned, indicating the corner where Cuckoo sat.

Without a word Lawler showed them out and closed the door. For another twenty minutes Cuckoo sat alone, glaring at the table by which these members of her sex had sat, and seeing no material objects but only—as is the way of humanity—her own point of view; the ladies saw only theirs. In this respect at least they closely resembled the lady of the feathers. When Lawler at length returned with his grave, "This way if you please, ma'am," Cuckoo rose to her feet with the inflexibility of some iron thing set in motion by mechanism, and marched in his wake to the doctor's presence.

The doctor was standing up by a bright fire; he looked very grave.

"I am very sorry to have kept you," he said, "very sorry. I did not think you could get here so quickly."

Cuckoo cleared her throat.

"I wish I hadn't," she answered bluntly.

"Why ?"

"It don't matter. I started directly your wire came."

"That was good of you. Please sit down."

Cuckoo sat, with a straight back in the straightest chair she could perceive. The doctor still remained standing by the fire. He appeared to be thinking deeply. His eyes looked downward at his gaily shining boots. After a minute or two he said :

"I speak to you now in strict confidence, trusting your secrecy implicitly."

The back of Cuckoo became less straight. Even a gentle curve made it more gracious if less admirable from the dancing mistress point of view.

"Honour !" she interjected rapidly, like a schoolboy.

The doctor looked up at her and a smile came to his lips. And as he looked up he noticed the neatness of her black gown, the simplicity of her hat, the absence of paint and powder. Being after all only a man, he was surprised at Cuckoo's appearance of propriety. The four ladies had been surprised at her appearance of impropriety. But the doctor seeing her so much better than usual, thought her—in looks—quite well, as indeed she was in comparison with the *tout ensemble* of her usual days. He looked from her black gloves, which held the thick black veil, to the winter sunshine sparkling, like a dancing eager child, at the window.

" Do you like driving ? " he said.

" What ? "

" Driving—do you like it ? "

" Pretty well, if the horse don't come down," said Cuckoo, at once concentrated on cabs.

" My horses won't."

" Yours ! "

" Yes. I have no more patients to-day. I have a half-holiday and I want to talk to you. Shall we go for a drive to Hampstead and talk out in the open air and the sunshine ? "

The four ladies, the illustrateds, the cough, dry as Sahara, were instantly forgotten. Cuckoo became all curves, almost like Jessie in moments of supreme emotion.

" Me and you ? " she exclaimed. " Oh I yes."

The doctor rang the bell.

" Take this lady to the dining-room and give her some lunch," he said to Lawler. " And please order the victoria round at once."

" Yes, sir."

" While you lunch," he said to Cuckoo, " Ill just get through two letters that must be written, and then we'll start."

Cuckoo followed Lawler with a sense of airy wonder and delight.

A quarter of an hour later she was seated with the doctor in the victoria, the veil tightly stretched across her face, her poor mode of living up to his trust in her, and deserving the honour now conferred upon her. The coachman let his horses go, and Harley Street was left behind. Such a bright day it was. Even the cold seemed a gay and festive thing, spinning the circulation like a gold coin till it glittered, decorating the poorest cheeks with the brightest rose as if in honour of a festival. To Cuckoo London, as seen from a private carriage, was a wonder and a dream of novelty, a city of kings instead of a city of beggars, a city of crystal morning instead of a city of dreadful night. She gazed at it out of a new heart as these horses—that never came down—trotted briskly forward. Through the silk of her gloves her thumbs and fingers felt silently the warm sables of the rug that caressed her knees. And she thought that this feeling, and the feeling in her heart, must be constituent parts of the emotion called happiness. If the four ladies could see her now I If they could see her now Cuckoo thought she would take off her veil, just for a moment. When the aspect of the street began to change, when little gardens appeared, and bare trees standing bravely in the sun behind high walls and iron gates, the doctor said to Cuckoo:

" Now I will tell you why I telegraphed to you "

And then Cuckoo remembered that she was in this wonderful expedition for a reason. The doctor continued speaking in a low voice, with the obvious intention of being inaudible to the coachman, whose large furred back presented an appearance of broad indifference to their two lives.

"You remember what I said to you the other day—that perhaps you could help Julian from great evil."

Cuckoo nodded earnestly.

"And you are prepared to do anything you can ? "

" Yes."

She had forgotten the smart carriage and the horses that never came down now.

"Good," said the doctor, shortly and decisively. "I will speak to you quite plainly to-day, for something leads me to trust you, and to say to you what I would say to no other person. Something leads me to believe that you can do more for Addison than any one else. Addison once implied it; but what I have observed for myself in your house leads me to be certain of it."

"Oh," said Cuckoo.

She had nothing more to say. She could have said nothing more. The stress of her excitement was too great.

" Look at that holly tree. What a quantity of berries it has ! " the doctor said. "That's because it is a hard winter. Miss Bright, you are right in your conviction. Valentine Cresswell is—has been—totally evil, and is deliberately, coldly, but with determination, compassing the utter ruin of the man who trusts him and believes in him—of Addison."

Cuckoo nodded again, this time with a strangely matter of course air, which assured the doctor in a flash of the long certainty of her knowledge of Valentine.

"Such a thing seemed to me entirely incredible," the doctor pursued. "I am forced—forced—to believe it is true. But remember this. I have known Mr. Cresswell for several years intimately. I have been again and again with him and Julian. I have noticed the extraordinary influence he had over Julian, and I know that influence used to be a noble influence used solely for good. Mr. Cresswell was a man of extraordinary high-mindedness and purity of life. He had a brilliant intellect," the doctor continued, forgetting to whom he was talking, as his mind went back to the Valentine of the old days. " But far more than that. He was born with a very wonderful and unusual nature. It was written in his face in the grandeur—I can call it nothing else—of his expression. And it was written in his life, in all his acts. But most of all it was written in all he did for Julian. Ah ! you look surprised ! "

Indeed Cuckoo's face, such of it as was visible under the black shadow of the veil, was a mask of blank wonderment. She looked upon the doctor as all that was clever and perfect and extraordinary, so this, as it seemed to her, idiocy of his outlook upon Valentine was too much for her manners.

"Well I never! Him!" she could not help ejaculating with a long breath, that was almost like a little puff.

"Remember," said Dr. Levillier, "this was before you knew him."

He had taken the trouble to ascertain from Julian the exact date of Valentine's first introduction to the lady of the feathers.

"Oh yes," said Cuckoo, still with absolute incredulity of the truth of the doctor's panegyric expressive in voice and look.

"Men change greatly, terribly."

"Oh, not like that," she jerked out suddenly, moved by an irresistible impulse to contradict his apparent deduction.

"No, there you are right," he answered with emphasis. "Sane men do not, can never, I believe, change so utterly."

"That's what I say. I've seen men go down, lots of 'em, but it ain't like that."

Cuckoo spoke with some authority, as of one speaking from depths of profound experience. She put her hands under the warm rug with a sensation of something that was like dignity of mind. She and the doctor were talking on equal terms of intellectuality just at this moment. She was saying sensible things and he was obliged to agree with her.

"Not like that," she murmured again out of the embrace of the rug.

He turned towards her so that he could see her more distinctly and make his words more impressive.

"Remember now that what I am going to say to you must not be mentioned to Julian on any account, or to any one," he said.

"I'll remember. Honour. I'll never tell."

"I have a very sad theory to explain this great change in Mr. Cresswell, from what he was as I knew him, and you must take his beauty of character from me—to what he is as you and I know him now. I believe that he has become mad." For the doctor had resolutely put away from his mind the fancies called up in it by the visit of Marr's wife.

Cuckoo gave a little cry of surprise, then hastily glanced at the coachman's back and pushed her hands under the rug, up towards her mouth.

"Hush," said the doctor. "Only listen quietly."

"Yes, pardon," she said. "But he ain't—oh he can't be."

"I am forced to think it, forced to think it," the doctor said, with pressure. "He has, in great measure, one of the most common, most universal, of the fatuous beliefs of the insane, a deep-rooted, an almost incredible belief in himself, in his own glory, power, will, personality."

Cuckoo tried to throw in some remark here but he went on without a pause :

"There are madmen confined in asylums all over England who think themselves the Messiah—this is the commonest form of religious mania—emperors, kings, regenerators of the human race, doers of great deeds that must bring them everlasting fame. On all other points they are sane, and you might spend hours alone with them and never discover the one crank in their mind that makes the whole mind out of joint. So you have been alone with Mr. Cresswell and have not suspected him. Yet he has a madness, and it is this madness which leads him to this frightful conduct of his towards Julian, conduct which you will never know the extent of."

Here Cuckoo succeeded in getting in a remark.

"Will," she said, catching hold of that one word and beginning to look eager. "That's what he was at all the time he was talkin' to me that night. Will, he says, is this and that and the other; will, he says, is everythin', I remember. Will, he says, is my God, or somethin' like it. He did. He did."

"Ah! you see even you have noticed it."

"Yes ; but he ain't mad though," Cuckoo concluded, with an echo of that obstinacy which she could never completely conquer. She said what she felt. She could not help it. The doctor was in nowise offended by this unskilled opinion opposed to his skilled one. He even smiled slightly.

"Why do you say that ? " he asked.

"He's too sharp. He's a sight too sharp."

"Madmen are very cunning."

"So are women," Cuckoo exclaimed. "I could see if a man was mad."

She was a little intoxicated with the swift motion, the bright sun, the keen air, the clang of the horses' hoofs on the hard roads, and, most of all, with this conference which the befurred coachman was on no account to hear. This made her hold fast to her opinion, with no thought of being rude or presuming. The doctor, accustomed to have duchesses and others hanging upon his words of wisdom, was whipped into a refreshed humour by this odd attitude of an ignorant girl, and he replied with extreme vivacity:

"You will think as I do one day. Meanwhile listen to me. When Mr. Cresswell came to you and broke out into this tirade, which you say you remember, on the subject of will, did he not show any excitement ? "

"Eh ? "

" Did he get excited, very hot and eager ?   Did he speak unusually loud, or make any curious gestures with his hands ? Did he do anything that you can remember, such as an ordinay man would not do ? "

" Why, yes," Cuckoo answered.   " So he did."

" Ah !   What was it ?   What did he do ? "

" Well, after he'd been talkin' a bit he caught hold of me and pulled me in front of the glass. See ? "

" Yes, yes."

" And he made me look into it."

" What for ? "

But at this point Cuckoo got restive.

" I—I can't remember," she murmured, almost sullenly, recalling Valentine's bitter sarcasms on her appearance and way of life.

" Never mind then.   Leave that.   But after ; what came next ? "

" While we was standing like that he seemed to get frightened or somethin', like he saw somethin' in the glass.   He was frightened, scared ; and he hit out all on a sudden, just where my face was in the glass, and smashed it."

" Smashed the glass ? "

" Yes.   And then he snatched hold of me and looked in my eyes awful queer, and then he burst out laughin' and says as the mirror was tellin' him lies.   That's all."

" He was perfectly sober ? "

" Oh, he hadn't been on the booze."

" Sober and did that, and then you can tell me that there is no madness in him."

The doctor spoke almost in a bantering tone, but Cuckoo stuck to her guns.

" I don't think it," she said, with her under lip sticking out.

" Well, Miss Bright, I want you to assume something."

" What's that ? "

" To pretend to yourself that you think something, whether you do really think it or not."

" Make believe ! " cried Cuckoo, childishly.

" Exactly."

" What about ? "

" I want you to ' make believe ' that Mr. Cresswell is not himself, is not sane."

" O-oh-h ! " said Cuckoo, with a long intonation of surprise.

" I do honestly believe it, you are to pretend to believe it.   Now remember that."

" All right."

" You are not to contradict any more, you see,"

" Oh," began Cuckoo, in sudden distress, " Pardon. I didn't——"

" Hush ! That's all right. Act with me on the make-believe or assumption that Mr. Cresswell is not himself at present."

" Ah, but that ain't no make-believe. He told me as he wasn't himself when he says—' I am Marr.' "

" Yes—yes," said the doctor. Secretly, almost angrily, he said to himself that Valentine, in some access of insanity, had actually confessed to the lady of the feathers that he knew himself to be mad.

" He says he ain't himself," she repeated again, with an eager feeling that perhaps, at last, she had got at the right interpretation of the gospel of Valentine.

" That is practically the same thing as his saying to you that he was mad. Now you have told me what you feel for Julian."

Cuckoo flushed, and muttered something unintelligible, twining her hands in the sables till she nearly pulled them from Dr. Levillier's knees.

" And you have seen the terrible change that has come over him, and that is fast, fast deepening to something that must end in utter ruin. You have not seen him these last few days I think—— ? "

" No," said Cuckoo, her eyes fixed hungrily on the doctor's face. She began to tug at her veil. " What's it ? Is he—is he ? "

She collapsed into a nervous silence, still tugging with a futile hand at the veil which remained implacably stretched across her face. The doctor looked at her, and said steadily :

" He has gone a little further—down. You understand me ? "

" I ought to," she said, bitterly.

" As you are mounting upward," the doctor rejoined, with a kind and firm gravity that seemed indeed to lift Cuckoo, as a sweet wind lifts a feather and sends it on high.

The bitterness went out of her face but she said nothing, only sat listening attentively while the doctor went on :

" My belief is this, and, if you hold it, you can perhaps act in this matter with more boldness, more fearlessness, than if you do not hold it. I believe that Mr. Cresswell, who played very foolish tricks with his nerves some time ago, just before he got to know you, has become mad to this extent that he believes himself to have a power of will unlike that possessed by any other man, an inhuman power, in fact. He fancies that he has the will of a sort of God, and he wishes to prove this to himself more especially. Everything is for self in a madman. Now he looks about for a means of proving that his will can do everything. He wants to make it do something extraordinary, uncommon. What does he find for it to do ? This, the ruin of Julian. And now I'll tell you why this ruin of Julian would be a peculiar triumph for his will. Originally, when Cresswell was sane and splendid, his splendour of sanity guarded Julian from all that was dangerous. Julian was naturally inclined to be wild. He has an ardent nature, and five years ago, when he was a mere boy, might have fallen into a thousand follies. Cresswell's influence first kept him from these follies, and at last taught him to loathe and despise them. And Julian, remember this, told Cresswell at last that he had been to him a sort of saviour. You can follow me ? "

" ' m," Cuckoo ejaculated with shut mouth and a nod of her head.

" So that Cresswell knew what his will had been able to do in the direction of lifting Julian high up, almost above his nature. Well, then followed certain foolish practices which I need not describe. Cresswell and Julian joined in a certain trickery, often practised by people who call themselves spiritualists and occultists. It decidedly had an effect upon them at the time, and I advised them earnestly to drop it. They disregarded my advice, and the result was that Mr. Cresswell fell into an extraordinary condition of body. He fell into a trance, became as if he were dead, and remained so for some hours on a certain night. I was called in to him, and actually thought that he was dead. But he revived. Now I believe that though he seemed to recover, and did recover in body, he never recovered from that insensibility in mind. I believe he went into that sleep sane and came out of it mad, and that he remains mad to this moment. Certainly ever since then he has been an altered man, the man you know, not at all the man he used to be. Since that night he, who used to be almost unconscious of the wonder of his own will, has become intensely self-conscious, and engrossed with it, and has wished to make it obey him and perform miracles. And what is the special miracle to which he is devoting himself at this moment, as you have observed ? Just this, the ruin of the thing he originally saved. It is like this," he said, noting that Cuckoo was becoming puzzled and confused, " Cresswell, by his influence, made Julian loathe sin. Coming out of this trance, as I believe a madman, he seeks to make his will do something extraordinary. What shall he make it do ? His eyes fall on Julian, who is always with him, as you know. And he resolves to make Julian love what he has taught him to loathe—sin, vice, degradation of every kind. So he sets to work with all the cunning of a diseased mind, and hour by hour, day by day, he works for this horrible end. At first he is quiet and careful. But at last he becomes almost intoxicated as he sees his own success. And he allows himself to be led into outbreaks of triumph. One of those outbreaks you yourself seem to have witnessed. I have witnessed another—on the night I dined alone with Cresswell, when he killed the dog, Rip, and threw him out into the snow. Cresswell is intoxicated with the mental intoxication of mania, at the degradation into which his will has forced Julian, who had learnt to love him, to think that everything he did must be right. And his intoxication is leading him to excesses. It is my firm belief that he intends to drag Julian down into intolerable abysses of sin, to plunge him into utter ruin, to bring him perhaps to prison, and to death."

Cuckoo was listening now with a white face—even her lips looked almost grey. The sunshine still lay over the winter world. The horses trotted. The sables were warm about her. They had nearly left the city behind them and were gaining the heights, on which the air was keener and more life-giving, and from which the outlook was larger and more inspiring. But the girl's gaiety and almost wild sense of vivacity and protectedness had vanished. For the doctor's face and voice had become grave, and his words were weighty with a conviction, which, added to her own knowledge of Julian and Valentine, made her fears unutterable. As the doctor paused she opened her lips as if to speak, but she said nothing. He could not but perceive the cloud that had settled on her, and his manner quickly changed. A brightness, a hopefulness, illumined his face, and he said quickly :

"This tragedy is what you and I, but you especially, must prevent."

Then Cuckoo spoke at last :

" How ever ? " she said.

" Remember this," he answered. " If Cresswell is mad we must pity him, not condemn him. But we must above all fight him. Could I prove his madness the danger would be averted. Possibly time will give me the means of proving it. I have watched him. I shall continue to watch him. But as yet, although I see enough to convince me of his insanity, I don't see enough to convince the world, or, above all, to convince Julian. Therefore never give Julian the slightest hint of what I have told you of to-day. His adoration of Valentine is such that even a hint might easily lead him to regard both you and me as his enemies. Keep your own counsel and mine, but act with me on the silent assumption that Cresswell, being a madman, we are justified in fighting him to the bitter end, you and I, with all our forces."

" I see," Cuckoo said, a burning excitement beginning to wake in her.

" Justified in fighting him, but not in hating him."

" Oh," she said, with a much more doubtful accent.

" Scarcely any human being, if indeed any, is completely hateful. How then can a human being, whose mind is ill and out of control, be hateful ? " said the doctor, gently.

She felt herself rebuked, and a quick thought of herself, of what she was, rebuked her too.

" I'll try not," she murmured, but with no inward conviction of success.

They were on the heath now, and the smoke of London hung in the wintry air beyond and below them. The sun was already beginning to wear the aspect of a traveller on the point of departure for a journey. His once golden face was sinister with that blood-red hue which it so often assumes on winter afternoons, and which seems to set it in a place more than usually remote, more than usually distant from our world, and in a clime that is sad and strange. Winds danced over the heath like young witches. The horses, whipped by the more intense cold, pulled hard against the bit, and made the coachman's arms ache. The doctor looked away for a moment at the vapours that began to clothe the afternoon in the hollows and depressions of the landscape, and at the sun, whose gathering change of aspect smote on his imagination as something akin to the change that falls over the faces of men, towards that hour when the sun of their glory makes ready for its setting. Still keeping his glance on that sad red sun in its net of radiating vapours, he said, in a withdrawn voice :

" We must hate nothing except the hatefulness of sin, in ourselves and in others."

Cuckoo listened as to the voice of some one on a throne, and tears that she could not fully understand rose in her eyes.

But now the doctor turned from the sun to the lady of the feathers, and there was a bright light in his quiet eyes.

" You and I must fight with all our forces," he said. " Have you ever thought about this thing, will, which Cresswell worships insanely ? Have you ever felt it in you, Miss Bright ? "

" I don't know as I have," Cuckoo said, secretly wondering if it were that strange and fleeting power which had come to her of late, which had made her for a moment fearless of Valentine as she defied him in the loneliness of her room, which had stirred her even to a faith in herself when she spoke with the doctor under the stars upon her doorstep.

" I think you have. I think you will. It must be there, for Julian feels it in you. He—he calls it a flame."

" Eh ? A flame ? "

" Yes. He sees it in your eyes, and it holds him near you."

So the doctor spoke, partly out of his conviction, partly because he had definitely resolved to put away from him all the things that fought against his reason and that his imagination perhaps loved too much. Such things, he thought, floated like clouds across the clearness of his vision, and drowned the light of his power to do good. So his fancies that had fastened on the mystery of the dead Marr and the living Valentine, connecting them together, and weaving a veil of magic about their strange connection, were banished. He would not hold more commerce with them, nor would he accept the fancies of others as realities. Thus, in his mind, Julian's legend of the flame in this girl's eyes, despite the doctor's own vision of flames, became merely a story of the truth of human will and an acknowledgment of its power.

"Is that why he looks at me so?" Cuckoo asked, in a manner unusually meditative. "But then he, Valentine, did the same! Why, could that be what scared him that night—what he struck at?"

"He too may feel that you have a power for good, to fight against his power for evil. Yes, he does feel it. Make him feel it, more. Rely on yourself. Trust that there's something great within you, something placed there for you to use. Never mind what your life has been. Never mind your own weakness. You are the home, the temple, of this power of will. Julian feels it, and it draws him to you, but it is as nothing yet compared with the power of Cresswell. You have to make it more powerful, so that you may win Julian back from this danger."

"Eh? How?"

"Rest on it; trust in it; teach it to act. Show Julian more and more that you have it. Can't you think of a way of showing that you have this power?"

"Not I. No," Cuckoo murmured.

The doctor lowered his voice still more. Quite at a venture he drew a bow, and with his first arrow smote the lady of the feathers to the heart.

"Has Julian ever asked you to do anything?" he said.

Suddenly Cuckoo's face was scarlet.

"Why? How d'you know?" she stammered.

"Anything for him that was not evil?" the doctor pursued, following out an abstract theory, not as Cuckoo fancied, dealing with known facts. "I know nothing. I only ask you to try and remember, to search your mind."

There was no need for the lady of the feathers to do that.

"Yes, he did once," she said, looking still confused and furtive.

"Was it difficult?"

She hesitated.

"I s'pose so," she answered at last.

"Did you do it?"

"No."

The doctor had noticed that his questions gave pain.

"I don't want to know what it was and I don't ask," he said. "I have neither the right to, nor the desire to. But can't you do it, and show Julian that you have done it? If you do I think he will see that flame, which he fears and which fascinates him, burn more clearly, more steadily in your eyes."

"I'll see," Cuckoo said with a kind of gulp.

"Do more than this. This is only a part, one weapon in the fight, Cresswell is always near Julian ; you must be near him. Cresswell pursues Julian ; you must pursue him. Use your woman's wit, use all your experience of men ; use your heart. Wake up and throw yourself into this battle, and make yourself worthy of fighting. Only you can tell how. But this is a fact. Our wills, our powers of doing things, are made strong, or made weak by our own lives. Each time we do a degradingly-low, beastly thing"—he chose the words most easily comprehended by such a woman as she was—"we weaken our will, and make it less able to do anything good for another. If you commit loveless actions from to-day—though Julian has nothing to do with them—with each loveless action you will lose a point in the battle against the madness of Cresswell. And you must lose no points. Remember you are fighting a madman, as I believe, for the safety of the man you love. If I could tell you what——"

The doctor pulled himself up short.

"No," he said, "no need to tell you more than that, within these last few days, I have found that all you said about Cresswell's present *diablerie*"—he shook his head impatiently at the language he was using to the lady of the feathers—"Cresswell's present impulse for evil is less horribly true than the truth. I shall watch him, day by day, from now. And, if I can act, I shall do so. If his insanity is too sharp for me, as it may well be, I shall be checkmated in any effort forcibly to keep him from doing harm. In that case I can only trust to you, and hope that some chance circumstance may lead to the opening of Julian's eyes. But they are closed—closed fast. In any case you will help me and I will help you. You shall have opportunities of meeting Julian often. I will arrange that. And Cresswell——"

He paused as if in deep thought.

"How to do it," he murmured, almost to himself. "How to bring this battle to the issue !"

Then he turned his eyes on Cuckoo.

She was sitting bolt upright in the carriage. Her cheeks were flushed. Her hollow eyes were sparkling. She had drawn her hands out from under the rug and clasped them together in her lap.

"Oh, I'll do anythin' I can," she said, "anythin'. And—and I can do that one thing ! "

"Yes," said the doctor. "Which ? "

"The thing what he asked me once, and what I said no to," she answered, but in such a low murmur that the doctor scarcely caught the words.

He leaned forward in the carriage.

"Home now, Grant," he said to the coachman. "Or—no—drive first to 400 Marylebone Road."

The doctor turned again towards Cuckoo. She was looking away from him, so much that he was obliged to believe that she wished to conceal her face, which was towards the sunset.

The sky over London glowed with a dull red like a furnace. It deepened, while they looked, passing rapidly through the biting cold of the late winter afternoon.

The red cloud near the fainting sun broke and parted.

Spears of gold were thrust forth.

"Flames," the doctor whispered to himself. "Flames! The will, the soul of God in nature."

BOOK V—FLAMES

CHAPTER I

VALENTINE INVITES HIS GUESTS

VALENTINE and Julian sat together in the tent-room at night, as they sat together many months ago, when Julian confessed his secret and Valentine expressed his strange desire to have a different soul. Now it was deep winter. The year was old. In three days it must die. It lay in the snow like some abandoned beggar waiting for the inevitable end. Some, who were happy, would fain have succoured it and kept it with them. Others, who were sad, said, " Let it go—this beggar. Already it has taken too many alms from us." But neither the happy nor the sad could affect its fate. So it lay in the snow and in the wind upon its deathbed.

The tent-room had not been altered. Still the green draperies, veiled walls, windows and door, meeting in a point at the ceiling. The fire danced and shone. The electric moons gleamed with a twilight softness. Only Rip was gone from the broad and cushioned divan upon which he had loved to lie, half sleeping, half awake, while his master talked and Julian listened or replied. The room was the same, and this very fact emphasised the transformation of the two men who sat in it. They leaned in their low chairs on each side of the fire, thinly veiled from time to time in cigarette smoke. No sound of London reached them in this small room. Even the voice of the winter wind whispered and sang in vain. Stifled by the thick draperies, it failed in its effort to gain their attention, and sighed among the chimney-tops the chagrin of its soul. The face of Julian was drawn and heavy. IIis eyes were downcast. His arms hung over the cushioned elbows of his chair, in which he sat very low, in the shrivelled posture of one desperately fatigued. From time to time he opened his lips in a sort of dull gape, then shut his teeth tightly as if he ground them together. The drooping lids of his eyes were covered with little lines and there were deeper lines at the corners of his mouth. The colour of his face was the colour of the misty cloud that haunts the steps of evening on an autumn day, grey, as if it clothed processes of decay and of desolation. Years seemed to crouch upon him like lean dogs upon a doorstep. Within a few months he had stepped from boyhood to the creaking threshold of premature age.

The change in Valentine was far less marked to a careless eye. There was still a peculiar clearness in his large blue eyes, a white delicacy in his features. The lips of his mouth were red and soft, not dry, as were the lips of Julian. The crisp gold of his hair caught the light, and his lithe figure rested in his chair in a calm posture of pleasant ease. Yet he, too, was changed. Expression of a new nature now no longer lurked furtively in his face, but boldly, even triumphantly, asserted itself. It did not shrink behind a soft smile, or glide and pass in a fleeting gaiety, but stared upon the world with something of the hard and fixed immobility of a mark. Every mask, whatever expression be painted upon it, wears a certain aspect of shamelessness. Valentine's was a hard and shameless face, although his features, if coarser than of old, were still noble and, in line, a silent legend of almost priestly intellectuality.

He was looking across at Julian, who held idly between his lax fingers a letter written with violet ink upon pink paper, which had a little bird stamped in the left hand corner.

" When did you get it ? " he said.

"Two or three days ago, I think. I can't remember. I can't remember anything now," Julian answered heavily.

" And you have had two since ? "

" Yes. And to-day she called."

" You were out ? "

" Yes."

" She shows herself very exigent all of a sudden. She is afraid of losing you. I told you long ago she cherished absurd ambitions with regard to you. Do you intend to answer her notes ? "

"Oh, yes," Julian said. " Cuckoo has always been very fond of me ; very fond."

He glanced at the absurdly vulgar little bird in the corner of the letter. " And that's something," he added slowly.

"You are weighed down with gratitude ? No wonder. Are you grateful to others who have always cared for you in a different way—unselfishly, that is ? "

"I don't seem to feel very much about anybody now," Julian said. " I do such a lot. The more you do the less you feel. Damnable life ! All cruelty. I can't feel satisfied. But there

must be something; something I haven't tried. I must find it,"
he said, almost fiercely, and stirring in a sudden energy, "I must
find it—or—curse you, Val, why don't you find it for me?"

Valentine laughed.

"The last novelty has failed? You are a very discontented
sinner, Julian. And yet London begins to think you too enter-
prising. I hear that Lady Crichton is the last person to shut her
doors against you. What did she hear of?"

"How should I know?"

He laughed bitterly.

"She oughtn't to be particular. She used to receive Marr. I
met him first in her yellow drawing-room."

"London had not discussed him, perhaps. You are rapidly
becoming a legend and a warning. That is fame. To be the
accepted warning for others."

"Or infamy; which is much the same thing."

"But you are only at the first posting-station of your journey,"
Valentine continued, looking at him with a smile. "If you are
dissatisfied, it is because you have not tasted yet half that strength
of the Spring we once talked of. You have not completely thrown
off the foolish yoke of public opinion. The chains still jangle about
you. Cast them away and you will yet be happy."

"Shall I? Shall I, Valentine?"

The exhausted, worn, and weary figure leaned abruptly forward in
its chair. Julian's tired eyes glittered greedily.

"To be happy I'd commit any crime," he said.

"Crime is merely opinion," Valentine answered. "Everything is
opinion. You will commit crimes probably. Most brave men do."

"But shall I be happy?"

"You are greedy, Julian, greedy of everything, of knowledge of
life, lust, joy. You are never satisfied. That is because you and I
fasted for so long. And the greedy man is never quite happy while
he is eating, for he is always anticipating the next course. And, let
philosophers say what they will, happiness does not lie in anticipation. Go on eating. Pass on from course to course. At last there
will come a time, a beautiful time, when your appetite will be satisfied and you will rest content. But, remember, not till you have
journeyed through the whole *menu*, played with your dessert and
even drunk your black coffee. Go on, only go on. Men and women
are unhappy. They think it is because they have done too much.
They reproach themselves for a thousand things that they have
done. Fools! They are unhappy because they have not done
enough. The text which will haunt me on my deathbed will be:
'I have left undone those things which I ought to have done.' Yes,
during my long cursed years of inaction, when I was called the

Y

Saint of Victoria Street. Ah! Julian, you and I slept; we are
awake now. You and I were dead; we are now alive. But we are
only at the beginning of our lives. We have those years, those
white and empty years, to drown in the waters of Lethe. They are
like monstrous children that should have been strangled almost ere
they were born, white, vacant children. And now, day by day we
are pressing them down in the waters with our hands. At last they
will sink. The waves will flow over their haggard faces. The waves
will sweep them away. Then we shall be happy. We shall redeem
those years on which the locust fed and we shall be happy."

"Yes, by God, we shall be happy, we will—we will be happy.
Only teach me to be happy, Valentine, anywhere, anyhow."

"Not with the lady of the feathers. She will not make you
happy."

"Cuckoo? No! For she's terribly unhappy herself. Poor old
Cuckoo. I wonder what she's doing now."

"Searching in the snow for her fate," Valentine said, with a
sneer.

*   *   *   *   *   *   *

It was not so. Cuckoo was sitting alone in the little room of the
Marylebone Road looking a new spectre in the face, the spectre of
hunger, only shadowy as yet, scarcely defined, scarcely visible. And
the lady of the feathers wondered, as she gazed, if she and the
spectre must become better acquainted, clasp hands, kiss lips, be day
fellows and night fellows.

*   *   *   *   *   *   *

"I am going to write to Cuckoo," Julian said a day later. "What
shall I say?"

Valentine hesitated.

"What have you thought of saying?" he asked.

"Oh, I don't know. First one thing, then another. Good-bye
among the number. That's what you wish me to say, Val, isn't
it?"

He spoke in a listless voice, monotonous in inflection and lifeless
in timbre. The dominion of Valentine over him since the supper at
the Savoy had increased, consolidating itself into an undoubted
tyranny, which Julian accepted, carelessly, thoughtlessly, a prey to
the internal degradation of his mind. Once he had only been
nobly susceptible, a fine power. Now he was drearily weak, an
ungracious disability. But with his weakness came, as is usual, a
certain lassitude which even resembled despair, an indifference
peculiar to the slave, how opposed to the indifference peculiar to the
autocrat. Valentine recognised in the voice the badge of serfdom,
even more than in the question, and he smiled with a cold triumph.
He had intended telling Julian now, once for all, to break with the

lady of the feathers, of whom, even yet he stood in vague fear. But the question, the voice of Julian gave him pause, slid into his soul a new and bizarre desire, child of the strange intoxication of power which was beginning to grip him, and which the doctor had remarked. If Julian broke with Cuckoo, repulsed her for ever into the long street that was her pent and degraded world, would not the sharp salt of Valentine's triumph be taken from him? Would not the wheels of his Juggernaut car fail to do their office, in his sight —there was the point! upon a precious victim? The lady of the feathers thus deliberately abandoned by Julian would suffer perhaps almost to the limit of her capability of pain, but Valentine would have lost sight of her in the dark, and though he would have conquered that spectral opposition which she had whimsically offered to him—he laughed to himself now thinking of his fear of it—he would not see that greatest vision, the flight of his enemy.

These thoughts flashed through his mind, moving him to an answer that astonished Julian.

"Good-bye!" he said. "Why should I wish that?"

"You said the other day, at the Savoy, that she hated you, that you and she must have a battle unless I chose between you."

"I was laughing."

The lifelessness left Julian's voice as he exclaimed:

"Valentine! But you were——"

"Sober and you were not. Can you deny it?"

Julian was silent.

"I so little meant that nonsense," Valentine continued, "that I have conceived a plan. To-morrow is the last night of the old year. The doctor asked us to spend it with him. We refused. Providence directed that refusal, for now we are at liberty to celebrate the proper occasion for burying hatchets by burying our particular hatchet. The lady of the feathers, your friend, my enemy, shall see the new year in here, in this tent-room where, long ago we—you and I, with how ill success, sought to exchange our souls."

Julian looked utterly astonished at this proposition.

"Cuckoo wouldn't come here," he began.

"So you said once before. But she came then and she will come now."

"And then the doctor! If he gets to hear of   We said we were dining out."

Valentine's hard smile grew yet harder, and his eyes sparkled eagerly.

"I'll arrange that," he said. "The doctor shall come here too."

It seemed indeed as if he meant that his triumph should culminate on this final night of the year, his year. He laughed Julian's

astonishment at this vagary aside, sat down and wrote the two notes
of invitation, and then went out with Julian, saying :

"Julian, come out with me. You remember what I said about
the greedy man ? Come ; Fate shall present you with another
course, one more step towards your *café noir* and—happiness.
Voilà !

Valentine was right in his supposition that both the lady of the
feathers and the doctor would accept his invitation, but he did not
understand the precise motive which prompted their acceptance.
Nor did he much care to understand it. Cuckoo, Dr. Levillier !
After all, what were they to him now ? Spectators of his triumph.
Interesting, therefore, to a certain extent, as an unpaying audience
may be interesting to an actor. Interesting, insomuch as they could
contribute to swell the bladder of his vanity, and follow in procession
behind his chariot wheels. But he no longer cared to divine the
shades of their emotions, or to busy himself in fathoming their exact
mental attitudes in relation to himself. So he thought, touched,
perhaps, with a certain delirium, though not with the delirium of
insanity attributed to him by Dr. Levillier.

The doctor had intended celebrating the last night of the year in
Harley Street with Cuckoo and the two young men. The refusal of
the latter put an end to the opening of his plan of campaign in this
strange battle, and he was greatly astonished when he received
Valentine's invitation. Still he had no hesitation in accepting it.

"So," he said to himself, as he read the note, "we join issue
within the very walls of the enemy—poor, deluded, twisted Valentine ! that I should have to call him, to think of him as an enemy !
We begin the fight within the shadow of our opponent's tent."

Literally that was the fact.

Cuckoo's thoughts were less definite, more tinged with passion,
less shaped by the hands of intellect. They were as clouds, looming
large, yet misty, hanging loose in torn fragments now, and now
merging into indistinguishable fog that yet seemed pregnant with
possibilities. Poor thoughts, vague thoughts ; yet they pressed
upon her brain until her tired head ached. And they stole down to
her heart, and that ached too, and hoped and then despaired—then
hoped again.

CHAPTER II

CAFÉ NOIR

SNOW fell, melodramatically, on the year's death night.   During the day Valentine occupied himself oddly in decorating his flat for the evening.   But although he thus seemed to fall in with the consecrated humours of the season his decorations would scarcely have commanded the approval of those good English folk who think that no plant is genial unless it is prickly, and that prickly things represent appropriately to the eye the inward peace and goodwill that grows, like a cactus perhaps, within the heart.   He did not put holly rigidly above his doors.   No mistletoe drooped from the apex of the tent-room.   Instead he filled his flat with flowers, brought from English conservatories or from abroad.   Crowds of strange and spotted orchids stood together in the drawing-room, staring upon the hurly-burly of furniture and ornaments.   In the corners of the room were immense red flowers, such as hang among the crawling green jungles of the West Indies.   They gleamed, like flames, amid a shower of cunningly arranged green leaves, and palms sheltered them from the electric rays of the ceiling.   The tent-room was a maze of tulips, in vases, in pots, in china bowls that hung by thin chains from the sloping green roof.   Few of these tulips were whole coloured.   They were slashed, and striped, and spotted with violent hues.   Some were of the most vivid scarlet streaked with black.   Others were orange coloured with livid pink spots, circus pink such as you see round the eyes of horses bred specially for the ring.   There were white tulips stained as if with blood, pale pink tulips tipped with deepest brown, rose-coloured tulips barred with wounds whose edges were saffron hued, tulips of a warm wallflower tint dashed with the stormy yellow of an evening sky.   And hidden among these scentless flowers, in secret places cunningly contrived, were great groups of hyacinths, which poured forth their thick and decadent scent, breathing heavily their hearts into the small atmosphere of the room, and giving a strange and unnatural soul to the tulips who had spent all their efforts in the attainment of form and daring combinations of colour.   As if relapsing into sweet simplicity, after the vagaries of a wayward nature had run their course, Valentine had filled his hall and dining-room with violets, purple and white, and a bell of violets hung from the ceiling over the chair which the lady of the feathers was to occupy at dinner. These were white only, white and virginal, flowers for some sweet woman dedicated to the service of God, or to the service of some eternal altar flame burning, as the zeal of nature burns, through all the dawning and fading changes of the world.

Thus Valentine passed his day among flowers, and only when the last twilight of the year fell had he fixed the last blossom in its place. Then he rested, as after six days of creation, and from the midst of his flowers saw the snow falling delicately upon London. Lights began to gleam in the tall houses opposite his drawing-room windows. He glanced at them, and they brought him thoughts at which he smiled. Behind those squares of light he imagined peace and goodwill in enormous white waistcoats and expansive shirt-fronts, red faced, perhaps even whiskered, getting ready for good temper and turkey, journalistic geniality and plum pudding. And holly everywhere, with its prickly leaves and shining, phlegmatic surfaces.

Peace and goodwill!

He glanced at his orchids and at the red West Indian flowers, and he thought of those crawling green jungles from which they should have come, and smiled gently.

Peace and goodwill!

He went to dress.

*   *   *   *   *   *   *

Meanwhile in the Marylebone Road the lady of the feathers achieved her toilet, assisted by Jessie. The only evening dress that Cuckoo possessed had been given to her long ago by a young man in the millinery department of a large London shop. For a week he had adored Cuckoo. During that week he had presented her with this tremendous gift. She went into her bedroom now, took it out and looked at it. The gown rustled a great deal whenever it was moved; this had been the young man's idea. He considered that the more a gift rustled the more aristocratic it was, and, being well acquainted with all the different noises made by different fabrics, he had selected one with a voice as of many waters. Cuckoo heard it now as in a dream. She laid it down upon the bed and regarded it by candle-light. The young man's taste in sound found its equivalent in his taste in colour. The hue of the gown was also very loud, the brightest possible green, trimmed with thick yellow imitation lace. Once it had enchanted Cuckoo. She had put it on with a thrill to go to music-halls with the young man. But now she gazed upon it with a lack-lustre and a doubtful eye. The flickering flame of the candle lit it up in patches, and those patches had a lurid aspect. Remembering that Julian had liked her best in black she shrank from appearing before him in anything so determined. Yet it was her only dress for the evening, and at first she supposed the wearing of it to be inevitable. She put it on and went in front of the glass. In these days she had become even thinner than of old, and more haggard. The gown increased her tenuity and pallor to the eye, and, after a long moment of painful consideration, Cuckoo resolved to abandon these green glories. Once her mind was made up she was out of the dress in an instan. Time was short. She hurriedly extracted her black gown from the wardrobe, caught hold of a pair of scissors, and in a few minutes had ripped the imitation lace from its foundations and was transferring it with trembling fingers to Julian's gift. Never before had she worked at any task with such grim determination, or with such deftness; inspired by exceptional circumstances, she might for twenty minutes have been a practised dressmaker. Certainly pins were called in as weapons to the attack, but what of that? Compromises are often only stuck together with pins. In any case Cuckoo was not entirely in despair with the new aspect of an old friend, and when she was ready was able at least to hope that things might have been worse.

Putting on over the dress a black jacket, she went out into the passage and called down to Mrs. Brigg, who, as usual, was wandering to and fro in her kitchen, like an uneasy shade in nethermost Hades.

" Mrs. Brigg! Mrs. Brigg, I say! "

" Well? "

" Where's the whistle? "

Mrs. Brigg came to the bottom of the kitchen stairs.

" What d'yer want it for? "

" A cab, of course," cried Cuckoo, in the narrow voice of one in a hurry.

" A cab!" rejoined Mrs. Brigg, ascending the dark stairs all the time she was speaking. "And what do you want with cabs, I should like to know? Who pays for 'em, that's what I say; who's to do it? "

Her grey head hove in sight.

" Where are you going? Piccadilly? "

" No; get the whistle."

" What—and no hat! "

She was evidently impressed.

" A toff is it?" she ejaculated, obviously appeased. " Well! so long as I get the rent I—— "

With a white glare Cuckoo seized the whistle from her claw, and in a moment was driving away through the snow.

Mrs. Brigg trotted back to the kitchen decidedly relieved. Cuckoo's suddenly altered mode of life had tried her greatly. The girl had taken to going out in the day and staying at home at night. Simultaneously with this changed *régime* her funds had evidently become low. She had begun to live less well, to watch more keenly than of old the condition in which her commons went down to the kitchen and returned from it on the advent of the next meal. By various little symptoms the landlady knew that her lodger was getting hardup. Yet no amount of badgering and argument would induce Cuckoo to say why she sat indoors at night. She acknowledged that she was not ill. Mrs. Brigg had been seriously exercised. But now her old heart was glad. Cuckoo was, perhaps, mounting into higher circles, circles in which hats were not worn during the evening. And as Mrs. Brigg entered her nethermost hell she broke into a thin, quavering song:

> "In 'er 'air she wore a white cam-eelyer,
> Dark blue was the colour of 'er heye."

It was her song of praise. She always sang it on great occasions.

When the lady of the feathers reached Victoria Street she found the little party already assembled. Valentine met her ceremoniously in the violet-scented hall and helped her to slide out of her jacket. His glance upon the imitation lace was quick and gay, but Cuckoo did not see it. She was gazing at the flowers, and when she entered the drawing-room and found herself in the midst of the orchids, the West Indian flowers and the palms, her astonishment knew no bounds.

"I never!" she murmured under her breath.

Then she forgot the flowers, having only time to remember to be shy. Dinner was immediately announced by Wade, whose years of trained discretion could not banish a faint accent of surprise from his voice. He was, in fact, *bouleversé* by this celebration of the death of the old year. Valentine offered Cuckoo his arm. She took it awkwardly, with a shooting glance of question at the doctor, who seemed her only spar in this deep social sea. Valentine placed her beneath the bell of violets, and took his seat beside her. Julian was on her other hand, the doctor exactly opposite. Wade presented her with *hors d'œuvres*. Cuckoo selected a sardine. She understood sardines, having met them at the Monico. Valentine and the doctor began to talk. Julian ate slowly, and Cuckoo stole a glance at him. His aspect startled her so much that she with difficulty repressed a murmur of astonishment. He had the appearance of one so completely exhausted as to be scarcely alive. Most people, however stupid, however bored, have some air, when in society, of listening even when they do not speak, of giving some sort of attention to those about them or to the place in which they find themselves.

They glance this way and that, however phlegmatically. They bend in attention or lean back in observation. It is seen that they are conscious of their environment. But Julian was engrossed with fatigue. The lids drooped over his eyes. His face wore a leaden hue. Even his lips were colourless. He ate slowly and mechanically till his plate was empty. Then he laid down his fork and remained motionless, his eyes still cast down towards the tablecloth, his two hands laid against the table edge, while the fingers were extended upon the cloth on either side of his plate. Cuckoo looked at him with terror, wondering if he were ill. Then, glancing up, she met the eyes of the doctor. They seemed to bid her take no heed of Julian's condition, and she did not look at him again just then. Trying to control her fears, she listened to Valentine's conversation with the doctor.

" Doctor's are sceptics by profession," she heard him say.

" I believe in individualism too firmly to allow that any beliefs or unbeliefs can be professional, Cresswell."

" Possibly you are right," Valentine answered lightly. " What a pity it is that there is no profession of which all the members at least believe in themselves."

" Ah; would you enter it ? "

" I scarcely think it would be necessary."

He glanced first at the doctor, then at Cuckoo as he spoke.

" I am thankful to say," he added in his clear, cool voice, " that I have no longer either the perpetual timidity of the self-doubter or even the occasional anxiety of the egoist."

" You have passed into a region which even egoism cannot enter ? "

" Possibly—the average egoism."

" The average egoism of the end of the century moves in a very rarefied air."

" Its feet touch ground nevertheless."

" And yours ? "

Valentine only laughed, as if he considered the question merely rhetorical or jocose.

" But we are getting away from the question, which was not personal," he said. " I contend that doctors as a body are bound to combat these modern Athenians who are inclined to attribute everything to some obscure action of the mind. For, if their beliefs are founded on rock, and if they can themselves sufficiently, by asceticism, or by following any other fixed course of life which they may select as the right one, train their minds to do that which they believe can be done, the profession of doctors may in time be abolished. Mind will be the universal medicine, Will not simply the cure, but the preventive of disease."

" And of death ? " the doctor asked quietly. " Will man be able to think himself into an eternity on earth ? "

Valentine looked at him very strangely.

" You ask that question seriously ? " he said.

" I ask seriously whether you think so."

It was evident that the doctor meant to make the question above all things a personal one. This time Valentine accepted that condition. He sat for a moment twisting his champagne glass about in his long fingers and glancing rapidly from the doctor to Cuckoo, who heard this conversation without very well understanding it. Indeed, she sat beneath her bell of violets in much confusion, *distraite* in her desire to command intellectual faculties which she did not possess. Valentine watched her narrowly, though he seemed inattentive to her. Perhaps he thought of his delivery of his gospel to her, and wondered if she recalled it at this moment ; or perhaps once more he began to rejoice in her mental distress and alienation.

" Wade," he said, ";the champagne to Mr. Addison. Well, doctor, suppose I acknowledged that I did think so—mind, I don't acknowledge it !—you might, on your side, think something too—that I am mad, for instance. Ah ! Miss Bright has knocked over her glass ! "

Cuckoo murmured a stumbling apology, gazing with nervous intentness at Valentine. It seemed to her that he had a gift of divination. Dr. Levillier laughed gently.

" I am not inclined to suppose all my opponents in thought mad," he said. " Still, such a belief would certainly indicate in the holder of it the possession of a mind so uncommon, so unique, I may say, that it would naturally rouse one to very close attention and observation of it."

" Exactly," Valentine rejoined.

A certain audacity was slowly creeping into his demeanour and growing while he talked. It manifested itself in slight gesticulations, conceited movements of the hand and head, in the colour of the voice and the blunt directness of his glances.

" Exactly. Attention and observation directed towards the object of satisfying yourself that the man—myself, let us say—was mad ? You don't reply. Let me ask you a question. Why should a profound belief in human power of will indicate madness ? "

" A belief that is not based on any foundation of proof—that is my point. An extraordinary belief, personal to one person, rejected by mankind in the mass, and founded upon nothing, no fact, no inference even, in the history of mankind, is decidedly a strong indication of dementia."

" But suppose it is a belief founded upon a fact ? "

" Of course that would entirely alter the matter."

The two men looked across at one another with a long and direct glance full in the eyes. Cuckoo watched them anxiously. Julian sat with his eyes cast down. He seemed unaware that there was any one near him, any conversation going on around him. Wade moved softly about, ministering to the wants of his master's guests. Course succeeded course.

" Do you propose to give me a fact proving the reasonableness of entertaining a belief that a man, by his own deliberate action of the will, can compass immortality on earth, or even prolong his life in such a way as this, for instance; by the successful domination, or banishment, of any disease recognised as mortal? I acknowledge that the will to live may prolong for a certain time a life threatened merely by the sapping action of old age. Do you propose to give me a fact to prove that?"

" I do not say that I intend to give it to you," Valentine answered, with scarcely veiled insolence.

"But you know of such a fact?" said the doctor, ignoring his host's tone.

" Possibly."

The voice of Valentine thrilled with triumph as he spoke the word. Again he glanced at the lady of the feathers.

" Cannot you convert the doctor?" he asked her, in tones full of sarcastic meaning. "You know something of my theories, something of their putting into practice."

" I don't know—I don't understand," she murmured helplessly.

She looked down at her plate, flushing scarlet with a sense of shame at her own complete mental impotence.

" What's the matter Cuckoo?"

The words came slowly from the lips of Julian, whose heavy eyes were now raised and fixed with a stare of lethargic wonder upon Cuckoo.

" What are they saying to you?"

His look travelled on, still slow and unwieldy, to the doctor and to Valentine.

" I won't have Cuckoo worried," he said. And then he relapsed with a mechanical abruptness upon the consideration of his food. Valentine seemed about to make some laughing rejoinder, but, after a glance at Julian, he apparently resigned the idea as absurd, and turning again to the doctor, remarked :

" It is sometimes injudicious to state all that one knows."

"Still more so all that one does not know. But I have no desire to press you," the doctor said, lightly. " This is wonderful wine Where did you get it?"

" At the *Cercle Blanc* sale," Valentine answered quickly.

It seemed that he was slightly irritated. He frowned and cast a glance that was almost threatening upon the doctor.

" Would you assume weakness in every strong man who refuses to take off his coat, roll up his shirt sleeve and display the muscle of his arm ? " he said, harshly.

"The case is not analogous. That muscle exists in the world is a proved fact. When I was at Eton, I was knocked down by a boy stronger than I was. Since then I acknowledge the power of muscle."

" And have you never been knocked down mentally ? "

" Not in the way you suggest."

Valentine shifted in his seat. It did not escape the doctor that he had the air of a man longing either to say or do something startling, but apparently held back by tugging considerations of prudence or of expediency.

"Some day you may be," he said at last, obviously conquered by this prompting prudence.

" When I am, the ' Christian scientist,' who once declared to me that she cured a sprained ankle by walking on it many miles a day, and thinking it was well while she walked, shall receive my respectful apologies," the doctor answered, laughing.

Valentine handed the lady of the feathers some strawberries. On her nervous refusal of them he exclaimed :

" I see you have finished your wine, doctor. No more ? Really ? Nor you, Julian ? "

Julian made no reply. He simply pushed his glass a little away from him.

" Then shall we accompany Miss Bright into the tent-room ? I thought we would have coffee there. You have never seen the tent-room," he added to Cuckoo, getting up from his seat as he spoke.

" I usually sit in it when I am alone or with Julian. You will not mind our cigarettes, I know."

He led the way down the scented corridor, scented with the thin, gently bright scent of violets.

"The tent-room has a history," he continued to Cuckoo, opening a door on the left. " It was once the scene of an—an absurd experiment. Eh, doctor ? "

They entered the room. As they did so the hot, sticky scent of the hidden hyacinths poured out to meet them. For a moment it seemed overwhelming, and Cuckoo hung back with an almost unconquerable sensation of aversion and even of fear. The aspect of this small room astonished her ; she had never seen any chamber so arranged. Certainly it looked very unusual to-night. The small fire was hidden by a large screen of white wood, with panels of dull green brocade. Only one of the electric lamps was turned on, and that was shaded, so that the diffused light was faint, a mere unflickering twilight. The masses of tulips hung like quantities of monotonously similar shadows from the tented ceiling, and the flood of scent caused the room to seem even smaller than it really was, a tiny temple dedicated to the uncommon, perhaps to the sinister.

" We will see the Old Year out and drink our *café noir* here," said Valentine. " Where will you sit, Miss Bright ? "

" I don't mind. It's all one to me," murmured Cuckoo. " What a funny room though ! " she could not help adding. " It ain't like a room at all."

" Imagine it an Arab tent, the home of a Bedaween Sheik in a desert of Nubia," said Valentine. " This divan is very comfortable. Let me arrange the cushions for you."

As he bent over her to do so, he murmured in her ear :

" And you, having tossed your will away, are nothing ! "

They had been the last words of his gospel, proclaimed to her that night on which she prayed !

The lady of the feathers looked up at him with a new knowledge, the knowledge of her recent lonely nights, of which he knew nothing as yet ; the knowledge of that glancing spectre of want whom, by her own action, she summoned while she feared its gaunt presence ; the knowledge of the doctor's trust in her ; the knowledge of her great love for Julian ; the knowledge, perhaps, that leaning her arms upon the slippery horsehair sofa in her little room, she had once thrown a muttered prayer, incoherent, unfinished, yet sincere, out into the great darkness that encompasses the beginning, the progress, and the ending of all human lives with mystery. She looked up at him with this world of mingling knowledge in her eyes, and Valentine drew away from her with a stifling sensation of frigid awe.

" What—what ? " he began. Then, recovering himself, he turned suddenly away.

" Sit down, doctor. Do you like my flowers ? Julian, are you still tired ? The coffee will wake you up. A cigarette doctor, or a cigar ? Here are the matches."

Julian came over heavily and sat down on the divan by Cuckoo. His unnatural lethargy was gradually passing away into a more explicable fatigue, no longer speechless. Leaning on his elbow, he looked into her face with his weary eyes, in which to-night there was a curious dim pathos. It seemed that the only thing which had so far struck him during the evening was still Cuckoo's confusion over her own misunderstanding at dinner, for he now again referred to it.

" Have they been chaffing you, Cuckoo ? " he said, striking a match on the heel of his shoe and lighting a cigarette, " have they been worrying you ? Never mind. It's only Val's fun. He doesn't mean anything by it. I say, how awfully pale you look to-night, and thin."

He paused, considering her with a glance that was almost severe.

" I'm all right," said Cuckoo, trying to repress the agitation she always felt now when speaking to Julian. " I ain't ill. Why don't you come to see me now ? " she added. " You don't never come."

Julian glanced over to Valentine, who was standing by the hearth talking to the doctor, who sat in an arm-chair.

"I've been busy," he said. " I've had a lot of things to do. Do you miss me, Cuckoo, when I don't come ? "

" Yes," she replied, but without softness. Then she added, lowering her voice almost to a whisper:

" Don't he want you to come ? "

Julian did not reply, but puffed rather moodily at his cigarette, glancing towards Valentine. He was thinking of the conversation at the Savoy and of the antagonism between Valentine and Cuckoo. Suddenly there came into his mind a dull wish to reconcile these two on the last night of the year—in Valentine's own words— to bury the hatchet. He sat meditating over his plan and trying to revolve different, and dramatic, methods of accomplishing it. Presently he said :

" Cuckoo, you and Val have got to be friends from to-night."

She started, stirring uneasily on the great cushions that were heaped at her back.

" We are," she said.

He shook his head.

" Not real friends."

" Oh, we are all right."

" D'you hate him still ? "

" He don't like me," she answered, evasively.

" Yet he invites you here," Julian said.   " Why does he do that ? "

" I dunno," Cuckoo said.

She wondered why. Not so the doctor, to whom it had become evident that Valentine had asked his guests out of vanity, and with a view to some peculiar and monstrous display of his power over Julian. While Cuckoo and Julian talked together on the divan Valentine came over to the doctor. His eyes still held an expression of awe created in him by the strange new glance of the lady of the feathers. He sought to conquer this sensation of awe, which fought fiercely against his intended blatant triumph of to-night.

" Your cigarette all right, doctor ? " he said, in a quick voice.

" A delicious one, thanks."

Valentine began touching the ornaments on the mantelpiece with nervous fingers.

" We didn't quite finish our conversation at dinner," he said.

" No ? "

" I did not give you a reason for my belief."

A deep interest woke in the doctor, but he did not show it. He thought :

" So, he must insanely return to this one subject, round which his brain makes an eternal tour."

" No," he said aloud, " you have a reason then ? "

" Yes."

His voice vibrated with arrogance. His hand still darted to and fro on the mantelpiece while he stood looking down at the doctor. There was something in his manner that suggested a mixture of triumph and of fighting anxiety in his mind. But, as he continued to speak, the former got the upper hand.

" A reason that might convince even you if you knew it."

" Convince me of exactly what ? " the doctor asked, indifferently.

His indifference seemed to pique Valentine, who replied with energy :

" That human will can be cultivated, has been developed, until it has moved the mountain, achieved the thing men call a miracle."

" By whom has it been so developed ? "

Valentine hesitated almost like one who fears to be led into a trap. The doctor could see " By me ! " trembling upon his lips. He did not actually utter it, but instead exclaimed, with a laugh :

" Some day you will discover."

And, as he spoke, he looked at Julian and the lady of the feathers. The doctor was anxious to lead him on, and, leaning easily back in his comfortable chair, occupied himself with his cigarette for a minute, as a man calmly at ease. Between his whiffs he presently threw out carelessly :

" This man has compassed eternity by his own will ? "

" Oh, I did not say that."

" He has contented himself with curing a sprained ankle by walking upon it, like my Christian scientist ? "

" Now you fly to the other extreme, from the very great to the very little. Take a middle course."

" Where would that lead me ? "

Valentine threw a glance round the dim, hot, scented little room, then once more his eyes rested on Julian and Cuckoo.

" What if I said—To this little room, to Julian and that girl, to myself ? " he answered in a low voice.

" And the miracle ? " said the doctor.

The door opened. Wade appeared with coffee.

CHAPTER III

THE HEALTH OF THE NEW YEAR

VALENTINE turned quickly with an air of mingled irritation and relief at the interruption.

"We must all take coffee," he cried. "It will give us impetus, vitality, so that as the old year dies we may live more swiftly, more strongly. I like to feel that my life is increasing while that of another—the old year for instance—is decreasing."

But the doctor noticed that his eyes had rested with a curiously significant expression upon Julian as he spoke the last sentence.

"Leave the coffee pot on that little table," he added to Wade, when the man had filled all four cups. "We may want it."

Wade obeyed him and disappeared.

"Your man makes wonderful coffee," the doctor said, sipping.

"Yes. Julian, have you reached that *café noir* I spoke of the other day?" Valentine asked laughingly, returning to his simile of the greedy man and happiness.

"I don't know. Not yet, Val, I think," Julian answered. This coffee seemed to give him life at last. The heavy weariness disappeared from his face. His eyes gleamed with something of their old youthfulness and ardour.

"If so, I must be close on happiness," he added.

As he spoke he looked into the hollow eyes of Cuckoo, seeming, strangely, to seek in them the will-o-the-wisp of which he spoke.

"Never look for it in unfurnished rooms," Valentine exclaimed with sudden violence.

This glance of Julian, so the doctor judged, precipitated his curious and subtle insanity towards an outburst.

"You will find it in the thing that is most definite, not in the thing that is most indefinite. Isn't it so, doctor? Happiness lies in the positive, not in the negative?"

"Happiness lies in many places. Each finds it in a different house."

"Perhaps you can't tell where I should find it, Val," Julian interposed, with a certain sturdiness of manner.

" No," said Cuckoo, eagerly.

The coffee, it appeared, had an effect upon her too. There was a life, a keen intentness in her thin, white face, not visible there before. Valentine turned round upon her. He was holding his coffee-cup in his right hand. With the other he put his cigarette to his lips.

" Can you tell us where Mr. Addison is likely to find happiness ? " he said. " Can you tell us, lady of the feathers ? "

" No. He can tell himself. That's all," she said " Let find it himself."

" Each for himself and God for us all, eh ? "

" I don't know about God," she said, looking towards the doctor as if for assistance.

" Each for another and God for us all is, perhaps, a better motto," the doctor interposed.

" Ah, Charity ! "

Valentine took out his watch and looked at it.

" Charity ! Midnight is approaching, and, of course, this is Charity's benefit night by common consent. Thank you, doctor, for the hint. Did the dying old year prompt you with its husky voice full of the wind and of the snow ? "

" Possibly."

" Let us have some more coffee. Julian, give me Miss Bright's cup You shall have your absinthe presently. Wade has not forgotten it.

" Absinthe ? " said the doctor.

" Julian drinks it every night. He has got tired of whisky. Doctor, your cup, too."

" We shall not sleep a wink to-night."

" All the better. Why should not we see the dawn in, as we did once before ? You recollect."

" Ah Val ! on the night of your trance."

" Yes. You were not here, then, lady of the feathers."

He spoke with a light mockery.

" I fainted, or died—the doctor was deceived into thinking so— and was born again in the dawn of the very day on which Julian first met you."

Cuckoo shivered with the recollection of Marr and her horror of that night.

" Why do you shiver? " Valentine continued. " Do you find the room cold ? "

" No, no."

Indeed, the heat and the over-powering scent of the hyacinths had previously weighed upon her physique, and increased the *malaise* into which her curious new dutifulness, and the faint spectre which drew near to her, had brought her.

z

" Perhaps you shiver in the influence of this little room," he continued, persistently. " Julian and I once did so. Eh, Julian ? "

" Yes, in those sittings."

" I didn't shiver," Cuckoo said, bluntly and very obviously lying. She quickly drank some more coffee.

" If you had it might not have been astonishing," said Valentine. " For this little room has seen marvels, and strange things that happen perhaps stamp their strange impression upon the places in which they happen. We ought to discuss the occult, doctor, on the last night of the year."

" By all means."

" How long ago it seems ! " Julian said suddenly, with a sigh.

" Yes," Valentine answered. " Because so much has happened in the interval. The greedy man has eaten so many courses, Julian."

He seemed to take a delight in throwing out allusions to one and the other of his guests, allusions which nobody but the person addressed could understand rightly. For he now went on, addressing himself to Cuckoo :

" In this little room was committed the great act of brigandage of which I once spoke to you. Do you remember ? "

She shook her head.

" Never mind. But, though you cannot remember, that might make you shiver."

" What act of brigandage, Valentine ? " Julian asked.

" Oh, the attempt—my attempt to seize upon a different soul."

" But you failed."

" Did I ? Do you think so, doctor ? "

His apparent audacity seemed to increase. In the twilight of the scented room he drew himself up as he stood by the brocaded screen that hid the fire. He closed and unclosed rapidly his left hand which hung at his side. His foot tapped the thick carpet gently.

" Did you not ? " the doctor answered quietly.

But Julian was roused to vivacity.

" What do you mean, Valentine ? " he said. " Of course you may have changed, or developed, or whatever you like to call it, since then. But to say you have got a different soul ! "

" Is absurd ? Yes, you are right. Because if I had got a different soul the original ' I,' that was dissatisfied with itself, must have ceased to be. Since the soul of a man—his will to do things, his will to feel things—is the man himself, if I had a different soul I should be another man. The former man would have ceased to be."

" Or would be elsewhere."

It was the doctor who spoke, and he spoke without special interest, simply expressing his thought of what might happen in so whimsical an event as that harped upon by Valentine. But Valentine seemed painfully struck by the almost idle words.

" Elsewhere ! " he exclaimed, with a lowering expression. " What do you mean, doctor ? What do you imply ? "

The doctor looked at him surprised.

" Merely that a thing expelled is not necessarily a thing slain. If you turn me out of this room I am not certain to expire on the door-mat."

Valentine broke into a nervous and uneasy laugh and cast a quick glance all around him, and especially on Cuckoo, who sat listening silently with her eyebrows drawn together in a pent frown of puzzled attention.

" I see, I see," he said hastily. And here Julian broke in.

" But the whole thing's impossible," he said with a laugh.

" You would say so, doctor ? "

Valentine addressed this question to Dr. Levillier in a very marked and urgent manner.

" You would say so, since the will of man cannot perform miracles ? "

" Certainly I should say so, despite the triumphs of hypnotism. A man may change greatly through outside influence, or perform occasional acts foreign to his nature under the influence of ' suggestion ' or hypnotism. But I do not believe he can change radically and permanently, except from one cause."

The last words were spoken after a moment of hesitation. Valentine rejoined quickly.

" What ? What ? One cause, you say ! You allow that—wait though ! What is the cause ? "

Dr. Levillier was silent. He was asking himself should he play this forcing card, make this sharp, cutting experiment. He resolved that he would make it.

" A man may change radically," he said, " if he becomes insane."

A short breath, like a sigh, came from Cuckoo. Valentine stood quite still, regarding the doctor closely for a moment. Then he said contemptuously :

" Mad ! Oh, madmen don't interest me."

The doctor had gained nothing from his experiment. It was impossible to gather from Valentine's manner that he was in any way struck by this suggestion, and indeed he abandoned all allusion to it with careless haste, and returned to that other suggestion of which the doctor himself had thought nothing.

" Supposing that soul of a man to be expelled," he said, abruptly, " where—where do you suppose it would go, would be ? "

It was obvious that he endeavoured to speak lightly, but there was a most peculiar anxiety visible in his manner. The doctor wondered from what cause it sprang.

"I have never formed a supposition on that matter," he said.

"Well—well—try to form one now. Yes, and you Julian, too."

He did not address himself to the lady of the feathers, but he looked at her long and narrowly. The doctor lit another cigarette. He seemed to be seriously considering this odd question. Julian, whose lethargy was changing into an almost equally pronounced excitement, was not so hesitating. As if struck by a sudden flashing idea, he exclaimed :

"How if it was in the air ? How if it was wandering about from place to place ? By God, Val !" he cried, with emphasis, "do you know what I read in a book I took up from your shelves the other day—something about souls being like flames ? It was in Rossetti : Flames !"

He turned to Cuckoo and stared into her eyes.

"I was half asleep when I read it," he said. "Why should I remember it now ? That flame—I saw that flame months ago." He seemed like a man puzzling something out, trying to trace a way through a tangled maze of thought that yet might be clear. "It came from you, Val, that night, with a cry like a lost thing. A soul expelled, did you say ?"

Suddenly his face was set in an awe-struck gravity.

"Why—but then, if so, that flame would be *you*, Valentine, that flame which seemed to haunt me, which I have seen in——"

He looked at Cuckoo again and was silent.

"Yes, Julian ? " Valentine said, in a hard, thin voice. "Go on, I am listening."

Julian stared at him with a strong excitement.

"And what are you then, Valentine ? Where do you come from ? " he said slowly.

"From Marr."

The words came from the divan, from the dry lips of Cuckoo. Dr. Levillier knew not why, but he was thrilled to the very soul by them as by a revelation throwing strong light upon the depths of things. Whether it was the influence of this strange scented room in which strange things had happened, or the influence of the hour and the climax and death of the year, or a voice in his heart speaking to him with authority, he could not tell. Only he knew that on a sudden all his guiding reason, all his knowledge, all his cool contemplation of the physician and common sense of the man were swept entirely away. His theory of insanity seemed in a moment the theory of a dwarf intellect trying to stick wretched, absurd pins through angels—white or black—that it thought butterflies. His conversation with Cuckoo on the Hampstead Heights seemed the vain babble of a tricked and impotent observer. His mind fell on its knees before the mind of the lady of the feathers. Reason was stricken by instinct. The confused feeling of the woman had conquered the logical inferences of the man. From that moment the doctor secretly abandoned the old landmarks which had guided him all his life, and entered into a new world—a world in which he would not have dreamed of permitting any of his patients to walk if he could help it. A strange, magic floated round him like a mist blotting out the crude familiarities of the normal world. The tent-room, with its shadowy tulips, its scented warmth, its pale twilight, its quick silences when voices ceased, was a temple of wonder and a home of the miraculous. And those gathered in it, what were they? Men and a woman? Bodies? Earthly creatures? No. To his mind they were stripped bare of the clothes in which man—governed by decrees of some hidden power—must make his life pilgrimage. They were stripped bare and naked of their bodies. They were warm, stirring, disembodied things—they were flames leaping, wavering, contending, aspiring. And he remembered the night when he sat alone in the drawing-room of Valentine, and saw the red walls glow, and the light deepen, and saw the stillness grow to movement, and the shadows come away from their background, and take forms—the forms of flames. Was that night a night of prophesy? Were those flames silent voices speaking to the ear of his mind? He looked around him like a man in a strange country, who takes a long breath and liberates his soul in wonder. He looked around, and the shadowy, thin girl leaning forward on the divan, with one arm outstretched as if she gave a message, was among the other flames as a flame upon an altar. At least his instinct had not played him false with regard to her. He knew it now. In the wild and sad streets, where feet of men tread ever, where tears of women flow ever, grow flowers of Paradise, strange flowers, leap flames from the eternal fires of heaven. And the voice of Cuckoo thrilled him as the voice of revelation.

Valentine turned upon the lady of the feathers, hearing her cry.

"Marr!" he said, "your lover who died! Ah!"

The brutality of the remark was so unexpected, so savage, that it struck all those who heard it like a whip. Cuckoo shrank back among her cushions trembling. Julian made a slight forward movement as if to stop Valentine. The doctor laid his hands on the arms of his chair and pressed them hard. He felt a need of physical energy. In the sudden silence Valentine touched the electric bell. Before any one spoke it was answered by Wade who carried a tray on which stood various bottles and glasses.

"We must counteract the exciting effects of our *café noir,*" Valentine said, addressing his guests in a group. "Otherwise we shall be strung up to a pitch of tension that will make us think the requiem of church bells, which we shall hear in a few minutes, the voices of spirits or of spectres. Julian, here is your absinthe. What will you drink, Miss Bright? Brandy, lemonade, whisky?"

"Lemonade, please," Cuckoo said, almost in a whisper.

The tears were crowding in her eyes. She dared not look Julian in the face. Never before had her past risen up before her painted in such grim and undying colours. The reprise of Valentine had been as the reprise of a Maxim gun to a volley fired by a child from an air tube. So Cuckoo felt. But how greatly was she deceived! Perhaps physical conditions played a subtle part in the terrible desolation that seized her now, after her outburst of daring and of excitement. The warmth and smallness of the room, the penetrating scent that filled it, even the movements of her companions, the sound of their voices, suddenly became almost insupportable to Cuckoo. She was the victim of a reaction that was so swift and so intense as to be unnatural. And in it both her mind and body were bound in chains. Then she was petrified. Her very heart felt cold and cramped and then hard, icy, inhuman. Her tears did not fall but were dried up in her eyes like dew by a scorching sun. She looked at Julian, and felt as indifferent towards him as if he had been a shadow on the grass in the evening time. Then he became remote, with a removedness attained by no shadow even. For a shadow is in the world and Julian seemed beyond the world to Cuckoo. She thought, even repeated, with tiny lip movements, the cruel words of Valentine, and they seemed to her no longer cruel, or of any meaning bad or good. For they came from too far away. They were as a cry of shrill music from a cave leagues onward behind the caves of any winds.

Valentine poured out some lemonade and gave it to her. She accepted it mechanically. She even put it to her lips and drank some of it. But her palate was aware of no flavour, no coolness of liquid. And she continued sipping without tasting anything.

Meanwhile Julian was saying to Valentine:

"I don't think I'll take any absinthe to-night. Give me some lemonade too."

"Lemonade for you? Nonsense. I ordered the absinthe specially. You must have some. Here it is."

As he spoke he poured some of the opalescent liquid into a tumbler and handed it to Julian. While he did so his eyes were on the doctor and they gleamed again with a sort of audacity or triumph. He seemed recovering himself, returning to his former mood and veiled intentions. And Dr. Levillier thought he saw the flame of Valentine's soul glow more deeply and fiercely. The three men, as if with one accord, ignored the lady of the feathers at this period of the evening. Valentine, having shot his bolt, left his victim to shudder in the dust. Julian and the doctor, full of pity or of wonder, were drawn instinctively to leave her for the moment outside of the circle of intimacy, lest the conflict should be renewed. They did not know how far outside of it she felt, how dim the twilight was becoming to her eyes, how dim the voices to her ears. She lay back on her pillows in the shadow of the divan, and they supposed her to be listening as before to what they said, to be drawing into her nostrils the scent of the hyacinths and into her soul—it might be—some fragments of their uttered thoughts. But for the moment they seemed to put her outside the door.

Julian did not protest against the absinthe. He took it and placed it on a small table beside him, and as he talked, he occasionally drank a little of it, till his glass was empty. Valentine had again looked at his watch.

"The flame of the year is flickering very low," he said.

This simile of the flame of the year, so ordinary, he had spoken against his will. He asked himself angrily why he had said flame, and again the doctor saw the flame of Valentine's soul trying to leap higher, to aspire to some strange and further region than that in which it seemed to dwell. Julian sat looking at Valentine with a gaze that was surely new in his eyes, the dawning gaze of inquiry which a man directs upon a stranger just come into his life. He had not alluded in any way to Cuckoo's startling and intense interposition. Valentine had killed that conversation with one blow it seemed. They buried it by deserting it. Yet the thought of it was obviously with them, making quick interchange of words on another subject difficult. Valentine had seized again on the poor, prostrate year, yet he had carried even to it the memory of that which seemed to encompass them as with a ring of fire. And that despite himself.

"We shall hear the bells directly," he added. "I hate bells at night. They will sound odd in this room."

"Very odd," the doctor said.

"We ought to sit reviewing our past year," Valentine went on. "Our past year and all it has done for us."

"Do you think it has done much for you, Addison?" the doctor asked. And, despite his intention, there was a certain significance in his tone.

Julian looked rather grave and moody, yet excited too, like a man who might burst into either gaiety or anger at a moment's notice.

"I suppose it has," he answered. "Yes, more than any year since I was quite a boy."

"It has taught you how to live," Valentine said quickly.

"Or how to—die," the doctor could not resist saying.

"Why do you say that, doctor?" Valentine asked sharply. "Julian is neither sick nor sad, are you, Julian?"

"Oh, I don't know. Don't bother about me."

But Valentine seemed suddenly determined that Julian should state in precise terms his contentment with his present fate.

"You are making your grand tour towards happiness," he exclaimed. "Dessert, *café noir*—then the cigarette and contentment."

"I have had the *café noir*," Julian said, indicating his empty cup, which Wade had, by accident, omitted to clear away. "I have had the cigarette."

"Well. What then? Are you unhappy?"

"I tell you I don't know. Give me some more absinthe."

The doctor watched his excitement growing as he drank. It seemed an excitement adverse to Valentine.

"One may have too much black coffee," he suddenly said.

"And that exerts a very depressing effect upon the nerves," said the doctor, taking him literally. "Neither you nor I are likely to sleep well to-night, Addison."

"I never sleep well now, doctor," Julian said.

All this time he continued to regard Valentine in the peculiar, observant manner of a stranger who is trying to make up his mind about the unfamiliar man at whom he looks.

"Then you should not drink black coffee."

As he spoke a very faint sound of bells penetrated to the tent-room.

"The psychological moment!" said Valentine.

And then they were all silent, listening.

To the doctor, the prey of magic art since the soft cry of the lady of the feathers, the bells seemed magical and strange to-night, thin and dreamy and remote. They rang outside the circle of the flames, yet they too had an eerie meaning. Nor did their music come, he thought, from any church tower, from any belfry, summoned by the tugging hands of men. Very softly they rang. Their sound was deadened by the thick draperies. They ceased.

"My year is born," Valentine said.

"Your year?" the doctor repeated.

"Yes. I feel that in this year I shall culminate, I shall touch a point, I shall put the corner-stone to the temple of my ambition. No one can prevent me now, no one. Look, she has fainted!"

He had been watching Cuckoo, and had seen her posture of mere rest change, almost imperceptibly, to the prostration of insensibility.

The doctor sprang up from his chair. Julian uttered an exclamation. Valentine only smiled. The door was opened. A fan was used. Air was let into the room. Presently Cuckoo stirred and sat up.

The three men were gathered round her, and suddenly Valentine said :

"My trance over again. The lady of the feathers imitates me."

Julian turned round to him with abrupt irritation.

"That's not so," he said. "Cuckoo is herself always." He turned again to her.

"Are you better?" he asked, touching her hand gently.

"Yes, I'm all right. It was them—them."

She glanced vaguely round at the tulips, as if searching for the cause of the scent which filled the room.

"There are hyacinths somewhere," the doctor said.

"Yes, they are hidden!" said Valentine. "A hidden power is the greatest power. But now you may see them."

And he drew from a nook guarded by some large ferns a pot of red hyacinths.

Cuckoo sat up and drank a little brandy, which the doctor gave to her. Some colour came into her pale and thin cheeks.

"I'm as right as ninepence now," she said, with an effort after brightness.

The bells began again.

"What's that?" she asked. "Not New Year, is it?"

"Yes," answered Valentine. "A happy New Year to you, lady of the feathers."

Julian was struck by a sudden thought.

"Val," he said, "Cuckoo, I want you to be real friends this year."

He caught hold of Valentine's hand, and placed it in Cuckoo's. But then again a bewilderment seemed to take hold of him, for even as he touched Valentine's hand he looked at him askance, and the eagerness died away from his face.

"I don't know," he muttered to himself, and getting up from the end of the divan where he had been sitting, he moved away towards the fire, leaving Cuckoo's hand in the hand of Valentine.

Valentine smiled coldly on Cuckoo.

"Lady of the feathers," he said, "we are to be allies."

"What's that?" she asked, pulling her hand away directly Julian had turned his back upon them.

"When people fight together against a common enemy they are allies."

"Then we ain't," she whispered, "New Year or not."

"You defy me?" he said, raising his voice so that the doctor might hear the words.

"Yes," she said.

"Doctor, do you hear?"

He seemed suddenly bent on forcing a quarrel. Dr. Levillier

felt again that sense of dread and horror which had attacked him now more than once of late in Valentine's presence. This time the sensation was so acute that he could scarcely combat it sufficiently to reply.

" I hear," he murmured.

" Julian ! " Valentine called. " Julian, come here. Miss Bright wishes to tell you something."

Julian turned round.

" Now, lady of the feathers ! "

But Cuckoo burst into a shrill little laugh. Her head was spinning again.

" I've nothing—nothing to say," she cried out. " Give me some more brandy."

" Very well. Let us all drink to the health of the New Year."

Valentine filled the glasses—Julian's with absinthe—and gave the toast.

" The New Year ! "

They all raised their glasses to their lips simultaneously. One fell with a crash to the ground and was broken. It was Julian's.

" I won't drink it," he said, doggedly, looking at Valentine.

There was a silence. Then Valentine said, calmly :

" Have you an animus against the thing you don't yet know ? "

It was sufficiently obvious that he alluded to the year just coming in upon London. But the words were taken by the doctor, and apparently by Julian, in a hidden and different sense.

" Perhaps because I don't yet know it thoroughly, and had thought I did," Julian answered, staring him full in the face still with that strange glance of mingled interrogation and bewilderment.

Valentine watched him.

" You are treating the poor thing—and my carpet—scurvily, Julian," he said. " And you have startled Miss Bright."

Cuckoo's eyes were shining.

" No," she ejaculated.

Valentine rang the bell and directed Wade to collect the fragments of glass. While the man was doing so silence again reigned, and the little room seemed full of uneasiness. Only Valentine either was or affected to be nonchalant. As soon as Wade had gone he said to the doctor :

" This room is destined to be dedicated to strange uses, and to influence those who come within it. Julian is not himself to-night."

" Are you ? " Julian asked.

" Myself ? "

" Yes."

" My dear Julian, we shall be forced to think the absinthe has been at work too busily in your brain. What is the matter ? "

" Nothing."

" One would think we had been having a sitting. You are so excited."

Julian suddenly drew his breath sharply, as if struck by a shot of an idea.

" Let us have one," he cried.

The distant bells rang faintly. The doctor thrilled to the suggestion, still bound by magic surely. For now, since the inspiring exclamation of Cuckoo, which had broken his theories on the wheel and swept his reason like a dead flower along the wind, he no longer condemned as a danger only that which had produced the trance from which, as from a strange prison, had come the new Valentine. The former sitting had, it seemed, beckoned that trance, and with the trance had beckoned an incredibly evil and powerful thing. What if that which had the power to give had also the power to take away ? Often it is so in ordinary conditions of life. Why not also in extraordinary conditions ? So his thoughts ran, fantastically enough, to the sound of the far-off bells.

" A good notion," he said on the spur of the moment and this quick reflection.

" You think so ? " said Valentine. " You who condemned us, even wrung a promise from us against sitting."

His regard was suspicious.

" Perhaps I have changed my mind. Perhaps I take the matter less seriously," said the doctor.

He had never been more near lying, nor was he ashamed of his dissimulation. There are creatures against which we must, whatever our principles, take up the nearest weapon that comes to hand. The doctor looked at Julian and at Valentine, and could have perjured himself a thousand times to wrest the one from the other.

" But Miss Bright is ill," said Valentine.

" No I ain't. I'm all right now," Cuckoo said.

She did not understand what was being proposed, but she gathered that the doctor desired it. That was enough for her. Valentine looked at them all three with eyes that plainly betokened a busy mind. Then a smile flickered over his lips. It was the smile of one in power watching his slaves creeping at their work—for him. He touched the point—of which he had spoken earlier in the evening— in that smile, a point of delirium.

" Let them try to break me," his mind said within itself. " Their very trial shall consolidate my empire."

And then his eyes left the others and rested only on Julian.

" Very well, we will sit," he said.

CHAPTER IV

THE FIFTH SITTING

JULIAN was painfully excited, but he strove to repress all evidences of his inward turmoil as he began to pull out a table and arrange it in the centre of the room. This act threw him with a jerk back into the days of the past, recalling so vividly the former life of himself and Valentine that he could not help saying:

"This is like last year."

"Like the year that the locust hath eaten," Valentine answered. "We must push our empty white years down into the water, Julian."

Julian made no reply. The table was soon arranged. The screen was drawn more closely round the fire which had been allowed to burn low. Four chairs were set. Valentine turned to Cuckoo who sat hunched on the divan staring with wide open eyes at these preparations.

"Will you come?" he said, with his hands on the back of one of the chairs.

"Whatever are we goin' to do?" she asked nervously.

"Something very simple—and perhaps very foolish," said the doctor, wondering, indeed, now the moment for beginning the phantasy was arrived, whether he was not to blame for encouraging a thing that in his under-mind he so thoroughly disapproved of. "We are going to sit round that table in the dark with our hands upon it, and wait."

"Whatever for?"

Her simple and blatant question caused the doctor actually to blush. His confusion was quite obvious, but it was covered by Julian, who exclaimed, rather roughly:

"Now, Cuckoo, don't chatter, but come here and sit quiet."

He drew her from the divan into a chair and sat down beside her. Valentine glided swiftly into the chair on her other side and said:

"Oh, doctor, I forgot the light. Do you mind turning it out?"

The doctor obeyed, felt his way to the chair opposite Cuckoo and sat down.

Almost at the moment he turned out the light the bells that rang
"*Le roi est mort, vive le roi*" ceased. Cuckoo was directed to lay
her hands on the table and to touch with her fingers the fingers of
her companions. She did so, trembling. This was a new experience
to her, and her entire lack of knowledge of what was expected to
happen filled the darkness with immoderate possibilities, and her
soul with awe and with confusion. Then to sit between the man
she loved and the man she loathed, thus in the blackness, was a
nerve-shaking experience which her preceding fainting fit did not
deprive of its normal terrors. The hand of Valentine and the hand
of Julian were as ice and as fire to her. The darkness seemed
crowded with nameless things. She could fancy that she heard it
whisper incessantly in her ear.

But the real interest of this sitting, to any little demon gifted
with a miraculous power of pushing its detective way into the minds
of the sitters, would have lain, perhaps, chiefly in the mind of Dr.
Levillier. It has been said that, suddenly struck to the soul by the
conviction with which the instinctive Cuckoo pronounced those
words, "From Marr," Dr. Levillier entered into a new world,
abandoning old landmarks. He remained in this new world of the
senses certainly, but already he was becoming accustomed to it,
clear-headed, keen-sighted, even reasonable in it. Moved by some
strange conviction that he was in the presence of an inexplicable
mystery, he no longer tried to explain it in some ordinary fashion.
He abandoned his theory of insanity, or it abandoned him. In any
case it was dead, buried, whether he would or no. He recognised a
mystery at present beyond his capacity to understand or to explain.
Having got thus far, and having entered, at Julian's word, into this
present circumstance of sitting, table-turning, or -rapping, or whatever you may choose to call it, he cleared any ordinary furniture of
doctor's prejudices right out of his mind—made a clean sweep of
them. That done—and the doing of it required some strong effort—
his mind was receptive, ready for anything, odd or ordinary, that
might come along. There he sat with his empty room waiting to be
filled—the only reasonable way of waiting for that of which we have
no knowledge. He did not clamour "I won't," or "I will." He
said nothing at all, only waited with the strict desire and intention
of recognising things to be what they truly were, neither dressing
them up nor tearing their garments off their backs. When he put
out the light and sat down, what he expected—so far as he expected
anything—was this, that the addition of darkness would add a cloud
to his mind, and endeavour to give various finishing touches to any
spurious excitement created in him, however much against his will,
by the enemy's doings. In this expectation he was entirely deceived.
The falling of darkness drew a veil from his mind, leaving his mental

sight singularly, even preternaturally clear. The falling of silence gave an amazing acuteness to his inner sense of hearing. Certain people are so made that they can, under certain conditions, and at certain moments, hear the workings of their neighbours' minds, as you and I can hear the whirr of machinery, or the cry of a child in the street. An ordinary man or woman can only hear a mind when lips, teeth, and tongue utter it with living sounds that set the air in vibration. These abnormal people hear, in these abnormal moments, the silent murmurs of the mind making no effort at all to utter itself through the usual speech apparatus. Till this moment the doctor had supposed himself to be an entirely normal man, but he had been sitting only a very short time before he began to become aware of the silent murmurs of these three minds around him. The darkness set his own mind free from clouds of excitement and from mists of unreason. That was the first step. But it did more. It developed in him this marvellous faculty of the hearing of silence, called by some divination. All his senses were rendered amazingly acute. A perfectly distinct impression of the precise feelings of Cuckoo, of Valentine, and of Julian respectively came to him as he sat there, although he could neither see nor hear them. Each of them seemed to pour his or her thoughts into the doctor's mind. Thus, at first, did his empty room become furnished with the thoughts of his companions. He was sitting in the circle between Julian and Valentine and held their hands. And it was Valentine who forged the first link in this strange chain of unuttered communication. As the darkness cleared the doctor's mind, and set him once more on his feet— although in a new world—an aroma of triumph floated to him softly, like a scent in a damp wood at night. He heard then the mind of Valentine murmuring in the stillness the Litany of its glory, a long and an ornate Litany, deep and full, and he knew that he had been right in supposing that Valentine had invited him to witness that glory. But the doctor became aware too, that at moments the Litany faltered, hesitated, as if the mind of Valentine grew uncertain or was assailed by vague fears. And these fears ran like little pale furtive things to Valentine from the lady of the feathers. By degrees the doctor could imagine that he actually saw them stealing back and forth. Now one would come alone as if to listen to the Litany, and then another would follow, and another, and growing brave, they would combine against it. Then Valentine would waver and become uneasy, as one who hears little voices crying against him in the night, and knows not whence they come or from whom. But the Litany would begin again and Valentine would triumph over the pale fears and they would shrink away. And in the Litany one name recurred again and again—the name of Julian. Over him was the triumph. In his ruin and fall and ultimate destruction the glory lived. To witness the complete possibility of this ruin, the complete sovereignty of this glory, the doctor and the lady of the feathers were there. And the doctor grew to feel that only some outside circumstance, alarming Valentine to anxiety, and waking Julian to a new observation, had hindered the intended triumph. What circumstance was that? He looked back along the past evening and found it in himself, in his theory that a soul expelled was not necessarily a soul dead. The rift in the glory of the Litany came with that. Valentine was trying to close it by this act of sitting, to impress the strength of his will upon his companions in the darkness. The doctor felt his effort like a continually repeated blow, stealthy and hard and merciless.

And now in the darkness and in the silence the doctor heard the mind of Julian. Another scent floated through that imagined damp and breathing wood from another—but how different—soul flower. No Litany of triumph murmured in the blackness where Julian sat, but a hoarse and broken solo, part despair, part fear, part anger, and all perplexed and flooded with bewilderment and with excitement. The doctor drew into him the murmur of Julian's mind until it seemed to become, for the time, the murmur of his own mind. He was conscious of a dreadful turmoil of doubt, and dread and perplexity, so strong, so painful, that it lay upon him like a dense and a suffocating burden. In that moment he knew utterly that the greatest load in the world laid on any man is the load of his own, perhaps beloved, sin. He was staggering wearily with Julian away from the light. His eyes were dim—with the eyes of Julian. His ears, like Julian's, were assailed with the dastard clamour of the calling sins. " Listen! Listen! you want me. I am here. Take me! Take me!" And the weltering seas of heavy flooding impotence rolled round him as they rolled round Julian. He grew numb and vacant and inert, then—alive ever to the murmur of Julian's mind—caught a glimpse, through the waters of that whelming sea, of far-away light, and heard that the voices of the importunate sins grew fainter. But whether the voices were loud or low, whether the seas flowed above his head or sank and failed, he was always conscious of the dominating mood of almost wild perplexity and a madness of bewilderment. For Julian stirred under the yoke that Valentine had laid upon him as if at last conscious distinctly that it was indeed a yoke, and that it galled him; as if at last conscious, too, that without that yoke was freedom. And he shot against Valentine in the darkness arrows of inquiry. But always he lived in doubt and almost in terror.

And then, detaching himself from the triumph, touched with anxiety of Valentine, and from the wild turmoil of Julian, Dr. Levillier opened the door of his mind wide, and the lady of the feathers entered in.

He heard the thoughts of a woman.

That was strangest of all—the most fantastic, eerie, wayward, wonderful music the doctor had dreamed of.

Have you listened to far-off and mingling melodies at night? melodies of things opposed and differing, yet drawn together, in strange places far from your home? Have you heard a woman wailing over some abominable sorrow in a dark house, and an organ—before which filthy children dance fantastically—playing a merry Neapolitan tune in front of it, while the mutter of scowling men comes from the blazing corner where the gin-palace faces the night? There you have sorrow, sunshine, crime, singing together in a great city. Or have you stood in a land not your own, and gleaned the whisper of an ancient river, the sough of a desert wind, the hoarse and tuneless song of a black man at a water-wheel, the soprano ballad of a warbling hotel English lady, and the remote and throbbing roar of a savage Soudanese hymn and beaten drums from the golden eastern night? There you have nature, toil, shrill civilisation and war claiming you with one effort in a sad and sweet country. Or have you, in a bright and dewy morning, heard the "murmur of folk at their prayers," the drone of a church organ, and, beyond the hedgerow, two graceless lovers quarrelling, and an atheist, leaning over the church gate, sneering to his fellow at the devotion of deluded Sabbath-keepers? There you have love of the hidden and faith, love of the visible and distrust, hatred of hidden love and faithlessness, making a symphony for you. Such mingled music is strange—strange as life. But to the doctor the music of this girl, Cuckoo, in the dark seemed stranger and more eerie far. Her mind sang to him of a thousand things in a moment, as is the fashion of women. Only men normally hear but one, at most two or three, of the many feminine melodies. And now Dr. Levillier heard them all, as a man may hear those differing songs already recounted, simultaneously and clearly. Degradation and the hopelessness that catches it by the hand, passion and the strength and purity of passion, hatred, fear, physical fatigue, ignorant nervousness, grossness of the gutter, which will cling even to a soul capable of great devotion and noble effort, and accompany it on the upward journey, very far and very high, resolve and shrinking, mere street boy virulence of enmity, and mere angel tenderness of pity—all these sang their song from the mind and heart of Cuckoo to the mind and heart of the doctor. It was a chorus of women in one woman, as it so often is in the dearest women we know. In that choir an outcast sat, hating, by girl who was all love and reverence. And they sang out of the same hymn-book; Jenny joining her voice with Susannah, Mary Magdalene and Mary Mother, so near together in one thing, so far apart in another, alike in this that both were singing. And in that choir—celestial and infernal—sang the jealous woman with grey cheeks and haggard eyes, and the timorous woman, and she of the fearless face, and the woman who could scale the stars for the creature she worshipped, and the woman who could lie down in the mud and let the world see her there, and the woman who had sold her soul for food, and a thin woman, such a thin, almost transparent, wistful creature, who was facing the thing men call with bated breath—starvation. She sang too, but, of all these women, she was the only one the doctor could not rightly hear nor rightly see. For she, as yet, was remote, far down the level line of that choir, hardly perhaps one with it yet, faint of voice, dim of outline.

The doctor heard the choir sing, and then——

His mind, as the time of the darkness grew longer, continued to grow more and more clear, until he felt thoroughly, and was able to try to analyse its unnatural condition. Scales had fallen from him and from his companions for him. Their bodies were clothed, their souls, their flames, seemed stripped bare and offered to him naked. He had examined them with this greedy, yet sane, attention and curiosity. He had led them into the empty room and stayed with them there. He had heard the Litany of the Glory of Valentine, and the suffocation, and the anger, and the stirring beneath his yoke of Julian. He had heard the many women sing in the heart of the lady of the feathers. But all this seemed leading him forward and onward, step by step, as to a threshold beyond which was some greater, some more importunate thing. And he took the last step with Cuckoo. It was as if he was handed on from one room to another, as is the fashion in the palace of a great king, his name being called in each, and sent before, like a voice sent on the wind, and as if Cuckoo was in the last ante-room that gave upon the audience chamber. Now he had arrived, and suddenly a great wave of mysterious expectation ran over him and filled the cup of his soul. He felt that he stood still and waited. The sense of Cuckoo, of all she felt and thought in the darkness, gradually dropped away from him, like leaves from a tree, till every branch was leafless. And this autumnal ravishment, like the ravishment of nature, was but a preparation surely for a future Spring.

The doctor waited outside that door, beyond which, perhaps, Spring blossomed and sang. He lost at last all sense of being in a company of people, and felt as one feels who is entirely alone, expectant, calm, ready. And still only the darkness and the silence. Nothing more at first. But presently what seemed to him a marvel.

He had by this time grown at ease with his power of thought-reading, at ease with this new sense of the hearing of silence. The differing scents of these three flowers hidden in the night had been breathed out to him. With infallible certainty he had recognised

each one, differentiated the one from the other. And as the scent
of one flower had failed, the scent of another had risen upon him
until he had known the heart of each of the three. Then for awhile
was the night scentless, silent, blank, empty. But presently the
doctor was aware of an uneasiness and of an anxiety stealing upon
him. Whence it came he could not tell. Only this he knew, that
he received it from something, but that it came neither from the
lady of the feathers, from Valentine, nor from Julian. From whom
then could it emanate, this weird eagerness, this fluttering, pulsing
fear and hope and intention? From himself only? He asked
himself that question. Was he communing in the dark with his own
soul? He knew that he was not. The scent of this knew and un
known flower grew stronger in the night, more penetrating and
intentional. Yet was it vaguer, more distant, than that emitted by
those other three flowers. The exact impression received by the
doctor at this moment was very subtle. Precisely it was this. It
seemed to him that he was gradually coming into communication
with a fourth mind, or soul, that this soul was actually more strong
more vehement, even more determined, than the souls of his three
companions, but that some barrier removed it from him, set it very
far off. The flame of a match held to a man's eyes may dazzle
him more than the flame of a great fire on the horizon. This new
flame was as the latter in comparison to match flames that had
been flaring in the doctor's eyes. And this great and distant flame
burned slowly in a smoke of mystery and upon the verge of dense
darkness.

Never had the doctor known so peculiar, and even awe-striking
an experience as that which now he underwent. What utterly be
wildered him was the circumstance of this undoubted new and
definite personality enclosed in this tiny room with him and with
his three companions. He was receiving the impression of the
thoughts of a stranger. Yet there was no stranger in the chamber
And he was vexed and curiously irritated by the fact of the impres
sion being at the same time very vague and very violent, like the
cry of a man which reaches you faintly from a very long distance,
but which you feel instinctively to have been uttered with the frantic
force of death or of despair. And the mind of this stranger was
tugging at the doctor's mind, anxiously, insistently. There was a
depth of distress in it that was as no mere human distress, and that
moved the doctor to a mood beyond the mood of tears or of prayers.
There came over him an awful sense of pity for this stranger soul.
What had it done? How was it circumstanced? In what ghastly
train of events did it move? It was surely powerful and helpless at
the same time; a cripple with a mind on fire with fight; Samson
blind. He felt that it wanted something—of him, or of his com-

panions, some light in its severe desolation. Deeper and deeper grew his horror and pity for it, deeper and deeper his sense of its ill fate. The woe of it was unearthly, yet more than earthly woe. Similes came to the doctor to compare with its dreadful circumstance : A child motherless in a world all winter ; a saint devoted to hell by some great error of God ; even one more blasphemous, and more terrible still : God worsted by humanity, and, at the last, helpless to reclaim the souls to which He had Himself given being ; lonely God in a lonely heaven, seeing far-off hell bursting with the countless multitudes of the writhing lost. This last simile stayed with him. He fancied he felt—not heard—the voice of this frustrate God calling to him : " Do what I could not do. Strive to help My impotence. A little—a little—and even yet hell would stand empty, the vacant courts of heaven be filled. Act—act—act."

" Doctor, why are you trembling ? Why are you trembling ? "

It was the voice of Valentine that spoke. The doctor, by an effort so painful that the memory of it remained with him to the end of his life, recalled his mind from its journey.

" Trembling ! " he said. " What do you mean ? I am all right. I am quietly in my place. How long have we been sitting ? "

" An immense time I fancy. It seems fruitless. Julian ! "

" Yes."

Julian's voice sounded heavy and weary.

" Don't you think we had better stop ? "

" If you like."

Valentine got up and turned on the light.

Then they saw that the lady of the feathers, leaning back in her chair, was fallen asleep, no doubt from sheer weariness. Her face was very white, and in sleep its expression had become ethereal and purified. Her thin hands still rested nervelessly upon the table. She seemed like a little child that had known sorrow early, and sought gently to lose the sense of it in rest.

" Cuckoo," Julian said, leaning over her, " Cuckoo ! "

She stirred and woke.

" I'm awfully done," she murmured, in her street voice. " Pardon ! "

She sat up.

" I seemed as if I was put to sleep," she said.

" You were," Valentine answered her. " I willed that you should sleep."

He looked at the doctor, and his eyes said :

" I have had my triumph. You witness it."

Cuckoo reddened with anger, but she said nothing.

" Did you feel anything Julian ? " Valentine asked.

Julian was looking strangely hopeless.

"Nothing," he said. "It's all different from what it was, like a dead thing that used to be alive."

It seemed as if the sitting had filled him with a dogged despair.

"A dead thing," he repeated.

Then he went over to the spirit-stand and poured himself out more absinthe.

"And you doctor?" said Valentine. "What did you feel?"

The doctor met his glance with a careful calm.

"I was thinking all the time," he said, "of other things. Not of the table or of table-turning."

When he and Cuckoo left the flat that night, or rather in the chill first morning of the New Year, they left Julian with Valentine.

He said he would stay, speaking in the voice of a man drugged almost into uncertainty of his surroundings.

CHAPTER V

THE LADY OF THE FEATHERS STARVES

Down in her dreary kitchen, among her dingy pots and pans, Mrs. Brigg was filled with an anger that seemed to her as righteous as the anger of a Puritan against Museum opening on Sunday. Her ground-floor lodger was going to the bad. Analysed, reduced to its essence, that was her feeling about the lady of the feathers. Cuckoo had lived at No. 400 for a considerable time. Being, in some ways, easy-going, or, perhaps one should say rather, reckless, she had given herself with a good enough grace to be plucked by the claws of the landlady. She had endured being ruthlessly rooked, with but little murmuring, as do so many of her patient class, accustomed to be the prey of each unit in the large congregation of the modern Fates. For months and years she had paid a preposterous price for her badly furnished little rooms. She had been overcharged habitually for every morsel of food she ate, every drop of beer, or of tea, she drank, every fire that was kindled in her badly cleaned grate, every candle that lighted her, almost every match she struck. She and Mrs. Brigg had had many rows, had, times without number, lifted up their respective voices in vituperation, and shown command of large and vile vocabularies. But these rows had not been on the occasion of the open cheating of the former by the latter. Fallen women, as they are called, seldom resent being cheated by those in whose houses they live. Rather do they expect the bleeding process as part of the penalty to be paid for a lost character. The landlord of the leper is owed for his charity and tolerance good hard cash. The landlady of the Pariah puts down mentally in each added up bill this item: "To loss of character—so much." And the Pariah understands and pays. Such is the recognised dispensation. Mrs. Brigg had had a fine time of robbery during the stay of Cuckoo in her ugly house, and, in consequence, a certain queer and slow respect for her lodger had very gradually grown up in her withered and gnarled old nature. She had that feeling towards Cuckoo that a bad boy, too weak to steal apples, has towards a bad boy not too weak to steal them. It could hardly be called an actual liking. Of that the old creature in her nethermost Hades was nearly incapable. But she enjoyed seeing apples off the tree lying in her kitchen, and so could have patted any hands that had gathered them nefariously. So far as she looked into the future she saw there always Cuckoo, and herself robbing Cuckoo comfortably, faithfully, unblamed and unrepentant, while the years rolled along, the leech ever at its sucking profession.

Now this agreeable vision was abruptly changed. This slide of the magic lantern was smashed to fragments. And Mrs. Brigg was filled with the righteous anger of a baulked and venerable robber. As a mother, dependent upon the earnings of her child in some godly profession might feel on the abrupt and reasonless refusal of that child to continue in it, so did Mrs. Brigg feel now.

The lady of the feathers had, for the moment, at least, given up her profession. She sat at home with folded hands at night. It was earth-shaking. It stirred the depths of the Brigg being. Quakings of a world in commotion were as nothing to it. And the sweet Brigg dream that had dawned on the last night of the old year, dream of a rich "toff" in love with Cuckoo and winding her up to gilded circles, in which the fall of night set gay ladies bareheaded, and scattered all feathered hats to limbo, died childless and leaving no legacies. Certainly Cuckoo was not making money on the quiet enough in one night to keep her as seven or fourteen nights would formerly have supplied. Mrs. Brigg questioned, remonstrated, stormed, sulked, was rude, insinuating, artful, blunt, and blackguardly—all to no purpose. Cuckoo would give no explanation of her conduct. In the day she went out, but Mrs. Brigg was not to be deceived by that. She based her observations and conclusions on weighty matters connected with the culinary art and with things about which her trained, disgraceful intelligence could not be deceived. Cuckoo was falling into poverty. In the eyes of Brigg she had formerly been in touch with riches, that is to say, she had—so the landlady considered—lived well. She had got along without falling into debt. The exorbitant rent, regularly earned, had been as regularly paid. The Brigg perquisites had not been disputed. No watchful eye had been directed upon the claws that grabbed and clung, the fingers that filched and retained.

But now was come a devastating change. Cuckoo grown, or growing, poor was no longer easy-going. Living much less well, she also began to keep a sharp eye on all she had. If it went mysteriously, without explanatory action of her own, she called loudly on Brigg for enlightenment. Where had it gone? The old lady, disgusted to be brought to subterfuge, a thing to which she was frankly unaccustomed, lied freely and with a good courage. But her lies did not stand her in much stead with Cuckoo, who had, from the start, no intention whatever of believing any word she might say. So war of a novel kind came about between them. Mrs. Brigg was forced to live and hear herself named thief, a distressing circumstance which she could scarcely surmount with dignity, whatever she might manage in the way of fortitude. Denial only armed forces for the attack. Battles were numerous and violent. Cuckoo, who had in some directions no perception at all of what was humiliating, took to measuring proportions of legs of mutton going down to Hades and re-measuring them on their return. If the inches did not tally, Mrs. Brigg knew it. Her soul revolted against such surveyor's work on meat that her own hands had cooked. She called Cuckoo names, and was called worse names in reply. But still the measurings went on, and still Cuckoo spent her evenings within doors, sometimes without a fire in the winter cold.

Mrs. Brigg therefore said within herself that Cuckoo had gone to the bad, and beheld, with fancy's agitated eye, a time in the near future when not only perquisites would be no more, but the very rent itself would be in jeopardy. Fury sparkled in her heart.

Meanwhile the situation of Cuckoo above stairs was becoming at once sordid and tragic. Starvation is always sordid. It exposes cheek-bones, puts sharp points on elbows, writes ugliness over a face, and sets a wolf crouching in the heart. Tragic it must always be, for a peculiar sorrow walks with it; but when it is obstinate, and springs from the mule in a human being, the tragedy has a lustre, a colour of its own. The lady of the feathers was for ever obstinate. She had been obstinate in vice, she was now obstinate in virtue. In the old days Julian had said to her, "Take some of my money and let the streets alone—even for one night." She had refused. Now Dr. Levillier had said to her, "Prove your will. Lean on it. Do something for Julian." She could only do this one thing. She could only leave the street! With frowning, staring obstinacy she left it. There was always something pathetically blind about Cuckoo's proceedings. She was not lucid. But once she had grasped an idea she was like the limpet on the rock. So now she sat at home. Out of her earnings she had managed to save a very little money. One or two men had made her small presents from time to time. For a little while she could exist. As she sat alone on those strange new evenings she did much mental arithmetic, calculating how long, with these reduced expenses, which brought Mrs. Brigg's so low, she could live without earning. Sad sums were these, whether rightly or wrongly worked out. The time must be short. And afterwards? This question drove Cuckoo out in the mornings, vaguely seeking an occupation. She knew that London was full of "good" girls, who went forth to work while she lay in bed in the morning, and came home to tea, and one boiled egg and watercress, when she started out in the evening. So she put on her hat and jacket and went forth to find out what work they did, and whether she could join in it. Those were variegated pilgrimages full of astonishment. Cuckoo would stroll along the road till she saw, perhaps, a girl who looked good—that is, as unlike herself as possible—descend into the frost, or the mud from a 'bus. Then she would dog the footsteps of this girl, find out where she went, with a view of deducing from it what she did. In this manner she once came to a sewing-machine shop in Praed Street, on the trail of a bright looking stranger, who walked gaily as to pleasant toil. Cuckoo remained outside while the stranger went in and disappeared. She examined the window—rows of sewing-machines, beyond them the dressed head of a woman in a black silk gown. What did the stranger do here to gain a living, and that bright smile of hers? Suddenly Cuckoo walked into the shop and up to the lady with the dressed head.

" A machine, ma'am ? " said the lady, with a very female look at Cuckoo.

Cuckoo shook her head.

" What can I do for you ? "

" I'd like some work."

" Work ! " said the lady, her voice travelling from the contralto to the soprano register.

" I ain't got nothing to do. I want something ; I'll do anything, like she does," this, with a nod in the direction of a door through which the pleasant stranger had vanished.

" Miss King ; our bookkeeper ! You know her ? "

" No. I only see her in the street."

" Good morning," came from the lady, and a back confronted Cuckoo.

The pilgrimages were resumed. Cuckoo visited dressmakers, bonnet-shops, A B C establishments, with no success. Her face, even when unpainted, told its tale. Nature can write down the truth of a sin better than art. Cuckoo learnt that fact by her walks. But still she trudged, learning each day more truths, one of which—a finale to the long sermon, it seemed—was that there is no army on earth more difficult to enlist in, under certain circumstances, her own, than the army of good working girls. The day she thoroughly understood that finale Cuckoo went home and had a violent row with Mrs. Brigg. A cold scragg of mutton was supposed to be the bone of contention, but that was only supposition. Cuckoo was really cursing Mrs. Brigg because the world is full of close boroughs, not at all because cold mutton has not learnt how to achieve eternal life, while at the same time fulfilling its duties as an edible. Not understanding this subtlety of emotion, Mrs. Brigg let herself loose in sarcasm.

" Why don't yer go out of a night ? she screamed, battering with
one hand on a tea-tray, held perpendicularly, to emphasise her
words. " What's come to yer ? Go out ; go out of a night."

" Shan't."

" Turned pious 'ave yer ? " sneered the landlady. " Or waitin' for
a 'usband ? Which is it to be ? Mr. Haddison, I dessey ! Hee,
hee, hee."

She burst into a bitter snigger. Cuckoo flushed scarlet and
uttered words of the pavement. Any one hearing her then must
have put her down as utterly unredeemed and irredeemable, a
harridan to bandy foul language with a cabman, or to outvie a
street urchin bumped against by a rival in the newspaper trade.
She covered Mrs. Brigg with abuse, prompted by the gnawings at
her heart, the hunger of mind and body, fear of the future, wonder
at the impossibilities of life. Her own greatness—for her love and
following obstinate unselfishness, without religious prompting or
self-respect, as it was, might be called great—turned sour within
her heart at such a moment. Her very virtue became as vinegar.
Mrs. Brigg was drowned in epithets and finally pushed furiously out
into the passage. Cuckoo turned from the door to Jessie yelping,
and directed a kick at the little dog. Jessie wailed, as only a toy
dog can, like the " mixture " stop of an organ, wailed and ran as one
that runs to meet an unknown future. Then Cuckoo pursued,
caught her, and burst into tears over her. The little creature's
domed skull and india-rubber ears were wet with the tears of her
mistress. And she whimpered, too, but with much relief, for she
was back in her world of Cuckoo's lap, and could not be quite
unhappy there. But in what a world was Cuckoo !

It will be said that Dr. Levillier knew of her circumstances ; but
anxiously kind and thoughtful though he was, he did not yet realise
the effect of his advice given to the lady of the feathers during the
drive on the Hampstead heights. He had told her to prove her
will by doing the thing that Julian had asked of her. But he did not
know what Julian had asked. And he did not comprehend the
bitter fruit that her following of his further advice to keep from
low and loveless actions must bring to the ripening. When he
spoke, as the sun went down on London, he was carried on by
excitement, and was thinking rather of the fate of Julian, the
diablerie of Valentine, than of the individual life of the girl at his
side. He was arming her for the battle. But he dreamed of
weapons, not of rations, like many an enthusiast. He forgot that
the soldier must be fed as well as armed. He said to Cuckoo,
" Fight ! Use your woman's wit ; use your heart ; wake up, and
throw yourself into this battle." And she, filled with determination, and with a puzzled, pent ardour to do something, did not know

what to do except—starve. So she began to starve for Julian's sake, and because the doctor had fired her heart. He had said, " Do what Julian asked you to do, and show Julian that you have done it." But something within Cuckoo forbade her to fulfil this last injunction. She could give up the street, but an extraordinary shyness, false shame and awkwardness had so far prevented her from letting Julian know it. If he knew it, he would understand what it meant for her, and would force money on her, and Cuckoo, having once made up her mind that money and Julian should never be linked together in her relations with him, stuck to secrecy on this subject with her normal dull pertinacity. So matters move slowly towards a deadlock. The lady of the feathers did not neglect the pawnshop. Her few trinkets went there very soon. Then things that were not trinkets, that green evening dress, for instance, the imitation lace, and one day a sale took place. Cuckoo disposed, for an absurd sum, of her title-deed, the headgear that had given birth to her nickname. She was no longer the lady of the feathers. The hat that had seen so much of her life reposed upon the head of virtue and knew Piccadilly no more. But Julian's present remained with her, and indeed came into every day use. And still Jessie sported her yellow riband. Later there came a terrible time when the eyes of Cuckoo—appraising everything on which they looked—fell, with that fateful expression not merely upon Jessie's yellow riband, but upon Jessie herself. But that time was not quite yet.

While Cuckoo endured this fate, Dr. Levillier was in a perplexity of another kind. The first round of that battle had ended in apparent decisive defeat of Valentine's accusers. During the evening the fortunes of war had certainly wavered to the doctor's side. Julian had displayed sudden and strong signs of an awakening; but the sitting had thrown him back into his dream, had pushed him more firmly beneath the yoke of his master. The doctor did not understand why. Although he recognised the fact, he could not divine the exact effect that disappointment would have upon sudden suspicious eagerness. Julian had been waked to wonder, to observe Valentine for an instant with new eyes, to look the mystery of the great change in him in the face, and know it as a mystery. Yes, he had even thought of Valentine as a stranger, and said to himself, " Where then is my friend ? " The new Valentine had risen out of the ashes of sleep. Julian pressed forward the sitting as a means, the only one, of searching among these ashes. In the old days each sitting had quickened his senses into a strange life, as the last sitting quickened the senses of the doctor. But to Julian this last sitting brought nothing but disappointment; the thing which had been alive was dead, and so the sudden hope which had come with the new wonder died too. He supposed that he had been the prey of an absurd fancy created by the idle words of the doctor, or by an idiotic movement of his mind, which had cried to him on a sudden : " If the Valentine you love and revere is really gone away, what are you worshipping now ? " Now, in his heavy disappointment he thought of this cry as a mad exclamation, and he sought to drown all memory of it, and every memory in fresh vices, and in his fatal habit of absinthe drinking. He lay down under the yoke beneath which he had previously crept, and so succeeded in going still lower. So that night Valentine had won his intended triumph, although for a while it had been in jeopardy.

Dr. Levillier was in perplexity; he had been brought to the very threshold of revelation, and then thrust back into an everyday world of thwarted hopes and broken ambitions. But the memory of magic was still with him, and gave him a feeling of unrest, and a pertinacity that was not to be without reward for ever. Valentine's triumph held for the conqueror a poison-seed from which a flower was to spring. The doctor's determination to continue the fight was frustrated at this time by Julian rather than by Valentine. Julian's disappointment plunged him in a deep sea of indifference, from which he declined to be rescued. The doctor's invitations to him remained unanswered. If he called, Julian was never at home. Several times the doctor met Valentine, who, with a deprecating smile, told him that Julian was away on some mad errand.

" I seldom see him now," he even added upon one occasion. " He has gone beyond me. Julian is living so fast, that my poor agility cannot keep pace with him."

It seemed as if the whole affair was going completely out of the doctor's knowledge, and that even Cuckoo had no longer any power of attraction for Julian. The doctor wrote to her and received an ill-spelt answer, telling him that Julian had not been near her since the last night of the year. In this event the doctor's only hope lay in keeping closely in touch with Valentine. To do this proved an easy matter. Valentine responded readily to his invitations, asked him out in return, seemed glad to be with him. The doctor believed he read the reason of this joy in Valentine's anxiety to prove the depth of Julian's degradation. He had now begun to play devilishly upon a pathetic stop, and sought every occasion to descant upon the social ruin that was overtaking Julian, and his deep concern in the matter. This hypocrisy was so transparent and so offensive that there were moments when it stank in the doctor's nostrils, and he could scarcely repress his horror and disgust. Yet to show them would be not only impolitic, but would only add fuel to the flames of Valentine's pyre of triumph. So the doctor, too, sought to play his part, and never wearied in seeking Julian, although his quest was in vain. From Valentine he gathered that Julian was now dropped even by the gay world, that his clubs looked askance at him, that men began to shun him, and to whisper against him.

"The stone is going down in the sea," Valentine said.

"Who threw it into the sea?" the doctor asked. "Tell me that."

Valentine shrugged whimsical shoulders.

"Fate, I suppose," he answered. "Fate is a mischievous boy, and is always throwing stones. Is the lady of the feathers disconsolate?"

The doctor did not trust himself to reply, but was silent, plotting another meeting to sit. For he had begun, still magic bound perhaps, to divine some possible salvation in that act which he had once condemned, led, as he thought, by knowledge and by experience, of the nervous system forsooth! Now he was led unscientifically by pure feeling, like a child by a warm, close hand. The instinct that had guided Cuckoo seemed to stretch out fingers to him. He must respond. But how to reach Julian? While he strove to solve this problem it was solved for him in a manner utterly surprising to him, although engineered by words of his.

Cuckoo wrought a strange work with the skeleton hands of hunger and of pain.

CHAPTER VI

THE SELLING OF JESSIE

ONE chill morning of earliest February, a stirring of Jessie at the foot of her bed wakened Cuckoo from a short and uneasy sleep. She opened her eyes to the faint light that filtered through the green Venetian blind. Jessie moved again, slowly rotating like a drowsy top, then suddenly dropped into the warm centre of a nest of bed-clothes, breathing a big-dog sigh of satisfaction that shook her tiny frame. She slept. But she had wakened her mistress, who lay with her head resting on one hand, deep in thought while the day grew outside. Cuckoo, having directed her steps down a blind alley had, not unnaturally, reached a dead wall, blotting out the horizon. Lying there, she faced it. She stared at the wall, and the wall seemed to stare back at her. Perhaps for that reason a dull blank-ness flowed over and filled her mind, and made her widely opened eyes almost as expressionless as the eyes of a corpse. For a long time she lay in this alive stupor. Then Jessie stirred again, and Cuckoo, as she had been before spurred into wakefulness, was stirred into thoughtfulness. She began to pass the near past, the present, even-tually the future in review. The past was a crescendo, solitude growing louder each night, poverty growing louder, obstinacy grow-ing louder, Mrs. Brigg growing louder. What an orchestra! Cuckoo had not seen Julian once. She had seen the doctor, to be told of his baffled efforts, of Julian's escape from all his friends, of Valentine's declaration of the stone going down in the sea, of utter deadlock, utter stagnation. For the doctor treated Cuckoo frankly as a brave woman, not deceitfully as a timid child to be buoyed on the waves of ill circumstance with gas-filled bladders. Cuckoo knew the worst of things, and by the knowledge was confirmed in her mule's attitude which so distracted Mrs. Brigg. Her hands were tied in every direction except one. She could only dumbly prove that Valentine was wrong, that her will was not dead, by exercising it to the detri-ment of her worldly situation. Doggedly then she put her whole past behind her, despite the ever-increasing curses of the landlady. She had given up her pilgrimages in search of honest work. They were too hopeless. She had pawned everything she could pawn, and sold every trifle that was saleable. Even Jessie's broad band of yellow satin had been included in a heterogeneous parcel of odds and ends purchased by a phlegmatic German with eyes like marbles and the manner of a stone image. Living less and less well, doing without fires, sitting often in the dark at night to save the expense of gas, Cuckoo had managed to pay her rent until a week ago. Then money had failed, and the great earthquake had at length tossed and swallowed the wretched Mrs. Brigg. The scene had been tropical. Mrs. Brigg was really moved to the very depths of her being. For days she had been, as it were, eating and drinking apprehension. Now apprehension choked her. She was shot up in the air by the cannon of climax. Limbs and mind were in the extreme of commotion. From her point of view it must be acknowledged that the situation was unduly exasperating. For Cuckoo would give no reason whatever for her reiterated formula of refusal to earn any money. And now she could not pay her week's rent, plunging Mrs. Brigg into the furthest depths of despair, and yet sat within doors day after day. Mrs. Brigg approached apoplexy by way of persuasion, was by turns pathetic and paralytic with passion. She coaxed with the ardour of an executioner inveigling the victim's neck to the noose and in haste to be off to breakfast. She threatened like Jove in curl-papers. Cuckoo was inexorable.

"Then out you go!" said Mrs. Brigg at last. "Out of my house you pack, you——" Nameless words followed.

Cuckoo got up from her chair with no show of emotion and moved towards her bedroom stonily to pack her box. She didn't care. She was in a mood to lie down in the gutter and wait the last blow of Fate, living only in her one obstinate determination to do what the doctor had told her, the one thing Julian had asked of her. She did not any longer war with words against the purple and hard-breathing landlady. And her silence and her movement of obedience awed Mrs. Brigg for the moment into another mood. She shuffled after Cuckoo into the bedroom.

" Eh ? What is it ? " she ejaculated. " What are you a-doing of ?"

" Goin'," Cuckoo threw at her.

" Now ?"

" Yes."

" Where to ? "

No answer. Cuckoo was thrusting the few things still left to her into the only box she now possessed in the world. Mrs. Brigg stood in the folding doorway watching, and making mouths, as is the fashion of the elderly when emotional.

" What are you going for ? " she said presently, as Cuckoo, bending down, stuffed a white petticoat into the depths,

" Can't pay," snarled Cuckoo.

" It don't matter—for a day or two," said Mrs. Brigg, reluctantly. She stumped downstairs torn by conflicting emotions. She had got accustomed to Cuckoo, and then both Julian and Valentine, Cuckoo's visitors, had taught her the colour of the British sovereign. They had not been near 400 lately, but they might come again. And then Dr. Levillier! Cuckoo had some fine friends, who would surely do something for her. Mrs. Brigg had no other possible lodger in her eye. On the whole, prudence dictated a day or two's patience, just a day or two's, or a week's, not more, not a moment more. Thus it came about that Cuckoo had now been another week beneath the roof of Mrs. Brigg without paying hard cash for the asylum. The previous evening the landlady had burst out again into fury, refusing to get in any more food for Cuckoo and demanding the fortnight's rent. She had even, carried away by cupidity and passion, striven to drive Cuckoo out to her night's work. A physical struggle had taken place between them, ending in the landlady's hysterics. Other lodgers had been drawn by the noise from their floors to witness the row. Two of them had come on the scene accompanied by men, and to them Mrs. Brigg had shrieked her wrongs and explanations of this swindling virtue of a woman who had formerly paid her way honestly from the street. The lodgers and their men had provided an accompaniment of jeering laughter to the Brigg solo, and Cuckoo, her clothes nearly torn from her back, had flung at last into her sitting-room and locked the door. That was last night—the past which she now reviewed in the morning twilight. What was she to do? She was without food. She was in debt, must leave Mrs. Brigg no doubt, but must pay her first, had no means to pay for another lodging. She might apply to Dr. Levillier. What held her back from taking that road was mainly this. She had the dumb desire to make a sacrifice for Julian, and the doctor had given her the idea of the only sacrifice she could make —retention of herself from the degradation that kept her free of debt. If she asked the doctor to pay the expenses of the sacrifice, whose would it be? His, not hers. So there was no banker in the world for Cuckoo. The dead wall faced her. The horizon was shut out. She lay there and tried to think—and tried to think. How to get some money? Something—the devil perhaps—prompted the sleeping Jessie to stir again at the bottom of the bed. Cuckoo felt the little dog's back shift against her stretched out toes, and suddenly a bitter flood of red ran over her thin, half-starved face, and she hid it in the tumbled pillow, pressing it down. The movement was the attempted physical negation of an abominable, treacherous thought which had just stabbed her mind. How could it have come to her, when she hated it so? She burrowed further into the pillow, at the same time caressing the back of Jessie with little movements of her toes. Horrible, horrible thought! It brought tears which stained the pillow. It brought a hard beating of the heart. And these manifestations showed plainly that Cuckoo had not dismissed it yet. She tried to dismiss it, shutting her eyes up tightly, shaking her head at the black, venomous thing. But it stayed and grew larger and more dominant. Then she took her head from the pillow, faced it, and examined it. It was a clear cut, definite thought now, perfectly finished, coldly complete.

Jessie was embodied money, an embodied small sum of money.

Long ago Cuckoo had said to Julian with pride :

"She's a show dog. I wouldn't part with her for nuts."

Now she remembered those words and knew, could not help knowing, that a show dog was worth more than nuts. At that moment she wished Jessie were worthless. Then the sting would be drawn from her horrible thought. Meanwhile Jessie slept calmly on, warm and cosy.

Cuckoo was cold and trembling. She knew that she was on the verge of starvation. The doctor had said that one day she could help Julian, only she. So she must not starve. Love alone would not let her do that. Between her and starvation lay Jessie, curved in sleep, unconscious that her small future was being debated with tears and with horror.

Long ago the little dog had entered Cuckoo's heart to be cherished there. Many wretched London women own such a little dog, to whom they cling with a passion such as more fortunate women lavish upon their children. A great many subtleties combine to elevate companions with tails to the best thrones the poor, the wicked, and the deserted can give them. A dog has such a rich nature to give to the woman who is poor, so much innocence at hand for the woman who is wicked, such completeness of attachment ready for the woman who is lonely. It is so beautifully humble upon its throne, abased in its own eyes before the shrine of its mistress, on whom it depends entirely for all its happiness. A little king, perhaps, it has the pretty manners of a little servitor. And even when it presumes to be determined in the expressed desire for the dryness of a biscuit or the warmth of a lap, with how small a word or glance can it be laid upon its back, in the abject renunciation of every pretension, anxious only for the forgiveness that nobody with a touch of tenderness could withhold. Ah, there is much to be thankful for in a companion with a tail! Jessie had winning ways, the deep heart of a dog. A toy dog she was, no doubt, but hers was no toy nature. Cuckoo could not have shed such tears as those she now shed over any toy. For she began to cry weakly at the mere thought that had come to her, although it was not yet become a resolve. Life with Jessie had been very sordid, very sad. What would life be without her ? What would such a morning as this be for instance ? Cuckoo's imagination set tempestuously to work, with physical aids—such as the following. She drew away her feet from the bottom of the bed where they touched the little dog's back. Doing this she said to herself, " Now, Jessie is gone." Curled up, she set herself to realise the lie. And perhaps she might have succeeded thoroughly in the sad attempt had not Jessie, in sleep missing the contact of her mistress, wriggled lazily on her side up the bed after Cuckoo's feet, discovering which, she again composed herself to slumber. The renunciation was not to be complete in imagination. Jessie's love, when present, was too frustrating. And Cuckoo, casting away her horrible thought in a sort of hasty panic, caught her companion with a tail in her arms, and made her rest beside her, close, close. Jessie was well content, but still sleepy. She reposed her tiny head upon the pillow, lengthened herself between the sheets and dreamed again. And while she dreamed the black thought about her came back to Cuckoo. It was assertive, and Cuckoo began to fear it. The fear of a thought is a horrible thing ; sometimes it is worse than the fear of death. This one made Cuckoo think herself more cruel than any woman since the world began. Yet she could ɪ ot exorcise it. On the contrary, she grew familiar with it as the day marched on, until it put on a fatal expression of duty. All that day she revolved it. Mrs. Brigg attacked her again. Food was lacking. Cuckoo's case became desperate. She turned over carefully all her few remaining possessions to see if there was any inanimate thing that she had omitted to turn into money. Jessie, poor innocent, assisted with animation at the forlorn inventory, nestling among the tumbled garments, leaping on and off the bed. Her ingenuous nature supposed some odd game to be in progress and was anxious to play a principal and effective part in it. Yet she was quieted by the look Cuckoo cast upon her when the wardrobe had been passed in review and no saleable thing was to be found. She shrank into a corner ready for whimpering. That night Cuckoo did not sleep, and through all the long hours she held Jessie in her arms, and heard, as so often before, the regular breathing of this little companion of hers. And each drawn breath pierced her heart.

Next morning she got up early. She was faint with hunger and with a resolve that she had made. She dressed herself, then carried Jessie to the flannel-lined basket, put her into it and kissed her.

" Go bials, Jessie," she said, with a raised finger. " Go bials."

Jessie winked her eyes pathetically, her chin resting on the basket edge. Cuckoo went out into the passage and called down to Mrs. Brigg.

2 B

"What is it?" cried Hades.

"I'm goin' out. I'm goin' to get some money."

Mrs. Brigg ran.

"Money!" she said in a keen treble. "Where are you going to git it?"

"Never you mind," said Cuckoo, in a dull voice.

She turned from Mrs. Brigg's flooding ejaculations and was gone. In her peregrinations about London she had sometimes encountered in a certain thoroughfare a broad old man with a face marked with small-pox, who wore a fur cap and leggings. This individual conveyed upon his thickset person certain clinging rats, which crawled about him in the public view while he walked, and he led in strings three or four terriers, sometimes a pup or two. Cuckoo had seen him more than once in conversation with some young swell, even with gaily-dressed women, had noticed that his terriers here to-day were often gone to-morrow, replaced by other dogs, pugs perhaps, or a waddling, bow-legged Dachshund. She drew her own conclusions. And she had seen that the old man's eyes, in his poacher face, were kindly, that his trotting dogs often aimed their sharp, or blunt, noses at his hands and seemed to claim his notice. Her morning errand was to him.

She walked a long time in search of him, trembling with the fear of finding him, inconsistently. Her mind, reacting on her ill-fed body, planted a crawling weariness there, and at last she had to stop and examine her pockets. She came upon two or three pence, went into a shop, bought a bun and ate it sitting by a marble-topped table. It nearly choked her. Yet she knew she needed it badly. With one penny the less she resumed her pilgrimage. But nowhere could she see the old man in his leggings, and suddenly a sort of joyful spasm shook her superstitiously. Fate opposed her cruel resolution. In a rush of eager contrition she started for home, walking as quickly as her abnormal fatigue would allow her. She had left the street in which the old man generally walked, and took care, as she turned its corner, not to cast one last glance behind her. She passed through the next street, and the next, and was far away from his neighbourhood, rejoicing, when suddenly she saw him coming straight towards her slowly, the rats resting on his shoulders, various small dogs in strings pattering on each side of him.

Cuckoo's heart gave a great thump, and then for an appreciable fragment of time stopped beating. She muttered a bad word under her breath and had an impulse to flee as from an enemy. She did not flee, but stood still like one condemned, while the old man stolidly approached with his menagerie. When he reached her she lifted her head and looked him in the face. The little dogs were jumping to reach his hands. Evidently they loved him.

" I say," Cuckoo said huskily.

The old gentleman stopped, lifted a rat from his shoulder, placed it on his breast, like a man who arranges his necktie, clicked his tongue against his teeth, and remarked :

" Parding lydy."

Cuckoo swallowed. She felt as if she had a ball in her throat shifting up and down.

" I say," she repeated. " You buy toy dogs, eh ? "

" I buys 'em and I sells 'em," answered the old man, with a large accent on the conjunction. " Buys 'em dear and sells 'em cheap. There's a wy to mike a living, lydy ! "

His small eyes twinkled with humour as he spoke.

Cuckoo swallowed again. The ball in her throat was getting larger.

" Want to buy one this morning ? " she asked. " A show little dog, eh ? "

She choked.

The old man did not appear to notice it. He looked at her with sharp consideration.

" Oh, you means selling ! " he remarked. " Where is it then ? "

" What ? "

" The show little dawg ? "

Cuckoo gulped out her address. All this time the old man had been summing her up, and drawing his own conclusions from her thin figure and haggard face. He scented a possible bargain.

" Trot along, lydy," he said, turning on his heels with all his little dogs in commotion. " Trot along. I'm with yer."

Cuckoo heard muffled drums of a dead march as she walked. She, who had lived a life so shameless, shivered with shame at the thought of what she was going to do. Her treachery laid her heart out in its winding-sheet. The old man tried to entertain her, as they went, by chatting about his profession, declaiming the merits of his rats, and spreading before her mind a verbal panorama of the canine life that had defiled through his changeful existence. Cuckoo did not hear a word. They turned into the Marylebone Road. She walked slower and slower, yet never had the street in which she lived seemed so short. At length the iron gate of No. 400 was reached. Cuckoo stopped.

" In 'ere, lydy ? " said the old man.

She nodded, unable to speak. He turned in with his crowd of pattering dogs, and proceeded jauntily up the narrow path. Cuckoo followed slowly and with a furtive step. She longed to open the front door, let him in, and then run away herself. Anywhere, anywhere, only to be away, out of sight and hearing of the cruel scene that was coming.

Now they were on the dootstep. The old man waited. She
fumbled for her latch-key, found it, thrust it into the door.
Instantly the shrill bark of Jessie was heard. Cuckoo's guilty
shining eyes met the twinkling eyes of the old man.

"That she a-barkin'?" he inquired, with a professional air.

Cuckoo nodded again.

"A nice little pype," he rejoined. "This wy, is it?"

The patter of feet in the oil-clothed passage roused Jessie to a
frenzied excitement. When Cuckoo opened the door of the sitting-
room, the little creature, planted tree-like upon her four tiny feet,
was barking her dog life into the air. Cuckoo, entering first,
snatched her up and gave her a sudden, vehement kiss.

It was good-bye.

Then she turned and faced the old man, who had paused in the
doorway. She held Jessie silently towards him. Transferring the
strings held in his right hand to his left, he took the wriggling dog
from Cuckoo, lifted her up and down as if considering her weight,
ran his eyes over her points with the quick decision of knowledge.

"'Ardly a show dawg, lydy," he said.

Cuckoo flamed at him.

"She is, she is, then," she cried vehemently, all her passion
trying to find a vent in the words. "You shan't have her, you shan't
if——"

"Neow, neow; I ain't sying nothink agin 'er," he interposed.
"She's a pretty dawg, a very pretty dawg. 'Ow much do yer sy,
lydy?"

Cuckoo sickened. She looked away. She could not have met the
eyes of Jessie at that moment.

"'Ow much, then?" repeated the old man, still weighing the
whining Jessie up and down.

"I dunno; you say."

The old man mentioned a price. It was bigger than Cuckoo had
expected. She nodded, moving her tongue across her lips. Then
she looked away out of the window. She heard the chink of
money.

"Put it on the table," she murmured.

He did so, looking steadily at her.

"You feels the parting, lydy," he began. "Very nat'ral, very. I
knows what it is."

He extended Jessie, now whining furiously, towards Cuckoo.

"Want to sy good-bye, lydy?" he said.

Cuckoo shook her head. The old man popped Jessie into one of
the capacious side-pockets of his coat and buttoned the flap down.

"Mornin', lydy," he said, turning towards the door.

Cuckoo made no reply. Her chest was heaving and her lips were working. The old man went out. Cuckoo heard the pattering feet of the little army of dogs on the oilcloth of the passage. The hall door opened and shut. A pause. The iron gate clicked. She had never moved. The money lay on the table. At last Cuckoo went out into the passage and called, in a strange voice:

"Mrs. Brigg."

The landlady came with hasty alacrity.

"Come here," said Cuckoo, leading the way into the sitting-room. "There—there's some money for you."

Mrs. Brigg pounced on it with a vulture's eagerness.

"'Owever did yer—— " she began.

But Cuckoo had rushed into the bedroom. The landlady stood with the money lying in her hand, and heard the key turned in the lock of the door.

CHAPTER VII

A MEETING OF STARVATION AND EXCESS

Now an awful loneliness, like the loneliness of the grave, fell round Cuckoo. Like Judas, she could have gone out and hanged herself, but for one thing, the love in her heart that seemed so useless. In her muddled, illogical way, and to stifle gnawing thoughts of the betrayed Jessie, she dwelt upon this love of hers for Julian. What had it ever brought her? What had it brought him? To her it had given many sorrows, humiliations. She remembered them one by one, and they looked at her like ghosts. Her dawning recognition of her own degradation, never yet come to sunrise; her tearing jealousy when Julian went out to do as other men did, preceded by, and linked with, the knowledge of that dreary incident in which she played the part of accomplice, that incident which she always believed had started him on his journey to destruction; her acquaintance with Valentine and the arrows planted in her heart by him; her despair when she learned from him her own impotence, not yet counterbalanced by full trust in herself or in her power for good, despite the faith of the doctor; her vision of the constantly falling Julian, of the stone going down in the deep sea; her desperate adherence to the doctor's request to prove her will, rewarded now by an apparently useless starvation, and by this treacherous sale of Jessie, her truest, trustiest friend. Cuckoo reviewed these ghosts and no longer prayed but cursed. So long as she had Jessie—she knew it now—she had never been really quite hopeless, often as she had thought herself hopeless. She had never even been utterly without self-respect, because Jessie had always deeply respected her and had thus given her little moments of clean and cheering confidence. And she had never been absolutely alone. Now she was alone, and felt like Judas, a betrayer. By turns she thought of Julian lost and of Jessie sold to strange hands, strange hearts, in a cruel and a bitter world. But even now she did not think much or often of herself, for Cuckoo was no egoist. Her very lack of egoism must have been the despair of any good woman trying to rescue her. She sat at home and starved and betrayed

now, not because her egoism shrank from the touch of the men of
the street, not because she had any idea of the great duty a woman
owes to herself—to keep herself pure ; but simply moved by the
dogged determination to do something for Julian. Were Julian dead
Cuckoo would have gone out into Piccadilly again as of old, and
earned the rent for Mrs. Brigg, and food for herself, and a sovereign
or two to buy back Jessie. The circumstances of her life had stuffed
cotton wool into the ears of her soul and rendered it deaf to the
voices that govern good women. Cuckoo was pathetically incomprehensible to most people, because she was pathetically twisted in mind.
But her heart grew straight and surely towards heaven.

The sale of Jessie had brought in enough money to keep Mrs.
Brigg quiet for a little while, but not enough to satisfy her claim
against Cuckoo or to give Cuckoo food. It went as an instalment
towards the rent. Now the landlady began to clamour again, and
Cuckoo was literally starving. One night her despair reached a
point of cruelty which drove her out into the street, not for the old
reason, not at all for that. Cuckoo was sheathed in armour from
head to foot against sin and its wages. Her obstinacy seemed to
her the only thing that really lived in her miserable body, her
miserable soul. It was surely obstinacy which pulsed in her heart,
which shone in her hollow eyes, tingled in her tired limbs, flushed
her thin cheeks with blood, gave her mind a thought, her will the
impetus to mark time in this desolation. Cuckoo was like a hollow
shell containing the everlasting murmur, " I'll starve—for him."
Whether her starvation was useless or not did not concern her at
this moment. She no longer even saw those ghosts. She seemed
blind and deaf and dull in a fashion, yet driven by an active despair.
Had Jessie been with her still she could have stayed within doors.
The little dog's faint and regular breathing, her occasional rustling
movements had made just enough music to keep Cuckoo still faintly
singing even when her heart was saddest. Now her room and her
life were empty of all song, and Jessie's untenanted basket—in
which the red flannel seemed to Cuckoo like blood—was a spectre
and a vision of hell.

So on this night, Cuckoo put on her hat and jacket. She meant
to go out, to walk anywhere, just to move, to be in the open air. As
she went into the passage she ran against Mrs. Brigg. The gas jet
was alight, and the landlady could see how she was dressed. Suddenly
Mrs. Brigg fell on Cuckoo and began slobbering her with kisses.

The old wretch even began to whimper. She had been sore
tried, and must have had a fragment of affection for Cuckoo
somewhere about her nature. For she did not want to part with
her, and the tears she now let fall were prompted not only by a
prospect of money coming into her, but also of pleasure in the

thought that Cuckoo had not entirely gone to the bad. She wept like the mother who sees her child return from its evil way.

Cuckoo thrust her away without a word, violently. Mrs. Brigg did not resent the action, but fell against the passage wall sobbing and murmuring, "My precious, my chickabiddy!" while Cuckoo banged the hall door and went out into the night. Then the land-lady, moved by a sacred impulse of pardon, bolted down to her kitchen and began to rummage enthusiastically in her larder. She knew Cuckoo had been near to starving, and had supported the knowledge with great equanimity while this prodigal daughter chose to wander in wicked ways of idleness. But now she killed the fatted calf with trembling hands, and made haste to set out a reverend supper in Cuckoo's parlour to welcome her on her return. The cold bacon, the pot of porter, the bread, the butter, all were Mrs. Brigg's symbols of pardon and of peace! And as she laid them on the table she sang :

"In 'er 'air (*whimper*) she wore a white cam-eelyer,
Dark blue (*whimper*) was the colour of 'er heye." (*Whimper.*)

It was like a religious service with one devout worshipper.

*　　*　　*　　*　　*　　*　　*

Meanwhile Cuckoo walked slowly along. It was a dark night, very still and very damp. The frost had gone. The stars were spending their brightness on clouds that were a carpet to them, a roof to poor human beings who could not see them. In the air was the unnatural, and so almost unpleasant, warmth that, coming suddenly out of due season, strikes at the health of many people, and exhausts them as it would never exhaust them in time of summer. Cuckoo, faint with hunger, fainter yet with sorrow, felt intensely fatigued. She did not consider where she was going, but just walked on slowly and heavily ; but the habit of her life, profiting by her unconsciousness, led her towards that long street in which she had passed hours which, if added together, would have made a large part of her existence. Piccadilly drew her to it, as the whirlpool draws the thing which inadvertently touches even the furthest outpost of its influence. Presently she was at the Circus. The little boys upon the kerb, crying newspapers, greeted her with excited comments and with laughter. They had missed her for so long that they had imagined her ill, perhaps dead. Seeing her turn up again, they were full of greedy ardour for her news. They put to her searching and opprobrious questions. She did not hear them. Soon she was in the midst of the crowd. Yet she scarcely realised that she was not alone. No mechanical smile came to her face. It seemed as if she had forgotten the old wiles of the streets, put off for ever the frigid mask of vice, that freezes young blood yet makes old blood sometimes run strangely faster. What was the street to Cuckoo now, or Cuckoo to the street? Once it had at least been much, almost everything, to her. And she had been perhaps as much to it as one of the paving-stones on which the feet of its travellers trod. Now things were changed. The human wolf was in the snow still, but it no longer feared starvation. Rather did it live in starvation with a fervour that was untouched by anything animal.

Cuckoo walked on.

The crowd flowed up and down, in two opposed and gliding streams. The warm heaviness of this premature air of Spring had brought many people out, and had even induced some of the women to assume costumes of mid-summer. There were great white hats floating on the stream like swans. Bright and light coloured dresses touched the black gown of Cuckoo as with fingers of contempt. She did not see them. Many women who knew her by sight murmured to each other their surprise at her reappearance. One, a huge negress in orange colours, ejaculated a loud and guttural, " My sakes ! "

Unheeding, Cuckoo walked on.

A few of the men looked at her. More especially did those observe her who love vice that is quiet, sedate, demure, and unobtrusive. To these her pale, unpainted cheeks, her unconscious demeanour, her downcast eyes, and severely plain black dress and hat appealed with emphasis. One or two of them turned to follow her. She never heard their footsteps. One spoke to her. She did not reply. He persisted. When at last she was obliged to heed him she only shook her head. He fell away, abashed by the dull glance of her eyes, and wondering discontentedly why she was there and what she was doing.

Forgetting him instantly, she walked on.

Some one she had known in old days met her. It was the young man in the millinery establishment who had loved her for a week, and given her the green evening dress trimmed with the imitation lace. Since those days he had become strictly respectable, had married an assistant in the shop, rented a tiny villa at Clapham, added two childish lives to the teeming world, and developed on Sundays into a sidesman at a suburban church. Now he was on his way to Charing Cross station from a solemn supper given by his employers at a restaurant to some of their staff. He recognised Cuckoo and the spirit moved him to speak to her. He touched her arm.

" Miss-er-Miss Bright," he said.

Cuckoo stopped.

" Miss Bright, you remember me ? Alf. Heywood ! "

He was a little man, with a whitish face and wispy light brown hair. Now his pale brown eyes glanced up at Cuckoo rather nervously under rapidly winking lids. She stared at him.

"Alf. Heywood?" she repeated, without meaning.

"Yes, yes; Alf. Heywood, as was in Brenton's millinery establishment, top of Regent Street. Him as give you that green dress. Don't you recall?"

Cuckoo shook her head.

"Green with white lace on it," he continued, with nervous emphasis.

Suddenly Cuckoo said:

"White; no, it was yellow."

Mr. Heywood was delighted at this evidence of recollection.

"So it was, so it was," he said. "But what I wanted to say was that I'm sorry to see you here still."

"Eh?"

"Sorry to see you here. I'm married, you know, turned over a new leaf, with two children of my own, and come to see the error of my ways. I hoped as you——"

Cuckoo walked on.

Her dream of despair was not to be broken by Mr. Heywood and his new-found respectability. Fate shattered it to fragments in very different fashion. A sudden thrill ran through the crowd, coming from a distance. People began to pause, to turn their heads, to murmur to one another, then to press forward in one direction, craning their necks as if to catch sight of something. The street was almost blocked and Cuckoo was entangled in this seething excitement, of which at first she could not divine the cause. Presently she heard shouts. The crowd swayed. Then a man's fierce yell cut the general murmur with the sharpness of a knife. Suddenly Cuckoo's dream fled. She pushed her way forward in the direction of the cry; she struggled; she crept under arms and glided through narrow spaces with extraordinary dexterity and swiftness.

"He's mad," she heard a voice say.

"No; only drunk."

"He'll kill the other fellow if he gets at him."

"The coppers will be on him in a minute."

Cuckoo was panting with her effort, but she passed the voices and came upon the core of the crowd, the man who had yelled—Julian. She saw in a moment that he was mad with drink. His hat was off; his coat was torn; his evening clothes were covered with mud. Apparently he had fallen while getting out of a cab. Two men—strangers of the street—were holding him forcibly back while he struggled furiously to attack another man, who faced him calmly on the pavement with a smile of keen contempt. This man was Valentine. Julian was screaming incoherent curses at him and wild threats of murder. The crowd listened and jeered.

Cuckoo caught Julian by the arm. He turned on her to strike her. Then his arm fell by his side. It seemed as if he recognised her even through the veil of his excess. The drunken man looked on the starving woman, and the curses died upon his lips. He began to shiver and to tremble from head to foot. Valentine made a step towards him, but some in the crowd interposed.

" Let him alone," they said. " You'll only make him worse. Leave him to her."

The cab from which Julian had apparently just alighted was drawn up by the kerb-stone. Cuckoo, who had not uttered a word as yet, drew Julian towards it. He staggered after her in silence, stumbled into the cab and collapsed in a heap in the corner, half on the floor, half on the seat. She got in after him, watched by the crowd, who seemed awed by the abrupt silence of this yelling madman at the touch of this spectral girl in black. Cuckoo gave her address to the cabman. Just as he was whipping up his horse to drive away, she leaned forward out of the cab as if to the crowd—really to one man in it.

" He's my man ! " she said, drawing her thick eyebrows together, and with a nod of her head. " He's my man. I'll see to him."

The cab drove off into the darkness.

CHAPTER VIII

AN AWAKENING

THAT drive in the night was taken in silence. Julian, a crumpled heap of degraded humanity, slept. Cuckoo watched over him, half supporting him with one thin arm. Exultation shone in her eyes and beat in her heart. The glory of being alone with this drunken creature, his protector, his guide, lay round the girl like a glory of heaven. As she looked at his white face, and pressed her handkerchief against the blood that trickled from his forehead, wild tears of triumph, passionate tears of joy and determination, swam in her eyes. She felt at last the pride and the self-respect of one who possesses a will, and who has exercised it. That was a justification of life to her mind. Something had given even to her the power to snatch this man to herself from the jaws of dark London, to carry him off, a succoured prey, from that world laughing at his degradation. She bent over him in the rattling cab and touched his face with her lips. Was that a kiss? She, who had known so many kisses, wondered. It was the going forth of her soul to purify with flame the thing it loved.

The cab stopped; Cuckoo shook Julian. He stirred uneasily, opened his eyes and shut them again, relapsing into something that seemed rather a sort of fit than a slumber. She called to the cabman to come and help her. Between them they carried Julian into the house and laid him out upon the horse-hair sofa.

"He'll come to all right, lady," said the cabby, with a pleasant grin of knowledge. "There's a many it takes like that. It ain't nothing."

He paused for his payment, and then Cuckoo remembered that she had no money. The thought did not worry her; it seemed too far off.

"I ain't got no money," she said.

Cabby's jaw dropped.

"Wait a second," she added. "Go out, I'll get some."

The man withdrew doubtfully, then Cuckoo robbed Julian. She, who had never yet taken money from him, stole the price of his fare to her protection. Then she let the cabman out, locked the street door and returned. She sat down by Julian, who still appeared to sleep. And now suddenly she felt that she was starving. She looked round the room, there was nothing upon the table. Mrs. Brigg, an hour after her song of praise, had been seized in the claws of reaction, and had repented of her generosity. Suspicions and doubts obscured the previous rapture of her mind. She bethought herself that Cuckoo might chance to return alone, still penniless; she remembered the rent still owing. Her impulse to kill fatted calves suddenly struck her as the act of a madwoman. As locusts clear a smiling country of all that nourishes, she swept the table of Cuckoo clear, impounding to her larder with trembling, eager hands the food that might never have been paid for. Thereupon she went to bed, nodding her old head, and muttering to herself with pursed lips.

So the eyes of Cuckoo looked in vain for something to stay the bodily misery that stole upon her as she watched by Julian. Starvation stripped away all the mists from her soul and left it naked with the burdened soul it loved. Despite her increasing pain of body, Cuckoo was conscious gradually of a light and airy delicacy of sensation that was touched with something magical. This awful hunger made her feel strangely pure, as if her deeds, which for years had clung round her like a brood of filthy vampires, were falling away from her one by one. They dropped down into the night; she was mounting into freedom. And, despite faint agonies which at moments threatened to overwhelm her, she had never felt so happy. Instinct led her to get away from the consciousness of her body by leaning utterly upon her mind. She sat down by Julian, bent over him, absorbed herself in him. One of his hands she took gently in her own. The little act baptized him hers in her mind, and she was aware of a great rush of happiness never known before. For she had him there in her nest, she alone. And she loved him. Even in his drunken sleep, even in his massacred condition of ugliness and hatefulness, he was so beautiful to her that she could have wept from thankfulness. The world, that had taken from her everything, the very little that she had ever possessed, the purity that every creature has once, the innocence that she had never understood, left her this tipsy, degraded, abandoned, tragic atom of evil. And a great glory was hers. She could have fallen upon her knees in blessing and thankfulness, forgetful of all her tribe of sorrows, conscious only that she was a woman crowned and throned. By degrees she forgot that she was starving, forgot everything in an ecstasy of pure passion and pride, an ecstasy that brought food, rest, calm to her.

In the dawn Julian stirred and murmured incoherent words. Cuckoo bent down to hear them. But he slept again. And as the dawn grew, the light and airy feeling within her grew, with it, till she seemed to be floating in the air and among soft billowing clouds. At first there was light through them, light of the sun, strong and beautiful. But then it faded. And darkness came, and strange sounds like far-off voices, and a murmur as of waters deepening in volume and rushing upon her. They reached her. She put out her hands and thought she cried out.

The waters swept her away.

*　　*　　*　　*　　*　　*

" Cuckoo ! Cuckoo ! What is it ? Cuckoo ! "

" She's a comin'—she's a comin' to."

" Give me some more water then."

Cuckoo felt it very cold upon her face, and fancied at first that it was those rushing waters of her dream. But the darkness parted, showing her two faces close together, one old and withered and yellow, one young but white and lined. At first she looked at them without recognition. Again she felt the cold drops of water dashing against her cheeks and lips, and then she knew Mrs. Brigg and Julian, and she saw her little room and that it was morning and light. They helped her to sit up. She glanced wearily towards the table.

" What is it Cuckoo ? " Julian said.

" Food ; I'm starving," she whispered, faintly.

Horror was written on his face.

" Starving ! What the devil does she mean ? "

He turned on Mrs. Brigg, who suddenly shrank away muttering :

" I'll get something ; breakfast—I'll get it."

Julian looked dazed. He was only recovering gradually from his drunken stupor.

" Starving—starving," he repeated vacantly, staring at Cuckoo, who said nothing more, only lay back, trying to understand things and to emerge from the mists and noises in which she still seemed to be floating. Presently Mrs. Brigg returned and shuffled about the table with a furtive, contorted face, laying breakfast. The teapot smoked.

" Come along my dearey," began the old creature.

But Julian thrust her out of the room. He brought Cuckoo tea and food, fed her, put the cup to her lips. At first she had scarcely the strength to swallow, but presently she began to revive and then ate and drank so ravenously that Julian, even in his vague condition, was appalled.

" Good God, it's true ! " he said. " Cuckoo starving ! "

He sat by her turning this piercing matter over in his mind. Its strangeness helped to sober him.

" You eat too," she said.

He shook his head.

" Yes, yes," she insisted feverishly.

To pacify her he made a sort of attempt at breakfast, and felt the better for it. Together they progressed slowly towards the normal. At last the meal was over. Cuckoo lay back, feeling wonderfully better and calm and happy. But Julian's eyes were searching hers insistently.

" What have you been doing Cuckoo ? " he said. " You've got to tell me. Starving ! What's the meaning of it ? "

IIis voice sounded almost angry and threatening.

" I ain't got any money," she said.

" Why ? "

She didn't answer.

" Why—I say ? " he repeated.

" Because I've give up the street," she said simply.

" Given up the street—Cuckoo ! "

He laid his hand down heavily upon one of hers.

" Since when ? "

" Oh—a little while. It don't matter how long."

He sat glancing about the room.

" Where's Jessie ? " he asked suddenly.

Cuckoo burst out crying.

" I had to—I had to," she sobbed.

" To do what ? "

" To part with her."

" What ! You've sold Jessie ! "

Julian stood up. This last fact struck right home to him, banishing all his vagueness, setting his mind on its feet firmly.

" Jessie_sold ! " he exclaimed again, in a loud voice. " Cuckoo, why have you done this ? Tell me—tell me at once."

She strove to control her sobs.

" I didn't know what to do to get you away from him," she said presently, flushing scarlet. " I didn't never see you ; I didn't know where you was. I knew as you didn't like me goin' on the street. Once you asked me not to. Remember ? "

Julian nodded, with a piercing gaze on her.

" So—so thinks I—I'll keep away ; p'raps it'll get him back."

" Me ? "

He sat down with a white face. All about him there was flame. IIe seemed to understand what he had never understood before, the wonder of the lady of the feathers, the mystery that had drawn him so strangely to her. He caught her in his arms.

" Oh Cuckoo, Cuckoo," he said, brokenly. " You love me."

He laid his lips on hers, and pressed her mouth in a passion of emotion that was almost an assault. And still the fire was about him. She clung to him with her thin arms.

" That's it ! " she whispered, in reply to his words.

Julian held her in silence, felt her heart beating, the piteous tenuity of her little body, the weak grasp of her arms round him. These things broke upon him one by one with a crescendo of meaning that came like a great revelation, came to him shod with flame, winged with flame, moving in flame, warm like flame.

" You starved for me, sold Jessie for me," he whispered. " How I love you ! How I love you ! "

And he crushed her close in an embrace that was almost brutal.

The door-bell rang. Julian let Cuckoo go.

" He has come for me," he said.

She knew it too, and looked at him with a piteous, greedy questioning.

" I hate him now," he said in answer.

The door of the room opened. They both turned towards it. Valentine entered.

" I thought I should find you here," he said, stopping near the door. " Are you better, Julian ? "

" Better ? "

" Last night you were not yourself."

" I have not been myself for a long time," Julian replied.

" I had not noticed any change."

Julian made no reply. A dogged expression had come into his face. He was still sitting close to Cuckoo. Now he took her hand in his. As he did so, Valentine moved a little nearer, as if urged by a sudden impulse. He bent down to gaze into Cuckoo's face, and uttered a short exclamation,

" The battle ! " he said.

An expression almost of awe had come into his eyes, and for a moment he hesitated, even half turned as if to slink away. But then, with a strong effort, he recovered himself and again fixed his eyes on Julian.

" Come, Julian ! " he said.

" I will not come."

" I have a cab here waiting." (Valentine spoke with an iron calm.) " We had arranged to go to Magdalen's."

Julian uttered an oath.

" That devil ! " he exclaimed. " I won't go to her. I am half dead. I am killing myself."

He pulled himself up short, then cried out savagely, and half despairingly :

" No, by God, you are killing me ! "

He began to tremble, and looked towards Cuckoo as a man looks who seeks for refuge.

" You are treating me very strangely, Julian," Valentine said frigidly. "Last night you were drunk. You seemed to take me for some enemy, and struck me. Many men would resent your conduct. I am too much your friend."

"You—my friend!" Julian exclaimed bitterly. "You!"

Abruptly he sprang up, tearing his hand out of Cuckoo's. He went over to Valentine and stared, with a passion of perplexity and of loathing, into his eyes.

"What, in God's name are you?" he said, in an uncertain voice. "Are you man or devil? You are not Valentine—not the man I loved. I'll swear it. You are some damned stranger, and I have lived with you"—he shuddered irrepressibly—"and never knew it till now."

"You say I am a stranger?"

"Yes, with the face of my friend."

"How can that be?"

Again a misery of confusion and of fear swept over Julian.

"Whence did I come then?" Valentine asked.

He began to have the air of a man bent on some revelation. An immense power infused itself through him. His blue eyes were utterly fearless. The moment of open battle had come at last. Well, he would not attempt to avoid it, to gain further uneasy peace. He would strike a final blow, secure of his own victory.

And Cuckoo sat watching silently. She remembered the night on which Valentine had half revealed the mystery to her, who could not understand it. Was he about to reveal it now to Julian? Her eyes flamed with eagerness, and again Valentine looked into them and faltered for a moment. Then he turned resolutely away from her, as if he gave his whole heart and soul to the business before him, to this Julian who at last began to shrink from him, to feel terror at his approach, even to repudiate him.

"From what have I come, then?" he repeated.

Julian paused, as if he sought an answer, looking backwards into the past. Suddenly he cried:

"From that trance! Yes; it was then. That flame going away it was—it must have been—Valentine."

"You talk like a madman."

But Julian did not heed the sneer. He was passionately engrossed by the flood of thoughts that had come to him. He was struggling to wake finally from the dreary and infamous dream in which he had been walking—deceived, tricked, tyrant ridden—for so long.

"But then Valentine is dead," he cried.

His face went white. He sank down, clinging suddenly to Cuckoo.

"Dead!" he repeated in a whisper.

The girl's touch was strangely warm on his hands, like fire. He looked up into her eyes, seeking passionately for that flame that now he began vaguely to connect with the Valentine he had lost.

"Or is he——?"

Julian hesitated, still gazing at the white and weary face of Cuckoo. Suddenly Valentine said loudly:

"You are right. He is dead."

He laughed aloud.

"I killed him," he said, "when I took his place. Julian, you shall know now, what the lady of the feathers knows already, what a human will can do, when it is utterly content with itself, when it is trained, developed, perfected. I came through Marr to Valentine. I was Marr."

"Marr!" Julian said slowly. "You!"

"And Marr, too, was my prey. Like Valentine he was not content with himself. His weakness of discontent was my opportunity. I expelled his will, for mine was stronger than his. I lived in his body until the time came for me to be with you. Have you ever read of vampires?"

Julian muttered a hoarse assent. He seemed bound by a strange spell, inert, paralysed almost.

"There are vampires in the modern world who feed not upon bodies but upon souls, wills. And each soul they feed upon gives to them greater strength, a longer reign upon the earth. Who knows? One of them in time may compass eternity."

He seemed to tower up in the little room, to blaze with triumph.

"When you see a man go down, sink into the mire, and you say: 'he is weak—he has come under a bad influence'—it is a vampire who feeds upon his soul, who sucks the blood of his will. Sometimes the vampire comes in his own form, sometimes he wears a mask—the mask of a friend's form and face. The influences that wreck men are the vampires of the soul at work, Julian, at work."

His face was terrible. Julian shrank from it. He turned to Cuckoo.

"They feed on women, too," he said. "On the souls of women. Men say that magic is a dream and a chimera. Women say that miracles are past, or that there never were such things. But the power of sin is magical. The death of beauty and of innocence in a soul is a miracle. My power over you, Julian, is magic. The bondage of your soul to mine is a miracle. Come with me."

"I will not come."

But Julian's face, his whole attitude, betokened the most piteous and degraded irresolution. This man, this creature, governed him despite himself. He felt once more for the hand of Cuckoo, and, finding it, spoke again more firmly:

" I'll not come," he said. " I'll stay with her. I love her."

Valentine cast a malign glance upon Cuckoo, but again fear seemed to draw near to him. He made no answer.

" Only once I'll come," Julian said. " At night I lost Valentine in the dark. In the dark I'll seek for him, I'll find him again. Cuckoo shall come too, and the doctor. That flame—it went into the air. I'll find it—I'll find it again."

" Come then—seek it—seek Valentine. But I, too, was with you in the dark. And in the dark I will destroy you. Till to-night then, Julian ! "

He turned and went out.

CHAPTER IX

"*THE LAST SITTING*"

THAT evening Julian drove Cuckoo down to Victoria Street. On the way they scarcely spoke. The doctor, summoned by a messenger, was there before them. He, although ignorant of what had passed between Julian and Valentine, was deeply expectant. Cuckoo was exhausted by the sleepless night of her vigil over Julian and by the severe joy, almost like pain, that had burst upon her with his avowal and with his savage embrace.

When she entered the tent-room followed by Julian, she looked like a shadow gliding wearily through twilight. The doctor was there with Valentine. Valentine's face was gay. His manner was ardent, almost tempestuous. The clear calmness so generally characteristic of him had vanished, swept away by the flood of his triumph perhaps. Julian seemed nervous, and his appearance was so haggard as to be engrossing to any one who was observant. There was a hunted, fearful look in his eyes. His hands were never for a moment still. He kept close to Cuckoo. He even held her hands as he sat by her, and she felt that his were burning hot. He scarcely noticed the doctor, who observed him closely. Valentine watched his feverish excitement with laughing eyes. Of those four people he alone seemed entirely untouched by any deep emotion, entirely master of himself. For even Dr. Levillier was curiously moved that night, and was unable to suppress every trace of abnormal emotion.

They sat down. There were no flowers in the room. Valentine explained that he had remembered Cuckoo's fainting fit and feared its renewal.

"I am afraid you are still scarcely yourself," he added, with a solicitude that was too elaborate to be agreeable. "You are looking pale and tired. You are sure to sleep again."

"I'll not sleep to-night," she answered, showing none of her usual fear of him.

The assertion of her will, her momentary rescue of Julian, Julian's avowed love for her, his clinging to her as to a refuge—all these things, so Cuckoo thought, built up in her a great fearlessness. In her bodily weakness she felt strong. Her faded, weakly frame held now a large spirit of which she was finely conscious. And she attributed this leaping spirit, so brave, so intense to these things, these facts of which she could make a list. She did not know that behind them all there was a motive power inspiring her, through them perhaps, but of itself. How often is the power behind the throne unsuspected, unheeded. Cuckoo did not recognise it in this crisis, although there had been moments in the past when the murmur of its voice had stolen upon her and stirred her to wonder and to perturbation. And Valentine, to whom the combat came, saw not his real foe. And Julian looked only into Cuckoo's faded eyes for refuge, for comfort. And Dr. Levillier——? At present he could only wait patiently in the hope, doubtful, fragmentary of revelation.

Conversation that night was uneasy and disjointed. Cuckoo's defiance of Valentine was fully apparent. Julian's fear, obviously grown up to hatred of his former friend, shone clearly. There was a nakedness about the manners of both tired woman and shattered man that was disquieting and unusual. Valentine did not seem to notice it or to be moved by it. Indeed it might be supposed to add to his pleasure an unnatural revelry in being hated. Dr. Levillier, glancing from him to Julian, found himself involved in remembrances of Rip and Valentine. The terror and the hate of the dog seemed to be reproduced vividly in the terror and the hate of the man. Valentine watched both with smiling eyes and drew draughts of power from that fountain of horror.

At last conversation failed entirely. Julian was half stretched on the divan, gazing at Cuckoo as one who aspires to salvation. It was apparent that he was fully awake to the terror of his own situation, that he pierced the depths of the abyss into which he had fallen, in which he lay crippled, prisoned, ruined. Yet a hope had dawned on him with the dawning of the full knowledge of his fall, of his fantastic self-deception. The great love in this woman's eyes shone down into the abyss, shone from that face pinched by starvation. There was Heaven in it. There was the flame. Yes, he saw it now, not literally as in the past days, when its mystery had plunged him in awe, when its presence had touched him with a great fear, but imaginatively, as men see flames of help, and of faith, and of purity, shining in the eyes of the good women they worship, with the reverence of earth for the distant wonder of the sky. He saw it now, without fear, but with a passion of desire, a sharp consciousness of his degradation, that swept over him like a storm. And even yet, in this new knowledge, this rapture of awakening, he was still a bond-slave, or feared he was, to this stranger with the face of a friend, this enemy with the presence of his former guardian angel. Only Cuckoo could save him, he said to himself, if indeed the day of salvation were not long ago past—only Cuckoo. For despite her many sins, the flame shone in her eyes. And where the flame shone there alone was even the shadow of help, a shadow within the shadow of those eyes.

In the silence that had come upon his guests Valentine turned to them, and said :

" We are supposed to be here for a sitting. Well, shall we have it ? "

" Yes—yes," Julian said, " a last sitting."

" Why—last ? "

Julian sat up on the divan, and his hands were clenched on the cushions.

" Because if nothing happens to-night, I'll give it up. I'll never sit again. And if Cuckoo sleeps——"

He paused.

" She will sleep," Valentine said. " I have the power to make her."

" No," said Cuckoo.

" Don't you think so, doctor ? "

" It seemed so the other night," the doctor answered.

" And with each sitting my power will increase. Do you hear, Julian ? "

" You're very fond of talking about your power," Julian said roughly.

" No. But I may be very fond of exercising it. Why help me, then, by sitting ? "

He spoke in a bantering tone. Julian began to look doubtful. Could it be that all was changed, that there was only danger in this act, that to grope thus in the darkness for lost hope, lost safety, a lost Valentine, with love, trust, beauty still clinging about him, was to stumble further into a deepening night ? It might be so. And if Cuckoo slept—— !

Valentine smiled at this wavering approach of indecision. But Dr. Levillier said decisively :

" I wish to sit. It interests me. Send me to sleep, too, if you can, Cresswell."

" I will," Valentine answered lightly. " Come."

The doctor saw him standing for a moment in the light, with a glory of power and of triumph upon his face, and remembered that glory, even seemed to see it, a clear vision, when darkness filled the room.

Out of the darkness came the murmur of a voice.

" The last sitting," it said.

Julian was the speaker. Nobody replied. Silence followed. As before, the doctor sat between Julian and Valentine and touched their hands. As before the darkness, and this mutual act in it, developed in him the faculty of hearing, or of thinking he heard, the voices of the thoughts of his companions. So far this night echoed the last night of the year. Would it echo that night farther still to the ultimate notes of this music of minds? The doctor wondered. He was soon to know.

Once again the notes of Valentine's Litany stole upon his heart. And to-night they seemed to him louder, more strident than before, as if blared from a soul that held a veritable brass band of shrill egoism within it. The doctor listened. He remembered presently that the former Litany had been broken sometimes, hesitating, that Valentine had been assailed by vague fears that stole upon him like ghosts from the lady of the feathers. To-night those little ghosts were laid. They came not. It seemed that Valentine had conquered them. No longer did they crowd to hear the bold fury of the Litany. No longer dared even one to creep along alone to bend and to listen. The doctor knew then that this night was not destined to be a mere echo of its forerunner. It was at first as if Valentine had closed the rift in his lute, had bridged the gulf between his trial and his triumph. A tremendous sadness came upon the doctor with this thought, enveloping him in a cloud of cold. His heart fainted within him, as at some great catastrophe. He could have wept like a man who finds the trust of his life ill-founded, the faith in which he has dwelt builded upon the quicksand. He fancied that Valentine instantly became aware of his distress and that the knowledge swelled the mighty tide of the music of the Litany. And this thought struck him and roused the man in him, like the call of circumstance on valour, crying: "Will a man say that anything is irrevocable, while there is breath in him to give the battle-cry, strength in him to stir a limb?" Then the faintness left him with the demeanour of that which is ashamed. The cold cloud evaporated. He heard the Litany without fear, but with a great desire to strike a lightning silence through it, with a fine hatred that destroyed his former hopelessness. This blatant will that sang ever the song of self, that had no desire but to itself, no glory but in its own deeds, no aim but to impress itself upon some slave, some Julian of this world, stood before the doctor's imagination like a personality, a devil embodied, more, like the devil of whom men and women speak, against whom religion prays, and strives and rears great churches, and consecrates priests. Egoism developed to the utmost limits, is that the Devil? The doctor asked himself the question, and the great shadow that dogs the steps of life went by him on its black mission in the likeness of Valentine singing. And all the modern world stood still to hear and whispered : "Hark! It is an angel singing! If we but echo the song we touch the stars. If we but echo the song we, who are weary of time, shall know eternity. If we but echo the song we shall lay grief to rest beneath many roses, and draw from its sculptured sepulchre the radiant form of joy. We shall sing and we shall be great." And the modern world lifted up its voice, and when it sang harmony was slain by discord.

The doctor shuddered. Yet the coward in him did not rise again. There was the gleam of a distant light upon him, unquenchable and serene. He doubted the eternity of the triumph of this Valentine, though he knew not why he doubted, nor upon what his doubts were based.

And as this doubt, which was a faith, blossomed within him he had a fancy that the music of the Litany wavered, faltered—that through it ran a thrill like a faint shadow of some dull despair.

At this moment Valentine spoke in the darkness.

"What are you doing, Julian ?" he asked, quickly.

"Nothing," Julian answered.

"I heard you whisper."

"I only said something to Cuckoo."

"We must not talk. Let us link our fingers instead of only touching each other."

They all did so and were silent once more.

* * * * *

And now a fear seized the doctor. He became aware that a drowsy spirit like the little sandman who throws the dust of slumber into the eyes of the children, stole round the circle. In his hands were poppy seeds and opiates, and his touch was magical with sleep. Valentine had surely evoked him by a strange effort of will. He came, and his feet were shod so that he moved without noise. He filled the atmosphere with heaviness, and with a murmurous melody, like the melody of the drooping streams that hang their silver ribands over the hills of the far Lotus land. Passing the doctor he stole to the place where Cuckoo sat between Julian and Valentine. And there he paused. The doctor divined his mission, to weave a veil and cast a cloud of sleep around the lady of the feathers. The weariness of Cuckoo's life lay like a burden upon her, a heavy burden to-night, despite the wild wakefulness of her spirit, the passion of her answered love, the strength of her resolution, the purity that drew near to her at last with ivory wings along the miry ways. She, who was at last awake, and conscious of the glory of a woman's will to rescue and to shelter, was to sleep again. The sentinel was to be overcome at her post that the enemy might penetrate the lines and seize the citadel. How heavy the air was! To the doctor it seemed alive with sleep, as the waters of the great sea are alive with death for the sailor who sinks down in them. He saw the weaving of the veil that was dropping gently round Cuckoo. He saw the cloud shrouding her in a scarcely palpable mist. Or was it his dream? Or was it his fancy? For it was dark. There stood the tiny, obstinate spirit by Cuckoo's side. His hands touched her forehead, and touched her white and weary eyelids, and the doctor knew that all the fatigues of her life trooped together, as at a word of command, and came upon her to conquer her. They pressed round, nameless wearinesses induced by acts which had made Cuckoo that which she was. And they seemed to whisper to her: "You cannot fight. You cannot protect—it is all over. You can only sleep—you can only sleep. Sleep! You are so weary. Sleep, for life which has taken everything else from you has left you that." Cuckoo's face was white with the story of her life, and with the wonder of her recent self-denial, and with the memory of her martyrdom when the little old man of the many dogs shuffled to the door, bearing from her the friend of her loneliness. Her eyes were hollow and desolate. It seemed that she gave heed to the voices and listened to the beautiful legend of the magic and the holiness of sleep. And as she seemed to give heed the devil of the egoism of Valentine rose again before the doctor, sharply outlined and distinct, and smiled with the triumph of the egoism—that modern vampire—of all the world, terrifically unconquerable. Would Cuckoo sleep? The doctor debated this question silently and with an agony of anxiety. He felt as if the fate of worlds hung upon it, and the destinies of kings.

Would she sleep?

The obstinate spirit stood by her always, and the song of Valentine was a procession of triumph in the night.

  *   *   *   *   *

Julian's thoughts broke upon the doctor fiercely, and swept him from his contemplation of Cuckoo. No drowsy poppy-bed was Julian's. The shadowy spirit of sleep strove not to influence him. No opiates gave him peace. No veil of gentle forgetfulness descended upon him. He was a human being plunged in the deepest abyss of fate, beneath the range of the starlight and the gaze of other worlds. He was trembling, stretching out his feeble hands in the blackness for guidance, sick with apprehension, betrayed, deluded. And now he began to writhe in the grasp of a new terror, for it seemed to the doctor that he, too, was conscious of the obstinate spirit that stood beside Cuckoo, and that he dreaded the approach of his doom in her slumber. He too, murmured silently, "Will she sleep? Will she sleep?" If indeed she slept at the word of Valentine—Julian's last hope was gone. For he had now concentrated himself almost utterly on Cuckoo. No longer did he draw near to her half in awe, half in derision, led to her by the presence of the flame that flickered, something strangely apart from her, in her sad eyes. No longer did he set her and the flame apart. To him she was the flame, the only refuge, the only safety. For he sought the lost Valentine indeed, but with a strange hopelessness of ever finding him again. She must not sleep. She must not sleep. In her slumber the flame would die down, flicker lower and lower to a spark, to grey, cold ashes. And Julian in his distraction thought of himself as inevitably lost should the flame die, should Cuckoo sleep, ruled by Valentine. The fight was between Cuckoo, the flame, and Valentine. Everything else fell away and left Julian's world bare of all things save this one contest. This the doctor learnt in the darkness. But still the spirit of sleep kept vigil by Cuckoo, and the air grew heavy and full of slumber.

The doctor began to feel that his own powers were being strenuously attacked. Inertia grew in his body. He sat almost like one paralysed. His limbs, at first heavy as if loaded with intolerable weights, gradually became numb, until he was no longer aware of them. He seemed to be merely a live mind poised there in the darkness, striving against the power that sought to sweep from its path all those that fought against it or dared, however feebly, to resist it. But his mind, poised thus in this strange circle of slumber, came by imperceptible degrees to have a grip upon the past. Imitating the mind that is enclosed within a drowning body it gazed upon the wildly flitting pictures of the years that were gone. Regent Street by night rose up before it. The doctor saw, painted upon the background of the dense gloom in which they sat, the huge and vacant thoroughfare in the last watch of the night. Faint figures wandered here and there, or paused beneath the shadow of the tall blind houses, assuming postures of fatigue or of leering and attentive evil. But one moved onward steadily, scarcely glancing to the right or to the left. The doctor's mind, watching, knew that this moving figure was himself, and, as if with bodily eyes, he marked its course down the long vista of the dim street until it passed into more private ways of the town. It passed into more private ways, but not alone. A shadow followed it, and the face of the shadow was turned away. The doctor could not see it, but there rose in him the horror and the fear which had attacked him long ago, when he turned to pursue the thing that dogged him in the darkness. And he saw the shadow waver, pause, then turn to flee. And as it turned he thought that it had the soul, though not the face of the new Valentine. Then suddenly a great anger against himself was born in him. Why had he been so blind, so deceived? He might have protected Julian. But he, too, had been a foolish victim of outward beauty, the prey of the glory of a face. He had not read the book of the heart. And other pictures succeeded this vision of the streets and of the shadows that walk in them by night. He saw Valentine singing while he and Julian listened. And the eyes of Valentine were as the eyes of a saint, but now he knew that behind them crouched a soul that was filled with evil. Slowly the air grew heavy. Slumber paced in the tiny room. The doctor struggled against it. But the colours of the brain pictures faded. He saw them still, but only as one sees the world in a fog; looming forms that have lost their true character, that have assumed a vagueness of mystery, outlines at once heavy and remote, suggestive yet indefinite. And still the spirit of sleep kept vigil by Cuckoo.

* * * * *

There was a slight hoarse cry in the night.

"What is that?" Valentine said, sharply.

There was no reply. The doctor could have told him that the cry came from Julian, and that the lady of the feathers, leaning low in her chair, had passed from consciousness to insensibility.

The spirit of sleep stole away. His work was accomplished. Julian sank forward upon the table with a gesture of utter abnegation. He thought that Cuckoo was dead. He felt that she was dead, as long ago he had felt that his loved friend, that Valentine who had protected him and taught him the right way of life, was dead in the night.

Dr. Levillier seemed to see Rip crouching down against the wall.

And now Valentine's will prepared to assert itself finally. It rose up to triumph, as it had risen up to triumph over Rip. Was that struggle going to be repeated? Nothing had intruded upon it except the marvellous tenacity of the dog, who had died rather than yield obedience, died fighting. That tenacity surely did not dwell in the nerveless Julian, utterly despairing, utterly wrecked.

The doctor trembled, feeling that the close of the strange mystery was at hand. And as he trembled he seemed to see in the dense darkness a tiny flame. It shivered up in the blackness where Cuckoo slept, moved away from her, like a thing blown on a light wind, and flickered above the bowed, despairing head of Julian. And, as he watched it, wondering, the doctor was conscious once more that there was a new presence in the room, something mysterious, intent, vehement, yet touched with a strange and pathetic helplessness, something that cried against itself, something that had suffered a martyrdom unknown, unequalled, in all the pale history of the martyrdoms of the world. The doctor recalled the sitting of the former night and his impression then—and again he was governed by the tragedy of this unknown soul. Its despair laid upon him cold hands. Its impotence crushed him. He could have wept and prayed for it. This was for a moment. Then a new

wonder grew in him. His eyes were on the fla
above the bowed head of Julian, and presently w
seemed to see, beyond and through it—as one who
lit window—the face of Valentine, the beau
Valentine whom once he had loved. The face wa
glory of endurance, and the eyes smiled like the ey
And the doctor knew comfort. For this face, alt
the shadow intense suffering ever leaves behind it,
the majesty of triumph. And the eyes were bent
Julian moved in the darkness and looked upwar
hope.

The man who sat by the doctor, and who was
him, was filled with a passionate fury. The docto
of his glory cease, and the long pulse of his hea
effort. His soul rose up, as the cruel spectre of t
had risen up to seize upon Rip, and moved
dominate him finally, to draw him into its own ete
and passion of degraded power. But Julian s
towards the flame which drew its brightness a
Cuckoo sleeping. That was a last battle of souls,
of it came clearly to the doctor's mind.

He divined, as in a vision, or as in a dream that
reality, the story of his friend, the true Valenti
had loved. He remembered Valentine's dissat
glory of his own beautiful nature, his mad desire t
dissatisfaction, that desire, had been the opportur
The soul that sighed in sorrow as it contemplated
had been expelled by the soul that was completel
own hatefulness. The weakness of the flame of p
the strength of the flame of impurity. And so l
out to wander in the wilderness of the air and ugl
body, its temple swept and garnished, like the s
Scripture. For how long a time had the wanderi
beauty been helpless, impotent, tortured by the a
of the soul of Julian whom it could no longer p
be at rest it had stayed to contemplate the dreary
gradual fall. It had seen his confidence in, his lo
whom he thought his friend and his protector.
delicate dawn, shrouded in the mystery of night
between the clasping hands of the angels of darkn
it had hung in the air above the solitary Juli
homeward after his vigil by the lifeless body of
a passionate effort it had sought to draw him t
the truth that he might wake from the dream
insecurity, at last his tragic danger. And faintl

sunbeam it had dawned upon him, once as he met the lady of the feathers, again as he bent his gaze upon the theatrical glories that attended the apotheosis of Margaret. And it had flickered behind the film of the tears in a woman's eyes, seeking to make itself known through the beauty of the love that clung inexorably to the heart of Cuckoo in the midst of the degradation and the corruption of her fate. Cuckoo had given it a home. She was alone. It approached her. She was an outcast. It stayed with her. She was beaten by the thongs of a world that teems with Pharisees. It clung to her. She had, through all her days and nights been put only to the black uses of evil. It sought to use her only for good. And now at last it drew strength and power from the soul of the lady of the feathers. And the doctor knew that the secret of Cuckoo's grand influence to succour lay in her completeness. Degraded, wretched, soiled, ignorant, pent within the prison house of lust—yet she loved completely. And because she loved completely the sad, wandering, driven soul of Valentine chose her from all the world to help him in the rescue of Julian. For she, like the widow, had given her all to feed the poor. Her starvation had set her on high more than the starvation and the mortification of Saints and hermits. For they crucify the flesh for the good of their own souls. Cuckoo thought ever and only of another. She had betrayed Jessie and touched the stars. Now in her slumber, physical allegory of her abnegation of self, she fought in this battle of the souls.

The flame above the head of Julian grew brighter. The flame of Marr, striving with the fury of despair, flickered lower.

Dr. Levillier held his breath and prayed. Again he thought of Rip. Would Julian, too, die rather than yield to the final grip of evil? Would he die fighting?

* * * * *

A strange thin cry broke through the silence. The doctor saw two flames float up together through the darkness. They passed before the face of Cuckoo and were lost in the air above her. Two happy flames!

She stirred suddenly and murmured.

The thing that sat by the doctor sprang up. Light flashed through the room.

As it flashed the doctor leaned towards Julian, who lay forward with his arms stretched along the table.

He was dead.

Valentine—the spirit, at least, that had usurped the body of Valentine—stood looking down upon Julian, dead, in silence.

Then it turned upon the doctor. The doctor stood up as one that nerves himself to meet a great horror.

He watched the light fade out of the eyes of this horror, the expression slink from the features, the breath remove from the lips the pulses cease in the veins and arteries, until an image, some life less and staring idol, stood before him.

It swayed. It tottered. It fell, crumpling itself together like things that return to dust. The flesh, formerly kept alive by the spirit, now deserted finally by that which had dwelt within it and sought to use it for destruction, went down to death.

Then the lady of the feathers awoke at last from her sleep. The doctor bent over her and took her hands in his. It seemed to him that she had won a great battle. He felt awestruck as he looked into her eyes. He tried to speak to her, but no words came to him except these, which he murmured at last below his breath :

" Your victory."

Cuckoo looked up at him. Her eyes were still lightly clouded with sleep, but they were smiling, as if they had been gazing upon the face of beauty.

For how long had Cuckoo slept ? Surely through all the length of her life, through all the tears that she had shed, through all the sad deeds that she had committed ! Now, at last, she woke.

Her slumber had been as the deep slumber of death.

And from death do we not awake to a new understanding and to a new world ?

Printed by BALLANTYNE, HANSON & Cö.
London and Edinburgh